PENGUIN BOOKS

Bronx Requiem

John Clarkson is the author of six previous novels, including *And Justice for One*. He spent many years in the New York advertising industry as a copywriter, and as a private consultant, running his own agency. He lives in Brooklyn, New York.

Bronx Requiem

JOHN CLARKSON

PENGUIN BOOKS

PENGUIN BOOKS

UK | USA | Canada | Ireland | Australia
India | New Zealand | South Africa

Penguin Books is part of the Penguin Random House group of companies
whose addresses can be found at global.penguinrandomhouse.com

First published in the United States of America by St Matin's Press 2016
First published in Great Britain by Michael Joseph
Published in Penguin Books 2017

002

Copyright © John Clarkson 2016

The moral right of the authors has been asserted

Set in 12.5/14.75pt Garamond MT Std
Typeset in India by Thomson Digital Pvt Ltd, Noida, Delhi
Printed in Great Britain by Clays Ltd, St Ives plc

A CIP catalogue record for this book is available from the British Library

ISBN: 978-1-405-92098-8

www.greenpenguin.co.uk

Penguin Random House is committed to a
sustainable future for our business, our readers
and our planet. This book is made from Forest
Stewardship Council® certified paper.

To Summer Clarkson Savina

Bronx Requiem

Prologue

James Beck had about ten seconds before bones broke and blood hit the floor.

It was his fourth day at Clinton State Prison in Dannemora, New York, and Beck knew he was about to be robbed.

He'd been in lockdown while they finished his intake process. Now he walked in a line of inmates, slowly making his way up a stairwell leading to the cell assigned to him on the fourth floor in A block. In his left hand, Beck carried a brown paper bag holding personal supplies: toothbrush, toothpaste, soap, shaving cream, tobacco, and papers.

Clinton was Beck's third prison. He'd been incarcerated for sixteen months. First in Rikers, then in Sing Sing. Long enough to know a new fish, a white guy, unaffiliated, holding a bag of supplies, would be a target.

Normally, there wouldn't have been so many prisoners on the stairwell, but guards on the third floor had decided to stop everyone and search them for contraband. When they finally let the inmates back onto the stairwell, Beck found himself surrounded in a tight space where the guards on the landings could only watch the line of men above them or below them, but not both.

The two inmates who had planned the rip-off didn't much care about what Beck carried in the paper bag. They wanted to know if the white-boy fish would give up his possessions without a fight. If so, they could feed off him forever.

Beck figured the man behind him would be the muscle. He had about fifty pounds on Beck. He'd do the grab. The one in front would do the snatch. Beck hoped he wouldn't try to shank him first. It would be impossible to defend against a blade in such a tight space.

But Beck wasn't going to wait to defend himself. He was going to hit first.

The moment the guard above looked away, Beck rammed his right elbow at the face of the big man behind him. But his attacker was already moving, too, trying to get one arm around Beck's throat, the other around his chest.

Beck's elbow banged into the bigger man's right fore-arm, missing the face, preventing the chokehold, but not stopping the attacker from getting his other arm around Beck's torso, trapping Beck's left hand. As Beck kept ramming his right elbow at him, the big man lifted Beck off his feet as the inmate in front of Beck turned and fired a punch at Beck's face.

Beck leaned back from the punch and drove both feet into the man in front of him, pushing all of his weight into the attacker behind. Beck and the bigger man fell onto the next inmate in line, knocking down him and three others. Beck landed on his attacker, whose head smacked into a stair with a wet, cracking sound, but he still kept his grip on Beck.

The inmate above grabbed the handrail and jumped up, trying to land both feet on Beck's chest.

Beck kicked up at the man, catching him midair between the legs, doubling him over. He fell onto Beck, who shoved him off, broke the grip of the half-conscious attacker under him, and rolled away from the pile of fighting, flailing inmates. Beck grabbed the handrail and pulled himself onto his feet, shouldered and elbowed his way out of the scrum of fighting, stumbling, cursing prisoners.

Guards from above and below shouted and pushed their way toward the melee, calling for help on their radios.

Beck joined the rush of men exiting to the tier below, running into more guards who grabbed and shoved the inmates against the wall, yelling for them to spread wide and get their hands up.

Beck felt a fist smack into his kidney, nearly sending him to his knees, but he managed to get into position, head down, hands against the wall, unmoving.

It took about an hour to sort everything out. Nine men were sent to keeplock cells, including Beck, where they were locked down for two days while the prison staff investigated what happened.

Nobody claimed they had been in the fight. Everybody professed ignorance, or said something vague about a guy who fell, or maybe got pushed by another guy.

The COs had little doubt about what had happened. Beck's supplies had been found on the steps. Clearly, the new fish had been attacked, but they couldn't prove that Beck had fought back.

Normally, the guard staff might have decided Beck was a victim and let him off, but word had already come to Clinton that James Beck was a cop killer. So even though Beck stuck to his claims that he had no idea what happened and had committed no violations, because he'd lost his supplies they'd found him guilty of violating Rule 106.10: "An inmate shall not lose, destroy, steal, misuse, damage, or waste any type of State property." Worse, they claimed it involved an assault and inflated the violation to a Tier III offense.

Beck received a sentence of sixty days solitary in the prison's Special Housing Unit (SHU).

They shackled his hands and ankles to a chain around his waist and shoved him into an isolation cell about the size of a parking space. There was an open shower in one corner, a toilet with no lid, a built-in bunk, desk, a shelf, and a door that opened to a cage outside tall enough for Beck to stand in, but only slightly bigger than what might be found in a dog kennel.

A nauseating stench, produced by human waste and unwashed bodies, permeated the airless cell.

With a Tier III violation, Beck was allowed two showers a week instead of the usual three, two books or magazines instead of the usual five, no television, no headphones for a radio, no personal possessions other than a small bar of soap and a roll of toilet paper. He received a change of clothes every ten days, one thin blanket that had never been laundered, one polyester sheet for his inch-thick foam mattress, no pillow. And no shampoo or comb. It took five days for him to receive a toothbrush, toothpaste, shaving cream, and disposable razor that had to be returned after one use.

On his shelf, he found a beat-up Bible and a February 1994 copy of *National Geographic*.

All meals were served through a slot in the heavy metal door.

Out of spite, the guards in the SHU made sure that for the first week Beck's meals consisted of water, a wedge of raw cabbage, and the infamous *brick* – a hardened loaf made out of carrots, potatoes, and bread dough. No human could possibly digest three daily servings of the brick. Beck managed to eat one brick per day by soaking pieces of it in water. He became so horribly constipated he had to stop eating on the fifth day. By the time they began serving him the usual prison food, he'd lost six pounds. He continued to lose weight during the rest of his time in SHU, eating food often delivered cold, sometimes with coffee grounds tossed on it, and three times consisting of nothing but an empty Styrofoam container.

From the moment he stepped into the small cell, Beck was determined to survive the Box. He immediately set out to clean his cell, which reeked of dried feces, urine, and general grime. Luckily, he had nearly a full roll of toilet paper. He folded a length of it into a tight block and used it to clean his sink, the rim of his toilet, and the floor around it before the wad of tissue fell apart.

He washed his hands, trying to conserve the half-used bar of soap, and spent the next hour doing calisthenics. Next, he tried meditating, first sitting, then walking methodically. After all that, less than three hours had passed on his first day.

Within four days, his notion of time slipped his grasp. Minutes could feel like hours. Days interminable. His concentration began fading in and out. His diet drained his energy, which made it harder to exercise.

He tried to find solace in reading, but found it increasingly difficult to absorb the archaic language in the battered

Bible. By the third week, he had read the *National Geographic* so many times, he loathed even touching it.

He had to force himself to step out into his kennel cage for his hour of *recreation* because it exposed him to the screaming abuse of other prisoners and manhandling by the guards, which caused nearly uncontrollable waves of rage to come over him. His only compensation was breathing fresh air, but one day he found himself dodging wet feces the guards had manipulated a prisoner into throwing at him. No one ever bothered to clean the shit off his cage.

His attempts at meditation turned into obsessing about revenge. Twice he fell into screaming outbursts he had to fight to control. As time passed, he had to exert more and more energy warding off panic attacks. His first hallucination came thirty-eight days into his sentence, in the middle of the night.

On the forty-second day he ran out of soap, and yelled at the CO through the door slot to give him another bar, but instead found his water supply shut off for two days.

Beck knew about men who had come into the Box for minor infractions, and committed so many offenses while in the SHU they'd had months, even years, added to their sentences. The prospect terrified him. As did his fear that the SHU was permanently damaging him.

By the fifty-second day he was yelling, slapping his face to pull himself out of his paralysis. He felt as if his brain had frozen inside his head.

He avoided looking at the walls of his 105-square-foot cell because it often made him feel as if they were closing in on him. He paced back and forth for hours, head down, burning away the tension, trying to force all thoughts of mayhem and retaliation from his mind, banishing any memories of the outside, any moments of time spent with family or friends.

On the day they released him from SHU, Beck dared not speak while they shackled him for transfer back to the general population out of fear he would slide into an incoherent rage that would land him back in the Box.

Once showered, changed into clean clothes, and placed in a cell with a man he had never met, Beck raised an open hand at his cellmate, mumbled he was sorry, and laid down on his bunk to sleep, but mostly to avoid any contact or conversation.

He fell into a sleep so deep it felt like only moments had passed when the five-thirty A.M. standing count arrived. He drifted through breakfast in the mess hall, feeling half comatose.

When they released him to the yard, Beck felt more awake and connected, but much more nervous and uncomfortable about being around so many inmates. Even though the temperature hovered in the teens, he had been anxious to get outdoors because he could still smell the stench of the SHU.

Beck barely held himself together until he reached the yard. He headed for the north end because the guards avoided that part of the yard. If prisoners wanted to go there and kill or maim each other, it was fine with them. They'd eventually arrive to clean up the mess.

Beck wanted to be as far away as possible from the COs. He didn't trust himself. He feared he might throw everything away and attack a guard to avenge what had been done to him, hoping they would shoot him, or beat him to death, and end the nightmare of his imprisonment.

The remaining sane part of James Beck forced him to do what he had done to survive the SHU – walk. Get away by himself.

There weren't many prisoners in the north yard. All were in small groups except for a solitary figure standing in a slice of sun, face raised to the warm light, his hands behind his back.

Beck decided he needed some of that sunlight. Absorb some of the cleansing warmth. He had to get into the light, and if it meant passing the lone figure to get to it, so be it.

Beck refused to walk with his head down, or with any hint of deference. He strode purposefully toward the man, but kept enough distance to indicate he had no intention of talking to him, or accosting him.

The sound of Beck's footsteps made the man open his eyes and turn toward Beck. Not surprising, since it would have been foolish not to watch someone approaching you in the north yard at Dannemora. Beck held both hands open, away from his pockets, to show there was nothing in them.

The other prisoner watched carefully. As Beck came closer, the prisoner's expression changed. Was it concern? Preparation to attack? Whatever it was, Beck found himself stopping, almost against his will, and meeting the man's gaze.

"What?" said Beck. One word, with enough of an edge to communicate to the man he'd better not give him any trouble.

"How long?" said the man.

It took a moment for Beck to get it. His brain still working slowly.

"Sixty days."

"First time in the SHU?"

"Yes."

The man nodded slowly.

"Did they win?"

Beck started to answer, then stopped. He thought about it. Really thought about it before he answered.

"No. Not yet."

Paco Johnson nodded again, communicating a deep, profound sense of empathy and encouragement, even though he was a complete stranger.

"Good," he said. "That's good."

Beck nodded back and walked on, feeling the human connection the man had made with him. It had only taken a handful of words, but whoever he was, Beck knew the man had changed his course.

Over the next days, months, and years Packy Johnson and James Beck forged a friendship and an unbreakable bond. At first, Packy concentrated on slowly guiding Beck back from the brink, asking him careful, pointed questions that pushed Beck to think and examine everything about himself, each question asked with the intention of helping Beck figure out what kind of man he wanted to be.

Packy Johnson had been incarcerated for most of his life, and had earned his status as a respected, righteous con long ago. Beck never asked Packy why he had decided to help him. Maybe it was part of Johnson's contrarian nature to help a white man. Maybe it was Johnson's curiosity about how a man with no criminal record had killed a cop. Whatever the reason, Beck didn't question it. Nor did he question the unspoken understanding that each of them would watch the other's back, share whatever they had, and suffer whatever the other suffered.

They might talk once a week, or every day. The conversations could be terse, or rambling. Beck learned how to do time, survive prison but, above all else, in the cauldron of hell that was Clinton maximum-security prison, James Beck learned the meaning and value of a true friend.

I

Tuesday, May 27, 6:30 p.m.
Nine years later

James Beck stood outside the Port Authority Bus Terminal on Eighth Avenue in Manhattan and checked his watch again. Demarco Jones had dropped him off in front of the main entrance, then driven off to park Beck's custom Mercury Marauder. Beck had ten minutes before the bus from Eastern Correctional Facility arrived. He wanted to be standing at the gate when Packy Johnson stepped off that bus, but he didn't know which of the 421 gates in the massive terminal was the right one.

Beck weaved around the line of people waiting for cabs and maneuvered past an obese black man wearing layers of clothing who'd parked himself in front of the entrance along with two overflowing shopping carts covered by a blue tarp.

Beck walked in, looking for the information booth. He saw it fifteen feet in front of him. A sign on the booth read: *Please go to the Information Booth located on the 1st floor of the South Wing, 8th Avenue entrance for assistance. Thank You.*

Shit.

He checked his watch. 6:32 P.M. He had eight minutes before the bus was due to arrive. Should he try to find the gate himself? He knew it was a ShortLine bus, but had no idea which gates were assigned to that bus line.

South wing. South wing. Maybe the ShortLine buses arrived in the south wing.

Beck turned and went back out onto Eighth Avenue and headed south, dodging slower moving pedestrians, sweating in the sultry New York heat and humidity. Typical New York spring. Last week, fifty-seven degrees and raining. Today, eighty degrees and sunny.

Beck remembered when he had come out of prison, five years ago. It was different for him. He wasn't released on parole, so he had no restrictions. It was a crisp fall day in October instead of a muggy day in May. And he hadn't spent the majority of his life incarcerated. Just eight years, but long enough so every connection to friends or family had withered or disappeared, so there was no one available to drive upstate and pick him up. He'd taken the exact same bus down from Eastern Correctional Facility just outside of Napanoch, New York. Because his conviction had been overturned, and he had a dedicated lawyer working for him, Beck had left prison with up-to-date identification, a working credit card, three hundred dollars in cash, plus an ATM card from Chase.

He had a change of clothes in a decent weekend bag and a very short plan of action. First stop – Smith's bar on Forty-fourth and Eighth for a few shots of Jameson and a cold beer. He'd been looking forward to hitting the old Irish dive bar for months. Maybe even getting a sandwich from the steam table. But his plan hadn't taken into account the passing of eight years.

There was no steam table. The bar had been renovated and expanded, gobbling up the ground-floor space next door. The old-school Irish bartenders in white shirts and black ties had been replaced by young girls who needed to be asked for everything: a glass for the beer. Another shot. A check. And they still acted like they were doing you a favor serving the overpriced booze. Amateurs.

Beck left the bar only slightly put out. All of New York City awaited him. The swirl of freedom and jolt of booze after a drought of eight years made him slightly disoriented, but also euphoric. He walked along the teeming streets, his weekend bag strapped across his shoulder, disoriented by the crush of cars, lights, and pedestrians. He hadn't crossed a traffic-filled street in eight years. Twice he waited on a corner to get his bearings before stepping out into the moving throng.

He zigzagged north and east until he reached the Plaza Hotel at Fifty-ninth Street. Even though he had a reservation, when he checked in he fully expected there'd be no record of it. But the name James Beck did appear on the computer. He did exist outside the walls of the New York State prison system.

Beck asked for a room on a high floor overlooking Central Park. The hotel clerk stared at his computer screen, moving his mouse and clicking his keyboard for an inordinate amount of time. It began to annoy Beck, and the aura of menace he had cultivated during his years in maximum-security prisons pulsed off him.

"What's the problem?" Beck asked.

When the hotel clerk looked up at Beck, he stopped fiddling with his keyboard and mouse and came up with a room that delivered most of what Beck wanted. Nestled on the eleventh floor but offering a view of Fifth Avenue. Good enough.

Beck remembered thinking the room felt huge after spending years in cells where he could spread his arms and almost touch the walls on either side. And the room felt almost unbearably quiet and luxurious. But it was the bathroom and the shower that had eased his soul that day. He still remembered the shower. He'd stood under the endlessly warm relaxing spray for twenty minutes, the extravagance and solitude almost too much to bear. Under that shower, for the first time in eight years, Beck felt his mind and body releasing the tension and dread he had been living with for so long.

The Plaza Hotel shower had given him a glimmer of what normal might be like, although for him *normal* would never be what it had been. He'd never lead the life most people lived, but he would construct a life he could be proud of and satisfied by, no matter who or what tried to stop him. His days of unbearable tension, of always being on the alert, suppressing who he was, were over. He knew two things: He would never return to prison. And no person, or institutions, or circumstances would ever stop him from being the man he wanted to be.

As he rushed into the south wing of the bus terminal, Beck knew Packy Johnson would also never be able to have a completely normal life after prison. He would help Packy find a job, and a place to live. Perhaps someday Packy might have a relationship with a woman. Be part of a family. But lurking under it all would be the decades of incarceration that had changed him forever.

Packy Johnson had gone to his first juvenile detention center at the age of ten with his twelve-year-old brother, Ramon. Their mother had been lost to drugs, and no family members had stepped up to take care of them. They had two older sisters, but they were barely able to fend for themselves.

Within a year, Packy and Ramon took every opportunity they could to escape the hell of that first juvenile facility, where abuse had been a daily occurrence. They'd find a way to slip out and run the streets of East Harlem trying to find their mother, living a feral existence until the cops found them and returned them to the prison-like juvenile institution, or later on to an overcrowded, repressive foster home.

By the time he was seventeen, Packy was a full-fledged drug addict and strong-arm robber. He was fearless, yet on some level utterly terrified by what he was capable of doing. He would rob anybody, at any opportunity, anywhere. He would take down a commuter walking to his car, a hooker and her john parked on a dark street in Hell's Kitchen, a pimp, another junkie, a businesswoman leaving an ATM, a drunk leaving a bar. He had a gun; he was strong; he burned with a crazed intensity, and could practically outrun a police car. Packy never hesitated. When he shoved his gun into somebody's face, opposition evaporated. He hit hard and fast and moved faster.

His only loyalty was to his brother, Ramon. When Packy went after two drug dealers who had threatened Ramon over a debt, he nearly killed both of them. The assault sent Packy to prison for the next seventeen years, much of his sentence served at Clinton, where he and Beck had formed their friendship.

Now, nine years later, on a muggy spring day in New York, James Beck's friend was about to take the monumental step from in prison to out of prison. Beck did not want to be one minute late for it.

Unfortunately, Beck burned up five minutes running to the south terminal and finding out Packy's bus would be arriving back at the main terminal.

He ran back to the main terminal and hustled through what looked to him like a cross between an old airport and a mall, trying to find the escalators that would take him up to gate 313.

He turned in to a long corridor with gate after gate angling into the passageway. Gate 313 was the farthest away. The only passengers in the entire area were standing in one ragged line, their bags resting on the floor at their feet, waiting at gate 310.

Beck checked his watch. Only four minutes late, but there were no passengers in front of gate 313. For a moment Beck thought, could I have missed everybody? No. Impossible. He checked the information board at the gate to make sure he was at the right place. The schedule listed all the small towns where the bus stopped. Various notes and pages of information were taped to the board. It all seemed messy and improvised, but it did list Eastern Correctional Facility as one of the stops.

Beck looked around for someone who resembled Packy. Nothing.

He checked back up the corridor and saw a blue rectangular booth with the company logo across the top: ShortLine. A fit-looking black man wearing a crisp white shirt sat at a desk in the booth. Beck tapped the window a few times to get his attention.

When the man looked over at him, Beck pointed down the hall and shouted through the speaker vent: "Hey, what's with the bus that's supposed to be at gate three-thirteen?"

The man motioned for Beck to hang on and picked up a phone.

Beck waited patiently, trying to tamp down the anxiety tightening his chest. *Why the fuck can't this go right today?*

Getting a prisoner released on parole from a maximum-security prison in New York State took an enormous amount of effort. Countless hours providing everything the facility parole officer required: Approvals for housing. Employment interviews. Enrollment in programs after release. Assignment of a supervising parole officer, a field officer, confirmation of jurisdiction. There seemed to always be one more thing to do.

Beck and his lawyer, Phineas Dunleavy, had been through it before. They had a third member of the team, Walter Ferguson, a senior parole officer who had helped navigate the rough patches, pushing and coordinating with the facility parole officer at Eastern Correctional to keep the wheels slowly turning. But if one person in the process went on vacation, or somebody dropped the ball, or lost a form, if a prisoner became sick, or suddenly got transferred to another facility, or any number of things happened, the process could be delayed for weeks and sometimes months.

Everything had been done, prepped, and set up. They had sent Packy's dressing-out clothes to Eastern, a pre-paid cell phone they were supposed to give him on release, and the maximum of two hundred fifty dollars in cash. It had all been arranged, and now this.

Finally, the bus employee got off the phone and shouted at Beck, "Bus broke down near Ridgewood, New Jersey. They're waiting for a new bus."

"When was that?"

"About forty-five minutes ago."

"So when will it get here?"

The bus employee gave Beck an apologetic look. "I don't know, buddy. They got to wait for another bus. Ridgewood is about forty minutes out. Depending on traffic."

"And the replacement bus hasn't arrived yet?"

"I don't think so."

Beck muttered a thanks and turned away. The man hadn't caused the situation, and he obviously couldn't do anything to help.

He checked his watch again. The bus probably wouldn't be in until around seven-thirty.

He walked back toward gate 313, pulled a slip of paper from his back pocket with Packy's cell phone number, and dialed it. The call went directly to voice mail, telling Beck the phone was turned off.

He left a message anyhow. "Packy, this is James. I'm at Port Authority to meet you, but I found out your bus broke down. If you get this message, call me back, but just hang in. I'll be at the gate when the bus comes in. Don't worry about being late. I'll be here whenever you get in. Call me when you get this message."

Beck recited his cell phone number twice. He hung up and was about to call Walter Ferguson, the parole officer in charge of Packy Johnson, to make sure Packy had boarded the bus, when he saw Demarco Jones approaching from the other end of the long corridor.

He raised a hand so Demarco would see him.

Demarco approached Beck with his usual effortless stroll. He wore a fitted black T-shirt, lightweight black cotton slacks, and Kenneth Cole slip-ons, no socks. His clothes and relaxed manner, however, didn't soften his appearance. When people saw Demarco Jones they generally walked around him, or quickly past him.

Beck asked, "Where'd you park?"

"Up top."

"It wasn't full?"

"Not for me it wasn't. What's up? Where's Packy?"

"Goddam bus broke down. Won't be here for about an hour."

"Always something. Did you call him?"

"Yeah. Straight to voice mail. I got a feeling he never turned the phone on."

Demarco squinted, trying to remember. "Were there cell phones when Packy went in?"

"Yeah, sure. 1998."

"I bet Packy never owned one."

"Probably not. Lot of shit he never owned in the last seventeen years."

"What do you want to do? There's more pleasant places to wait than here."

"How much time you got before you have to meet your client about that security job?"

Demarco checked his watch. "Twenty-two minutes. But she's always late."

"Not this time."

"You're probably right." Demarco pulled the parking ticket for Beck's car from his back pocket and handed it to

Beck. "You might as well take the Mercury. I can walk to where I'm meeting her."

"Okay. Hey, how'd you find out which gate to come to?"

"Asked the parking guy. He didn't know the exact gate, just said the three hundred terminal. Sorry I can't hang with you, James. Tell Packy I'll see him later."

"Will do."

Demarco said, "It'll be fine. This stuff happens all the time."

"I know, but I wanted to get him settled in with the mother-in-law tonight."

"You have time."

"That old crone made no bones about not wanting him in her home. I hope she hasn't locked us out by the time we get there."

Demarco gave Beck a look. "What old lady is going to keep you and Packy locked out from anywhere?"

"You haven't met this one."

"Don't worry. She'll hold up her end of the bargain. She wants the rest of her money."

"I suppose."

"Come on, James, it was the mother-in-law's or a shelter, and the last place we want Packy is in a shelter."

"I know."

"Hell, most guys get dropped off in a parking lot with a couple of dollars in their pocket, wearing the same dirty clothes they wore into the joint, and maybe a bed in a halfway house or shelter. Packy's way ahead of the game."

"Waiting makes me edgy."

"Packy's been waitin' seventeen years. Another hour or two won't make any difference."

Beck stood. "You're right. I'll walk you out. I'm going to grab a beer."

"Let's go."

Neither of them spoke until they exited the terminal and said good-bye on Eighth Avenue. Beck continued east on Forty-second Street, heading for a hotel bar usually overlooked by the hordes of Times Square tourists because it was located on the eleventh floor of a building mid-block.

He stepped off the elevator and made it halfway to the lobby bar when his cell phone rang.

Beck didn't even check the caller ID.

"Packy?"

"No, James, it's Walter."

Beck stopped in the middle of the lobby, bracing himself for bad news.

"Oh, Walter, yeah, I'm glad you called. The bus broke down. It's late. He made it onto the bus, right?"

"Yes, yes. He made it. He just called me."

"Oh. Great. What's the story? Is he on his way in?"

"Well, I'm not very pleased."

Beck stepped toward the windows overlooking Forty-second Street. "Shit. What happened?"

"He's at his mother-in-law's place."

Beck checked his watch. 7:32 P.M.

"What? How the hell did he get there?"

"He hitchhiked. Came over the George Washington Bridge and took a livery cab to the old lady's apartment."

"You're kidding me."

"No. I'm not. It was incredibly stupid. He could have been violated back to prison if he got caught hitchhiking."

"Unbelievable. I'm going to call him now."

"Don't bother. His phone battery is dead. It was dead when they gave him the phone. And I'm not sure he even has a charger. He called me from a pay phone near his mother-in-law's."

Beck wanted to curse and complain about the prison personnel, but didn't bother.

"Do you have her number? I don't have it with me."

"I've called her many times, James. She never answers her phone. Listen, don't worry about it. He's there. He's where he's supposed to be. I told him to report to me first thing tomorrow at eight-thirty, my office in Brooklyn."

"Maybe I should go up to the Bronx and make sure everything is okay."

"James, I believe that might be too much right now. I gave him hell for that stunt. But between us, I think it might be positive. He took charge of his situation. The trick is to channel that in the right direction. I think we should let him settle down. Get himself together. He'll check in with me tomorrow, and I'll bring him around to see you right after."

Beck thought it over, nodding to himself. "All right, Walter. By the time I get up there he might be asleep anyhow. All right, let him settle down. Tomorrow, then."

"Tomorrow."

Beck cut the call. He stared out the window looking down at the dazzle of Forty-second Street below him. A crushing feeling of loneliness came over him. He had been looking forward to seeing his friend Packy Johnson, perhaps in more ways than he realized. The last place he wanted to be was in a hotel bar amid strangers.

He turned away from the window and headed back to Port Authority to get his car.

2

Amelia Johnson sat naked, trembling, hunched over in a locked dark closet asking herself how did this happen? She had been hanging around in the bedroom she shared with another one of Derrick Watkins's prostitutes. It was early afternoon. She still had on the clothes she had slept in: green-and-black-striped sleep pants and a T-shirt decorated with a picture of a Yorkie and the words, *Dream On*.

Derrick Watkins walked into the bedroom and yelled, "Princess, what the fuck are you doing?"

She answered "Nuthin'."

That was all it took. Derrick Watkins grabbed the back of her neck and dragged her out of the bedroom. He pushed and kicked her down the hall into his bedroom, screaming at her, "Nothing? Fucking nothing? How the hell you think nuthin' does me any good, you goddam useless bitch?"

Amelia was a tall, strong, athletic girl, but no match for the strength of a grown man. Derrick slammed the bedroom door. The unprovoked attack had been shockingly violent from the first moment, and it just got worse. Hard stinging slaps to her head, kicks, punches, clothes torn off, throat choked, violent, brutal rape and sodomy. All done under the guise of outrage. All justified by Amelia Johnson's supposed ingratitude.

Amelia had known Derrick Watkins was a pimp. A low-echelon criminal, like many of the young men in her neighborhood around the Bronx River Houses who dealt in drugs, theft, and prostitution. She knew the game. And she knew how to use her austere beauty and flawless body to make men and boys do what she wanted, so she figured should could play Derrick like she had played so many men in her past. When she let Watkins take her in, give her food, clothes, and a place to stay, Amelia knew she had entered into a dangerous game. But knowing the game didn't make her able to win at it.

Derrick Watkins had played his role perfectly. Start by acting concerned. Make her feel special. And even though Amelia knew it was a con, she couldn't help but enjoy the feeling, because at a deep, unspoken level, Amelia Johnson did feel special.

She thought she could deal with the bargain being made. She'd slept with Derrick, going along with the pretense that he was her boyfriend. And eventually she'd agreed to sleep with a few of Derrick's *friends*. In the last few weeks, of course, there were more and more of the *friends*. Amelia knew where she was heading with Derrick Watkins, but she fooled herself into thinking she could control the situation. Get out before things got too bad.

Any notion of that evaporated as the rape and beating continued. And when Amelia screamed and cried, Watkins became even more infuriated. Thrusting harder. Hitting harder.

It ended when Derrick demanded to know why Amelia was so ungrateful. Why had she treated *him* so bad? Made *him* do this to *her*.

By then he had reduced Amelia to a sixteen-year-old girl who could muster nothing but a hysterical, hopeless answer: "I don't know."

An answer that gave Derrick Watkins a reason to drag her naked to the hall closet and lock her in the small space, telling her, "Bitch, you stay in there until you come up with a better fucking answer than 'I don't know.'"

The closet was only three feet deep and five feet wide, so Amelia had to sit with her back against the end wall, her knees bent, the side walls inches away from her shoulders.

It took an hour for her to stop trembling and crying as she sat with her elbows on her knees, her face in her hands, trying to come to terms with what Derrick had done. She'd had sex forced on her before. The first time at the age of twelve. But never with such violence and raw entitlement.

Her first partner was her mother's boyfriend, who kept telling her just this once so they would be close, be a family. She'd finally given in to get some peace, but it had simply given him license to want more. After months of the abuse she'd run away, sleeping over with school friends until her mother found her. Amelia didn't say why she'd run off, she just said she wasn't going back. Her mother didn't argue with her. She couldn't afford to lose the meager supply of money and drugs her boyfriend supplied, so she turned Amelia over to the Child Protective Services office in the Bronx.

It was supposed to be temporary. But then her mother went into a rehab program. And then her mother left the program. And then her mother died of an overdose.

Amelia drifted through a series of foster homes. By the time she reached fifteen, she had developed into a tall young girl with a model's shoulders and a lovely figure, which meant sexual predators were a given, but she made sure to get something for giving *it*.

There was the tough boy who lived in her foster home who'd protected her from the neighborhood kids in return for *it*. The foster parent who'd fondled her in exchange for a room of her own. There was the older brother of a schoolmate who'd given her the release of cheap vodka mixed with orange soda in return for *it*. And, inevitably, the neighborhood handyman who had simply given her money. The slow, inescapable slide into prostitution had happened. Amelia had given away something priceless and irreplaceable for a pathetically small return.

The quid pro quo of sex became an accepted reality. A concession to the necessities required in order to survive. But not quite a full concession. Some part of Amelia never gave in completely. Which is why she had ended up in a dispositional hearing in family court for throwing a rock at a car driven by a man who had been stalking her. The judge ordered that she be placed in a supervised group home, telling her this was her last break. Next time, it would be a secure facility run by the State of New York.

And then, Amelia had been caught shoplifting clothes she'd needed for school. Macy's security showed zero mercy. They called the cops. A bored patrolman issued her a desk appearance ticket, and when she failed to appear in Brooklyn Criminal Court, a warrant had been issued for her arrest. Her days in family court were over. She was officially a fugitive.

Amelia had been living with her grandmother, Lorena Leon, an unstable, angry woman who nagged and criticized her, constantly telling Amelia she was becoming like her worthless mother.

With a warrant hanging over her, and her grandmother becoming intolerable, Derrick Watkins had swooped in like a vulture smelling death. Older, confident, the pimp appeared at just the right moment armed with the right lies and promises. Derrick told Amelia he'd take care of the warrant. He told her it was time to stop living with the old lady. He'd find her a place to stay. Even help her get a job.

So she'd moved in with Derrick in his apartment at Bronx River Houses. For the first couple of weeks, Derrick allowed her to stand by and watch him run his group of whores. He had taken to calling her Princess. And treating her as if she were different from the others, instinctively playing to Amelia's weakness – thinking she really was different from the others.

Until she wasn't.

Now, she had to face a reality that she had refused to admit because, despite all the warnings, Amelia Johnson never believed Derrick Watkins would actually do this to *her*.

By the time she opened her eyes in the dark closet, the crushing claustrophobia panicked her so much she immediately closed them again.

Then came the pain from sitting for hours on her tailbone. To relieve the agony, she slid down onto her back.

But in order to do that, she had to raise her feet high up and rest them against the far wall, which placed her head down on the closet's filthy carpet and forced her to breathe in the dusty, moldy smell, which made her more claustrophobic.

Of course, the blood quickly drained out of her feet so she had to pull her legs down, bending her knees, clutching them close to her chest, making it harder to breathe. She almost lost herself to panic, but she turned onto her side, which helped.

She managed to fall into an exhausted, fitful sleep, but in the middle of the night, without clothes, she began shivering. A filthy old overcoat hung at the far end of the closet. She pulled it off the hanger and tried to maneuver in the tight space to get it under and around her, which caused an excruciating muscle cramp that gripped her right hamstring and brought tears. She scrambled into a bent-over standing position, banging her head into the shelf above her.

She turned sideways and tried to stretch out the cramp. Finally, the pain subsided. She felt like crying again, but just kept shaking her head, telling herself over and over, "No, no, no, no," afraid that if she began to cry she might become hysterical, and Derrick Watkins would hear her, and she didn't think she could survive another beating.

She finally managed to lay on the floor in a fetal position, on top of the overcoat, her face toward the door, trying to breathe the air seeping in between the door and the saddle.

She lay there trying to keep calm so she wouldn't get another horrible muscle cramp. She began inventorying all the places she hurt. The places she didn't worry about, like her hip where Derrick had kicked her and the back of her head where he'd punched her; and the places that frightened her like the back of her throat and between her legs.

She fell asleep again, but a full bladder pulled her awake. She had to urinate, badly, and she knew she would never be able to hold it in until they let her out of the closet. After the horrible degradation she'd endured, this last indignity finally crushed her spirit to the point of hopelessness that had caused so many women in her position to consider ending it all. But she quickly recoiled from the feeling, knowing if she allowed any of those thoughts she would not make it.

She cursed silently, letting the misery and pain fuel her anger. Letting it build, and turn dark and mean, and burn away any thought of killing herself, replacing it with visions of killing Derrick Watkins.

Just before noon the next morning, the closet door lock finally turned. Queenie, a retired prostitute who had worked for Derrick's older brother Jerome, pulled open the door. Too old and too heavy to earn her way as a prostitute, Queenie had been passed on to Derrick to help run his prostitution business, and act as a poor excuse for a madam to the young women Derrick exploited.

Queenie's first words were, "Oh, Lord."

She fanned her hand under her nose, as if that would help. Amelia lay on her side with her back facing Queenie.

"Come on out of there, girl." Amelia felt stuck, frozen in position. "Come on, now, he's lettin' you out. Let's go."

Amelia rolled onto her back, blocking the sudden light with her forearm.

"Let's go girl, you got to stand up now. I can't lift you with my bad back. C'mon, or I'm gonna shut this damn door and leave you in there."

Amelia rolled out of the closet, gradually getting up on her hands and knees. She used the doorknob on the closet door to slowly pull herself upright, but a sudden spasm in the small of her back stopped her. She had to remain bent over.

Queenie told her, "You'll be all right. Just go slow."

Amelia didn't answer. She looked up at Queenie with eyes that made the old whore step back. Defiance. Queenie knew that look from decades of experience. A look that always ended in more pain, and often death.

Queenie took another step back.

"I'll run a tub for you. You clean yourself and then you clean this closet. Derrick said you gotta dress up for dinner. Says you gotta work tonight." And with that Queenie moved down the hallway, getting as far away from Amelia Johnson, as fast as she could.

3

By eight o'clock Tuesday evening, Amelia had done what she could to recover from her night in the closet. She sat alone in the back bedroom of Derrick Watkins's apartment. No one would go near her. She had dressed in clothes she knew Derrick would approve: denim short-shorts, a tight-fitting pink T-shirt displaying a Playboy-bunny logo formed out of cheap rhinestones, platform heels that emphasized her long legs, and no bra. She had applied enough mascara, eyeliner, and lipstick to look ten years older, and had fitted a wig of shoulder-length red synthetic hair over her straight black hair.

During the time she had prepared herself, she fought down a panicky desire to flee. To wrap a bundle of normal clothes and drop them out the window, so when Derrick let her out of the apartment she could change and make a run for it. But where would she go? She used to have a few friends she could stay with, but nobody would take her in now. Everybody knew she was with Derrick Watkins. No one would risk his retribution. She couldn't stay with her grandmother. That would be the first place they looked.

Most important, she needed money. Derrick would be sending her out to work. If she didn't earn enough, the beatings would continue. She was trapped and, to make it worse, she feared he was going to make her prowl the

Hunts Point Market area. There were still whores working those streets, but only the very dregs: older, overweight women with missing teeth, longtime drug addicts, HIV-afflicted transsexuals.

And then she heard Derrick yelling at her from the living room. He didn't bother to come get her. He just shouted, "Princess, get your ass out here. Now, goddammit."

She walked into the front of the apartment, head down. She carried a small gold purse on a chain, and a light-weight, pink, cotton/polyester hoodie folded, half-hidden by the purse. Inside the purse were condoms, lipstick, a cheap cell phone, and a packet of Kleenex.

Derrick sat at the head of a table set up outside the kitchen presiding over a dinner consisting of two large buckets of lukewarm KFC extra-crispy chicken and assorted sides. The chair on his right was empty. Queenie sat in the next chair over. On the left side of the table next to Derrick sat Tyrell Williams, and next to Tyrell one of the youngest girls in the *family*, a fifteen-year-old runaway Derrick had named Duchess.

Derrick barely glanced at Amelia and told Duchess, "Move down a seat, honey." He pointed to the empty chair next to Tyrell, making sure Amelia sat next to some-one she loathed.

Derrick Watkins, thirty-two years old, six feet tall, about twenty pounds overweight, wore ordinary clothes pur-chased from popular chain stores like Gap: tan khaki pants, a button-down white collar shirt, nondescript can-vas boat shoes with rubber soles.

Derrick dressed low-key because his older brother Jerome dressed that way. And because the top man in their gang set, the feared Eric Jackson, dressed low-key. Plus, Derrick considered himself too smart and too diversified in his criminal activities to be labeled as just a pimp. So, no tattoos. No bling. No fancy car. Derrick worked hard to project his image, using his basic math skills to track every dollar earned by his prostitutes and every penny spent on them.

But the carefully cultivated exterior didn't obviate the fact that Derrick Watkins seduced and recruited the vulnerable, both male and female. The young men he controlled through fear and promises of money. The women and girls by alternating between affection and terror, savage punishment and pitiful rewards, just like every other pimp.

Without looking at Amelia, Derrick told her to eat. She took a cold chicken leg along with a spoonful of gelatinous mashed potatoes.

Derrick ate the greasy chicken with his hands, using a white plastic fork when necessary to scoop mashed potatoes or coleslaw into his mouth. He ate with his mouth open as a sign of privilege, using napkin after napkin, which he dropped on the table.

As he ate, he made a point of ignoring everybody while still giving the impression he was always keeping track. He also kept his gun on the table next to his plate – a forty caliber compact semi-automatic Taurus. Derrick pretended to be a gun aficionado, but had actually picked the gun because it looked cool with its lightweight polymer frame.

Derrick had forced Amelia to sit next to Tyrell because he knew how uncomfortable he made her feel. Derrick used Tyrell Williams, a hulking, twenty-five-year-old high school dropout, as an enforcer, messenger, and particularly as an informer. Tyrell had a talent for knowing how to find out if any of Derrick's prostitutes broke any of his rules.

Derrick had four women working for him. Their family names were Jewel, Duchess, Destiny, and Princess – Amelia's working name. All of them were underage except for Destiny, who had been passed on to him by his brother Jerome. Derrick preferred underage girls because they were easier to intimidate and bully. They were the ones who had the least and feared the most.

Amelia knew the dinner would continue for some time. Often during these meals various members of Derrick's crew would visit. Derrick had one of his new recruits, a gangly eighteen-year-old named Leon Miller, sitting out in the living room to guard the front door. There would be a knock. Leon would take out his proudest possession, a beat-up Glock 17, and stand by the door. Tyrell would lumber out, vet whoever had arrived, then escort them to the dining table.

The visitor would sit in the empty chair next to Derrick, who would do a poor version of a Mafia don chewing food while somebody talked in his ear.

Forty minutes into the meal, Derrick finally addressed Amelia.

"So how you feelin', Princess? You still feelin' special?"

Amelia didn't look at Derrick. That was one of Derrick's most important rules. For now, Amelia didn't care because she didn't want to see his face.

"No."

"Good, cuz you ain't. Too bad you got to learn that the hard way."

Amelia didn't comment.

Derrick wiped his mouth with a greasy paper napkin and sat back in his chair. He looked at Amelia.

"Yeah, as a matter of fact, unless I missed somethin', you ain't like no doctor or lawyer are you?"

"No."

"Actually, you ain't even made it through high school. Did you?"

"No."

"That's right. You didn't. Oh, wait, you got some rich daddy out there give you a big trust fund?"

"No."

"No. You don't. You ain't got shit, girl. All you got is what I give you. The food on my table, the roof over your head, and the clothes on your back, bitch."

Derrick leaned forward, moved his gun nearer to his right hand.

"Look at me, bitch."

Amelia raised her eyes, making sure to keep her expression neutral.

"You understand how this works, right? I know you ain't stupid. I wouldn't have you in this family if you was stupid. It's just economics, girl. You got to earn your way. And as far as I can tell, you ain't got any way to do that other than selling that ass of yours." He leaned back, sucked at a piece of chicken between his teeth, and frowned. Speaking to himself he said, "Hm. Well, we'll see about that. Don't even know that for sure."

He slid his gun back to where it had been and scooped more food into his mouth.

Finally, at 9:45 P.M., while the others remained seated, Derrick told Amelia, "Okay, Princess, you've had enough of my food and shelter. Time to go out and prove to me you worth keepin' in this family."

Amelia knew the others were watching her closely, especially Tyrell. If she said the wrong thing or displayed anything less than the proper demeanor, a sudden burst of violence could erupt, accompanied by curses, slaps, and food overturned.

"You get your ass down to the Point, girl, and get me my money. I come by there, I'd better see you working it. You understand?"

"Yes."

"Yes, what?"

"Yes, Daddy."

Derrick frowned, nodded, looked at Amelia like she would never stop disappointing him. "Go on. Get the hell outta here."

Amelia, head down, walked to the front door of the apartment, half expecting something to be thrown at her before she stepped out and shut the door behind her.

She walked out of Bronx River Houses, still sore and stiff from Derrick's assault and the hours of confinement in the closet. She headed south on 174th Street, wondering if maybe she should continue to Bronx River Avenue and hustle a livery-car driver for a ride to Hunts Point, or maybe to a lounge on Southern Boulevard, where she might pick up a trick, or run into someone she knew who might help her. Maybe, maybe, maybe.

As she walked, Amelia attracted the attention of male pedestrians and drivers on the wide, two-way street. Her clothes, makeup, and red wig left little doubt about why she was walking the streets at night. She ignored the drivers who slowed down to look at her. She did not want a cop to pull her over and arrest her for soliciting. After surviving Monday night, she knew a night in the holding pen at Central Booking might break her completely.

Staring straight ahead and walking quickly, Amelia Johnson didn't see the man wearing dark clothes heading in her direction on the other side of 174th Street. Nor did the man walking with intensity and purpose notice his daughter passing by. Even if Packy Johnson had seen Amelia, he would have never connected her with the delightful three-year-old he'd once seen on the other side of a plastic barrier in a prison visiting area fourteen years earlier.

As Amelia approached the corner of Bronx River Avenue, a blue Ford Taurus pulled over to the curb next to her. The driver lowered his passenger-side window and leaned over to ask, "Yo, what's up?"

He sounded drunk, slurring his words so much Amelia was surprised he could drive. She looked around. No other cars in sight. If for no other reason than to get off the street, Amelia decided to take advantage of the opportunity. She walked over and leaned in the open window. The sickly smell of digesting alcohol filled the air. She checked the backseat to make sure it was empty before she slipped into the passenger seat.

"What you want?"

"Get my dick sucked."

Amelia said fifty. He said twenty. She said forty. When he hesitated, Amelia opened the door and turned to leave.

The driver said, "Wait."

She turned back. With the door open, the interior lights gave the mark a better view of Amelia.

"Okay," he said.

Amelia smiled and closed the door. She held out her hand for the money, carefully watching where the man pulled it from. Unfortunately, he dug the bills out of his shirt pocket, handing them to her and slurring something Amelia couldn't make out.

She quickly checked the bills. Two twenties. She stuffed them into her back pocket and asked, "What are you drinking?"

The man smiled and opened his eyes wide like he was going to tell her a big secret. He reached under the driver's seat and pulled out a pint of Johnny Walker Red, unscrewed the cap, and handed the half-empty bottle to Amelia. She smiled back, tipped the bottle up, sipped a small amount, and handed it back. She didn't have to encourage him. He took a healthy swallow.

She asked, "What's your name, honey?"

"Bill. What's yours?"

"Princess."

"Princess what?"

"Okay, Bill, let's get to it, huh? Pull over there around the corner, baby, and find a quiet spot."

"I asked you a question. Princess what?"

"Princess I-wanna-suck-your-dick. Let's go, baby. Time is money."

Amelia caressed Bill's thigh, moving her hand toward his crotch.

"Come on, baby."

Bill put the car in gear and followed Amelia's directions, finding a dark spot under a linden tree on Elder Avenue.

By the time he'd pulled over, Amelia had the condom out. She opened his belt and zipped open his trousers. She worked fast, her heart pounding at the risk she was about to take. She said the things she had to say. She did what she had to do. She even let the drunk's hands wander, all the time keeping a discrete eye on him, watching to make sure his head was tipped back and his eyes were closed.

She kept working him toward a climax, hoping he wasn't too drunk to come, keeping him occupied while she felt the outsides of his pants pockets. She could tell there was nothing but a set of keys in one pocket, a cell phone in the other.

She kept working him, angry at her bad luck. He'd obviously hidden his money somewhere. Maybe in his sock.

She put a hand on Bill's knee, then shifted around so she could lightly brush her free hand past his ankle. Instead of a wallet or money hidden in a sock, she'd felt the outlines of a gun in an ankle holster. Her heart pounded. Could this be a cop? Off duty? Or a bad guy with a gun? Either way the danger level had suddenly escalated enormously.

And now Bill had his hand on the back of her head, pushing her head down, adding to Amelia's panic.

She braced her left hand on the seat and lifted off him. Trying to keep the fear out of her voice she said, "Hey, take it easy, honey. Don't be rough. I'll do you good. Be nice." And as she said that, her left hand slid into the crease between the driver's seat bottom and seat back. Her fingers touched something. She started in on him again, carefully pushed the fingers of her left hand farther into the crease. His wallet. He'd hidden it there.

She worked faster. Making sounds like she was uncontrollably excited.

The drunk slurred encouragement, telling her. "Keep going, bitch. That's it. Come on. Come on you fucking whore."

She did, finishing Bill off as she slid the wallet out from between the seat crevice and into her back pocket. Fear sent her heart banging against her ribs. She knew if this drunk caught her, he would beat her senseless, or quite possibly shoot her.

She smiled, she flirted, she complimented Bill, and got out of the car as fast as she could without creating suspicion, making sure to tell him she'd keep an eye out for him. She left the condom on him to keep him busy.

The moment she closed the car door, she walked across the street, turned south, hurrying away, trying to find an opening between houses she could duck into.

Every driveway was blocked with a chain-link fence, except for the second to last house on the block, which had a wrought-iron gate. Amelia checked and found it unlocked. She slipped past the gate into a narrow driveway between two houses, trying to move silently in her ridiculous platform shoes. Walking sideways between the house and a car, she made it to the end of the driveway and crouched down out of sight behind a second car and a small garage.

She pulled the wallet out of her back pocket and ripped the cash out of it, trying to count the money in the dim light. She heard a dog bark. The sound sent a wash of fear through her. She lost count. Started over. Two hundred, sixty-three dollars. She shoved the bills into her front pocket, and tossed the empty wallet under the car.

She had to make a quick decision. Hide until Bill gave up looking for her, or make a break right now, catch a livery cab on Bronx River Avenue, and get the hell out of the neighborhood.

She took off her wig, pulled up the pink hoodie, and zippered it closed.

She maneuvered through the next driveway, climbing over a short fence, and made her way out to the next street over. She took a deep breath and stepped out onto the sidewalk, walking as fast as her platform shoes would allow, heading for Westchester Avenue. From the waist up she looked different, but there was no way to cover her long bare legs and platform heels.

She made it to Westchester Avenue, feeling more exposed on the open busy street, but there wasn't much she could do about it. She half-walked, half-ran two blocks looking for a cab or livery driver, all the while keeping an eye out for Bill's Taurus.

She saw a beat-up Nissan Sentra with a livery-car license plate stopped at a traffic light ahead. She slipped into the backseat before the driver could pull away.

The driver, a tired-looking Middle Easterner told Amelia, "No. You get out now."

Amelia was in no mood to take any shit from the driver. She yelled, threatened to call 911, 311, and the cops. She showed him money and argued about the fare. She even had to fend off a stupid proposition that he'd take her if she showed him her tits. When she threatened to call her pimp and have him come shoot the driver, he finally agreed, but only after Amelia paid him first.

She gave him thirty dollars for a ride that should have cost twenty and slumped out of sight in the backseat.

When she got to Hunts Point, Amelia put her wig back on and unzipped her hoodie. She walked around, talking to a few of the other women, asking how things were going, making sure she was seen.

Amelia wouldn't risk robbing again. Not at the Point. Too many people knew she was with Derrick Watkins, there were few places to hide, and the area was too isolated to get out quickly.

She already had a good start with her successful robbery, so she could be selective. Pick men who looked like she could hustle. Take her time. Work each trick to get the most dollars. Beg, taunt, make up a story, whatever she could think of to separate them from their money as efficiently as possible.

By 5:35 A.M., Amelia had amassed four hundred and eighty dollars along with a receipt from a street food truck for six dollars and fifty cents she'd had to argue to get. It was a good amount of money, especially for working the Point. She was too exhausted to work a minute longer. Her entire body ached.

As a hazy pre-dawn light seeped into the streets, Amelia wheedled a ride from one of the older women who called herself Staci, promising her five dollars for gas. When Staci asked Amelia where she wanted to go, Amelia surprised herself by giving Staci her grandmother's address. She didn't really know when she'd made the decision. She wasn't even sure what she was going to do when she got there, beyond getting out of her whore clothes, showering, and sleeping on the couch until Lorena found her and woke her up.

Long ago, Amelia had hidden a key to her grandmother's back entrance in the courtyard that separated Lorena's buildings from a duplicate set of buildings one street over on Vyse Avenue. Amelia knew when Lorena found her sleeping on the couch she would yell at her. Ask what she was doing. Amelia didn't have an answer yet. All Amelia Johnson knew for sure was that she was done being Derrick Watkins's whore.

She and Staci were walking in the street, twenty feet from Staci's car, when a green Chevy Malibu screeched to a halt next to her.

Staci disappeared without a word. Amelia froze. Tyrell yelled out the open passenger window. "Yo, bitch. Get in the car. Now."

She turned toward the leering brute, unmoving.

"Fucking get in. I ain't telling you again."

Amelia put her head down and closed her eyes. Running was impossible. Her feet hurt. Her back hurt. She'd probably twist an ankle in her stupid platform heels. And running would just give Tyrell an excuse to hurt her more. She took a breath, feeling the life drain out of her. She walked to the car and got into the passenger seat.

Tyrell couldn't wait to tell her, "You in for it now, girl."

"What?"

"You fucking heard me."

Amelia wouldn't give him the satisfaction of asking him why she was in trouble.

"I'm taking you to the Mount Hope Place apartment."

Amelia felt like someone had just punched her in the stomach. The apartment on Mount Hope Place was used by Derrick and his brother Jerome as a low-rent whorehouse for clients responding to "in-call" ads in *Craigslist* and *Backpage*. Amelia knew the Watkins brothers often made women work for days at a time in that apartment.

Servicing clients in one of the dingy bedrooms on Mount Hope Place, knowing it wouldn't be quick condom-covered blowjobs, but full-on penetration almost made Amelia open the car door and jump out. She looked at the car's dashboard clock. Just past six A.M. Maybe there wouldn't be many customers at this hour.

As if reading her mind, Tyrell told her, "Don't worry. You ain't going to be workin'. Gonna be a lot worse than that."

A flood of questions hit Amelia. She couldn't imagine what could be worse. She turned to Tyrell, waiting for more information. He gave her nothing but a self-satisfied smirk.

The ride to Mount Hope Place took less than ten minutes. Tyrell pulled her out of his car by the arm and turned her toward the house. Amelia wrenched her arm free and yelled at him, "Get off me."

Tyrell raised a hand to hit her. Amelia screamed at him, "You hit me I'll kill you. I'll fucking kill you. You ain't my pimp. You ain't got the right."

Tyrell gave her a hard look and nodded at her, as if to say, okay, just wait.

He followed her into the house and walked behind her as Amelia made it up three flights of stairs to the top floor, knowing the disgusting Tyrell was staring at her ass all the way. Tyrell unlocked the front door and told her to go into the first bedroom.

She told him she had to go to the bathroom first.

He said, "Hurry the fuck up."

As soon as Amelia entered the bathroom, she locked the door and dug out the cash from her pocket. She took three twenty dollar bills, folded them into a small bundle, and took off her wig. She carefully hid the bills in her thick black hair, holding them in place with a barrette. She put the wig back on, used the toilet, and stepped out of the bathroom.

Tyrell locked her in the nearest bedroom. Amelia was too exhausted to do anything more than lay down on a bed stinking of stale perfume and body odors. Within seconds, she fell into a sleep so deep it felt like death.

4

In the pre-dawn light, the body spilling off the curb looked like a large bag of garbage.

Detective John Palmer eagerly stepped out of the unmarked Impala he'd pulled over at the corner of 174th Street and Longfellow Avenue. His partner, Raymond Ippolito, pulled himself out with a grunt and walked slowly behind him, frowning at the sight of a corpse jammed between the curb and a parked car.

The report came in thirty minutes before the end of their Wednesday midnight-to-eight shift at the 42nd Precinct in the Bronx. A dead body lying in the gutter. There wasn't any particular reason to believe it was a murder. In fact, there hadn't been a murder in the Four-Two in thirteen months. Not like the old days. But if this was a murder victim, Palmer knew it would provide a rare chance for recognition and advancement toward his goal of Detective First Grade.

For Ippolito, a murder, an accident, a heart attack – it didn't matter. It was all just bad luck.

Clouds obscured the rising sun. The air felt heavy with humidity and hotter than normal for the end of May. In the dim light, with a stunted elm tree shading the area, Ippolito wondered how long it had taken for someone to spot the body.

Both detectives stopped about ten feet away, stood next to each other on the sidewalk, a vest-pocket park behind them, and gazed at the corpse in front of them.

Two first-on-the-scene uniformed cops were stringing NYPD crime-scene tape, forming a thirty-foot rectangular boundary around the body.

Palmer told the cops, "Hey, you gotta close off a bigger area, guys. Take the tape across the street, run it up the whole block, and bring it back over to this side."

Ippolito watched the cops, a tall African-American and a short Hispanic, react to Palmer's take-charge order with deadpan expressions. They didn't seem to wonder why the younger detective was giving the orders. Ippolito was clearly the senior detective. At fifty-two years old, too overweight to close the top button of his white shirt, wearing a rumpled sports jacket and stained tie, he was nearly twice Palmer's age. Palmer wore a trim-fitting dark suit, blue shirt, and skinny tie. He'd been a detective for a little over a year.

Palmer said, "Hey, Ray, think we should pull the car across the intersection there, let people know they can't drive through?"

"The tape should be enough, John."

"Right, right."

Palmer walked over to the body. He slid on a pair of blue latex gloves from his back pocket and squatted next to the corpse, just looking.

The body lay sideways, facing away from him, the head and upper body jammed between the curb and a Honda Odyssey. Most of the face was pressed against the front tire.

Palmer had to lean over to see the profile, but the section of sidewalk where he squatted had been cracked and lifted by the roots of the elm tree so he had to place a hand against the SUV to keep his balance.

He leaned farther over the victim and bumped his head on the parked car.

In the dim dawn light, Palmer couldn't tell if the man's zippered sweatshirt and T-shirt were dark blue or black. The pants were definitely dark blue jeans. He bent closer, looking down at the side of the dead man's face. He could just make out a swollen bruise on the left cheek.

Palmer looked for blood. He didn't see any on the clothes or sidewalk or curb, although there could be blood under the dead man.

The victim's right arm and hand were under the body. The left hand jammed between stomach and car. Palmer carefully pulled the lifeless left hand free. He took out a small Maglite from the inside pocket of his suit jacket and focused the bright white light on the hand. There were open scrapes and cuts on almost every knuckle.

Ippolito stood close behind Palmer, watching, saying nothing.

Palmer held up the man's hand.

"Looks like he was in a fight."

Ippolito made a small noise of agreement.

Palmer pulled back the unzipped sweatshirt, shining his light along the length of the torso, playing the part of a careful investigator looking for blood, stab wounds, bullet wounds. There were none.

He slowly ran the light toward the neck and head. They both saw it at the same time.

"Ah," said Ippolito.

Palmer leaned closer, moving the dark hair aside with his right forefinger, uncovering more of the angry red bullet hole, the edges stippled and stained with gunpowder. The bullet had entered about two inches below and slightly to the right of the man's left ear.

"Shot."

"Yep."

The long hair made it difficult to see the wound clearly, even under the glare of the Maglite.

"Guess we'd better turn him over. See if it came out the other side."

Ippolito was down next to Palmer now. It was much harder for the older, heavier man to squat. He balanced himself with one hand against the Honda and craned his head down and around, almost even with the street.

"Nah, no blood under his head. Bullet's still in there. If it'd come out there'd be blood all over the place."

Palmer asked, "Nothing under him?"

"No," said Ippolito, "I think he got shot and the impact sent him down right here."

"Let's lift him onto the sidewalk. Roll him on his back."

The body was wedged so tightly between the car and the curb it took an unexpected amount of effort. When they finally managed to free the dead man and lay him flat, Ippolito let out a hiss.

"Fuck. Somebody beat the shit out of this poor guy."

Even without the Maglite, Palmer could see that the face had been damaged. Some of it might have been from the pressure created when the bullet entered the head, but clearly the victim had been beaten. Both eyes were filled with blood, blackened underneath, a cut split the bridge of his nose, both upper and lower lips were lacerated. There was a swollen lump at the corner of the left jaw.

Ippolito stood up with a grunt. Palmer joined him. They stared down at the victim.

Palmer asked, "You want to look around for a shell casing?"

"Size of the hole, I'm betting a twenty-two." Ippolito gave the area a cursory look. "Gonna take a lot of work to find it, all this mess around here. Let the CSU guys do it."

Palmer frowned and nodded. Another patrol car had arrived. One of the uniformed cops joined the others to keep passersby away from the crime scene. The other cop waited near Palmer and Ippolito for orders.

Palmer pulled out his police radio and called the precinct dispatcher, telling her to send a sergeant and request a Crime Scene Unit.

Ippolito looked down at the body. Frowned, shook his head, and said to himself, "All I fucking need, end of my goddam shift."

Ippolito watched Palmer check the pockets of the dead man. He pulled out a single key on a beaded chain, a thin wallet, a wad of folded papers in the back pocket.

"What's in the wallet?" asked Ippolito.

"Couple hundred bucks. A little more. Guess it wasn't a robbery."

"No ID?"

"No. Wait a second." Palmer found a single laminated card in the wallet. "Shit."

"What?"

Palmer held it up. "Department of Correction ID. Name is Paco Johnson."

Ippolito squinted at the ID. "Ah, Christ. What's this guy, on parole?"

Palmer unfolded the papers he'd pulled from the victim's back pocket. "Jeezus, this son of a bitch just got out yesterday."

"What?"

Palmer handed the discharge forms to Ippolito, who checked the dates.

"You fucking kidding me? This guy ain't been out even a day." Ippolito squinted at the dates again. "Christ, he was in seventeen years."

Palmer stared down at the inert body and shook his head, trying to look concerned while thinking: *Shit, man, people are gonna be all over this one. Department of Correction. The Parole Division.*

He took the papers back from Ippolito.

Paco Johnson had been discharged from Eastern Correctional Facility at 2 P.M. yesterday, Tuesday. He checked his watch. Palmer could already see the headline: PAROLEE DEAD SEVENTEEN HOURS AFTER SEVENTEEN YEARS IN PRISON.

He took out his notebook and carefully wrote down the time, place, victim's name, and the name of parole officer assigned to him: Walter Ferguson.

5

Wednesday morning a little after eight, Walter Ferguson walked from his apartment on Livingston Street to his office three blocks east. As the highest-ranking member of the staff, he tried to be the first one in every morning. This morning, two men were waiting for him. Walter quickly made them for NYPD detectives. One older. One younger.

The veteran detective looked like he had definitely worked past his normal shift and wanted to get home. The younger one appeared to be ready to go another shift and another after that if needed.

Walter went through a quick mental inventory of parolees who might have caused two detectives to show up. Unfortunately, it was a long list.

By ten thirty, James Beck had finished most of his morning routine and sat restlessly in his usual spot at the far end of an old oak bar on the ground floor of his building in Red Hook. Sections of the morning edition of *The New York Times* lay stacked on the bar in the order Beck had read them.

Demarco Jones stood cleaning the back-bar shelves and wiping down bottles, his puttering around adding to Beck's restlessness.

Beck thought about calling Ferguson, but decided to wait. Walter would be busy enough dealing with Packy's hitchhiking stunt.

Just then the front door opened, and Walter Ferguson entered.

Beck saw the expression on Walter's face. Noted he was alone. A sick feeling hit him just below his solar plexus.

Walter Ferguson, normally a vigorous, distinguished African-American man, looked sallow, tired, barely able to move. He was dressed as usual in a suit and tie, but uncharacteristically the top button of his shirt was open and the tie pulled loose.

"What happened?"

Walter stepped to the bar, placing his right hand on it for support. He neither looked at Beck, nor answered his question.

Walter cleared his throat and said, "Demarco, may I have a whiskey, please."

Demarco's brow furrowed. He had never seen Walter Ferguson drink alcohol. He poured Johnny Walker Black into a rocks glass. No ice, no water.

They waited for Walter to take a long sip.

Walter put his head down and rested his foot on the bar rail, waiting for the burning in his throat to subside.

He looked up, his eyes distant, his voice choked with emotion, and said, "Paco Johnson is dead."

Nobody moved, as if moving would confirm the truth.

Beck stifled an anguished curse. He came off his bar stool and took a step toward Ferguson. "Walter, what the hell happened?"

Walter turned to Beck. The older man looked so distraught that Beck involuntarily reached out and put a hand on his arm.

Walter responded in a flat, toneless voice.

"Two detectives showed up at my office this morning. From the Forty-second Precinct in the Bronx. They discovered Packy's body on the street this morning. I forget the exact location. Somewhere, I . . . I'll have to look at a map. They said a man opening a bodega saw the body and called it in about six o'clock. They found ID on him and my name and address on his release papers. They came to my office this morning for information."

"Wait a minute, wait a minute," said Beck. "What happened to him? Where was this?"

"Northern Bronx. Near where the, uh, mother-in-law's apartment is. Where he was staying."

Beck turned away, gripping the bar with both hands, grimacing, trying to fight off the anguish and helplessness.

"What happened? Did he have a heart attack or something? What was he doing out on the street at six in the morning?"

"James, this is bad. Very bad."

"Walter, please, just tell me."

Manny Guzman had come out from the bar kitchen. Dressed in his usual work clothes, Manny looked like a tough, old short-order cook, except for the prison tattoos peeking out from the collar and cuffs of his canvas work shirt.

He had heard Walter's report and walked slowly, solemnly, to stand on Walter's left. Demarco remained behind the bar with no expression.

Walter took a small sip of his scotch and spoke calmly in a more normal voice.

"Here is what they told me. And trust me, I used every bit of my authority to get as much information as I could.

"They responded to a nine-one-one call at about six o'clock this morning. Near the end of their shift. Two uniformed patrol cops were already at the scene. Packy was half on the sidewalk, half in the street.

"They did a preliminary exam. They said it looked like Packy had been in a fight, but what killed him was a gunshot to the head. Small caliber." Walter pointed his forefinger to a spot behind his right ear. "Right here. No exit wound. Bullet still in him."

Walter paused, blinked, and then continued.

"The younger cop said they didn't find any shell casings or anything near the body. They left when the Crime Scene Unit arrived to come to my office, but before the medical examiner showed up. They're still processing the scene. The only witness so far is the store clerk who reported seeing the body. The area was most likely deserted when it happened, but they're canvassing for witnesses.

"I asked them about when they thought it happened, but they wouldn't guess. Said they'll wait for the M.E. report. They reassured me there'd be a thorough investigation."

Walter paused for a moment, and then continued.

"The older detective asked me if and when I'd talked to Packy. I told him about seven-thirty last night." Walter turned to Beck. "What time did I call you, James?"

Beck had to focus to answer. "Uh, yeah, yeah. Seven-thirty."

"Okay. So, sometime last night between then and six in the morning. I told them Packy called me from a pay phone near his mother-in-law's place."

"Are the cops going to talk to the mother-in-law next?"

"Yes."

"You think Packy went to her place after he talked to you?"

"Yes. I think so. And they found him near the mother-in-law's. I told them her address, they said it was within walking distance of where they found the body."

Beck had forced himself to calm down even though he was seething, guilty, hovering between devastated and determined.

He said, "I should have . . ."

"No, James. I told you not to go up there." Walter rubbed his face with both of his big hands, pulling himself together, standing up straight to his full height of just over six two. He cleared his throat.

"Packy Johnson was the responsibility of the Division of Parole from the moment he stepped out of that prison. He had an officer in my group assigned to him, a man under my supervision. I was the one in charge of Packy. He was my responsibility. I should have gone to see him last night after he hitchhiked into town, but I made an error in judgment." Walter shook his head at the recollection. "I don't know what I thought, but I made a terrible mistake, and now Packy is dead."

Beck said, "Walter, you can't . . ."

Walter waved him quiet.

"What I'm saying is, Packy was my responsibility. And still is until everything is resolved, and he's had a decent burial. I will follow up with the homicide investigation, with the medical examiner's office, with whomever. I'm not letting this go."

Beck said, "Yes, Walter, of course. When did the cops leave you?"

Ferguson checked his watch. "About forty minutes ago."

"Okay."

The question alerted Walter. He turned toward Beck. "James, you can't get involved in this."

Beck stepped back from the bar and nodded. "I know."

"James, we don't know what happened yet. You have to let the police handle this. If you get in the way, go out there and do anything foolish" – Walter paused and looked at Demarco and Manny – "it won't do anybody any good."

"I'm not disagreeing with you, Walter. And like you said, you'll follow up on everything."

"I will."

Beck placed a hand under Walter's elbow, put his arm around the taller man, and gently guided him toward the front door.

"You promise you'll let me know whatever you find out. As soon as you find out."

"Of course."

"After they're done, after they find out what they need to find out, we'll make arrangements with you about the burial. We'll cover whatever it costs. You know that, right? Can you claim the body? There's no other next of kin is there?"

"Packy has a daughter, but as far as I know there hasn't been any contact between them for years."

"Right, right. I think I knew that. But can you be in charge of the body? I mean, claiming it and all so we can make the funeral arrangements."

"Yes. Packy is still the responsibility of the division until the case is resolved. I'll try to find the daughter and notify her, but I'm responsible."

"Okay. Fine. Good."

Beck had walked Walter Ferguson to the door.

"How'd you get here, Walter?"

"Car service. I told him to wait."

Beck opened the door and saw the car parked across the street.

"Okay, good. I'm – I'm at a loss here, Walter. I don't know what else to say."

Walter stepped out of the bar into a day that had continued to be gloomy and overcast. He turned to Beck. "What can you say?"

The two men shook hands solemnly. Beck watched as Walter walked slowly toward the car. After a few steps he turned back and faced Beck.

"James."

"What?"

"Thank you."

"For what?"

"For listening to me."

Beck nodded, grimacing at the effort to contain the emotions overtaking him. Three seconds after the car pulled away, Beck turned back into the bar, not even bothering to close the door. He let out a primal curse of rage and slammed a fist down on the nearest table.

Manny Guzman, baleful and solemn as ever, had already taken off his apron, heading back to the kitchen for his guns.

Demarco pulled Beck's gun lockbox out from under the bar and placed it on the bar top. He took out a Benelli

M2 Tactical Shotgun with a pistol grip from a cabinet in the back bar. He laid it on the bar, pulled his Glock out from his waistband at the small of his back, and brought out boxes of ammunition from under the bar.

Demarco asked, "What's the old lady's address?"

Beck spoke slowly, trying to keep his anger in check.

"I'll give you directions. Goddam fucking parole board. We had to use her place so it looked like he was with a relative. So it would look good on his fucking COMPAS score. But she wasn't a blood relative. She was nothing to Packy."

Manny returned to the bar room, the old gangster's expression without affect. Maybe old friends like Beck and Demarco could see an extra intensity smoldering in his dark eyes, but even without it, Manny Guzman, a stocky Hispanic man in his fifties, looked to be a man intent on a reckoning.

Manny had a gun in both of his front pants pockets. A Charter Arms .357 Magnum Bulldog revolver for up close. A Smith & Wesson .38 Special for longer distance.

"Do we need Ciro?" Demarco asked.

"I don't know," said Beck. "But Packy was one of us. We have to call him."

6

After their meeting with Walter Ferguson, John Palmer and Ray Ippolito pulled up to an address on Hoe Avenue located seven blocks from where they'd found the body of Packy Johnson.

Palmer parked their unmarked car in front of a row of redbrick two-story buildings that ran the entire block. The public housing had been built in 1958. Each building held four apartments. From the outside, everything looked well maintained. All the windows had child-safety bars on them. The garbage cans were lined up neatly out front.

Palmer checked the address he had written down in his notebook and pointed to the entrance two sections to their right.

"Over there," he said.

"Think she's gonna have anything to tell us?"

"Let's find out."

Ippolito knew the best chance to find a lead usually happened in the first hours of a murder investigation. Despite needing sleep, he knew they had to keep going for as long as they could, even though he didn't have high hopes. Most murders were committed by someone who knew the victim. But Paco Johnson hadn't been on the streets for seventeen years. Maybe this was a simple drug deal gone bad, just another guy out of prison looking to score. It happened so often it was a cliché. But

Ippolito didn't think so. The man had clearly been in a fight. He still had his wallet on him with over two hundred dollars in it. And where they'd found him wasn't a known location for drug deals.

He put it all out of his mind and followed Palmer toward the entrance. Ippolito knew Palmer saw this case as an opportunity for advancement. He was the most ambitious young man he'd ever known. It ran in the family. Palmer's father, John Palmer Senior, had a reputation for being a hard-charger. He was a well-known lobbyist and political operator with clients both in Albany and Washington. Ippolito had zero doubt that John Junior fully intended to use his father's connections and influence to advance his career.

More power to him, thought Ippolito.

They found Lorena Leon's buzzer. After three rings, a garbled voice came over the intercom.

"*¿Qué?*"

Ippolito leaned toward the speaker. "*Policía*. Lorena, *abra la puerta, por favor.*"

Palmer said, "You sound like you know her."

"Exactly."

A buzzer sounded. They pushed open the entrance door, stepping into a musty interior. The humid weather seemed to intensify the cooking odors, cat piss, and general mustiness of the old building.

Both men trudged to the second floor. They passed cinder-block walls painted institutional green. The linoleum floors were worn down to black in the center of the stairwells. Ippolito found apartment 2G. At the second knock, the door opened to the width of a safety chain.

The weathered face of a short, thin Hispanic woman peered out at them.

Ippolito held his police identification in front of her eyes. *"Policía."*

She squinted at the identification. *"¿Qué deseas?"*

"Estamos aquí para hablar con usted acerca de Paco Johnson. *¿Se puede abrir la puerta, por favor?"*

Palmer added, "Ma'am, don't be alarmed. Just open the door so we can ask you a few questions."

The door closed. Ippolito and Palmer listened for the sound of the chain being removed, but heard nothing. They exchanged looks. Palmer raised a fist to bang on the door when it suddenly opened wide.

Lorena Leon stood in the doorway, defiantly blocking entrance. She had once been a good-looking woman. Even now, after a lifetime of hard years, she made sure to color her gray hair a deep brown with something she bought off the shelf at the local Duane Reade. But she couldn't cover the deeply etched lines in her skin, or hide the anger and defiance in her eyes. She wore a pair of old jeans that hung off her bony hips and a clinging, faded white top with navy blue horizontal stripes that emphasized her sagging breasts.

Ippolito asked, "Okay if we come in?"

She stepped back and hacked a phlegmy smoker's cough.

Old, cheap furniture crowded the small living room. For some inexplicable reason, an iron skillet filled with fried ground beef sat on a heavy 1950s coffee table in front of a beat-up red couch.

Drooping green drapes covered most of the room's two windows, blocking the gray daylight outside. A tired window air conditioner ground away, doing very little to change the fetid air filled with cooking smells.

Both detectives stepped in, but neither moved very far into the apartment so as not to upset her. She stood with her arms crossed, waiting for whatever trouble they had brought to her.

Palmer hung back, letting Ippolito continue.

"Mrs. Leon, I'm afraid we have some bad news."

She shook her head and turned away from them, moving over to the couch, sitting down at the edge, as if she didn't want to hear the bad news while standing. She didn't offer the detectives a seat so Palmer and Ippolito walked toward the couch and stood opposite her.

Palmer held his notebook and pen, ready to take down any information Ippolito might pull out of the old lady.

Ippolito knew from his interview with Ferguson that Lorena was Paco Johnson's mother-in-law, so he put on a sympathetic demeanor, informing her, "Your son-in-law was found dead this morning, not too far from here."

Lorena looked up at Ippolito confused. He translated. *"Su yerno fue encontrado muerto."*

Maybe it was his accent, but Ippolito's translation seemed to confuse her even more.

She responded with a voice degraded by decades of cheap menthol cigarettes. "What?"

Palmer glared at the woman and raised his voice in case there was something wrong with her hearing. "Paco Johnson has been murdered."

"He's dead?"

"Yes. He's dead."

"Why?" she asked.

Good question, thought Ippolito.

"That's what we're trying to find out. Do you have any idea why?"

She looked down at a frayed green carpet and shook her head. Palmer couldn't tell if she was somehow trying to deny Packy had been murdered, or deny them an answer.

She looked up at them and frowned.

Ippolito said, "Can you tell us anything that might explain what happened?"

"He should never come here. Never."

"Why, Mrs. Leon? Why should he have never come here?"

She shot her right hand up as if to slap away the trouble that had entered her home. She sat up straighter.

"He don't belong here. He knows nothing. I never see him for years. He no care about me, about my house."

"So why did he come here?" asked Ippolito.

"From prison. For a place to stay. He no want to be here. You are the police. You already know these things? You know he was in prison."

Palmer said, "Why did you let him come here, if you didn't want him to?"

Now the old lady looked up at the two men. First Palmer, then Ippolito. Something in her hardened. She shook her head again, digging in, a stubborn scowl twisting her face.

Ippolito was tired. The hot, stuffy apartment and odor of the fried beef aggravated him. The old lady's raspy smoker's voice annoyed him. If this was their only lead, they were going to be fucked on this case.

He walked to the dining area and came back with a chair, part of an old red Formica dining set. The vinyl on the back of the chair had split apart years ago. He dragged the chair near where Lorena Leon sat and placed himself in front of her.

Palmer stood where he was, watching, listening carefully.

Ippolito poked the old woman's knee, perhaps harder than he'd intended. She jerked away from him and looked at him, angrier now. Ippolito didn't care.

He dropped his attempts at Spanish, not wanting to give her any cover. "Listen to me, lady. This is serious. This isn't drugs, or burglary, or some petty bullshit. This is homicide. Murder. Understand?"

Ippolito made sure to get his face right in front of the older woman's. He looked at her carefully, letting what he'd said sink in. Although her skin had creased with age and taken on a web of fine lines from years of smoking, the woman had strong features. This wasn't some shy old lady. She still had plenty of fire in her.

She didn't look away. She met Ippolito's direct gaze.

He spoke slowly and forcefully. "We don't forget about murders. We will find out everything. Everything. If you help us, if you tell us what you know, it will be better for you. What's the matter, don't you want to know who killed your son-in-law?"

"No. I don't want to know. I don't care."

Ippolito ignored the response and forged on. "Did he come here like he was supposed to when he got released from prison yesterday?"

"Yes. He come here like he was supposed to."

"What time was that?"

"Last night. About eight."

"How long was he here?"

"I give him some food. Maybe an hour he stays. Then he went out."

"Where?"

"I don't know."

"He didn't tell you?"

"No."

"You didn't ask?"

Again she stopped talking, but Ippolito and Palmer had no doubt she knew more than she was telling them. Palmer took a soft approach, speaking to Lorena Leon as if the two of them trusted each other. Not like the other cop in the chair staring at her.

"Come on, Mrs. Leon, it's okay to tell us. Don't worry. Where did he go? He must have said something."

Lorena responded with a quick shake of her head. She grabbed the iron skillet with the pungent ground meat and stood quickly, her agility surprising both men.

Palmer took a half step back, thinking for a moment she was going to toss the greasy ground meat at him, or worse, try to hit him with the iron skillet.

Ippolito stood, thinking the same, and how embarrassing it would be to take down an old lady trying to hit them with a damn frying pan.

But the moment passed quickly as Lorena stepped around the coffee table, moving away from them, heading toward her kitchen.

She didn't turn to them as she spoke. She yelled out, "He went to find his *mandria* daughter."

Palmer whispered to Ippolito, "What's *mandria* mean?"

"Worthless."

Both men followed at a distance as Lorena walked into her small, cluttered kitchen. Now Ippolito hung back, letting Palmer stand in the doorway asking his questions.

"What's his daughter's name?"

"Amelia."

"Johnson?"

"Yes, what other name?"

"Why did he want to find his daughter?"

She continued answering in a shout, never looking at Palmer. She dropped the skillet on the counter with a bang. Pulled out a bowl from a cupboard over the counter. Scooped and scraped the ground meat into the bowl. Shouting out information.

"Why shouldn't he go see his daughter? He didn't see her for so many years. He wants to see her, so I told him. Go to the Bronx River Houses. She's in there. With her pimp. Derrick. Derrick Watkins. I know what she does. Like her mother. A whore and a drug addict."

Palmer wrote quickly and carefully in his notebook.

"The same, the same. Always the same. Such a beautiful girl. Like her mother. And look what she does."

Lorena was crying now, talking, ranting as the tears ran down her face, seemingly unconnected to any anguish. Her face remained without expression as she angrily wiped her tears with the back of her hand, as she continued to fuss with the food and the bowl and the skillet, scraping up the ground meat and wiping away the drip under her nose, as annoyed and angry at her crying as she had been at the two men who had come into her apartment. No sobbing, no hitch in her voice. Her tears seemed to be an independent part of her that she simply couldn't control. Just like she couldn't control what was happening around her.

She dropped the skillet into her sink and pushed past Palmer before he could step out of her way. She headed back to her small living room, away from them. She was done with them.

But Ippolito wouldn't let her get away. He yelled out after her as she walked past him, putting enough into his voice to let her know this wasn't over yet.

"Hey, Mrs. Leon!"

Ippolito walked after her into the living room. Palmer hung back. She stopped and turned to him, her old wet eyes blazing, arms crossed.

"What?" she yelled.

Ippolito saw Lorena was reaching a point he didn't want her to go past.

"Just one more question, okay? Why did you let him come here?"

She lifted her chin at him as she answered, "Go ask the parole man. The black man and his friend."

"What friend?"

"Someone who knew Paco in prison." She paused, remembering the name. "Beck. His name is Beck. They made me take him, that's why. They make me do it. Okay?"

Ippolito said, "You know his first name?"

"James. He and the black man, they say he can't get out of prison without a place." Lorena's mouth formed into a tight line. She looked like a defiant child refusing to eat. She suddenly yelled, "They make me take him, okay?"

With that, she walked out of the living room, down a short hall to her bedroom, and slammed the door behind her.

70

7

As usual, Demarco Jones drove the customized, all-black Mercury Marauder. Beck in the front passenger seat. Manny content to be alone in the back.

Nobody spoke much. Each of them dealing with their memories, sorrow, and anger.

Beck felt the pain more intensely than the others, for he had been much closer to Packy Johnson. He struggled with the loss of a true friend. And the terrible loss of a last chance for Packy.

Packy Johnson had lived forty-two years, thirty-two of which had been spent in juvenile institutions, foster homes, or prisons. Eighty percent of his life confined, focused mostly on simply surviving. And now, the chance for Packy Johnson to finally experience what a life freed from incarceration might have to offer him had been completely and irrevocably destroyed.

Demarco glanced at Beck brooding. He had never seen him give in to such a dark, angry mood. A mood Demarco knew might turn Beck reckless. And that would be very dangerous.

In the backseat, Manny Guzman showed little except for the imperceptible clenching of his jaw and occasional pursing of his lips.

Demarco cleared his throat.

"I left a message for Ciro."

Beck nodded once. "Good."

Demarco pushed it, wanting to get Beck talking.

"What do we know about this old lady?"

Beck scratched his nose with the knuckle of his fore-finger. His mouth twitched. "Not much. Walter and I went to see her in order to get the housing issue cleared with the parole board. She's a hard case."

"How old is she?"

"I don't know. I'd guess in her seventies."

"And what is she to Packy? An in-law?"

"Barely. I don't know if she's anything to anybody."

"What about his daughter? He has a daughter, right?"

Beck knew Demarco's questions were his way of pulling him out of his silent brooding so he went along with it, barely.

"I don't know much about her. I think she's sixteen or seventeen."

"Who's she live with?"

"I don't know. It wasn't something we asked the mother-in-law about."

"Was Packy close to her? The daughter?"

Beck lapsed into one-word answers.

"No."

Demarco persisted. "So you and Packy first met up at Clinton, right?"

"Yeah."

"How long before you got sent there? I forget."

Beck shifted in his seat. They were entering the Brooklyn Battery Tunnel. His thoughts narrowed like the car lanes entering the underpass, remembering back when he had been unjustly sentenced to a term of ten to thirty years for first-degree aggravated manslaughter.

"After my trial was finally over, which took almost two years, they sent me to Sing Sing for about eight months, which is where a lot of guys go until they get sorted out."

"But that judge tried to get you exiled right away up to Clinton, right?"

"He tried. He put a target on me with the Department of Correction as much as he could, but DoC moved at its own pace."

From the backseat Manny said, "You killed a cop, man. He wanted to make an example of you."

"I killed a drunken loudmouth in a stupid bar fight that consisted of a chest bump and one punch. The prosecutor tried to screw me by withholding evidence, the judge fucked me with the jury instructions and the way he ran the trial, and he fucked me again in the sentencing and the assignment. It all gave Phineas more grounds for appeal, but at the time, it put me in a nearly constant state of rage. Pissed off at the judge, the trial, my lawyer, myself."

Manny nodded at his memory of Beck in Dannemora. "And what, couple days after that they threw you in the SHU?"

"Yeah. When I got out of the Box, I was ready to go after anybody. Inmates. Guards. I was right on the edge." Beck shook his head at the memory. "If I hadn't run into Packy, I wouldn't have made it."

Manny spoke while staring out the car window, almost as if he were talking to himself. "Those sadist pricks like driving men to suicide."

Demarco asked, "How'd you connect with Packy?"

"Day after I got out of the SHU. Ran into him in the north yard." Beck shook his head at the memory. "He'd been in a long time by then. He took one look at me and just said what I needed to hear. He saved my life. He changed my life."

Demarco glanced at Beck, waiting for Beck to explain more, but he didn't, and Demarco let it go.

The car emerged from the tunnel. Demarco eased over to the left lane heading for the FDR.

A sad silence descended in the car. No one spoke for a while. And then, without preamble, the grizzled, oldest, perhaps toughest of them, Manny Guzman, leaned forward and placed his hand on Beck's left shoulder. He let his heavy hand remain there for a moment, and then patted Beck's shoulder one time. Suddenly, everything Beck had been feeling penetrated into him. And he allowed it. Allowed the deep, terrible unremitting loss to stream into him and flow back out.

Beck blinked, feeling the sudden sting of tears welling up. He stared straight out the windshield, silent and still. Nothing seemed to touch him now as he let the tears spill from his eyes. He wiped his face with an open palm, in the same way he would wipe away sweat.

In the backseat Manny Guzman nodded to himself slowly.

In the driver's seat Demarco Jones blinked and cleared his throat.

Beck turned in his direction and smiled ruefully, shaking his head. "Jeezus."

Demarco tipped his head in acknowledgment.

Beck began talking again to fend off the emotion.

"Packy and me met first." Beck pointed a thumb toward the backseat. "A month or so later, me and the OG there connected."

"After he got ahold of himself."

"After I helped you with the Crips thing."

"That, too. D, once we got together it wasn't long before we ran our part of that place. I mean, we ran that thing and half the dopes in there didn't know we was running it. That was the beauty of it."

Beck said, "The warden knew it well enough."

"I guess."

"No guessing about it. That's why they sent me the hell out of there. Warden didn't bother trying to arrange another max prison for me, he just sent me back to Sing Sing. It was just as bad as it was when I'd been there the first time. Too many new guards training there. Too many assholes coming in from Rikers still in the middle of some war that started in that shit hole. Seemed like half the prison had a blade of some sort. Sneaking around, scheming for a way to jump somebody."

Manny said, referring to Demarco, "That's when you and the *maricón,* here, met, right? Your second bit at Sing Sing."

Beck looked at Demarco. "You were there, what, about a year when I got back the second time?"

"About a year. Little more. I was on A block. You were on B."

Beck nodded, remembering. "Too many fucking grudges and fights in that place. You remember the guy who stomped that poor bastard's head out in the yard?"

Now it was Demarco's turn to be terse. "Yes."

Beck said, "The tower guard shot him, but not before he crushed the guy's skull."

Demarco said, "Got him in the leg, which was a good shot from that distance."

Manny said, "I'm glad they kept me at Clinton."

Beck turned and said, "That's cuz they didn't want you starting a war at another prison. They kept you there and moved everybody away from you."

Demarco accelerated the Mercury onto the FDR and said, "How long before you left for Eastern?"

"About a year. By then Phineas was going all guns on my appeal. He'd pretty much cracked it open. The timing came together on a lot of moving parts. Taschen was going to retire. . . ."

"The cop who finally came forward?"

"Yeah. He didn't have to worry about being blackballed or losing his rank or anything. That broke it open. All the Brady violations came out. Prosecutor withholding exculpatory evidence. The bad jury instructions. Phineas tore down the temple, man. He got me transferred out of Sing Sing up to Eastern. Much better joint. Calmer. Max security, but a better place. And they had a bunch of programs up there. Including the Bard College thing."

"And Packy was there by then."

"Yep."

Demarco continued up the FDR, maneuvered the car into the right lane, lining up to head over the Willis Avenue Bridge. Beck watched the slimy water of the East River slide by on his right, remembering his past.

"I didn't know he was at Eastern. I was sitting out in the yard by myself. Early summer night, a couple of weeks after they transferred me there. Around this time of year. They have a big athletic field next to the main building. The walls weren't very high on that side. You could see the sky. You could see the Shawangunk Ridge off in the distance. It almost felt like you were outside, not trapped in a prison.

"So I'm sitting on this bench near one of the ball fields, and I see this guy heading toward me from about fifty yards away. The sun was behind him, so I couldn't really make him out. He had his hands in sight, which helped, but you know – prison. You don't take anything for granted. So I get up on my feet. He stops, laughs. Calls out my name. Now I see it's Packy. We do the handshake, the brother hug. How're you doing? Blah, blah, blah. Thirty seconds later, no warning, no explanation, he asks me to help him learn to read better."

"Just like that."

"Yep. That's the way it was with Packy. No preamble. No explanation. He always got right to it. So I agreed, but it's fucking hard to teach an adult how to read. You ever do it?"

"No."

"I don't recommend it. I never knew what prompted him to ask me. And he never went overboard thanking me. It was just understood. He'd do the same for me if he could, so that was it."

Demarco said, "And with no strings attached like with most cons who only do something as part of a hustle."

"Yeah, that endless, goddam running the con."

Manny said, "They can't help it."

"You're right. They cannot stop themselves. Packy was way beyond that shit."

The men stopped talking and turned their attention to the neighborhood. They had skirted the edges of Hunts Point and maneuvered into the section of the Bronx where Lorena Leon lived. Everyone's attention focused. Manny scanned everything out of both windows from the backseat. Beck's eyes shifted constantly. None of them was very familiar with this neighborhood.

The area had evolved from bad to decent. Many of the buildings they passed were four- and five-story brick apartment buildings that looked fairly well maintained, interspersed with two-story houses. There were also dozens of newer buildings where there had once been rubble-strewn empty lots. Plus, signs of renovation were everywhere: scaffolding sheds covering sidewalks, buildings being gutted, some of them covered in netting with multiple Dumpster bins out front.

A few of the lots had been turned into little parks or, in some cases, rough community gardens. One entire block of attached two-flats looked like they could have been pulled out of Astoria, Queens. The cars parked on the streets were fairly new.

But the people on the streets were still overwhelmingly black and Hispanic. Splashes of graffiti marred the neighborhood, and most ground-floor doors and windows were protected by iron bars.

Demarco maneuvered along one-way streets to Lorena Leon's address. As they moved farther north, the density decreased and there were fewer people on the streets.

The Mercury rolled past a boarded-up three-flat. Two gangbangers sat in front of the abandoned building on lawn chairs. One man stood at the top of the stoop, scanning the street.

They gave Beck and his men hard looks as they cruised by. Drug dealing still had its place in the Bronx.

They pulled up to Lorena's housing complex. Seeing the low-rise buildings again from the outside reminded Beck that the inside was much more grim.

"D, hang out here while Manny and I go in and talk to her."

"Take your time."

"We're not going to need much."

8

At 11:45 A.M., not quite six hours after they'd found the body of Paco Johnson, Palmer and Ippolito parked on Harrod Avenue in front of Bronx River Houses, located in the Soundview section of the Bronx. The complex was bounded by East 174th Street, Harrod Avenue, and Bronx River Avenue, but further isolated by the Cross Bronx Expressway and the Bronx River Parkway – large multi-lane roads of fast-moving traffic that left Bronx River Houses cut off from the rest of the city, metastasizing out of sight and out of mind.

Smaller than most New York housing projects, Bronx River Houses had nine twelve-story utilitarian high-rises set around a central building that served as a community center and offices for the New York City Housing Authority.

When they were first built in the fifties, the apartments housed working poor. Through the seventies and eighties, drugs and urban decay turned the place into a locus of violence, crack cocaine, and misery. In the nineties, the NYPD took over from the Housing Police and began a campaign to crackdown on crime and lawlessness. The FBI Violent Gang Task Force also came in and prosecuted gang members and affiliates using RICO statutes, arresting large groups of young black and Hispanic men and prosecuting them in federal courts.

Raymond Ippolito knew the history of the Bronx River Houses much better than his partner, but he had no interest in giving John Palmer a history lesson. During the drive from Lorena Leon's apartment, Palmer had immersed himself in nonstop phone calls, texts, e-mails, and research, oblivious to what was going on in the streets around him.

When Ippolito pulled in front of the Houses, Palmer announced the results of his research.

"Okay, Mr. Derrick Watkins is officially a piece of shit. My contact on the FBI Gangs Task Force checked his records. They have him connected to an offshoot affiliated with United Black Nation, called HAV."

"What's that stand for?"

"Harrod Avenue Villains."

Ippolito sneered. "Same shit, different name."

"I also talked to the Narcotics Task Force in the Five-O. Watkins and his older brother, Jerome, have been around a long time. He said Jerome Watkins does a lot of financial transactions for the UBN."

"UBN. HAV. Fucking morons."

"What does it mean that Watkins and his brother do financial transactions for them?"

"The way it works, the top assholes use guys in their set they trust, like these Watkins pricks. Say the big boys make a deal for drugs, or guns, or whatever. Some skel shows up at an apartment rented to somebody with no connection to the top guys. Watkins is at that apartment. He collects the cash owed for the merchandise.

"In a second apartment nowhere near where the money changed hands, another asshole picks up the goods when

Watkins calls and says he's got the dough. The top guys are never near the goods or the money."

"Who are the top guys in the UBN?"

"What's your FBI org chart say?"

"I didn't ask for that information."

"Well, you don't need it." Ippolito tapped his head. "It's all in here. The top two Mau Maus in this neck of the woods are Eric 'Juju' Jackson and Floyd 'Whitey' Bondurant. Jackson is the boss, the brains. Whitey Bondurant is Jackson's muscle. He is one crazy, vicious motherfucker. You do not want to run into that guy."

"How'd he get the name Whitey?"

"He's a goddam albino. Weirdest looking asshole you've ever seen. Big. Big bones. Big head. Got this reddish, white hair he wears in dirty-looking dreads. Always wears sunglasses because of his eyes. The shit I've heard about him."

"Really?"

"Oh yeah, he definitely don't give a fuck. Guy's a freak. An outcast. The albino thing made him into a mean son of a bitch."

"I guess the good news is you'd know him if you saw him."

"Trust me, you don't want to see this guy. If you do, shoot him. Seriously. Just shoot him. Empty your fucking gun."

Ippolito stared out at the housing complex.

"Look, John, the gangs in these projects work just like every other organized crime group. The money flows from the bottom up. I know about these UBN assholes. You can trace Juju Jackson all the way to the Black Spades.

It got all mixed up with factions and wars and alliances, but it's basically the same shit. The wannabees underneath run around doing crime, whatever they can pull off. They send money up the chain. The head guys use the money to do bigger crimes, cull out the best earners, and let them in on bigger deals. Everybody else mostly scuffles around until they get locked up, shot, or quit. And not many quit."

"I suppose it's all they have."

"You suppose right."

Palmer took in everything Ippolito said. If Derrick Watkins was connected to a bigger gang and more crime, it meant he had a chance to arrest more people and make a bigger name for himself.

Ippolito interrupted Palmer's thoughts, asking, "What's his arrest record?"

"Watkins?"

"Yeah, who the fuck else we talking about?"

Palmer clicked through his computer.

"He got popped for second-degree possession of a controlled substance about nine years ago. He did five months in Rikers, took a plea bargain for time served and probation. Five years later, he gets arrested on a murder charge. Spent another eight months in Rikers awaiting trial. Charges dropped for lack of witnesses."

"Amnesia caused by a gun to their heads."

"He's been under the radar since then. FBI has him as an unindicted co-conspirator on the usual range of charges: conspiracy to commit murder, drug trafficking, firearms possession, prostitution, money laundering."

"Yeah, yeah, who isn't an unindicted co-conspirator? The prostitution fits with what the old lady said."

Palmer answered absentmindedly, "Yeah. My Fibbie McAndrews says it's the latest thing now. The gangs are running prostitutes to make up for lost income since their drug businesses are dwindling."

"He's right. But they've always run prostitutes. They're just doing it more now."

"McAndrews says they're going to nail all these guys at some point."

"Oh, fuck the FBI. Those assholes take five years to put together a jaywalking case. If this prick Watkins popped Paco Johnson, we take him down now."

"And anybody else connected to this," said Palmer.

Ippolito gave Palmer a look. "Hey, don't get too far ahead of yourself on this, Johnny Boy."

"What do you mean?"

"John, look at me. How long I been doing this? I know what you're thinking before you're thinking it."

"What?"

"What? So far we got two precincts involved, the Four-Two, and now the Four-Three since our lead has brought us to the venerable Bronx River Houses. You got FBI investigations. Plus, Department of Correction. We both know this thing could bounce up to the borough or division level in a heartbeat. And we both know you're gonna ride this as hard as you can."

"What's wrong with that?"

"Up to you, just don't get ahead of yourself."

"Fine. And, by the way, I did a quick check on James Beck."

"Who?"

"The guy who hooked Johnson up with the mother-in-law. The guy the old lady copped to."

"Who gives a fuck about him?"

"Hold on. The guy killed a cop."

"What are you talking about?"

"James Beck fucking killed a cop."

"You kill a cop, you're supposed to fry."

"Not if your conviction is overturned."

"How the hell did that happen?"

"I don't know but get this — last year a warrant was issued for his arrest on an assault charge, and then quashed."

"This guy must have some lawyer."

"He's a bad guy, Ray."

"Yeah, along with a million other bad guys. John, he's not our problem. We got enough crap on our plate right now. I know you want to arrest everybody within a hundred miles of this thing, but don't start going off on other assholes before we even figure out what to do with the assholes in front of us."

Palmer knew better than to argue, but he wasn't the least bit dissuaded. Ippolito shut off the car engine.

Palmer asked, "Where should we start? The housing office."

"Yes. Assuming Derrick Watkins has an apartment here in his name, which is a big fucking assumption. And assuming we're lucky enough the asshole is home instead of hiding out after whatever happened last night."

Palmer took out his service revolver, a SIG Sauer P226 9 mm, and chambered a round.

"Jeezus fuck, John, take it easy."

"I just want to be ready. Especially if he's got some of his crew around."

"Relax. We find him, we talk to him. Things get shitty, we call for backup."

"Hey, you're the one who always says get it done fast and simple. Right?" He slid the SIG into the holster at his waist. "Let's go."

"And if he's not here, we go back, report in before the bosses get pissed, and then we get some sleep. Or I get some sleep, and you can do whatever the fuck you want with your networking and politicking and all your Junior-G-man-buddy bullshit. But we gotta report to the lieutenant. And he's going to have to fill in the precinct commander, and he's going to have to liaise with the commander in the Four-Three because this shit hole is in their jurisdiction, which we happen to be operating in without telling anybody jack shit about anything."

"Exigencies, Ray. Time is of the essence. We have a right to follow this lead as fast as we can."

"Yeah, yeah."

Ippolito popped open the car door and stepped out onto the street. It felt like the sun might try to break through the gray skies, but the day was still overcast and muggy. There were trees scattered through the projects' grounds, and lawns in between the walkways and buildings, but the presence of green did little to dispel the institutional atmosphere created by a crowd of massive redbrick buildings.

Ippolito and Palmer made their way to the administration building to check with the Housing Authority office.

"I give you ten to one, even if this guy does live here, he ain't home."

"Maybe," said Palmer looking at his watch. "It's not even one yet. He could be still in the sack. Pimps keep late hours, don't they?"

"In which case, he won't open the door."

Palmer said, "In which case, maybe Amelia Johnson will, and we can find out from her what happened when her ex-con father came calling. Which doesn't take a genius to figure. Things turned nasty, Derrick and his boys beat the piss out of him, and put a bullet behind his ear."

"But first they dragged him ten blocks away on 174th Street?"

"Why not? It makes sense. They're not going to pop him outside their doorstep."

Ippolito noted that Palmer had expanded the murder to include Watkins's fellow gang members. By the time this was done, Palmer would have everybody in Watkins's crew arrested.

What the hell, thought Ippolito, he might be right.

The Housing Authority office confirmed Derrick Watkins occupied an apartment in building six. And was current on his rent. The only mark on his record had to do with him never responding to a request for access to his apartment to check on the source of a water leak.

They located Watkins's apartment on the seventh floor and banged on his door, but there was no answer. Nobody else on the floor answered except for one elderly black woman who lived the farthest down the hall from Derrick Watkins's apartment. She told them Derrick's mother had died about eight years ago, Derrick had taken over the lease on her apartment, and his dear, departed mother would be ashamed of him.

Palmer asked a few people on the way out if they knew Derrick Watkins, or had seen what had happened last night. Same result. Not much.

As they approached the car Ippolito said, "What'd I tell you?"

"It was worth a try. So what do you want to do?"

Ippolito leaned against their unmarked sedan. Scrunched his face in thought.

"We have to figure an angle here. We can't just wander around hoping this mutt is going to show up, or some moron is going to know where he is and tell us."

"What do you have in mind?"

"I don't know. I'll think of something."

Palmer had the impression Ippolito was holding out on him, but he knew enough not to push.

Ippolito levered his backside off the Impala's fender and opened the driver's door.

"Let's get back to the precinct. We gotta report to Levitt."

Before he stepped into the car, Palmer took a last look around. The sky had cleared enough for the sun to turn the weather from muggy to hot and muggy. Palmer ran a hand through his thick brown hair. He felt a nagging fatigue creeping into him. He checked his watch. He'd gone almost twenty-four hours without sleep. And he'd be working four or five more hours before he could rack out.

"All right," he said, "let's get back. Check with the skip. And then we can catch up with the medical examiner's office and Crime Scene . . ."

"You can catch up. After we talk to the lieutenant, I'm out until midnight."

"Fine. I'll bunk at the precinct. Keep on top of this."

Palmer didn't talk any more about the case on the drive to the precinct. He knew Ippolito could be lazy, bigoted, and racist. But he also knew Raymond Ippolito was a top-notch investigator and had a ton of connections on both sides of the law in the Bronx. So, for now, Palmer decided he would do all the write-ups, report to the bosses, keep the files current, and make sure their immediate supervisor knew what they were doing so he could cover for them.

And when it all went down, take all the credit.

9

Lorena Leon surprised James Beck, buzzing him in without asking who it was. Maybe she expected him to show up now that Packy had been shot. By the time Beck hurried up to Lorena's apartment on the second floor, Manny had fallen behind. Beck stood in front of Lorena's door and waited for Manny to catch up and take a position next to the door. Beck raised a hand, but before he knocked, Lorena Leon opened her door partway, holding an old .38 six-shot revolver pointed at Beck. He reflexively kicked the door into her. She fell backward, pulling the trigger. A bullet ripped past Beck's right shoulder and buried itself in the concrete-block wall behind him. If the door hadn't hit her, the slug would have gone through Beck's heart.

The old lady went down hard, but she still held on to the gun.

Beck jumped through the doorway and kicked the gun out of Lorena's hand, sending the old .38 spinning across the floor.

Manny pulled his gun, stepped in behind Beck, looking for anybody else in the room.

Beck straddled Lorena. He'd knocked the wind out of her. He bent down, grabbed her under the arms, and lifted her onto her feet, holding her in front of him.

Beck said, "Breathe. Come on, take a breath."

Manny closed the door behind him, wondering if anyone had heard the gunshot.

Suddenly, Lorena gasped, slapped at Beck, and yelled at him to let her go.

Beck held her tighter and shouted. "Stop it!"

He pivoted her to the couch and sat her down. He held both of her thin wrists with his left hand to keep her from flailing at him, while trying not to hurt her. He knelt on one knee in front of her.

"What the hell's the matter with you? Settle down."

Lorena kept struggling until Manny Guzman placed the short barrel of his Charter Arms revolver firmly against her temple and slowly cocked the trigger.

Her tantrum ended. She looked up at Manny Guzman, her back straight, her face twisted into an angry grimace.

Beck released her wrists. He took a long, deep breath, calming himself.

"What the hell are you doing coming to the door with a gun? You could have killed me."

She sat tight-lipped, saying nothing.

"Answer me."

Finally, she spat out, "I no want you here. You cause me all this trouble. I no have any problems until you make me take Packy in. Now he's dead. Now the police come to me. Yell at me. Now what? Now you come and hurt me." She turned to Manny. "He puts a gun to me. Leave me alone. I don't want no more problems."

Beck looked at Manny and tipped his head, silently telling him to move his gun. Manny stepped back, taking the barrel from Lorena's temple, but still holding his revolver.

He said, "If you don't want any problems from me, tell me what I need to know, and you'll never see me again."

She yelled, "What do you want to know? What?"

"Where did Packy go after he came here?"

With a disgusted look on her face she answered, "To find his daughter's pimp."

Beck took a second to absorb the information.

"Who's that?"

Lorena looked like she had a bad taste in her mouth as she said the name. "Derrick Watkins."

"How did Packy know his daughter was being prostituted?"

"He knows."

"You didn't tell him?"

Lorena shouted at Beck. "He know when he come here."

"Did he ask you where he could find Derrick Watkins?"

"I tell him at the project. Bronx River Houses."

"What's his daughter's name?"

Lorena stopped shouting her answers. "Amelia."

"How long has she been with this pimp?"

"I don't know."

"Did she live with you before?"

"Yes."

"And before that?"

"Foster homes. And with her mother."

The change of subject seemed to calm Lorena.

"Does Amelia keep clothes here? Any of her belongings?"

"Top drawer in my bedroom. She sleep on the couch."

Suddenly, the old, angry woman buried her face in both hands. Beck wasn't sure why. Perhaps talking about her daughter and granddaughter brought it on. Maybe it was just exhaustion and fear. All her anger had dissipated. She seemed smaller, diminished by the burden of constantly scraping by and the years of torment brought into her life by drugs and addiction and jail sentences. Beck suddenly felt terrible that the police had come to her door. And now he had appeared with his anger and urgency for revenge.

He placed his large hand on her shoulder.

"I'm sorry, Lorena. I'm sorry."

She pulled away from Beck's hand.

He spoke more softly. "When did the police come here, Lorena?"

She dropped her hands but kept her head down.

"This morning."

"What did you tell them?"

"Same as I tell you."

"Anything else?"

She looked up at Beck. She appeared to be exhausted. "What else is there?"

Beck nodded. He assumed she'd told the police he had convinced her to let Packy stay with her. Which meant now the cops knew about him and his connection to Paco Johnson. So be it.

He couldn't think of anything more to ask the defeated, angry woman.

He checked his watch. If anyone had called 911 about the gunshot, they didn't have much more time. While Manny watched Lorena, Beck quickly searched the apartment.

He found a small duffel bag that belonged to Packy on top of the refrigerator. He rifled through it as he made his way back to Lorena's small, stuffy bedroom. A change of clothes and the cell phone Packy had never used were inside the duffel. Nothing else.

In the bedroom, heavy old curtains had been pulled across the one small window in the room. He pulled the curtains back to brighten the room enough so he could see the contents of the top dresser drawer. The pressed fiberboard drawer had warped under the cheap plastic veneer, and he almost pulled the loose knob off opening it.

Inside were a few of Amelia's things: flimsy thong panties, two bras, costume jewelry, condoms, a disposable lighter, a few receipts stapled together, an old cell phone, makeup and brushes in a rectangular plastic case. He stuffed everything into Packy's duffel bag, took a quick look at the rest of the dresser drawers, the closet, glanced around the room. There didn't seem to be anything else that belonged to Packy's daughter.

As he walked toward the living room, he reached into his pocket and pulled out a fold of cash. From the center of it, he took five one-hundred-dollar bills then, realizing the woman might have trouble breaking hundreds, he added another hundred in twenties.

When Beck emerged into the living room, Lorena was still sitting on the couch, immobile, waiting for this latest intrusion on her to end.

Beck sat down next to her. As Manny watched out the front window, Beck placed the folded bills into her hand. He said, "I'm sorry, Mrs. Leon."

She made no response.

Beck didn't repeat the words. They felt empty and worthless.

She had taken the money with her left hand. He looked at her right hand, trying to remember how hard he had kicked the gun out of her grip. He reached for her hand, lifting it so he could see if he'd hurt her. She didn't resist.

Beck walked to her small kitchen and opened the freezer. Old, cloudy ice cubes filled an ancient aluminum tray. He dug out two.

He could feel Manny behind him, restless to get out of the apartment.

Beck wrapped two thick ice cubes in a threadbare kitchen towel, returned to the living room and placed her hand on the covered ice.

He didn't look at her. He couldn't. They left quickly, walking past the old revolver still on the floor.

10

Demarco turned the Mercury onto Harrod Avenue bordering Bronx River Houses forty minutes after Ippolito and Palmer had left.

"I remember coming here when I was a kid. My Auntie Esther and her husband, Mickey, lived here back in the day."

Beck asked, "How many aunts you got, D?"

"Lots. In my community aunts come in varying degrees."

Manny said, "Back in the day?"

"When this place was known for all the hip-hop stuff going on." Demarco peered out the windshield. "Man, I remember there being a lot less grass and trees, and a lot more junkies back then. Place looks livable now."

"Still the damn projects," said Manny.

"True. They're like gulags, these places," Demarco eased the Mercury alongside the curb. "If Derrick Watkins is in one of these buildings, I'll find him. My cousin Giles still lives here. My Aunt Esther's oldest."

"You think your cousin is still around?" asked Beck.

"Doesn't matter. I know you're burning to get in there, James, but give me a little time to look around before we storm the place."

Demarco slipped out of the Mercury before Beck could answer and ambled into the projects. As Beck watched Demarco walk away, his cell phone rang. He checked the caller ID. Ciro.

He quickly told Ciro Baldassare where they were, and what was going on. Ciro told him he was heading north on the Henry Hudson and would be there in about thirty minutes.

Beck answered, "Okay, let me know when you're in the area and I'll tell you where to meet us."

When he broke off the call, Manny asked from the backseat, "You hungry?"

Beck looked up and down the block on the other side of the street. The only place that appeared to sell food was a Pioneer Supermarket.

"Better than sitting here waiting."

Beck and Manny killed time walking the cramped aisles of the little market. Beck found a sealed bag of cashews, unsurprised at the high prices typical of stores in minority neighborhoods. He matched it with a single can of beer from a limited selection, particularly since he didn't drink malt liquor. Manny picked out a banana.

Beck paid for the food. They crossed back to the other side of the street and ate leaning against the Mercury, watching the comings and goings of the housing project residents, almost exclusively minority women and young kids.

Beck could feel the heat of the midday sun seeping into his back and shoulders.

Demarco hadn't been gone very long, but Beck was restless. He remembered the duffel bag he'd taken from Lorena's apartment. He reached into the backseat, pulled out the bag, and dropped it on the trunk of the Mercury. The items he'd taken from Amelia's dresser drawer were on top of Packy's clothes. He shoved aside flimsy undergarments that looked inappropriate for a teenager, trying to ignore them. He felt inside the pants pockets of Packy's slacks. Checked the shirt pocket. Nothing.

He looked through Amelia's things, seeing nothing of interest until he spotted the small bundle of receipts. Beck pulled them out of the bag and thumbed through them.

Most of them were for amounts under ten dollars. Some were from fast-food outlets. There were several cab receipts, and one for $83.68 from Old Navy. Who were these records for? Beck decided they had to be for Amelia's pimp. The thought both saddened and angered him.

Beck dropped the receipts back into the duffel bag and tossed it into the backseat. He was almost ready to go into the housing project and find Demarco when his cell phone vibrated.

He answered it, seeing Demarco's caller ID.

"Yeah?"

"Walk in on that path I took. Go past three buildings. I'm sitting in front of Derrick Watkins's building."

"Good work. On my way."

Beck cut the call. He opened the trunk of the Mercury and pulled out a three-foot steel crowbar. He positioned it under his right arm to conceal it, and hustled into the complex to find Demarco. Manny followed as quickly as his bowed legs allowed.

Demarco Jones sat on a bench wearing black cotton slacks, an extra-long designer T-shirt, Allen Edmonds slip-ons with no socks. Despite the expensive clothes, most would have thought twice before they sat on the same bench. He looked like a man who wanted to kill somebody, and could easily do it.

Beck walked into the courtyard and headed quickly toward Demarco. Manny Guzman lagged behind, taking time to check his surroundings, look for security cameras, take note of every person nearby.

There were two elderly black ladies on a bench about twenty feet away. A young woman wearing a halter top and blue shorts stood near the front entrance of Watkins's building rocking a double stroller with her left hand as she yelled into a cell phone in her right hand, warning whoever listened at the other end they better goddam remember to pick up some motherfucking Pampers.

Beck sat next to Demarco, let the crowbar slide from under his arm down next to his right leg, and asked, "What do you have?"

"A lot of bad news." Demarco glanced at the crowbar. "We have to be careful. I got his apartment number, but I don't want to bust in there without knowing what's on the other side of the door."

Manny sat down on the other side of Beck. Beck tapped the curved end of the crowbar on the asphalt.

"What'd you find out?"

Demarco motioned toward the two elderly black ladies sitting on the bench.

"Had a talk with those lovely ladies."

"And?"

"You ever spend much time in the projects, James?"

"No. They didn't build anything special for us in Hell's Kitchen. It was ghetto enough the way it was."

Demarco nodded, still intent on making his point. "These projects go back a long way. Thirty, forty, fifty years. There are housing projects in every borough. Hundreds

99

of thousands of people. Acres and acres, pretty much cut off from everything around them. People hardly ever think about it."

"Your point being?"

"I could make a lot of points." Demarco nodded toward the two old ladies he'd been talking to. "But for now, my point is — all the time these places have been around, those old ladies and thousands like 'em have been defending 'em. They're the sentinels, always watching. They know everything. Even back in the worst days, they were watching, defending the turf. Not just against the bad boys, against everybody. Drug dealers, cops, Housing Authority, everybody."

"Except you," said Beck.

Demarco smiled, "Me, they like."

"What'd they tell you, Demarco?"

"Told me our man Packy was here last night around ten. He came in hot. Blazing hot. Packy walked right out front of Derrick's building and called the man out. And his daughter. Just yelling for blood and his kin."

"Calling out for what, exactly?"

"For his daughter to get the hell out of Derrick Watkins's apartment."

"Then, what?"

"Watkins's family has been around here a long time. This is home ground. Bunch of his crew live in this project. By the time Watkins came out, there were five, six guys backing him up."

"Christ. Then what?"

"One of the ladies, Miss Margaret, lives on the sixth floor there." Demarco pointed to the building in front of them. "She had the best view. Said it went down mostly in front of the entrance over there. She could see, but not hear what was said. There was shouting. Packy and Watkins having it out. She called the cops. She's sure other residents called the cops, too, but before they arrived, everything blew up. They swarmed Packy. He fought back, but there were too many. They beat him down. Kept pounding on him until they heard sirens, then disappeared like cockroaches when you turn on the lights."

"And Packy?"

"The other lady, Maxine, said they left Packy on the ground, but before the cops pulled in Packy got back on his feet and walked away."

"Did the cops stop him?"

"Not that she could see. He was out of view when the cops showed."

"What the hell was he thinking? What was so important he couldn't wait until the next day and come talk to us? Come in here with some backup. Make a plan before he came into some goddam pimp's turf and got killed."

Manny said, "Maybe that was it."

"What?"

"Maybe Packy figured he'd just be dealing with a low-life pimp. Nothing he couldn't handle himself."

Beck said, "I don't know. But like I said, why the hell come in here blind? Why risk hitchhiking into town and rushing over here first thing?"

Demarco said, "Obviously he wanted to get his daughter out of her situation. Why he was in such a damn rush is something we'll have to find out."

Beck pulled out his smartphone and clicked on his map app. He waited impatiently until a street map of the area appeared and a blue dot showed his location. He traced the route from where they sat to where the police found Packy's body near Longfellow Street.

"Based on where they found him, it looks like he went straight out onto 174th Street, across the bridge over the Sheridan Expressway, and then walked three more blocks. Watkins and his gang might have scattered when the cops came, but they could have easily followed him and shot him once he was out of here."

Manny grumbled, "Goddam cowards."

Beck tapped his crowbar on the ground, looked around the area where they sat. There was a small playground within sight. Two women with four kids among them had drifted into the park. An older man in neat slacks, a square-cut short-sleeve shirt wearing a straw Kangol cap sat down on the bench with Miss Margaret and Maxine.

Beck said, "We're not going to find out anything more sitting here. I want to see if Derrick Watkins is home."

Demarco asked, "You open to a suggestion?"

"If it's an idea on getting into his apartment."

Before Demarco could explain, Beck's cell phone buzzed.

"Ciro." Beck paused and listened, then told Ciro Baldassare where to meet them.

Demarco asked, "Ciro's coming?"

"Yeah."

"Then I think we should definitely try it my way before we start a war in here."

11

When Derrick Watkins kicked the bed and yelled at Amelia to wake up, it took her a full four seconds to struggle back to consciousness, and another few moments to remember where she was.

"I said wake up, bitch. We got shit to talk about. Get your ass out of here."

He left the bedroom, kicking the door out of his way.

Amelia forced herself out of bed. She staggered barefoot to the bathroom. She splashed cold water on her face, used the toilet, and checked the folded twenty-dollar bills she'd hidden in her hair. She was taking a huge risk, but she'd be damned if she was going to give Derrick Watkins everything.

She put her red wig back on and walked out to the front room.

The moment she stepped to the threshold, she froze. Not only Derrick, but his brother, Jerome, and five members of his crew turned toward her with hard looks.

What had happened? They looked like they wanted to kill somebody. How could it have anything to do with her? Knowing that it couldn't did not dispel the paralyzing fear that she was going to be the target of a roomful of male anger and hate.

Her next thought was – if he finds the sixty dollars in front of his crew, he'll beat me to death.

She desperately wanted a gun, a razor, something, anything to defend herself. She remembered hearing Derrick kept a gun in the freezer of the old refrigerator in the kitchen. She thought about making a run for the kitchen, but she knew she wouldn't make it halfway.

All of them continued staring at her: Derrick, Tyrell, Johnny Morris, all longtime members of his crew, plus two newer members. One called Eddie. The other, a dull-looking boy she didn't know. Last, and certainly worse than all the others, sat Derrick's older, larger brother, Jerome Biggie Watkins.

Derrick said, "Sit down, Princess."

He motioned toward an empty spot on the old couch between him and Biggie. Amelia took a few steps toward the dirty couch, the upholstery scabbed by years of stains and worn spots, her head down, making sure to avoid eye contact with any of the others.

She sat between the two brothers, feeling the tension and anger in the room directed at her, still trying to figure out why.

"You got my money, bitch?"

She turned to Derrick, pulled out the cash and receipt for food from her front pocket, and handed them to him.

Derrick pocketed everything without looking at it. A bad sign. He didn't even count the money. As if he were done with her. Why? She had earned. What was going on? Sitting between the brothers on the filthy couch, all the members of his crew staring at her, Amelia could not shake the idea that Derrick had decided to let them all pull one last brutal chain of serial rape and then kill her.

She kept her head down, feeling a constricting sensation that made it difficult to breathe. A flush of panic and fear came over her. She began to sweat.

Derrick narrowed his eyes at her and said, "Why didn't you tell me your father was out of prison?"

Amelia flinched in confusion for a moment, but then answered without hesitation. "I didn't know."

"Liar."

She kept her head down, still confused, but grabbing at the chance to respond. "I'm not lying. I don't know nuthin' about that man. I ain't seen or heard from him in years."

Derrick told her, "Look at me. Look me in the eyes so I know if you're lying."

That's when she saw Derrick's left eye was nearly swollen shut and his lower lip had been cut.

She looked him in the eyes and said, "Last time I seen my father I was maybe three years old. I ain't heard one word from him since then. I don't even remember what he looks like. How am I supposed to know he got out of prison?"

Derrick stared back, trying to find any hint of a lie. Amelia had the sense not to try to convince him.

Tyrell interjected, "She's a motherfuckin' lying bitch."

Derrick glanced at him, annoyed. "Shut up." He turned back to Amelia, "You ain't never heard from him?"

"No, never. What happened?"

"Goddammit bitch, don't you ask me no fuckin' questions. Who tol' him you was workin' for me?"

The question confused Amelia for a moment. She could barely grasp that her father knew anything about her, much less that he knew her connection to Derrick. She concentrated, trying to come up with an explanation.

"I don't know. Maybe my grandmother told him. I don't know. I didn't. I got no business with him. I never talked to him my whole life."

Derrick shifted at his end of the couch, going through a calculation Amelia couldn't fathom. He seemed to be trying to come to some decision, but none of his options worked for him.

He looked to his older brother, Jerome, for a moment. The big, stolid man sat on the couch with a blank expression, neither moving nor saying anything.

Finally, Derrick spoke.

"Your old man come up to the Houses to find you." He waited for a reaction from Amelia, but didn't get one. "He's lucky he didn't come lookin' for you with a gun, cuz I'da shot his ass right then and there."

"When?"

"Last night. The fool walked up outside my building shouting my name. Callin' me out. Like I'm some punk."

She asked, "What . . . ?" but stopped.

"What, what, bitch?"

"What happened?"

"What you think happened? Someone call me out, they callin' all of us out. Like I said, if he'd had a gat, he'd be dead. Dumb son of a bitch threatened me unless I give you up. Shit. If you hadn't been out getting me my money, I might a kicked you to the curb right then and there. Instead, we fucking beat the shit outta him, that's what happened."

Amelia quickly looked at the others. She noted that a few of them hadn't come out unscathed. She struggled with her feelings. She'd never had a father, and certainly never had a man who was willing to fight for her. But what the hell good had it done?

Amelia swallowed, sitting motionless and silent so as not to ignite any reactions. Clearly, Derrick and his crew were blaming her, wanting her to pay for what had happened. It felt like she was surrounded by vicious dogs working themselves up to attack her. Any one of them might make a move at her, particularly Tyrell.

And then, perhaps sensing control slipping away, Jerome Watkins stood up and spoke.

"Get up girl. Go back in the bedroom. Derrick, come with me."

Amelia moved fast, taking the opportunity to get away from Derrick's crew. Jerome and Derrick followed her. She went into the bedroom. Jerome came to the door. Before he locked her in, he told her, "Don't make a goddam sound in here."

He motioned for Derrick to follow him back to the kitchen. They sat across the table from each other. Jerome was forty pounds heavier than Derrick and six years older. He spoke more slowly, with less emotion. He leaned toward his younger brother.

"We got trouble here."

"Why? Fuck that bitch. I'ma cut her loose. She ain't no fuckin' earner anyhow. More trouble than she's worth."

"It's past that now."

"Why? Cuz her asshole father gonna try to cause us trouble? If I put a bullet in her head and dump her, what's he gonna do about it?"

"Listen to me. You don't know the whole story."

"What do you mean?"

"I fucked up. Eric told me to get word to you. Wanted you to kick her out."

"When?"

"Day before yesterday. I was going to tell you yesterday, but I didn't get around to it. I didn't know it was like a right-away thing."

"Why? Why Juju want me to get rid of her?"

"I don't fuckin' know. He don't explain shit. Just do this, do that."

"So whatever. We'll kick her ass out now. Let her run back to her bust-out father."

"Might be too late for that. Might be we have to make her disappear like you said. I don't know what's going on with Eric. Or what's behind all this mess. I gotta get with him and tell him what's happening. He probably already knows, but we got to wait to hear from him now."

Derrick said, "All right. No big thing. I got to lay low anyhow. Cops piled in the Houses after we beat the shit out of that guy. I'm sure they be looking for me."

"All right. Lay low. And keep the bitch locked up and out of sight." Jerome lowered his voice and leaned closer to Derrick. "Comes down to it, who you want to use to get rid of her?"

"That one's easy. Fuckin' Tyrell. I won't even have to pay him. I tell him he can do what he wants with her for a couple of hours, then get rid of her. That's all the pay he'll need."

"All right, but make sure after he does her, he meets me with the body. I got to know it's done and make sure to dump her someplace nobody's gonna find her. Can't rely on no retard like Tyrell to do that right."

"What about the father?"

Jerome gave his brother a baleful stare and said, "I suspect that ship is sailed. He might already be gone if Juju heard about this mess and put Whitey on it."

By the time John Palmer had filed his reports, checked in with Lieutenant James Levitt, the supervisor of the 42nd Precinct's detective squad, and liaised with the 43rd Precinct, where the Bronx River Houses were located, it was 2:35 P.M. He'd already dipped into his private stash of Adderall to keep going. He still had to write up a report for the other detectives in the squad, check with the M.E.'s office, and circle back to his FBI contact. Then he would try to locate Derrick Watkins.

He had feelers out with two contacts. Gregory McAndrews at FBI Violent Gangs Task Force, and Peter Malone, a detective from the 50th Precinct who worked gangs and narcotics. Malone would take his sweet time getting back to him, so he planned on driving over to the Five-O to run down the information with him personally.

Gregory McAndrews was a different story. Even though the FBI was notorious for keeping information under wraps, McAndrews would check his files and call him back as soon as possible because McAndrews wanted to cultivate a connection with his father, John Palmer Senior, a powerful lobbyist, lawyer, and well-known advocate for law enforcement unions in New York State and City. Palmer Senior's influence extended into the NYPD, the Department of Correction, New York State Police, numerous local police forces, as well as the Justice Department, and

Homeland Security. Palmer Senior had long ago mastered the art of greasing the revolving doors between law enforcement personnel and the private sector. A phone call from him could help McAndrews jump ahead of a hundred other special agents when it came time for a career change.

Palmer knew he shouldn't reach out to a federal agency without clearing it through his bosses, but protocol had never stopped him before and it wouldn't stop him now. Palmer could already see his path forward. Step one, make Detective First Grade. He had to have that. Then a few more years in the Detective Division. After that, start taking the necessary civil service exams and rise through management positions. Palmer's ambition and hubris would not end until he became the NYPD commissioner. Nothing less. And after that, who knows, maybe even mayor of New York.

Palmer checked his watch. Not quite three o'clock. If he moved fast and got everything in the works, he might even be able to get a bead on Watkins's location before end of day. Then take five milligrams of Ambien and be in a precinct bunk by around six. Get a good five hours of sleep, and be ready to organize an arrest team and start hitting places after midnight when Ippolito came back on duty. Wrap this whole fucking thing up in less than twenty-four hours. That's how you made a name for yourself.

What else? Oh right, the daughter. Find Amelia Johnson. She might be a valuable witness.

And don't forget James Beck, the guy who got away with killing a cop. Sending him back to jail would go a long way toward making a name for himself. He'd have to find out everything he could about Beck, including his connection to Paco Johnson. But, fuck, he barely had time to do what he had to do.

Just then, Palmer saw Tim Witherspoon, the youngest detective on the precinct squad. A crew-cut, eager-to-please straight arrow, but with just enough smarts to brown-nose his way into a spot with the big-boy detectives.

Palmer watched Witherspoon approach, wearing a buy-one-get-one-free Men's Wearhouse suit, and a permanent-press white shirt from Macy's, ready to start his four-to-midnight shift.

Palmer yelled, "Yo, Timster, what's up?"

Witherspoon couldn't resist basking in the glow of John Palmer.

"Ah, you know, the usual, man, how's it going?"

Palmer mustered up a beleaguered look, taking Witherspoon into his confidence, giving him the impression he could really use his help.

"Ah, you wouldn't believe it. Suddenly everything went from same old shit, to the shit hitting the fan this morning."

"Really?"

"Yeah. Ray and I caught a homicide just near the end of our shift. I've been going full blast ever since."

"Wow." Witherspoon knew an opportunity when he saw one. "Anything I can do to help?"

Palmer paused, as if genuinely giving it some thought. As if he hadn't planned on getting Witherspoon to work for him from the moment he saw him.

"As a matter of fact, now that you mention it, there is something you can do."

"Name it."

Palmer motioned Witherspoon over to his desk. He opened a folder and extracted a printout of the NYPD file on James Beck. He handed it to Witherspoon.

"This guy is connected to my homicide. He's got an interesting history. Right now, I'm not sure how he fits in, but I can't let any lead slide. This could be really important, Tim. Trouble is, I got so much other crap I have to follow up on there's no way I can get to it now. If you're up for it and have some time, I'd really appreciate anything you can come up with on him. I'll clear it with Levitt. Tell him I need your help."

"Sure, man. No problem. I can fit it in. Anything you're looking for specifically?"

"Don't know yet. Just find out everything you can about him. Known associates. Known addresses. Whatever is available."

"Okay. How much time do I have?"

"ASAP, man," said Palmer. "ASAP."

13

They were four serious men. All ready to beat down doors and anybody behind them, walking slowly and patiently toward Derrick Watkins's apartment on the seventh floor in building six led by a ninety-one-year-old woman riding her Rascal scooter.

She neither looked behind her, nor worried about what was in front of her. Belinda Halsted Smith was on a mission concerning Derrick Watkins, whom she had known from the time he was an annoying toddler and through all the years of his unremittingly destructive criminal life. In Belinda's firm opinion, the best that could be said of Derrick Watkins was that his older brother Jerome was worse.

Now, for some reason, a day of reckoning seemed to have arrived for Derrick, and Belinda Halsted Smith was eager to lead these men to their task.

She wore plain, practical clothes: a dark pleated skirt, white blouse buttoned to the neck, and support hose. She peered through thick glasses to compensate for failing vision, but it did not prevent her from rolling in a straight line toward apartment 720.

Belinda smacked her sturdy wooden cane on Derrick's door, demanding in a surprisingly loud voice. "Derrick, open up. You open this door now."

The four men took up positions on either side of the doorway, Beck and Demarco on the right side, Ciro and

Manny on the left, all of them ready to fight their way into the apartment with fists, or guns, or both.

Belinda ignored all of them and banged harder.

"Derrick, open up now. It's me, Miz Smith. You open up this minute."

She rapped four times, each one harder than the previous.

Beck was just about to send Belinda back to her apartment and use his crowbar when he heard feet shuffling on the other side of the door.

Just as Belinda raised her cane for another smack, the door opened. A tall, thin young man wearing only boxer shorts and a white T-shirt appeared, hovering over the old matriarch and her red Rascal scooter. He hadn't opened the door for the cops. He wouldn't have opened the door for Beck and his men, but he really couldn't bring himself to defy Belinda Halstead Smith.

"Damn, what you want . . . ?"

He never got the last word out. Beck spun into the doorway, grabbed the insolent youth by the throat, lifted him off his feet, and threw him to the floor.

Manny and Ciro rushed into the apartment, guns in hand.

Demarco deftly turned Belinda's scooter around and guided her back toward her apartment, patting her shoulder, and telling her everything would be all right.

Beck kept his grip on Leon Miller's throat and quietly asked, "Anybody else in here?"

Leon couldn't speak with Beck choking him. He shook his head no.

Manny and Ciro moved fast to check each room.

Demarco walked with Belinda until they reached her apartment at the end of the hall. Thankfully, there were no sounds of shouting, body parts being hit, or gunshots back in Derrick's apartment.

Demarco leaned down to tell Belinda, "Miz Smith, you've been a wonderful help here today. My friends and I are going to find out what's going on in that apartment, and I guarantee you whatever nonsense those boys are up to, it's going to end."

Belinda stared up at Demarco, her bottom jaw jutting out, eyes narrowed behind her thick glasses. For a moment, she wondered about who she had helped get into Derrick's apartment, but looking at the big handsome young man with such a sincere smile, she decided it must to be all right.

And then Demarco touched her gently on the arm as he continued speaking quietly. It had been a long time since a man had touched her, much less spoken softly to her. There was a kindness to it.

Before she knew it, the young gentleman gently guided her into her apartment, one hand on the handle of her Rascal, the other on her upper back, a hand so large in comparison to the diminutive Belinda, it covered most of the space between her shoulders.

Belinda rolled into her apartment and turned the Rascal around to face Demarco, who held the door open.

"Thank you, dear," he said, smiling a dazzling smile.

Belinda found herself smiling back as he closed her door. She blinked, intent on preserving the memory of Demarco Jones's kind face as her door clicked shut.

Demarco quickly walked back to Derrick Watkins's apartment, his kind look replaced with a scowl. He stepped into the living room and saw a young man sitting in his underwear on an armless wooden chair taken from the kitchen, Beck standing over him.

Manny and Ciro appeared from the back of the apartment.

Beck asked, "Anybody else?"

Manny said, "No. There's three bedrooms back there. Lot of women's clothes and makeup and shit, but no women, or anybody else."

Manny took a position next to the chair holding his short-barrel revolver, looking like he wanted to shoot the boy. Ciro stood on the other side, his thick arms crossed, straining against his black Gucci short-sleeve shirt, waiting for a reason to hit the sullen youth.

Beck pulled up a second chair and sat in front of their captive, staring at him, saying nothing.

Demarco closed the front door and leaned back against it. He knew they had gotten into the apartment without much noise, but he kept his position at the door just in case.

Beck finally spoke.

"What's your name?"

The youth tried to speak, but had to swallow and clear his throat. Beck had nearly crushed his trachea.

"Leon." It came out as a croak. "My name is Leon. I don't . . ."

Beck raised a hand to silence him.

"Stop. Just answer my questions. I don't want to hear anything else. Understand?"

Leon nodded.

"If you hesitate, if you tried to bullshit me, if you act stupid, my friend here will start hitting you." Beck paused as Leon took a quick look at Ciro Baldassare.

"And let me tell you something, Leon, if that man hits you, you will never be the same. Do you believe me?"

"Yes."

"Good. Is this Derrick Watkins's apartment?"

"Yes."

"Where is he?"

"I ain't sure. Derrick called me and told me to come up and watch the place. He and his brother have other places. Probably he went to one of those other apartments."

"Last night a friend of ours came here about ten. Were you here?"

Leon answered quickly. "No."

"Do you know what happened?"

"Yeah. Guy called out Derrick. Some beef about his daughter or somethin'. Derrick and his crew got into it with your friend."

"What do you mean, got into it?"

"You know – words was exchanged. Ended up in a fight. I guess they beat him up."

"You guess?"

"No, no. They gave him a beat down."

"How do you know that if you weren't here?"

"One of his guys told me. He was here when I got here."

"Everybody else was gone?"

"Yeah."

"Where's the guy who was here when you got here?"

"I don't know. He left. I came to take his place."

"What time was that?"

"About midnight."

"How many of you assholes are in Derrick Watkins's crew?"

Leon paused, wary of saying the wrong thing. Beck repeated his question.

"How many?"

"It varies." Leon made a seesaw motion with his hand. "Not everybody has the same status, you know. Just figuring the ones close to him, maybe five, six. But you know, there's others who float in and out."

"How many others?"

"Maybe a dozen?"

"And you?"

"I ain't official yet. You got to buy your way in. Then you get recognized."

"Why does he need you watching the place?"

"He wants to know if the cops come by. Or if someone wants to get in touch with him."

"Did the cops come?"

"Yeah. Couple hours ago."

"I'm not a cop, am I, Leon?"

"No."

"So that makes me someone who wants to get in touch with him. How do I go about doing that?"

Leon Miller hesitated.

"Careful, Leon. You said Derrick and his brother have other places. How many are there?"

"That I know of?"

"Ask me another question, and I'll fucking kill you."

Leon quickly answered, "Three. I know three of them."

Beck stood.

"Get dressed."

14

As soon as Derrick and Jerome locked her in the bedroom, Amelia tried to stifle the paralyzing fear gripping her. She paced around the room, taking deep breaths, thinking through what was happening. Her father, whoever he was, whatever he'd been trying to do, had ruined any chance she might have had to escape.

Worse, now there was no way Derrick would want her around. Not after being called out. But he couldn't just let her go. That would be like admitting he was afraid of her father. So he had called on his brother Biggie to figure out what to do.

Suddenly, with absolute clarity and soul-crushing certainty, Amelia Johnson knew they had only one option: kill her. Make her disappear. Jerome and Derrick were sitting in the kitchen planning it right now.

Amelia Johnson stopped pacing. She felt her own death approaching. She couldn't take a full breath. Her legs felt so weak she had to sit down on the rumpled bed. The small bedroom closed in on her. There was nothing between her and death except a battered old wooden door with a flimsy sliding bolt lock that could be broken with one kick.

There was no way out of the room. There was a small window that had been painted shut for years with bars on the outside. Breaking the window and screaming for help would do nothing. They'd be punching and kicking her long before anybody could respond, assuming anybody would even hear her cries.

She looked around the room and under the bed, searching for something she could use as a weapon.

Survival pulled her to the other side of her fear. She rushed to the closet. Nothing but a few empty wire hangers hung on a pole. Maybe she could get the pole out of its holders. Use it to fend them off. Or twist the wire hangers into something she could slash at them with. Use the weapon pimps had used on their whores for decades.

No. That was stupid. Wire hangers against fists and guns? And they'd probably beat her to death with the pole if she tried to use it.

She sat back down at the foot of the bed, facing the door. She had nothing. She didn't even have her shoes; they were in the other bedroom. She hardly even had clothes. All she had was a useless fold of three twenty-dollar bills hidden in her hair that once discovered would make her death even worse.

Her anger hardened into silent cursing. She cursed the father she never had who should have protected her instead of ensuring her death. She cursed her mother for being a hopeless, selfish drug addict who died and left her alone. And her grandmother for being such a crazy, angry, volatile, nagging shrew. She cursed Derrick Watkins to hell and everybody around him – that hulking fool Tyrell, and Derrick's heartless brother Jerome, and all the stupid boys in his crew scuffling and thieving, ducking and dodging, trying to be criminals. And she cursed the stifling, dark, fearful presence of the mythic Eric Juju

Jackson sitting on top of it all, ready to send out his insane assassin Whitey Bondurant. Slowly her hate and fear and anger hardened into a desperate resolve. Whoever they sent for her, she knew he would have a gun. And somehow, through stealth or seduction, she would get close to that gun, grab it, fight for it, and pull the trigger. She would pull and pull until they cut her down and ended her miserable life here and now, once and forever.

15

While Beck and the others filtered out of the Bronx River Houses one at a time, Demarco stayed behind with Leon while he dressed. They walked out of the complex side by side, as if they were friends, and headed over to Harrod Street where the Mercury Marauder sat, engine running.

Manny opened the back door and shoved Leon in next to Ciro, then climbed in after him. Beck sat in the passenger seat as usual. Demarco took the wheel.

Beck turned to Leon.

"Leon, don't waste our time. You said there are three possibilities. Take us to the best one first."

Leon Miller directed them to a three-flat house on Mount Hope Place. The drive took less than ten minutes.

Nobody in the car spoke until Demarco parked about fifty feet south of the house.

Beck asked Leon, "Why don't you call your buddy Derrick and find out if he's in there."

Leon answered, "Don't have to." He pointed toward the end of the block. "That's his car."

"What? The black Jeep Cherokee?"

"Yeah."

"So what's your man Watkins doing here?"

Leon had relaxed a bit. Enough time had gone by with Beck and his men that he no longer feared they were going to kill him. He responded to Beck's question with a sullen attitude.

"Hell if I know."

Without a hint of warning, Ciro Baldassare slammed the side of his right fist down onto Leon's left thigh. He hit him so hard that even though the femur was the thickest bone in Leon's body, covered with layers of muscle, the blow nearly cracked the bone. The pain was so intense and unexpected that Leon gasped, and then as waves of more pain followed, he bent forward grunting and moaning.

The fact that Leon dared to utter any noise further angered Ciro. He grabbed Leon by the back of his neck and rammed his forehead into the front seat.

"Straighten up your attitude you fucking ignorant hump, or I'll kill you. Are you too goddam stupid to get what's going on here?"

Beck knew he had seconds before there would be no way to stop Ciro. He needed Leon Miller. He turned quickly and said, "Ciro, do me a favor and don't kill him just yet. He's going to cooperate."

Ciro snarled at Leon, "Answer his fucking questions."

Beck waited as Leon struggled to get control of himself, knowing the boy had never felt anything like the pain pulsing through his thigh. Leon grimaced and talked as fast as the pain and fear would allow him.

"I can't say for sure. I'm figuring he wants to get somewhere away from the Houses after that fight. But he might be doing some deal up there. I seen his brother Jerome's car about a block back that way."

"What kind of deal?"

"Could be anything. He and his bro handle money for a lot of deals."

Beck nodded. "Do they own the whole house?"

"Yeah, everything but the top floor is mostly for stuff he stores."

"Like what?"

"Stuff they got to buy or sell. Whatever they gotta hide until it gets where it's s'posed to be."

"What do they do on the top floor?"

"Run hookers mostly."

"What's the layout?"

"There's a front room, a hallway, a bathroom, two bedrooms for his whores, kitchen, and a small room in back they also got a bed in."

"How many women is that pimp running?"

Leon shook his head, knowing he did not know the actual number, but reluctant to say out loud that he didn't know.

"Guess," said Beck.

"Between him and his brother, I'd say 'bout fifteen, twenty. Maybe more."

"So we got two pimps hiding out up there, and most likely some whores."

"Could be some of his guys up there, too. You know, hangin' with him. Layin' low."

"Okay," said Beck, "D, cruise around a bit. Leon, keep your eyes open and let me know if you see any other cars you recognize."

Demarco drove until he'd covered every street on the three blocks surrounding Watkins's whorehouse. Leon picked out two more parked cars he recognized. They arrived back where they'd started out.

Demarco turned in his seat slightly so he could talk to Beck as well as Ciro and Manny in the backseat. "So, what do we figure? Five, six, ten guys up there? Maybe a couple of hookers?"

"The more the merrier as far as I'm concerned," said Beck. "Better chance we find the one who pulled the trigger on Packy."

The comment didn't go unheard by Leon Miller. Up until that moment, he didn't know the man who had started the beef with Derrick had been shot. Were these guys setting out to kill Derrick and his crew? Couldn't be. Derrick and the others wouldn't go down without a fight. And how did these four figure on getting in there? Maybe they were crazy enough to try it, but there was no way they would all come out alive.

Beck asked Leon, "Is there any back door out of there?"

Leon swallowed, distracted by his thoughts. "What?"

Ciro turned to look at Leon.

"Sorry. Sorry. You mean up top? No. No, there ain't no back door or back stairs. There's just a window in the kitchen that opens onto a fire escape."

"How many shotguns do we have?" asked Beck.

Demarco answered, "Two. Both in the trunk. Manny's Winchester and my Benelli."

Beck checked his watch. 3:10 P.M.

"Okay, look, we're never going to get all these assholes in one place again. I'm not losing this opportunity. D, you take the Winchester and go around to the back of the house. See if you can make your way up the fire escape. When you hear us bust in the front, break the window if it's locked, and get into the kitchen. Make sure nobody runs out the back. Anybody points a gun at you, drop 'em."

"Ciro, you take the Benelli. I'll go in the front door. Manny behind me. You last. We put everybody we see on the ground. If it takes a couple of blasts, so be it, but try not to kill anybody unless you have to. I need information."

Leon asked, "What about me? I done everything you asked me to."

Beck opened the Mercury's glove compartment and pulled out a pair of handcuffs joined with a three-foot chain. He handed the cuffs back to Manny, who quickly fed the chain through an eyebolt welded to the back floor of the car and cuffed Leon's wrists.

"So far you're good, Leon," said Beck. "You wait here for us to get back."

"What?"

"You heard me."

"What if you don't make it back?"

"If I was you, I'd start praying we do. If we don't and they do, they're going to find your ass sitting here. How long you think it'll take them to figure you ratted them out?"

"Wait a second."

"For what?"

Leon thought it over for a moment and then said, "I wanna tell you where they hide the key to the front door of the house. That's the only way you gonna get in there without them knowing you're coming."

"Good thinking, Leon."

16

John Palmer hadn't wasted time at the 50th Precinct, but it still took him thirty minutes to find out Peter Malone had nothing useful on Derrick Watkins. The file Malone handed him was pathetically thin. Palmer flashed a tight smile, telling himself he would remember this incompetent prick.

He headed back to his unmarked car and called his FBI contact, Gregory McAndrews, who unlike Malone, had come through for him. He provided addresses for two locations used by the Watkins brothers. He told Palmer there were probably more, but they hadn't uncovered them yet.

Palmer thanked McAndrews and asked him to stay in touch. He envied the FBI their resources and efficiency, but still preferred the NYPD where he could cut corners, ignore procedure, and take risks under the protective cover of his father.

Palmer climbed into his car, pulled up Google Maps, and checked the two addresses McAndrews had provided. One was north, about a mile in the opposite direction. The other he could check out on the way back to his precinct.

Palmer ached for sleep. He was way out on a limb, following information provided by a source outside the department, working alone. Real cowboy stuff, but fuck it, he thought. Nobody will bitch if I nail this thing. Even if the location didn't pan out, he'd sleep better crossing it off his list.

He checked the address on Mount Hope Place one more time.

17

By the time Beck, Manny, and Ciro arrived at the second landing of the rickety wood-frame building, the creaking and squeaking of the wood steps made Beck raise a hand and tell everyone, "Hold it."

Beck held his Browning Hi-Power pointed down, tight against his right leg. Manny held two guns, his long-barrel .38 Colt Special in his left hand and his Charter Arms Bulldog .357 in his right. Ciro Baldassare had the Benelli cradled in his left arm. He'd shoved his Smith & Wesson M&P .45 in the front of his pants where he could reach it easily.

Besides being worried about the noise they were making, Beck wanted to give Demarco time to make it up the fire escape at the back.

Of the three of them, Demarco was best suited for a stealthy climb three stories up a fire escape. Ciro was by far the strongest. Manny Guzman was the oldest of the four, the shortest, and the least physically capable, but in a fight he would be the one with the most focus, least encumbered by nerves or tension. Beck didn't have the athletic skill of Demarco, the strength of Ciro, or the stone-cold nerves of Manny, but he always managed to do what had to be done.

While the others held their positions, Beck slowly edged toward the apartment door on the second-floor landing and pressed his ear against it. He heard nothing, just like he'd heard nothing on the first floor.

He turned his attention to the apartment above them, thinking it through one more time. He turned to Manny and Ciro, speaking in a whisper.

"They're going to hear us coming up this last flight of stairs no matter how slowly we go, so I'm going to take it all in one shot and hit the door hard."

Beck shoved his Browning under his belt in front, pushing it down low so it would be as secure as possible. From his pants pockets he slid out a pair of custom-made brass knuckles cut from a single piece of solid nautical brass, highly polished, no seams. He slid the brass over both his fists.

"We move fast. We put them down. Don't kill anybody unless you have to."

Beck turned and stepped up the last flight of stairs, slowly at first, taking the steps one by one. He quickly picked up speed. By the time he reached the top half of the stairway, he was moving as fast as he could, taking two steps at a time. By the time he reached the landing he was moving at full speed. His right foot hit the door with so much force the handle lock, dead-bolt lock, and one of the hinges all broke through the frame.

Beck's forward momentum carried him into the front room. Everybody in the room jumped up, but Beck went straight for the biggest within his reach and overhanded a punch into the middle of Tyrell Williams's face, breaking his nose and cracking his right cheekbone. Tyrell fell back, knocked out, hitting the floor hard. Beck felt rather than saw a body closing in on his right. He whipped a backhand in that direction and connected with something that felt like a head.

Manny and Ciro came in right behind Beck, yelling for everyone to get on the floor. Beck heard the slap-cracking sounds of blows landing on body parts, shouts, curses, and the kitchen window in the back shattering. Somebody tried to grab him from behind, but Beck spun him off. Two deafening blasts from Ciro's Benelli exploded. Chunks of plaster and lath fell. Everyone ducked and froze in place. Beck swept the feet out from under somebody standing near him, yelling, "Get down."

Manny whipped the long barrel of his .38 against someone's head to put him down. Ciro rammed the butt of the Bennelli into the last man standing.

It took nine seconds from the time the door broke open until everyone lay flat on the floor.

Beck felt his heart pounding. He was out of breath. He wiped his brass knuckles off on an old upholstered chair then slipped them back into his pockets.

Demarco walked into the room holding the Winchester shotgun in one hand and the arm of a barefoot young woman showing a good deal of skin in his other hand. He sat her in a straight-back chair near a beat-up red velour couch.

All the shouting had stopped. Ciro kept his shotgun pointed at the crew while Manny went from prone body to prone body, telling them to put their hands on the back of their heads as he searched them for weapons and ID. When he found a gun, he tossed it on the ratty couch.

Beck heard gasping from the man he'd knocked unconscious, the kind of labored breathing that occurs when a brain has shut down except for the autonomic reactions that keep a heart beating and lungs working. He rolled Tyrell Williams over on his side so he wouldn't choke on the blood flowing from his broken nose.

He looked for the one he thought he'd skulled with the brass-knuckled backhand, hoping he hadn't killed him. He found him lying flat on the floor, his right hand pressed against a bleeding forehead. It was Derrick Watkins, quietly cursing at the pain.

Beck walked to the front door and wedged it into the cracked frame, sealing off the apartment from the landing. Demarco took a position near the door, his shotgun held low, aimed at the group.

Beck asked Demarco, "Anybody else in the back?"

"Nope."

Ciro firing the Benelli had caused a lot of noise, but it certainly helped put a stop to anybody fighting back. Nobody was dead. None of Beck's crew was injured. So far, so good, as long as the two shotgun blasts didn't bring the police.

Beck waited until Manny finished disarming and collecting identification from the last man on the floor, then he sat on the scabby red couch and gathered the guns and other weapons into a pile.

There were six men of various sizes and ages on the dirty floor of the Mount Hope Place apartment. All of them had been armed, but none of them had been able to get off a shot.

Beck looked at the girl sitting to his right. She was dressed in a way that revealed nearly everything about her body. Her short-shorts and tight T-shirt made it difficult for Beck not to stare, which, of course, was exactly the point of the clothes.

He didn't want to hear the answer to the question he was about to ask, but he asked it.

"Young lady."

Amelia looked over at Beck.

"What's your name?"

She paused for a moment, staring at Beck with an expression he couldn't quite decipher. She seemed stunned, yet, at the same time, strangely alert. She took a quick look at the bodies on the floor, and then answered, "Princess."

Beck paused. Speaking carefully, he said, "No. I don't mean your working name. What's your real name?"

"Why?"

"Are you Amelia Johnson?"

She stopped looking at Derrick's crew on the floor and turned to Beck. "Who are you?"

"My name is James Beck. I was a friend of your father's."

He saw a look of confusion on the young girl's face. It confirmed two things. She was, in fact, Amelia Johnson, and she probably didn't know her father had been shot and killed.

Amelia asked, "What do you mean, was?"

Beck hesitated. "It's been a long time since I've seen him. Which one of these is Derrick Watkins?"

Amelia didn't answer, but tipped her head toward Derrick.

Beck said to Amelia, "Would you do me a favor? Go in the kitchen and get a towel or something. Run cold water over it, wring it out, and give it to Derrick."

Amelia stared at Beck for a moment, then got up to do as he'd asked.

Beck turned to the bleeding man on the floor.

"Derrick, get up and go sit in that chair."

Derrick lifted his head off the floor to glare at Beck, but made no move to get up. Manny Guzman stood closest to him. Without a second's hesitation, he began kicking Derrick Watkins – hard, fast, brutal kicks into his leg and ribs. Derrick scrambled away from the kicks and got to his feet. He staggered over to the chair and fell into it more than sat on it.

The others watched, but didn't move.

Amelia returned from the kitchen with a threadbare hand towel she had rinsed as Beck had asked. She'd also put on her pink hoodie, zipping it up to her neck. She handed the towel to Derrick without looking at him.

Beck thanked her and said, "One more favor. There are bedrooms back there, right?"

"Yes."

"Go back and find me a couple of pillowcases if you can, and bring them out here."

Beck spoke to Amelia, but stared at Derrick Watkins, taking in the sight of him. Coming to an opinion about him.

Derrick sat in the upholstered armchair, holding the wet towel to his bleeding head.

Beck took note that Derrick appeared to be older than most of the others in the room. He wore better clothes than expected: a square-cut oversized shirt that hung out over black, pleated slacks, and black suede sneakers.

Beck figured him for mid-thirties, about twenty pounds overweight, mean, blank eyes. He had none of the expected gang tattoos or garish jewelry, but he did have a typical hateful, defiant expression.

One other person on the floor also looked to be older than the others. He was the largest in the room, and like Derrick dressed in conventional clothes instead of the baggy jeans and T-shirts the others wore. Beck figured him for close to 230 pounds and had the feeling he was the kind who used his size to intimidate. Maybe he could actually back that up, thought Beck, but he had the feeling the guy would probably be more likely to pay or coerce somebody else to do his violence for him.

The question was, which one of these had shot his friend Packy Johnson?

Beck turned his attention back to Derrick Watkins.

Amelia Johnson returned carrying two pillowcases that at one time must have been white, but were now discolored with indelible stains where too many dirty heads had lain. She handed them to Beck without a word. She also had a small handbag over her right shoulder and had put on a pair of platform high-heeled shoes.

Beck thought, maybe she thinks I'm going to let her leave now, but she sat back down on the chair near the couch.

Beck looked carefully at her face, trying to see signs of drug addiction or fear or depression in her eyes. She looked alert, although he did see a remoteness in her eyes he couldn't quite figure out.

Beck used one of the pillowcases to methodically wipe down all the guns they had taken from the crew. He divided the guns evenly into the two pillowcases, tossing in a few knives Manny had also collected. Then he tied off both pillowcases and laid them on the couch.

Finally, Beck spoke to Derrick Watkins.

"Why are you and all your friends here?"

Derrick stared back at Beck, saying nothing.

Beck held his gaze on Derrick Watkins, resisting the urge to put a bullet in one of Derrick's limbs and asked again.

"All right, Mr. Watkins, let me explain something. Just so you understand. If I ask you something and I hear anything that sounds like bullshit, I'm going to have my friend shoot off your left foot."

Ciro Baldassare pumped the Benelli and pointed it at Derrick's foot.

"Then we'll tighten a belt around your calf and I'll ask you again. Make a second mistake, and we'll blow off your right foot. Think you can make it past your hands?

"One more time. What are you and all these others doing here?"

Derrick shifted in the overstuffed upholstered chair. Ciro stood unmoving, the unwavering shotgun aimed directly at Derrick's left foot.

Derrick pointed his chin at Amelia. "Had a run-in with her father. I figured it was best to clear out of the area for a bit. Any shit happens over in Bronx River Houses, cops always come knockin' on my door."

"You're getting close to losing a foot, Derrick. Why are *all* of you here?"

"It's my fuckin' crew, man. We hang together."

Beck looked at Ciro. Ciro lowered the shotgun so the muzzle was even closer to Derrick's foot. Derrick moved his foot back. "Wait, wait. It wasn't just me. We all took him down. Someone calls me out, they call all of us out."

"Uh-huh. So it took all six of you lowlife cowards to beat up one guy?"

"He's the one who came lookin' for trouble, man. And it wasn't all six. Just five of us."

"Oh, so who wasn't there?"

Derrick hesitated. From the floor, Jerome Watkins spoke. "I wasn't there."

"And who are you?"

"I'm his brother."

"What's your brother doing here, Derrick?"

"We got business to talk over."

"What business?"

Derrick tilted his head toward Amelia again. "Got to decide what to do with that bitch. Guy comin' around causing all sorts of trouble, bringing attention on me. Fuck it. Time to cut her loose. Goddam, broke-ass bitch can't even earn a pimp his money. So we discussed kickin' her to the curb. Lettin' her go back to her broke-ass father."

Beck looked at Amelia for a moment. She stared intently at Derrick. Beck turned back to Derrick, thinking about his answer. It didn't escape him that Derrick Watkins talked as if Packy Johnson were still alive.

"Just like that. Let her go? Like everything is okay? She doesn't owe you anything?"

"Hell yeah, she owes me. But like I say, fuck it. She a bad investment. A mistake. Smart businessman cuts his losses. What the fuck is the problem? Her father's the nigger who started all this mess. He come into my hood

138

callin' me out, what you think is going to happen? He got a ass whipping. So what? Why you all up in here with guns and shit?"

Beck leaned forward, "Because after the ass whipping, you or one of your crew followed Packy Johnson out of that housing project and shot him in the back of the head like the sneaking, pimping, lowlife cowards you are."

Derrick Watkins pulled the bloody towel from his head. His reaction was immediate.

"Fuck we did. Nobody . . ."

But the thunder of a gun exploding in the enclosed room obliterated Derrick's words.

Amelia Johnson stood firing a handgun at Derrick Watkins, a gun still cold from the kitchen freezer, its barrel hissing as the exploding gunpowder heated the barrel.

The first bullet hit Derrick in the upper chest, slightly to the left. As the recoil bucked the handgun higher, the second bullet hit his mouth, taking out most of the lower third of his face. The third bullet hit him slightly off-center in the middle of his forehead, blowing most of his brains out the back of his skull. The fourth bullet missed entirely, burrowing into the wall behind Derrick Watkins.

Ciro and Manny both ducked and turned their weapons on Amelia, but their discipline held, and they didn't shoot her.

Beck was about to lunge off the couch to knock her down, but held back, knowing if she kept pulling the trigger she might hit Manny as she fell.

And then, as quickly as it had started, the gunfire stopped.

While she pulled the trigger, she'd kept her eyes on her target, but now Amelia swept the gun from side to side, yelling, "Stay back. Back away," as she walked toward the front door.

Beck held up a hand. Manny kept his gun lowered. Ciro did the same with the shotgun. Demarco stood between the door and Amelia. He had laid down the Winchester and now held his Glock 17 behind his back, his eyes never leaving Amelia as she moved toward him. He glanced at Beck, knowing the safest thing would be a head shot, killing her instantly, eliminating any chance she could pull the trigger and injure one of them.

The decision had to be made now. Shoot her, or let her go. Demarco glanced again at Beck. He gave him a quick headshake, no. Demarco reached up, grabbed the top of the battered door, and tipped it open, holding it between him and the girl, his Glock still ready behind his back. Amelia pointed her gun at Demarco as she slipped out the door.

As soon as Amelia disappeared, Demarco, Manny, and Ciro turned to Beck. He knew he didn't have much time to make several crucial decisions. In fact, he had no time.

18

As John Palmer drove down Jerome Avenue toward Mount Hope Place, he thought he heard the sound of four, quick, distant gunshots. But the strain of the last hours combined with his fatigue made him unsure. And then he realized how close he was to a known location for Derrick Watkins. Gunshots, definitely.

He flicked on the grill-light flashers and stopped in the middle of Jerome Avenue to report shots fired at the address he had been given for Derrick Watkins. He called for assistance from any available units in the area, turned on the rest of the unmarked Dodge Charger's emergency lights, and accelerated forward, tapping his siren when needed to clear away traffic. He glanced at his GPS screen and saw the turnoff onto Mount Hope Place was two blocks away.

Beck cursed in frustration. Where the hell did she get that gun? It must have been hidden somewhere in the apartment. She'd brought it back in the pocket of her hoodie. No time to worry about it now.

He patted his shirt pocket to make sure he had the IDs Manny had collected from Derrick's crew. In three seconds, he ran through a series of decisions.

Let Derrick's crew go. He didn't want them around identifying him. If he had to, he'd find them.

He confirmed to himself that he'd wiped down the guns they'd collected enough to obliterate Manny's prints. Leave them. Too dangerous to be caught with two pillow-cases filled with guns.

Anything else? Gather the cartridges from the shots fired by Amelia? No. There'd be nothing about them that could lead to Beck or his men.

Beck stood, yelling at the five on the floor. "Get up. Get the fuck out of here. Now! Use the fire escape out back. You come out the front door, we'll shoot you. Go."

They didn't need any encouragement. Four jumped up and scrambled toward the back of the apartment. Beck and Manny had to lift Tyrell Williams to his feet and push him in the right direction. He wobbled away, bracing himself against the hallway wall.

"D, get the car."

Demarco tossed his shotgun to Beck and ran out the door, using the handrails to fly down the stairs four and five at a time.

The others shoved their guns into pants pockets and waistbands and rushed after Demarco. By the time they were halfway down the stairs, Demarco had the Mercury fired up. He pulled out into the street just as John Palmer turned onto Mount Hope Place.

Demarco saw Palmer's lights flashing behind him at the top of the block.

Up ahead, Beck and Manny stepped out of the house, followed by Ciro a few paces behind. They walked quickly, Beck and Ciro holding the shotguns down out of view.

Demarco accelerated toward them, the Mercury's wide tires screeching and melting rubber into the asphalt.

Palmer noticed immediately. He turned his sirens on full blast and accelerated after the black car up ahead, taking note of the two men heading toward the street, followed by a third man.

Demarco screeched to a halt. Beck jumped into the backseat, climbing over Leon Miller, Manny coming in behind, leaving the front passenger seat for Ciro.

The unmarked NYPD Charger closed the distance fast.

Without a second's hesitation, Ciro Baldassare strode into the middle of the street, raised the Benelli and pumped round after round of 12-gauge shot into the onrushing police car.

His first blast blew apart the grill, radiator, and emergency lights. His second two shots tore the front tire off the right wheel. The Charger swerved on its bare spinning rim and crashed into a parked car. But Ciro wasn't finished. He blasted two shots into the engine block, and two more into the front window.

When the Charger smacked into the parked car, John Palmer pitched forward into the exploding steering wheel airbag. The impact momentarily paralyzed him, but he quickly shoved aside the deflated bag and threw himself down behind the dashboard as shotgun pellets disintegrated the windshield above him and tore through the upholstery and interior of the car. Palmer didn't even think about returning fire.

Walking backward toward the Mercury, Ciro expended his last shell into the wrecked hulk of Palmer's police car and calmly slid into the passenger seat.

Demarco floored the accelerator and the Mercury flew down the block. He braked hard and slid into a left turn the wrong way on a one-way street, then took a quick right onto another one-way street, but this time going in the correct direction.

They heard the deep *woop, woop* of police sirens coming from multiple directions.

Demarco slowed down. He drove quickly and precisely, determined to get as far from where the police were converging as fast as possible.

Leon Miller sat with hands covering his bowed head, repeating quiet curses over and over.

Beck and the others braced themselves as Demarco braked and turned and maneuvered. About a half mile from the shooting, Demarco finally stopped at a red light. In the backseat, Beck unlocked Leon's handcuffs. He told Demarco, "Pull over for a second."

When the car reached the curb, Beck stepped out, dragging Leon with him.

He made sure the slim youth was on his feet and steady, and then said to him, "Here's what you are going to do. Are you listening?"

He got a blank look from Leon. Beck slapped the side of his head.

"Look at me, Leon. Derrick Watkins is dead."

"Shit."

"Shut up. There were five guys from his crew up there. Including his brother. They got out alive. They're going to figure out you're the one who led us to them. You have to disappear, Leon. For a long time. Do you understand?"

"Yes. Yes."

"Go somewhere nobody will find you." Beck stared at him to make sure Leon got the message. "Got it?"

"Yes. Yes. Disappear. I got peoples in South Carolina. I can go there."

"Good." Beck shoved a wad of bills into Leon's front pants pocket. "Go. Now."

Beck jump back into the Mercury as the light turned green. He didn't bother to watch Leon Miller run away.

19

Amelia Johnson clomped down the worn wooden stairs of the Mount Hope house as fast as she could, her ears ringing from gunfire, the acrid smell of gun smoke clinging to her clothes. She felt a mixture of joy, fear, and excitement that made her shiver.

By the time she reached the bottom of the stairs, she was out of breath. Her legs felt wobbly. She stopped at the interior door, forcing herself to take deep breaths and concentrate.

She realized she was still holding the gun in her right hand. She shoved it into the kangaroo pocket of her hoodie, feeling both the hot barrel and the cold body of the gun against her stomach.

She checked her red wig, making sure it was in place, and then she stepped out onto Mount Hope Place, moving with an urgency fueled by exhilaration and fear.

Without knowing when the idea had come to her, she turned and walked toward Derrick's black Jeep parked near the end of the block. When she reached the car, she quickly crouched down near the left-rear wheel well, feeling inside the top of the rear panel for the magnetic key case Derrick used to store a spare key. She located the case, extracted a single key for the Jeep, and opened the driver's-side door.

She climbed in the driver's seat, fired up the engine, and drove away, nearly sideswiping the cars on the other side of the street. She'd driven a car only twice in her life. Never anything as big as the Jeep. She drove hunched over, gripping the wheel, staring straight ahead, concentrating on keeping the Jeep in the middle of the narrow street. When she managed to get three blocks away, she pulled over to an empty section of curb on Mount Hope Place, bounced the right front wheel up onto the sidewalk, and braked hard. She put the car in park. It was only then that she figured out how to adjust the seat, strapped on her seat belt, and positioned the rearview mirror.

She slipped off her red wig, pulled the gun out of her hoodie, wrapped the wig around it, and shoved both under the passenger seat.

Her hands still shaking slightly, she fished out the bills she'd hidden in her hair, stuffed them into her front pocket, and pulled the hoodie over her head. She drove back out into the street without hitting anything, but cut off a driver coming up behind her who beeped furiously at her.

"Shit, shit, shit."

She put all her attention on driving straight forward. Mount Hope Place quickly dead-ended at Jerome Avenue, forcing Amelia to make a nervous left turn onto the busy two-way street. The traffic ran in narrow lanes squeezed between huge iron girders supporting the elevated subway tracks, bordered by cars parked block after block on both sides.

Minutes ago, Amelia had the courage and strength to shoot a man, but now she felt like a teenager who had stolen the family car and was worried about getting into a traffic accident. The adrenaline that had fueled her escape and sharpened her concentration had worn off. She felt weak, almost faint. She hadn't eaten anything except a chicken leg the night before, and a cup of coffee and a stale donut eleven hours earlier.

Up ahead, she spotted a McDonald's. She managed to turn into the parking lot without hitting anything and park the Jeep in an empty space. She kept her hood up and walked into the fast-food restaurant, ignoring the looks her bare legs and platform heels attracted.

She got her food and took a seat in a corner, as far back from the front window as possible. She forced herself to eat her meal slowly, but sitting in a public space where anybody might see her gave her a nearly unbearable feeling of dread and anxiety.

Unless those friends of her father had killed everyone else in the room, and she hadn't heard any gunfire after she left, she knew it wouldn't be long before Biggie got the word to Eric Jackson about what she'd done. Once that happened, dozens, maybe hundreds of neighborhood punks would be out looking for her along with the dreaded Whitey Bondurant.

She kept her head down and her hoodie pulled up, pictured Biggie Watkins or Whitey bursting into McDonald's, walking up to her, and shooting her in the face.

God help her if Whitey Bondurant found her. She'd been around him only a few times, but he was the scariest man she'd ever seen. Big, with a creepy albino face and dead, weird-looking pink eyes. Usually, Bondurant wore sunglasses to protect his eyes, but if he talked to you or looked at you he always took them off to see you better. Nobody wanted those crazy grim-reaper eyes staring at them.

Amelia forced herself to stop thinking about it. She'd done what she'd done. They were going to kill her. Maybe they'd still kill her, now in an even more horrible way. At least she'd die knowing she had killed Derrick Watkins first.

So now what?

She stank from fear and tension, and working all night at the Point. She needed regular clothes, not this whore outfit smelling of gun smoke. And shoes. And a place to hide. Her sixty dollars was down to fifty-three and change. She needed money, but not by turning tricks. Never again.

She had a gun, but knew she couldn't do a strong-arm robbery.

She blinked and sniffed, fighting off the need to cry. She thought about what she had done to earn the money sitting in dead Derrick Watkins's pocket. Forget about it, she told herself.

She thought about those men who were supposedly friends of her father. Maybe she could find them. Maybe they would help her. But how could she find them? She didn't even know who they were.

She finished her last french fry and the rest of her Coke. The food had revived her. She had to move on. But where? And how long could she last without money? And how long before they found her and killed her?

20

Crouching below the dashboard of the Dodge, Palmer heard the fading squeals of the Mercury Marauder's tires telling him his attackers had fled. The wail of police sirens told him help and protection were on the way.

He half fell, half crawled out of his wrecked car. Palmer stood and drew his service gun. There was nothing to shoot at, but he wanted to look like he might have been shooting.

The first patrol car appeared at the top of the block.

Palmer walked out into the middle of the street, holding up his badge wallet, shouting his name, rank, and precinct number at the cops piling out of their patrol cars.

In the small, empty yard behind Derrick's house, the last of his crew except for Tyrell Williams dropped down onto the ground from the fire escape ladder. They ran through the backyard, climbed over a wrought-iron fence, scattering in all directions. Biggie Watkins struggled over the gate last and then lumbered off toward Jerome Avenue.

Back at the fire escape, Tyrell, still woozy and off balance from the brass-knuckled fist to his face, had taken a long time reeling down the steep fire escape. He'd just managed to get onto the drop-down ladder that hung about five feet above the ground behind the Mount Hope house. Near the bottom of the ladder, he lost his footing, dropping hard enough to make his legs buckle, and fell to the side, smacking his head on the packed dirt.

Everything turned black for him again.

Out front, Palmer had been yelling a description of a black sedan into a police radio, possibly a Ford Crown Vic with four armed men leaving the scene of a shooting. He would have bet money one of the men was James Beck, but he kept that to himself.

He quickly organized the four uniformed cops on the scene into a raiding party. As two more arrived he told them, "Go search the back."

One of the cops broke open the front door, and they all headed up the stairs of the rickety three-flat. They quickly searched the first two floors, finding them empty. On the top floor, the broken front door of the last apartment stood half open. Palmer moved to the front of the pack. He held his SIG in a two-handed grip, kicked the broken door out of his way, and shouted, "Police! Everybody down. Down!"

He leaned into the room and saw the bloody, bullet-riddled corpse of Derrick Watkins, slumped in the armchair. He stepped into the apartment, motioning the cops behind him to enter.

He walked to the body and stood in front of the dead man, as if claiming ownership of it. He told the other cops to check the apartment. Three of the four cops made their way to the rear of the apartment, while the fourth cop stood next to Palmer, who holstered his gun and bent over to get a closer look at the body, wincing at Derrick's destroyed face. Whoever had shot him had done a thorough job of it.

Cops filtered back into the front room, talking to each other in raised voices, their police radios crackling. The cop who had stayed with Palmer pulled out his radio and reported in to his precinct about the discovery of a deceased black male shot multiple times. It annoyed Palmer. He considered this his case, but he was too tired to say anything.

He checked his watch. Almost 4:27 P.M.

Palmer asked, "Anything back there?"

All three cops confirmed the apartment was empty.

"All right, guys, this is a crime scene. Let's seal this place off."

He ordered one cop to go downstairs and close off the entrance to the building. He ordered two others to search the lower floors more carefully for weapons, drugs, or other bodies, and then to check the buildings on each side to see if they could find witnesses.

He told the cop who had stayed with him, "Okay, you and I are going to search this place more thoroughly."

The cop had already discovered the two pillowcases on the couch filled with guns. He opened one of them and tilted the makeshift bag toward Palmer, who walked over and looked at the pile of guns. He bent down to take a sniff. "Doesn't smell like any of them have been fired. Just leave them there. Go in the back and work your way to the front. See if you can find anything. Guns, drugs, money. The usual."

"Got it," said the patrol cop.

"Be thorough. You got gloves?"

The uniformed cop pulled out a pair of blue latex gloves and slipped them on, as did Palmer. As the patrolman turned toward the back of the apartment his radio crackled with the information that the cops on the street had captured somebody.

Palmer smiled. *This just keeps getting better and better.*

21

Out in the McDonald's parking lot, Amelia climbed back into the driver's seat and steered the Jeep onto Jerome Avenue. She drove south, determined to get something else to wear. It was difficult enough for her to drive, but now she had to scan the stores along either side of Jerome Avenue. She passed empty lots, food stores, bodegas, pharmacies, automotive-supply stores. Finally, she found what she wanted: a discount clothing shop.

She parked the Jeep next to a fire hydrant, unworried about getting a ticket, and walked back to the store. She found an off-brand pair of jeans that fitted her. She found a gray women's T-shirt decorated with an image of a fedora with a pink feather and the words: *Thinking about the summer vacation makes me lighthearted*.

Amelia didn't bother to read the words as she quickly shoplifted the T-shirt. In another section of the store she found a cheap pair of red ballet flats. By the time she bought the jeans and shoes she was down to thirty-eight dollars.

She walked back to the Jeep, changed in the front seat, and dumped her old clothes and shoes in the back. She still needed a shower, her hair felt filthy, she had no bra, but at least she didn't have to wear the stinking, cut-off, rhinestone-decorated T-shirt, short-shorts, and stupid whore shoes.

Night was coming on as she turned off Jerome Avenue worried that someone would see her driving Derrick's Jeep. She drove south on local streets, forcing herself to keep going so she could put more distance between her and Derrick's neighborhood, but she soon found herself squinting into the darkening streets because she didn't know how to turn on the Jeep's headlights. Finally, she had to pull the Jeep over and stop. She turned off the engine and rested her forehead on the steering wheel, fighting off the urge to cry.

She looked around and found herself in an isolated, mixed residential and commercial section of Shakespeare Avenue. Across the street she saw a derelict two-story brick house with all the windows covered in sheets of plywood. Next to it, occupying the corner, was a three-story building with a bar on the ground floor, closed off behind roll-down security gates. It looked like it had gone out of business long ago.

Amelia stared at the abandoned house. She'd known kids on the run who had squatted in such places. But she'd never done it herself. She never thought she would have to, until now. Beyond everything that plagued her, she had an overwhelming urge to hide. To hide from the men and boys and guns coming for her.

She slipped out of the Jeep, walked back, and lifted the hatch door. She rummaged around until she found a car cover, which she pulled out and folded into a bundle small enough to carry under her arm. She also found a tire iron, which she hid in the folds of the car cover, and a partial roll of paper towels, which she stuffed into the pocket of her hoodie.

She went to the passenger side of the Jeep and took the gun out from under the seat, threw aside the red wig, and slipped the gun into her hoodie with the paper towels.

She pulled the hood over her head and walked around the corner until she reached a chain-link fence blocking access to the backyards behind the houses on Shakespeare. Past ragged bushes and stunted ailanthus trees, Amelia could see the back of the abandoned house. Much of the back wall was covered in large sheets of plywood.

There was a gate made of corrugated metal attached to the chain-link fence, secured with a padlock and an eye-bolt welded to an iron pole. Amelia looked around, then placed the tire iron in the eyebolt, turning and twisting it until she broke the eyebolt off the pole. She pulled back the corrugated metal fence and slipped into the backyard, waded through the overgrown area, and climbed over another chain-link fence to get behind the abandoned house. She had to step over junk and around discarded furniture to reach the back of the house. Once there, she spotted two half-windows at ground level. One was sealed by concrete blocks, the other by a set of iron bars in front of a piece of plywood.

Amelia squatted down and used the tire iron to pry the bars out of one end of the window frame and pulled them away as if she were opening a stuck gate. She punched the end of the tire iron into the plywood blocking the window until it dropped into the basement with a thud.

She peered into the dark space, unable to make out anything. She shined the light of her cell phone screen into the dark, but it revealed almost nothing.

The basement smelled moldy and damp, but she didn't detect the stink of urine or feces that would signal someone might be living down there.

She heard a sudden movement in the overgrown grass and bushes behind her. She let out a short scream and turned, half expecting to see Biggie Watkins or the hulking Whitey Bondurant behind her with a gun pointed at her.

"Shit, shit, shit."

Must have been a cat or something, but she hardly believed it, the noise had been so loud.

She pulled the iron bars open wider, laid the car cover over the sill, and turned over on her stomach. She maneuvered her feet into the window opening and squirmed backward, lifting herself over the bottom of the frame so the gun and paper towels in the pocket of her hoodie wouldn't catch. Fearful that she might be dropping into a hole she would never get out of, she lowered herself all the way in. Even hanging full length from the windowsill, her feet didn't reach the ground. She looked down. She thought she could see the floor, but could only hope that once she let go, she wouldn't land on something that would hurt her.

The remains of Derrick Watkins stank. Even though Palmer and the others had opened all the windows, with the outside temperature hovering around eighty and the temperature in the decrepit top-floor apartment creeping higher as more crime-scene investigators and police personnel began to arrive, the stench of the dead body, along with the blood, bones, and brain splattered on the walls, grew worse.

With his fatigue pressing in on him, Palmer wasn't sure how much more of the smell and heat he could take. And then it all went away when the uniformed cops brought Tyrell Williams up to the third-floor apartment.

Palmer knew a man in bad shape when he saw one. Dried blood matted Tyrell's face, and he wobbled around, clearly not fully conscious. It didn't matter to Palmer. This was a possible eyewitness.

He told the two cops holding Tyrell, "Take him to the first bedroom down the hall."

Palmer followed them and watched the cops lay the young black man on a rumpled bed, setting him on top of the dirty sheets and a bare, badly stained pillow.

Palmer figured him for about twenty-five years old. Big, wearing a blue polo shirt with the large logo, jeans, and New Balance sneakers. Somebody had obviously hit him in the face with something more than a fist. The skin across the bridge of his nose had split open, and the nose looked fractured and swollen, as well as the area under his left eye. Blood stained not only the front of his shirt, but also his jeans.

He would need stitches and some attention to the broken nose.

Palmer looked at him lying on the bed with his eyes closed and wondered if he were playing up his injuries. Then again, the cops did say they'd found him passed out back behind the building.

Fuck it, thought Palmer. Let's see what we have here. He told the cops who had brought him into the bedroom, "All right, guys, give me a minute."

Palmer waited until the cops left before he knocked the back of his fist against Tyrell's shoulder.

"Hey. Wake up."

Tyrell stirred, but kept his eyes closed.

Palmer shook him gently.

"Yo, c'mon. Wake up."

Tyrell cracked one eye.

Palmer pulled over a battered chair from the corner of the room and placed it near the head of the bed. He sat down and leaned close to Tyrell.

"Listen to me. This is important. Can you follow what I'm saying?"

Tyrell turned toward Palmer and mumbled, "Huh?"

"C'mon, listen up. My name is John Palmer. I'm the detective in charge here. My men found you out back. I need to know something. You were here when the guy in the front room got shot, right?"

Tyrell had both eyes open now.

Palmer repeated, "You were here, right?" Making it sound more conspiratorial.

Still no answer.

Palmer lowered his voice, looked behind him to make sure no one was hovering outside the door. He leaned closer to Tyrell. "When that guy got shot, you were here."

This time it wasn't a question.

"Yeah," answered Tyrell.

Palmer nodded.

"Good, that means you have a chance to help yourself out. What's your name?"

"Tyrell. Tyrell Williams."

"Okay, Tyrell, you're going to need medical attention for your injuries. You need to be taken care of, you know what I mean?"

"Yeah."

"It doesn't look to me like you could have pulled any trigger. Doesn't seem like you even had a gun."

"No. I didn't have no gun."

Palmer kept going, knowing he was completely leading his witness. Describing to him the answers he wanted.

"I pulled up outside here in time to see three guys coming out of this house in a big hurry. They got into a black car. Look like a black Ford Vic, or maybe a Lincoln Town Car."

Tyrell listened, and waited.

"There were three plus the driver," said Palmer. "One of 'em was white. Had a shotgun. He fired at me."

Still Tyrell didn't comment.

"You know who they were, Tyrell?"

"I don't know who they were, but they was up here." Tyrell pointed to his face. "One of 'em did this to me."

"Really?"

"Yeah."

Palmer asked the next question softly. As if he and Tyrell were friends.

"I'm assuming they shot the guy out in the front room."

Tyrell hesitated only slightly before he gave Palmer the answer he was seeking, making sure to use the plural as Palmer had. "Yeah. Yeah, they shot him."

"You know why?"

Tyrell thought carefully before he answered. "Something about a friend of theirs."

"I see. How many were there?"

"Four. Two whites. One brother. One spic."

"Who's the guy they shot?"

"Name is Derrick. Derrick Watkins."

"Which one shot him, Tyrell?"

"The white guy. There was two white guys." Tyrell pointed to his face. "The one who did this to me shot Derrick."

Palmer mustered a look of sympathy. "Really. Think you could identify him?"

"Hell yeah I can identify him."

Palmer patted Tyrell's shoulder. "Good. Good. All right, I want you to take it easy. Don't worry about anything. I'm gonna make sure you're okay. You know. Get somebody in here to look at your injuries. Give you something for the pain."

As he spoke, Palmer unlocked one of Tyrell's handcuffs and attached it to the frame of the bed.

"Don't worry about this cuff. This is just procedure. Something I have to do until I get things set up. Understand?"

Tyrell lifted his left arm and held his wrist in front of Palmer.

"You arrestin' me?"

"No, no. Just procedure until I get you looked after."

"Yo, cuz I ain't done nuthin' but tell you what you want to know. I don't want to be cuffed like this for too long. We on the same page?"

"Sure. Sure. Don't worry. I just need them on until I get you set up as a witness. Just work with me here."

"Yeah, because I'm still a little dizzy and all. I want to be able to recall what you need."

Palmer nodded. He didn't like the implied threat, but at least it showed his *witness* had a brain. "Well, if you want to do yourself a favor, you'll make sure you do recall what I need. Otherwise, all kinds of problems come into the picture. Problems about who actually shot that guy out front. You understand what I'm saying?"

"Yeah, I got it. Ain't no need for any confusion. I can identify all them motherfuckers. All four of them. Show me their pictures and I'll pick 'em out for you. All four."

"And the white guy who shot Derrick."

"Him especially."

Palmer stood above Tyrell Williams and smiled down on him.

"Good. That's real good."

Tyrell nodded at Palmer, saying nothing more. He'd play along with this detective. Let the fucking cops go after those four motherfuckers. Lock their asses up. Then tell Juju Jackson what really went down. Help him and Biggie find that bitch Amelia and make her pay for what she did. Make her pay like she'd never paid in her goddam life. The shit he would do to her was going to be legend. Tyrell Williams closed his eyes picturing how he would strip that fine bitch, tie her up, and rape her for days.

John Palmer took one last look at his prize witness, lying on the sour-smelling bed, eyes closed, like all was right with the world.

He'd better call Witherspoon and get him to come over with a photo array with James Beck's picture. Palmer smiled. Wait'll Ray finds out how close he is to sending a cop killer back to jail. Forever.

23

Demarco Jones had taken a route back from the shootout that avoided security cameras and eluded the cops. Now James Beck and the others sat on couches surrounding a massive coffee table made of petrified wood on the second floor of his three-story waterfront building at the south end of Red Hook – the smell of gun smoke still in their clothes, still ramped up from their brawl with Watkins's crew, still picturing Derrick Watkins blown away by three shots at close range.

Beck's building at the far end of Red Hook provided a measure of safety and security for them. It had taken him a year to renovate the place with help from an assortment of local workers and ex-cons. He'd restored the ground-floor bar, gutted the second and third floors, and built them to meet his needs. The top floor had bedrooms, bathrooms, storage areas, and a workout space. The second floor was an open loft divided into an office space, kitchen/dining area, and seating area.

Manny and Beck sat on one couch, Demarco and Ciro on the facing couch, all of them finishing a meal Manny had put together in the large upstairs kitchen accompanied by an ample supply of amber lager.

Demarco asked, "How long you think before the cops come after us for shooting Derrick Watkins?"

Ciro said, "Maybe never. That cop might have seen us, but he couldn't identify anybody with me blasting the crap out of his vehicle."

Beck said, "He doesn't have to. I caught a glimpse of him. He fits the description Walter gave us of the cop who showed up at his office this morning."

Ciro asked, "Walter Ferguson? The parole guy you work with?"

"Yeah. That cop and his partner told Walter Packy had been shot. Walter said they were going to interview Packy's mother-in-law after they talked to him. I gotta figure she told them about me. How me and Walter persuaded her to take Packy in, so he knows I'm tight with Packy. He'll figure I went after the crew responsible for shooting my friend. It won't be a big leap to say I killed the guy who I think killed Packy."

Demarco said, "Except you didn't."

Manny said, "So what. Cops get someone they can hang a murder on, they ain't gonna bust their ass trying to find anyone else. In the meantime, James, that girl did everyone a favor getting rid of that lowlife pimp, but I don't think he shot Packy. He didn't sound to me like he even knew Packy got shot."

Ciro said, "How do we know he wasn't lying? Guys like that, if their lips are moving they're lying. Shit, I'd lie my ass off if someone had a shotgun pointed at my foot."

Beck said, "Maybe. But I think Manny is right. I don't think Watkins shot Packy."

Ciro said, "Then who did?"

"I don't know. Maybe one of his crew. I also don't know why the girl shot him. I did not see that coming."

Manny said, "Neither did the pimp."

Beck said, "She didn't have a gun on her when you found her, right D?"

"Absolutely not. The way she was dressed, she had no place to hide a gun."

"So every time she left the room, she got something she needed. The hoodie to hide the gun. Then the gun. Her purse. Her shoes."

Ciro nodded. "She made her bones, man."

Beck said, "What is she? Sixteen? Seventeen?"

Manny said, "Old enough to have a reason to kill somebody."

Beck asked, "But what was the reason? She didn't know Packy had been shot either. She jumped on me when I said I *was* a friend of her father's. She set up everything, getting the gun and all before I announced her father had been shot."

Manny said, "I don't think Packy had shit to do with it. Girl like that, getting whored out? That means she's getting beaten, raped into submission. Maybe drugged up on top of it. She had enough reasons on her own to pull the trigger. We come along and give her the opportunity."

Demarco said, "Agreed, but there was more to it. When I found her, she was locked in one of the bedrooms. She looked crazed. I think she believed they were going to kill her. I think that whole crew was going to pull one last train on her, and then get rid of her."

Manny made a sour face, thinking it over. "Animals. But that don't explain why they wanted to kill her in the first place. Maybe it was because her father raised hell at the projects."

Beck said, "Which brings me back to my main question. Why was Packy raising hell? I keep trying to figure out what made him risk his parole hitchhiking into town, and then rush over to that housing project minutes after he arrives ready to take on a whole crew?"

Ciro said, "Because his daughter was getting turned out. Ain't that enough of a reason?"

"Maybe. But it wasn't as if Packy and the girl were all that close. And the Packy Johnson I knew didn't do things on the spur of the moment. The better play would have been to come to us for help. There had to be more to it."

"What?"

"I don't know. But I guarantee you I'm going to goddam find out."

Demarco asked, "How?"

Beck sat forward. "First, you guys have to find the older brother." Beck pulled out the IDs Manny had gathered out of his shirt pocket, held one up, and dropped the rest on the coffee table. "Jerome Watkins. If anybody knows what the hell is going on, it's him. You've got to find him, and find him before he gets to Packy's daughter. If he was going to kill her before, what do you think he'll do to her now that she shot his brother?"

Demarco, "She'll be begging for a bullet before he's done with her."

Manny asked, "And while we're doing that?"

"I'll be looking in the only other place that might have the answers to all this."

Ciro asked, "Where?"

"The place Packy Johnson had been up until seventeen hours before his death. Eastern Correctional."

24

It took nearly three hours to process the crime scene and remove the bloody remains of Derrick Watkins. All the windows in the apartment were opened, and surfaces in the front room were sprayed with an enzyme solvent and deodorizer to cover the lingering odors and make it bearable for the police personnel gathering at the scene.

Palmer talked to Tyrell Williams twice more. Once, making sure Tyrell picked out James Beck from the photo array as the man who shot Derrick Watkins. And once to make sure Tyrell understood he shouldn't talk to anyone else but him.

Since the crimes connected to the shooting of Derrick Watkins involved two precincts, the 42nd, where Paco Johnson had been found, and the 43rd, where Derrick Watkins had been shot, it meant double the number of police brass.

The bosses from the Four-Two included Lieutenant James Levitt and his sergeant Billy Clovehill, plus Levitt's boss, the precinct commander Captain Dermott Jennie. From the Four-Three came the precinct commander, a deputy inspector named Kenneth Walker who brought with him a veteran homicide investigator, Richard Albright.

The last police official to arrive was the man who would decide what happened next, Borough Commander Edward Pierce.

Palmer, Levitt, the two precinct commanders, and Pierce occupied five seats around the kitchen table in the back of the whorehouse/apartment. Richard Albright and Billy Clovehill stood watching. Palmer had called Ippolito for help with the bureaucratic battle, but he hadn't shown up yet.

Even though Palmer had never presented a case before so many bosses, his sense of entitlement and unbridled ambition enabled him to speak calmly and lay out the facts as if he were convinced everything he said was actually true.

He started with the murder of Paco Johnson in the Four-Two, claiming it had been done by Derrick Watkins in retaliation for Johnson threatening him at Bronx River Houses.

He then explained that Paco Johnson's ex-convict friend, James Beck, tracked down and shot Derrick Watkins to avenge the Johnson's murder, making sure to emphasize Beck's history as a cop killer who got away with murder once, but shouldn't get away with it again.

His presentation ended with an appeal that he and his partner be allowed to pursue both cases, obviously under the supervision of Lieutenant Levitt and Captain Jennie, based on Palmer's involvement in both murders. He'd caught the original murder in the Four-Two, had followed a lead on that crime to the scene of the second murder, where he'd survived a shotgun attack, and had been able to secure an eyewitness to the shooting in the Four-Three.

Edward Pierce, the borough commander, let the two precinct commanders argue for jurisdiction, but Pierce ended up giving both cases to the Four-Two, saying Palmer's eyewitness tipped the scale against Deputy Inspector Walker and the Four-Three. Although it was unsaid, everybody at the table knew Edward Pierce's decision was influenced by his wanting to stay in the good graces of Palmer's father.

And, as if on cue, just before Pierce rendered his opinion, Raymond Ippolito entered the kitchen. Pierce knew Ippolito and considered him a reliable veteran investigator.

He asked Ippolito, "Ray, are you up to speed on all this?"

"Pretty much."

Pierce pointed to Palmer. "If I give this youngster his head on these cases, can I trust you to ride herd on him?"

Ippolito answered the borough commander without hesitation. "Absolutely, sir."

Pierce looked around the table once, made sure he sounded decisive, and pointed his index finger at John Palmer. "Okay, I'm going to let you see this through with your bosses keeping tabs on you. You've got a lot of i's to dot and t's to cross. You need hard evidence for all your allegations."

"Understood."

"You know where to find Beck?"

"Already working on it. He's based in Red Hook."

"What's that, the Seven-Six?"

"Yes, sir."

"Which means another jurisdiction we have to deal with." He turned to Levitt and Jennie. "You two run interference and coordinate." He turned back to Palmer. "You get this witness of yours processed and squared away. I want a signed statement tonight. And you make damn sure you don't lose track of him, or he becomes a problem for us. Then you and Detective Ippolito follow through on every loose end. You have a long way to go before you convince the DA's office they can win these cases, much less issue warrants."

Pierce turned his attention back to Levitt and Jennie. "I'm letting the Four-Two run with this, but if you haven't nailed everything down in a few days, I'm putting together a task force to take over. And let me know immediately if you run into problems. I don't want to be the last one to find out about problems. Understood?"

Everybody at the kitchen table indicated they got it loud and clear. The borough commander walked out of the kitchen trailed by the Four-Three's Kenneth Walker and his homicide detective Richard Albright, who smiled at Ippolito and whispered as he passed him, "Good luck, butt hole."

Once the others were gone, Levitt told Palmer and Ippolito, "Get it done, guys. No screw-ups. Let me know if you need assistance. See you back at the house."

Palmer waited for Levitt, Jennie, and Clovehill to leave and quickly filled in Ippolito about what had gone down and how he'd set up Tyrell Williams, who could be heard snoring through his broken nose in the bedroom down the hall.

"Ray, I'd say we're close to nailing this whole thing down tight."

Ippolito raised his eyebrows in response and said, "Jeezus fuck, John, you got any idea how far out on a limb you are? With me right next to you?"

"Don't worry. It'll work out. Hey, I'm about to lay down on this table I'm so fuckin' tired. Let's get this mutt Tyrell back to the precinct. You take his statement while I grab some sleep. Go easy on him. Help him out, you know what I mean?"

"Yo, John, the brass is gone. It's me you're talking to. Does this scumbag understand the deal? You explained the facts of life to him?"

"He understands."

Ippolito didn't believe Palmer fully realized what he was trying to pull off, but he made a quick decision. In less than two weeks, he would be officially retired. It was time to play the smart move and go with Palmer.

"All right, fuck it, I'm not going to ask you if he really saw anything. Just tell me you got it into his head what he has to do."

"It's pretty simple, Ray. He testifies Beck shot Derrick Watkins, or I'll put the murder on him."

"Yeah, it sounds simple but, I'm telling you, the first thing that can bite us in the ass is some cock-sucking double-dealing *mulignan* of a witness. Fucking shines, you know you can't trust them, John."

"Hey, rely on him doing what's good for him. He was here. He saw it. What the hell else do we need?"

Ippolito stared up at the ceiling.

"What?"

"Those words, *rely on*. All right, the hell with it. First thing we have to do is run down his record. I guarantee you he's dirty."

"If he wasn't, he wouldn't be in a room where a guy got shot three times."

"Obviously, let's just hope he's not a complete piece of shit. After we find out his record, we have to work on getting corroborating witnesses."

"I'll get witnesses if I have to arrest every asshole in that crew and break every one of them."

"All right, all right, let's not get ahead of ourselves. One step at a time."

"Hey, c'mon, Ray, give me some credit. I told you that asshole Beck was important, didn't I?"

Ippolito lowered his voice. "How do you even know it was Beck who was here? I mean seriously."

"First of all, I got an eyewitness who says he was here. Second, *I* can identify Beck leaving the scene."

"While another guy was shooting at you with a twelve gauge? Careful, John."

"I saw what I saw, Ray. And it all lines up. Beck is connected to Paco Johnson. We know that from Lorena Leon. Paco Johnson threatened Derrick Watson. We'll get a half a dozen witnesses at the Bronx River Houses to verify that. Watkins, or one of his guys, popped Johnson. Beck does Watkins in revenge. All the dots connect."

"Yeah, well the first dot we gotta establish is Derrick Watkins puttin' a bullet in Paco Johnson. You do see the challenge here, right John?"

"Tyrell will back me up."

"You can't put all your eggs in that broke-ass basket."

"It's a start."

"Okay, John, just be realistic, okay? We got a long ways to go before we convince an ADA on this mess. And don't forget now you got a shitload of bosses looking over your shoulder."

"Agreed. Absolutely. But if we make good on all this, it's going to be good for us, Ray. Real good. The links are there. Stick with me, big guy. We are going to make out great."

Ippolito smirked, taking note of the word *we*, and not believing for a second that Palmer meant anything other than *me*.

25

The cell phone alarm signal started slowly. It wasn't until it reached its fastest, most insistent beeping that John Palmer finally forced himself out of a deep sleep.

He rolled over and sat up on the cot in the 42nd Precinct bunk room. He cursed, rubbed his face, stood up wearing only his boxer shorts and socks. The dark room felt airless. He shuffled into the precinct locker room, rinsed his face in the sink, washed his armpits, and splashed water over his torso. He used paper towels to dry off.

He padded to his locker, slathered on deodorant, and dug out a fresh shirt, before climbing back into his rumpled suit. It was almost 11:30 P.M. He'd slept for two and a half hours. It would have to do.

As he made his way into the precinct, Palmer wondered how Ippolito had done shepherding the case along. Ippolito lived to complain, but he knew how to get things done. Palmer hoped he had gotten a statement out of Tyrell Williams. If Tyrell had balked, there were ways to coerce him. He could threaten to lock up Tyrell as a material witness. There might be some outstanding warrants on Tyrell he could use for leverage. Or, if things had really blown up, he'd turn the tables and arrest Tyrell for the murder of Derrick Watkins. Tyrell might figure the charge would never stick, but at the very least it would mean a long night at

Central Booking. Then arraignment on a murder charge, or on conspiracy to commit murder, which would certainly convince a judge to send him to Rikers without bail.

Palmer had plenty of ways to keep Tyrell on the team. But when he walked out into the detective's work area, he saw Tyrell sitting next to Ippolito's desk, with Ippolito diligently typing on an old IBM Selectric. A legal pad with Tyrell's written statement sat on Ippolito's desk.

Palmer walked up to them and asked, "How's it going?"

"Good," said Ippolito. "It took me a while to get to this, but we're almost done with Mr. Williams's statement."

"Great. Great. How're you feeling, Tyrell?"

"Like shit, man. All they would give me was goddam Tylenol. I wanna get the fuck out of here."

"Absolutely. As soon as possible. So where are we, Detective Ippolito?"

Ippolito leaned back from the typewriter and pointed to a file folder sitting on the mess of paperwork littering his desktop. "Detective Witherspoon has a rather extensive file for you, Detective Palmer."

"Good, good. And do we have an ADA heading our way?"

"As we speak."

"Okay," said Palmer as he picked up the Witherspoon folder. "We'll get a copy of your statement, Tyrell, meet with the assistant DA, and we'll be all set. We'll have you out of here in no time."

Tyrell made a face to show he knew Palmer was bullshitting him.

Ippolito stood up and said, "Tyrell, I'm gonna talk to Detective Palmer for a second."

Ippolito walked a few desks away, Palmer following him, asking, "Jeezus, Ray. What the fuck's taking so long?"

"Waiting for you so you can see this mutt's record before you jump in with this asshole. John, this skel's sheet goes back to when he was thirteen."

"Shit. Anything horrible?"

"Define horrible. He's been arrested for drugs, assault, possession of an unlicensed firearm, for which he did a mandatory twenty-four months."

"Anything else?"

"Of course. There's also a bunch of charges before he turned eighteen, which are sealed."

"Okay, so just the one prison term, right? C'mon, that's not so bad. It's the same for plenty of guys in his neighborhood. He's never testified before, has he?"

"Not that I can tell."

"Good. We got that going for us."

"John, that's not exactly the point. You gotta see Witherspoon's file on James Beck. His conviction for killing a cop in a bar fight was overturned. Completely exonerated, plus he got a couple million in damages. Technically, he's clean. As far as the system is concerned, he has no criminal convictions. Nuthin'. Not even a parking ticket."

"How'd he beat a charge like that?"

"Fuck, I don't know. Brady shit, or something the judge did. Beck is Kryptonite, or he had a hell of a good shyster, or both."

Palmer shot back. "James Beck isn't clean. He's an ex-convict. He was at the scene of a brutal execution where a guy was shot three times. He shot his fucking face off. He fled the scene with a guy who unloaded a shotgun at me. There's shit in Beck's file about an assault charge last year. We'll find whatever there is to discredit Beck. He's an ex-con, a murderer, and a cop killer who everyone in this department would love to see back in jail where he belongs."

"With a lawyer who'll portray him as a victim of the NYPD. John, all I'm saying is you're going to need more than one bust-out skel of a witness like Tyrell fucking Williams."

Palmer said, "I'm going to make these cases, Ray. I'm going to use anybody and everybody in the New York Police Department to help me do it, and in the Bronx DA's office, and the FBI, and any other place that can help me. You can jump on board or keep an arm's distance or whatever you want, Ray. It's up to you."

Ippolito raised both hands and said, "Yo, relax, man, I'm on your side." Ippolito checked around them to make sure nobody was within earshot. He leaned closer to Palmer and lowered his voice. "Just hear me out, kid. This is Uncle Ray talking. I been doing this a long time. You want to go after this asshole, Beck, trust me, you're going to need more than your buddy, Tyrell."

"I know that."

"So listen to me, John. You ain't got time to run around the Bronx trying to persuade some nitwits from Watkins's crew to be witnesses for you. They live their whole lives getting it pounded into their heads never to rat. Stitches for snitches and all that shit. You'd need a thirty-year bit hanging over one of them to get 'em to turn. It just ain't going to happen. Not in two or three days. No way."

"Tyrell turned."

"For now. He fell into your lap, and he knows you'll try to hang a murder on him if he doesn't play along."

"All right, so what do you have in mind, Ray?"

Ippolito looked around again to make sure nobody was within earshot. He bent closer to Palmer and said, "Look, I was going to float this to you back when we were looking for Watkins at Bronx River Houses, but I figured well, whatever."

"Float what?"

"I think we gotta go to the head honcho and make a deal here."

"The head honcho?"

"The guy who runs all these mutts."

"Eric Jackson?"

"Yeah, Eric Juju Jackson."

"What kind of a deal?"

"We give him something, he gives us witnesses."

"Why should he help us?" Palmer asked.

"For starters, murder investigations aren't good for him. He'll want to shut this thing down as fast as we do. The only way to make that happen quickly is to prove Derrick shot Paco Johnson. Jackson should be happy to get us a couple of witnesses who'll claim Derrick Watkins did it. Stitchin' up a dead guy for shooting Johnson is zero skin off Jackson's ass."

Palmer nodded. "Makes sense. What about helping us with Beck?"

"Why shouldn't he? Beck shot his boy Derrick. We ask him nice, he'll give us a couple of assholes to back up Tyrell's testimony."

Palmer said, "Just ask him nice?"

"Well . . . plus offer him the same thing they all want, John."

"What?"

"Information. Information that will keep him and his crazy enforcer, Whitey Bondurant, out of jail. Fuck, even disinformation. I don't give a shit. We both know the Fibbies have got multiple cases they're developing. Hell, even our dumb asses in Gangs are always looking at Jackson and Bondurant. They've been trying to nail those two pricks for years."

Palmer looked at Ippolito. "Christ, Ray, giving a guy like Eric Jackson inside information? If that ever got out . . ."

Ippolito raised his hands and said, "John, you don't have to do anything you don't want to. I'm just telling you how I see it. It's up to you. My clock gets permanently punched in two weeks one way or the other. Makes no difference to me. I'm tryin' to help you if you want to go for it. No risk, no reward."

Palmer nodded. And then asked, "You ever make a deal with Eric Jackson?"

"No comment."

Palmer said, "I assume you know how to get to him."

"You assume correctly. Listen, John, don't make any decision now. Take what you've got – your theory of the murders, Tyrell's statement, what you saw at the scene, whatever. Present everything to the ADA. Hear what he says. Then decide."

John Palmer nodded slowly, but both he and Ippolito knew he had already decided.

26

Walter Ferguson walked into Beck's second-floor loft space looking like he had aged about five years. He sat alone on the unoccupied third couch, so he could face all four men.

Manny asked him, "You hungry, Walter? Let me heat up a plate for you."

"No thank you, Emmanuel. I'm fine."

"Something to drink?"

"No, thank you."

Beck said, "Long day?"

"Yes. Quite a lot to deal with in one day." Walter checked his watch. 10:14 P.M. "Didn't realize it was so late. Sorry I kept you all waiting."

"Don't worry about it. What can you tell us?"

"Jacobi Hospital isn't the easiest place to deal with. I waited at the medical examiner's office there until after eight, and they still didn't have the report finished. Unfortunately, I don't have a relationship with the doctor in charge, a fellow named Meyers, so he wouldn't take the time to talk to me. I had to stay there to read the preliminary notes."

"They find anything you didn't expect?"

"Not really. They followed procedures. The notes confirmed he was in a fight. Which the detectives already told me."

Beck didn't comment.

"They listed all the scrapes on his hands and trauma to his head and torso, including a diagram showing the location of each injury." Walter pointed to places on his body as he spoke. "A cracked rib. A bruised spleen. A big contusion on his hip. A note said the hip bruise probably impaired his ability to walk. Hands. Face. Broken jaw." Walter didn't have the heart to go into more detail. "Be that as it may, the death certificate stipulated the cause of death was a single gunshot to the back of the head.

"There were notes about which parts of the brain the bullet destroyed, but I didn't read them. They recovered the bullet. A twenty-two. Fairly intact."

"Time of death?" asked Beck.

Walter pulled out a notebook from his breast pocket. Flipped through the top pages. "Estimated time between eleven P.M. and one A.M."

Beck and the others had been listening stoically to what had happened to Paco Johnson. None of them commented, but Beck's expression clouded with anger. His friend, a man who had saved his life, a man who had been trying to save his daughter's life, had lain dead in a gutter for hours before anybody even came to look at the body.

Beck cleared his throat, but said nothing.

Now that Walter had delivered the hardest part of his news, he hurried through the rest.

"So, I contacted a funeral director nearby in Carroll Gardens. I know a man who's worked there many years. He promised to make sure the funeral home takes care of everything correctly." Walter tore a page out of his notebook and placed it on the coffee table. "Here are his name and contact numbers. He'll have to wait for the official death certificate. It should be issued tomorrow. Friday latest. It's all web-based now. They e-mail copies. The second he gets the death certificate and the body is cleared, he'll go get Packy and bring him down from Jacobi. Then we can make whatever arrangements we want."

"Okay," said Beck. "Thank you, Walter."

"Of course."

"You have any report from the police who are investigating this?"

"No. It's still early, James, but I assure you I will follow up with them."

"Good. Good. That will be very helpful, Walter. You've done everything you could for Packy. And for us." Beck paused, "But I'm going to ask you to do more."

Walter turned to Beck, somewhat surprised, but he recovered and said, "Whatever you need, James. Whatever I can do."

"First, a simple thing. Can you describe the cops who came to see you this morning?"

For a moment, Walter seemed confused at Beck's request.

"I know you told us before, but can you tell us again, Walter?"

"Of course. There were two of them. A younger man who seemed to be in charge. And an older detective who looked like someone who's been at the job too long. About thirty pounds overweight, salt-and-pepper hair, combed straight back. Italian. Name is Raymond Ippolito."

Beck interrupted him. "And the other one?"

"I'd say early thirties. Tallish. Maybe six two. Thin. Brown hair. Styled to look disheveled, which I suspect takes some time to achieve. He impressed me as someone who thinks he's smarter than everyone around him. Or better. I don't know which. Maybe both."

"What's his name?"

Walter thought for a moment. "Palmer. John Palmer. They both work out of the Forty-second Precinct. I have their contact information if you want it."

"Hang on to it," said Beck. "Last question, Walter. Would you consider taking a trip with me up to Eastern Correctional?"

"When?"

"Now. Tonight. We'll get there, check in to a motel, and then visit the facility tomorrow morning. I'll have you back in Brooklyn by end of day tomorrow."

"I don't have any other clothes with me."

"We'll stop by your place. I'm already packed."

"What do you want to do at Eastern?"

"I'll tell you what I have in mind on the way."

Walter looked at the men sitting around him. None of them offered any comment. Walter looked back at Beck. This was an unusual request. He wanted to ask Beck more, but he simply said, "All right, James."

27

Captain Jennie had left hours ago, but he told Levitt they could use his office for their meeting with the Bronx assistant district attorney.

Levitt sat behind Jennie's desk. Palmer and Frederick Wilson, the ADA, sat facing each other from opposite corners of the desk. Ippolito stood by the door. The ADA's assistant, a heavyset, conservatively dressed Asian woman, sat alone on Jennie's battered couch, contributing nothing to the meeting except intermittent frowns and adjustments of her wire-rim glasses while Palmer and Frederick Wilson sparred.

Palmer ran down the history of the two murders, the status of the investigation, backgrounds on his suspects, his theory of the murders, ending with emphasizing the advantage of having an eyewitness to the murder of Derrick Watkins.

Levitt made optimistic comments, trying to back up his detective.

Ippolito said nothing.

Wilson, a tall, impeccably groomed black man wearing stylish tortoise-shell-framed glasses had an air of confidence about him. His crisp white shirt and off-the-rack brown suit fitted him well. His shoes were polished to a shine, somewhat matched by his gleaming bald head.

When Palmer finished, Wilson took no time to focus on the weakest part of his case.

"Look, Detective, I know you have your eyewitness to the second murder." Wilson checked the notes on his legal pad. "Mr. Tyrell Williams. And hopefully, your witness will hold up against scrutiny."

Palmer tried to speak, but Wilson raised a hand.

"Please, don't try to sell me on him. We both know he's as bad as the criminal who was murdered. And we both know what can happen to a witness between now and two years from now, when we go to trial.

"But, putting all that aside, you need more than a witness. You need motive. You assert that this fellow Beck shot Derrick Watkins in revenge for Watkins killing his friend Paco Johnson. That in itself is problematic, proving that level of friendship. But the bigger problem is you don't have any evidence proving Derrick Watkins shot Paco Johnson. Without it, you have no motive for Beck."

Palmer opened his mouth to respond, and again Wilson put up a hand.

"Please, let me warn you. Do not tell me Tyrell Williams will verify Watkins shot Johnson. I'm not going to prosecute two murders on the testimony of one witness who could have shot Paco Johnson himself. Or Watkins, for that matter."

Palmer worked his tongue around in his dry mouth, wishing he had a decent cup of coffee to help him focus. His fatigue had made him irritable. He realized he'd have to keep calm. Ippolito had been right. They were going to need a lot more.

"Mr. Wilson, it's not surprising at this stage that we haven't nailed everything down yet. But the connections are there. Paco Johnson goes to confront Derrick Watkins. There's an argument. A fight ensues. Watkins and his crew beat up Johnson. We can prove that."

Wilson interrupted. "You're simply repeating what you've already told me."

Palmer raised his voice to keep Wilson at bay. "We're going to get you proof that Derrick Watkins, or one of his men under his orders, shot Paco Johnson. But even without that, right now we have enough to arrest James Beck. He had motive to revenge the death of Johnson. He was Johnson's friend. We know he arranged housing for Johnson after his release. We'll nail down how much time Beck was incarcerated with Johnson, but clearly they had a close relationship. Beck and his men tracked down Derrick Watkins. We'll find out how. My eyewitness will testify Beck shot Watkins." Palmer pointed to his chest. "*I* can put Beck and his men at the scene seconds after the shooting. I'm also in the process of identifying the man who shot at me, who I believe is a known associate of Beck's."

Finally, Wilson interrupted.

"Again, you're simply repeating what you've told me. I don't care about the man who shot at you. I don't care that you saw Beck at the scene. If you want to charge Beck with shooting Watkins, I need motive. You have to get me proof that Derrick Watkins, or one of his men on his orders, shot Paco Johnson. *And* that Beck knew Watkins shot Johnson."

Palmer tried to stay calm, but couldn't stop himself from raising his voice. "We already have leads. We'll get corroboration. Trust me, we'll follow this trail, we'll connect the dots, we'll get all the witnesses and confirmation you need, and this will end in a success. For you, your office, for all of us. I'm sure the Bronx DA's office will be happy to get convictions on a double homicide with all the people involved."

Wilson gave Palmer an insincere smile and said, "Thank you for your career guidance, Detective Palmer, but frankly, I'm not interested in it. Just provide what I've asked for. Please."

Ippolito interrupted before Palmer responded to Wilson.

"Okay, so we know what we gotta do. Right? We'll pull this all together as fast as we can, and your office can start drawing up a warrant for Beck on suspicion of shooting Derrick Watkins. And once we identify his associate, who fired a shotgun at Detective Palmer, we'll ask for a warrant for him, too. Assault on a police officer with a deadly weapon. Agreed?"

Wilson said, "I'm not going to say it again. Get me the evidence I've asked for; you'll get your warrants."

Palmer jumped on Wilson's comment. "We have enough to arrest Beck right now as a suspect in a brutal murder. We should get warrants now. Beck could be fleeing our jurisdiction as we speak. I've got an eyewitness. What more do I need for a warrant? The sooner we get him locked up, the better."

Wilson shot back. "No. That's how mistakes are made. Beck is going to have first-rate representation. Look at his history. Very few people get a conviction overturned like he did. When you arrest him, he's going to argue for bail and most likely get it, and most likely have the financial resources to post bail when it's granted. And then what? Then we have a major problem. If this case does become as strong as we hope it is, Beck gets to decide whether to stay, or run, or eliminate witnesses. Or, sue us for false arrest. I want to arrest Beck as much as you, but when we do, I want it so no judge would even consider granting him bail."

Again, Ippolito spoke before Palmer. "Fair enough. It's your call. We'll get you the evidence you need."

Lieutenant Levitt stood up and said, "Okay, gentlemen, we all know what we have to do. Let's go do it. Let's keep this case on track."

Palmer forced himself to stop arguing. Wilson and his assistant left the office. Nobody offered a handshake.

Levitt told Palmer and Ippolito, "You two have a lot of work to do."

Ippolito led the way back to the detective bullpen, followed by the fuming John Palmer. Tyrell Williams was still at Ippolito's desk, but now with his arms on the desk pillowing his head, sleeping.

"Jeezus," said Ippolito. "He's probably drooling all over my stuff."

"Take it easy," said Palmer. "And please don't tell me how much he's going to fuck me again."

"Okay."

"And don't tell me you were right about the ADA."

"I don't have to. Meanwhile, don't overlook his fat Chink assistant sitting there. Every time you said something she looked like she wanted to take a shit. Guarantee you that see-you-next-Tuesday is going to yammer at

Wilson all the way back to their office about all the stuff we don't have: murder weapons, timelines, motive, corroborating witnesses, blah, blah, blah."

"Well fuck her, too. I sent all those guns from the murder scene for ballistics. Maybe one of 'em will match the bullet they took out of Johnson's head, and we'll have a murder weapon for the Johnson hit."

"Good. I hope so."

"Shit. Sorry, Ray. I'm just pissed at that asshole ADA."

"That's his job. He's going to break our balls for as much as he can get before he steps into a courtroom." Ippolito lowered his voice. "So where are you on the other thing?"

Palmer tipped his head and they walked slowly toward a far corner of the detectives' bullpen.

"Okay, you were right. I'm with you on the witness thing, but tell me – what can we give Jackson to make him help us without jamming ourselves up?"

"It shouldn't take much. Like I said, Eric Jackson will want to make this go away as much as we do. Listen, you've been nurturing your contact at the FBI for months. Now's the time to get something out of it. Go to your guy. Find out what they have on Jackson and his boy Bondurant, we'll give it to him, and keep this shit show moving."

"Man, that's a big one, Ray."

"What the fuck, they'll never know where Juju got the info from."

"The FBI isn't stupid."

"But they're busy. And they're running tons of investigations." Ippolito dropped his voice even lower and said,

"And listen, a little way down the line, we feed your FBI guy something that'll help him. Maybe even help them take down Jackson and Bondurant. Tie up all the loose ends, you know what I mean?"

Palmer stared at his partner. Reality began to set in. The ruthlessness of it. The willingness to double-cross everybody if necessary. But it would have to start with betraying Gregory McAndrews.

Ippolito watched Palmer struggling with the risk involved. He had no doubt Palmer would do it. As soon as he convinced himself he could do it without getting caught.

"All right, Ray. Set it up."

"It's the only way, John."

"I know. I know." Palmer rubbed his face, rousing himself for the next task. "All right, let me get Tyrell home. I want to see where he lives. It'll help me keep track of him."

"Sure. And John, go home after you drop off that shit bag, crank one out, and get some sleep. You look like hell."

"Thanks for the advice."

Ippolito watched Palmer head over to get Tyrell. He smiled to himself. *Now we'll see what the boy wonder is made of.*

28

Walter Ferguson had lived in the hundred-year-old building on Livingston Street at the southern edge of Brooklyn Heights for twenty-seven years. Some would have avoided such an old building, but it very much suited Walter and his wife, Phyllis. They had an affordable one-bedroom on the fourth floor with a classic layout that had everything they needed, including a surprisingly spacious bedroom overlooking Packer Collegiate Institute across the street.

The building went co-op in 1989, and with their two incomes they managed to scrape together the down payment and qualify for a mortgage. Phyllis taught in the New York public school system. Walter worked as a paralegal in a law office on Joralemon Street after graduating from Hunter College. During his time at the firm, he'd considered enrolling in law school, but Walter worked such long hours it didn't seem feasible. Nor was he at all sure the never-ending relativism of a legal practice aligned with his core values.

Instead, Walter took several civil service exams, including one for the NYPD. Phyllis worried about a reserved, young black man with a studious bent joining the police department. She had visions of Walter being hurt, or shot, or marginalized. Walter understood Phyllis's concerns. When he also passed the exam for a position as a parole officer in the Department of Correction, and Phyllis urged him to take the safer job, he agreed.

Over the years, Walter worked hard and made his way up the ladder. They both worked in various locations around the city. Phyllis never landed a teaching position in their neighborhood, but she didn't mind traveling by subway and bus to wherever she had to go. She used the time to read, or listen to music, two of her favorite pastimes.

After a number of years, Walter ended up in the parole office within walking distance of their peaceful, comfortable apartment.

They lived quiet, almost contemplative lives. Phyllis was the one who pushed to see an interesting exhibition at the Met, found discount tickets for Broadway shows, or persuaded Walter to see an art film at BAM. Walter agreed to accompany her, mostly to please her. She would playfully chide him about being such a homebody. It never rankled or upset him. Any attention from Phyllis made him happy.

For his part, Walter was more likely to ask Phyllis if she'd like to go for a walk. Walking seemed to help the tall man unwind. Phyllis wasn't as athletic as Walter, and sometimes she had a little trouble keeping up with his long strides, but she never minded the effort. Being with Walter was the most important thing. And the long walks gave them time to talk about whatever was on their minds, as well as comfortably lapse into silence when the mood hit them. Most of the time Phyllis talked while Walter walked and listened.

They were an attractive couple. Walter, tall, handsome in a down-to-earth way, his demeanor a bit solemn. Phyllis, a perfect match for him in terms of height and bearing, more pretty than beautiful, with a quick, winsome smile that won over nearly everyone she met.

Walter, of course, had his challenges. There were many, many parolees who came through his office he knew were never going to escape the horrors of the debilitating penal system. For those, he tried to make the inevitable more bearable. For the few who still hadn't committed crimes that would condemn them to decades of incarceration, Walter tried to piece together whatever stepping stones back to society he could. A GED course. An internship at a corporation willing to offer one. A program that helped people in the penal system with résumés and clothing suitable for interviews.

He relentlessly pursued companies that might qualify for a grant or a subsidy to employ ex-convicts: super-market chains, restaurants, warehouses. It was slow, tedious, often heartbreaking work. Many times, just when he had a candidate qualified and next in line for a job, something would destroy all his efforts. Little things and big things. An arrest for doing something impulsive or stupid like shoplifting, or jumping a turn-stile. A lapse back into drug or alcohol addiction. Unexpected pregnancies. Traveling out of state. Even being in the company of the wrong person could send a parolee back to prison, back to square one where Walter might have to wait years to start over.

Phyllis's job challenged her, too, but brought her almost daily rewards. She loved teaching. And she loved the kids. For Phyllis, reading was the key to awakening minds. She knew if she could teach a child to read, the entire world, whole and wonderful and complete, would open up to them.

In such things, as in all other matters, Walter and Phyllis shared with each other a complete, quiet, confident love that sustained them. Until the day when Walter lost Phyllis much too early to breast cancer at the age of fifty-six. Just when they were envisioning the next phase of their lives, retiring and growing old together.

The loss shocked Walter to his core. Phyllis had always been such a vibrant, vital woman, with picture-book perfect posture. And strong. She'd been blessed with a wonderful body that Walter loved to hold and touch. And then everything had betrayed them. And she was gone, and Walter was alone, sliding into a world bereft of those special things Phyllis brought. Occasionally, he would force himself to go to a museum or a movie. But gradually, his life became mostly his work. The only other mainstay was his church, but too often the quiet solitude and peaceful atmosphere of St. Charles Borremeo's felt very lonely to Walter.

Walter made sure not to think about Phyllis too much. But as he packed a small carry-on bag opened on the bed where the two of them had slept together for so many years, he couldn't help but remember her.

He thought about Phyllis until he felt too sad, and then turned his attention to thinking about what he was doing with James Beck.

Ah, Mr. Beck, thought Walter. He had come into his life a couple of years after Phyllis's death, bringing a rough, aggressive vitality that both worried Walter and energized him. James Beck shared Walter's dedication to helping men trapped in a ruthless, dehumanizing penal system. Not many. Just a few whom Beck and his inner circle had taken on as their own. But once committed, Beck would stop at nothing to make sure that man never saw the inside of a prison again.

The *stopping at nothing* both worried Walter and invigorated him. He had to admit, Beck had resurrected him. Walter knew Beck had saved him from falling into a debilitating depression after Phyllis. Without Beck, Walter could never have imagined himself packing a bag late at night to take a spur-of-the-moment trip offering unpredictable consequences.

Walter smiled. Shook his head. Even now, before he'd set out, Beck had made him feel a bit young and reckless.

But not so reckless as to overpack. Just enough for one day

Walter smiled ruefully. He could have packed for a week, or a month, or a year. There was no cat. No houseplants. Nobody on Livingston Street waiting for him.

Walter put that last thought out of his mind and concentrated on the task at hand. Pack for one night. Think about how he could help Beck find out what had happened to Paco Johnson, and why. And then come home to his empty apartment.

29

Tyrell Williams's apartment building on Daly Street was about a five-minute walk from Bronx River Houses. When John Palmer dropped him off, he made a point of saying to Tyrell, "So this is where you live?"

"This is it."

Tyrell pulled himself out of the patrol car. Palmer watched him enter a five-story brick building and kept watching until the lobby door shut behind him.

During the drive from the precinct, Palmer had alternated between threatening Tyrell with all the bad things that would ensue if he didn't come through as a witness versus the good things that would happen if he did.

Tyrell entered the building and walked up one flight of stairs before he turned around, went back to the lobby, and left the building. He walked to the Bronx River Houses and went straight to Derrick's apartment, arriving at 1:15 A.M. Tyrell was one of the few who knew about the spare key Derrick had taped under the handrail out in the stairwell between the sixth and seventh floors.

He let himself into the apartment, turning on lights as he made his way through the rooms. News of Derrick's death would have already swept through the neighborhood so he wasn't surprised to see Leon Miller had disappeared. It wouldn't be long before Biggie or someone else came to clean out the apartment of anything incriminating or valuable. Worst of all, it wouldn't be long before word spread that the cops had arrested and released him. Juju Jackson would assume that meant he was working for the police, so Biggie, or God forbid Whitey Bondurant, would be coming for him soon. Time to quickly scavenge what he could, and then go convince Biggie he had no intention of ratting anybody out to the cops, and see if Biggie and Juju would agree to let him testify against the white guy. Hopefully, they'd see it was the right move. Keep the cops running in the wrong direction while he and Biggie hunted down that bitch Amelia and made her pay for what she did.

Tyrell walked back to Derrick's bedroom. He lifted the queen-size mattress off the box spring and tried to prop it against a wall, but the cheap mattress folded onto itself and sagged onto the floor. Wrestling with it sent a jolt of pain through Tyrell's broken nose and cracked cheekbone. He lost his balance and became dizzy for a few seconds. Tyrell cursed the son of a bitch who had sucker punched him. He vowed he would do everything he could to see that bastard dead or in jail.

He kicked the box spring away from the mattress and tore off the flimsy cloth covering the wood frame. In between the springs were three bundles of cash, two guns, two boxes of ammunition, and two ledger books.

Tyrell stuffed everything into a pillowcase barely big enough to hold it all.

He carried his plunder with him as he rifled through drawers, looked into closets, checked the freezer in the kitchen, the tension building in him as he progressed from room to room. Even though it was after two in the morning, he feared Biggie Watkins might come busting in on him at any moment.

He decided he needed something better than a pillow-case. Anyone seeing him in the dark of night with a stuffed pillowcase, especially cops, would know he'd robbed somebody.

He found a red nylon laundry bag in one of the closets. He shoved the full pillowcase into the bottom of the laundry bag, then added a sheet from Derrick's bed for cover.

All right, he told himself, time to get the fuck out of here.

30

James Beck and Walter Ferguson pulled in to the small courtyard of the old motel on the outskirts of Napanoch, New York, at one-twenty on Thursday morning. Walter had recommended the place, having stayed there on previous visits to Eastern Correctional Facility.

It was a no-nonsense, utilitarian motel from a time gone by, set back off the road with a half-circle gravel driveway leading to a reception office. A line of ten rooms ran to the right of the office.

They parked the Mercury and approached the office door. An envelope had been taped to the locked front door labeled: W. Ferguson. Beck pulled the envelope off the door. Inside were two keys to two rooms. The keys were attached to old-fashioned plastic fobs with the room number.

Beck felt like he had stepped back in time. That, combined with their discussion about Eastern Correctional on the drive up, brought back memories and feelings Beck would have rather let lie dormant.

He and Walter exchanged quick good nights and agreed to meet at seven-thirty for an early breakfast before they set out for the prison.

Beck knew before he entered his room that it would be clean, functional, without frills. It was. Not even a TV. A little more worn down than he might have preferred, but no matter.

He showered quickly and slid in between the stiff sheets. There was a blanket covering the bed, too thin to keep him warm against the falling temperature. Much like in prison. Worn sheets and blankets, small foam pillows, and cells that were always too hot or too cold.

Beck closed his eyes, exhaled slowly, trying to dispel the sense of dread and anger and loneliness sweeping over him. When he'd left Red Hook, he had expected these emotions to intensify. He'd felt them to one degree or another nearly every time he'd lain down to sleep in the years since he'd been released from prison. But now he could feel the behemoth that was Eastern Correctional Facility looming a few miles away; its presence imposing on him, intensifying the familiar feelings.

He muttered a curse and rolled over on his side. He focused on his breathing, letting the simple in and out of his breaths occupy his mind. He tried to let his thoughts drift, even though they kept returning to the pain he'd lived through, and a man who had helped him deal with that pain and saved him from infinitely more – Packy Johnson.

He kept at it, breathing in and out, trying not to think about his deceased friend. His thoughts drifted to Walter and Manny and the rest of his crew. Beck focused on the living and his reason for being in an old motel on the edge of a scrub forest in Napanoch, New York, until he fell into a cold, fitful sleep.

Amelia Johnson let go of the basement window sill and released herself into a dark void, bracing for the unknown. Unable to gauge the distance, she couldn't prepare for the impact and fell onto her knees when she landed. Fortunately, there wasn't anything sharp enough to cut her, or uneven enough to twist or break an ankle.

The only light illuminating the basement came from the half window above, and that light was quickly fading. The first thing she did was pull the car cover in after her. Then she looked around for something she could stand on so she could pull the iron bars back into place.

She saw dirty pieces of corrugated cardboard, broken slats of wooden lath, a few shelves, empty paint cans, old bundles of magazines, and piles of junk. But then, along the wall, she saw an old, stained porcelain toilet bowl. She dragged it over to the window, managed to balance herself on the rim, reached up and pulled back the iron bars almost all the way over the opening. For now, she left the plywood cover off so as to catch the last of the dying daylight.

She slowly picked her way around the area until she found a set of stairs leading up to the ground floor. She moved cautiously up the stairwell, feeling pieces of broken glass under her flimsy ballet flats until she reached a wooden door reinforced with three-quarter-inch plywood. She turned the door knob, pushed and pulled.

There was no give at all. The door had been nailed to the frame. She felt relieved knowing nobody would be able to come down, but disappointed that there was no way out except back through the ground-level half window.

She made her way back down to the bottom stair and sat on it, closing her eyes, trying to convince herself she was safe. From somewhere behind her, she heard what sounded like dripping water. She followed the sound until she found an empty laundry room. There were no appliances, but the faucet on the wall where the washing machine had been attached dripped steadily. She opened the faucet until she had a small stream of water running.

She used her cell phone to illuminate the room and found a nearly empty box of powdered laundry detergent. She stripped off all her clothes, except for her ballet flats, scraped the hardened soap from the bottom of the box, and squatted under the water faucet.

She used her hands to soap herself with the gritty detergent and rinse with the cold water. Soon, she was shivering almost uncontrollably, but she persisted, soaping, scrubbing, cleaning off the sweat and dirt and stink from every part of her. She washed her face, over and over, working the gritty soap into her skin, rubbing and rinsing away every last vestige of makeup.

At last, she felt clean, scoured down to the point where she finally felt separated from where she had been and the things she had done.

She turned off the water and carefully stepped out of the puddle soaking through her cheap shoes. There was almost no light in the laundry room now, but she was able to pull out the roll of paper towels from her hoodie. There wasn't much left on the roll, so she started with one piece, using it to get as much water as she could off her smooth, dark skin, squeezing out the piece of paper towel, rubbing herself with it until it became useless. Then another piece, and another until she felt like she had buffed her skin raw.

Much of her back was still wet when she put her clothes back on, but once dressed, her shivering subsided into a weird quivering centered in the pit of her stomach.

She found the remains of a cardboard box and used it to scrape a clean space until she had a big enough area to set down another piece of corrugated card. She lay down on top of the cardboard and wrapped herself in the car cover. She found an old paperback book, which she used as a pillow.

She stretched out in stages, trying to ignore how hard the floor felt underneath her. She thought about finding more boxes to flatten and lie on, but she was too tired. Too enervated. She remained flat on her back, not on her side, because she knew her hip and shoulder would ache against the concrete floor.

Her quivering subsided. She closed her eyes and wondered how she could escape from the Bronx, and Biggie and Juju and Whitey, and wondered if she would die trying.

32

Manny Guzman had been awake since his usual time, five A.M. He came out from his small kitchen on the ground floor of Beck's building in Red Hook to sit at the old oak bar with Demarco Jones, who had come down just after seven.

They were eating breakfast burritos Manny had made and drinking strong black coffee. Laid out on the bar were the IDs they had taken from Derrick Watkins's crew.

Both men ate without rushing. Their day was going to be filled with tracking Biggie Watkins and trying to find Amelia.

Demarco pointed his fork at the IDs on the bar top.

"I know we have to find the brother, but we might have to start with one of the others so I scanned those and sent copies to Alex last night."

"Mr. Computer."

"Yeah. He's probably run them through every database in the world by now."

"Does he ever sleep?"

"Sleep is a problem for Alex." Demarco said as he took another bite of his burrito. "He once told me for a year he only slept two times a week. On Wednesdays and Sundays."

"Why?"

"I don't know. To see if he could."

Manny shook his head. "That's a good way to die faster." Manny wiped his mouth and mustache with a napkin and said, "How do you want to do this?"

"Start with the older brother. See how it goes. Decide from there."

Manny nodded and said, "Between us, we have to know somebody in the Bronx who can put us onto that *chulo*."

"Agreed. And maybe Alex came up with something. I'll give him a ping before we hit the road."

"A ping?"

"A text."

"That's not an e-mail?"

"No. Over the phone. Not the Internet."

Manny stared at Demarco. Demarco said, "Never mind. How's the coffee? I made it strong."

"You're getting there, amigo."

The coffee in the diner where Beck had gone for breakfast was only passable. From the motel, he and Walter found a classic highway diner set off the main road between Ellenville and Napanoch surrounded on three sides by a large parking lot.

Beck ordered ham and eggs, no potatoes, rye toast, coffee. He was pleased to see the diner served a proper slab of ham steak.

Walter ordered cottage cheese and a bowl of mixed fruit. As they ate, Walter outlined his plan.

"So, James, I'm going to try to find out if any of the staff knows something about what was going on with Packy before his release."

"How're you going to do that?"

"I'll check in with the warden first. Tell him what happened. Make sure he understands I have to investigate Packy's death. That'll clear the way for me to talk to the staff."

"Okay."

"I'll start with Packy's facility parole officer. Then work my way down from the supervising guards to the COs on the floor. I have to tell you, James, I expect them to close ranks on me."

"See what happens and then press them. Ask as many of the staff as you can about anything that would explain why Packy got murdered. Remember, you're investigating a murder. That ought to give you some leverage."

"And you're going to work the prisoner side?"

"Yes. I gave Alex Liebowitz a list of guys I knew in Eastern. He's running a check to see if any of them are still there. I'll start with them."

"How?"

"I'll put in calls. Letters, if that doesn't work. I'll get on their visitor lists if I have to get in to see someone."

"Getting on a visitor's list won't be easy, you being a former inmate there."

"I'll work around it."

Walter didn't ask how.

Beck said, "My end is going to take time. I'm figuring you can get to most of the staff before the day is out."

"Everybody but the night shift."

Beck finished his first cup of coffee and said, "Do what you can, Walter, and we'll see what happens. Hey, not only are you entitled, you're obligated to investigate Packy's murder."

"I'll do my best."

"I'm sure you will. Somebody in that prison knows something. Packy didn't get shot down in the street for no reason."

Walter nodded, but said nothing. They finished their food and Beck motioned to the waitress for a check.

"What are you going to do while I'm in there?" asked Walter.

"Me? I'm gonna shop for another vehicle to use while I'm up here."

"Really?"

Beck smiled. "I can't be driving around redneck country in a customized Mercury Marauder. Plus, I gotta send you home in it. I'll get some piece of crap truck like all the local yokels around here drive."

"How long are you planning on being up here, James?"

"As long as it takes."

Walter stared at Beck, unhappy with Beck's vague answer.

"James, you do understand my position here."

"Of course I do, Walter. And I'm sure you understand mine."

"That's what worries me."

"You know who I am, Walter."

A pensive look came over Ferguson's face. He said, "James, we both know you only reveal part of yourself. Not because you're duplicitous. Because you feel like you have to protect the people around you. People like me."

Beck tipped his head toward Walter, neither agreeing or disagreeing.

"James, anyone anywhere near the penal system finds themselves immersed in a tidal wave of misery. The chances of standing against it, ameliorating even a small part of it, are beyond daunting. Paco Johnson did that for you. And then, against all the odds, you got a chance to help him. And that rare chance was snatched away from you, suddenly, tragically, irrevocably."

Beck leaned across the table and looked Walter directly in the eyes. "And your point, Walter?"

"I'm worried."

"About what?"

"About how that has affected you. About what you might do."

Beck sat back, taking a moment to think before he spoke. "I won't do anything that hurts you, Walter. You should know that."

"I never thought you would. What about others?"

"What about them?"

Walter stopped talking and looked down, feeling his way with it. Beck remained silent. Finally, Walter looked up and said, "Okay. I have an obligation to see this through for Packy. He was my responsibility. So I'll go into Eastern and find out what I can. But James, can you promise me one thing?"

"What?"

"If I learn something that helps you find out what led to his death, or who killed him, can you promise me you will bring that information to me? Let me at least give the system a chance to investigate and arrest whoever did it. A chance to do this legally?"

Beck stared intently at Walter Ferguson.

"Legally."

"Yes."

"The system that incarcerated me illegally for eight years? That tried to break me, that took everything away from me? The system that institutionalized Packy Johnson from the age of eleven, then spat him out on his own to try to build a life from nothing? From worse than nothing? The system that does those things every day to hundreds of thousands of people whose main crime is being black or brown or poor? The legal system that doesn't give one goddam about Packy Johnson? You want me to give that system a chance to investigate and prosecute whoever killed Packy? Legally?"

"I'm part of that system, James. And I give a damn."

Beck's voice softened. "I know, Walter. I know. But what about the others in that system? The ones who are corrupt, or inept, or too overworked and battered themselves to give a shit?"

"They can't stop me from trying."

Beck saw the pain his question had caused his friend who had spent decades trying to make the system work, experiencing every disappointment and frustration that meant.

Beck nodded. "Fair enough, Walter. If there were more people like you, there wouldn't be a need for someone like me." Beck leaned forward. "How about this? We're partners. So I promise you, I will share everything I find out, whether it's from a lead you come up with, or from something I find out myself, or from any other source. You can use the information to do whatever you think is right."

Walter paused, making sure he had heard Beck correctly, then said, "I can't ask for more."

"Good. And will you promise me the same thing, Walter? Will you promise me you'll follow through with what the cops are doing about Packy, good or bad, and share the information with me?"

"What will you do with the information?"

"Same as I'm asking you to do. Whatever I think is right."

Walter looked away, staring out of the diner's large window into the parking lot and beyond. Without seeing it coming, Beck had maneuvered him into a checkmate. There was no comeback. He supposed he had known it would end up this way. Was he with Beck, or against him?

He turned to Beck and nodded his assent.

"Agreed."

33

They finished their breakfast in silence and Beck drove Walter to the entrance of Eastern Correctional. He had been locked up there for nearly two years, but had never clearly seen the outside until the day he'd left. Seeing the prison now, it seemed more foreboding than ever. From the road, the immense structure looked like a massive Germanic medieval fortress that had been dropped in the middle of the countryside.

The four-story-high center of the prison had been built out of huge brown blocks of stone, topped by a massive pyramid-shaped roof. All four corners ended in battlement towers and cone-capped turrets. Long cell blocks made of the same massive blocks of stone flanked the center section. The structure looked so imposing it seemed able to hold its own against the jagged Shawangunk Ridge in the background.

Beck had spent a relatively good time in the prison. Eastern had a reputation for being perhaps the easiest maximum-security prison in the system. But prison was prison, and Beck didn't want to be anywhere near the place for a moment longer than he had to.

He dropped Walter off and told him to call when he was ready to be picked up.

Beck sped out of the parking lot and took Route 209 toward Ellenville. As soon as he entered town, he turned in to a hospital parking lot, pulled out his smartphone to call Demarco, but changed his mind. He wanted to hear Demarco's plan to find Jerome Watkins. He wanted to urge him to find Packy's daughter, knowing Watkins would be looking for her to avenge his brother's death. He wanted to warn Demarco to watch out for that cop, John Palmer, who would also be looking for Watkins and the other members of his crew.

But Demarco didn't need a call from him. Demarco knew what was at stake, and he had Manny Guzman, who could give him any counsel he needed.

Beck realized he wanted to make contact with somebody who understood his reaction to Eastern Correctional. And perhaps he wanted to share his misgivings about getting any information from the prisoners in Eastern. Packy wouldn't have shared his plans with very many. Finding the one or two who might know what had sent Packy off on a tear to get his daughter wouldn't be easy.

Forget it. Demarco and Manny have enough to deal with.

Instead of calling Brooklyn, Beck used his smartphone to find a local car dealer that might have what he wanted.

Twenty minutes later, he pulled up in front of a small house with an oversize garage and about twenty vehicles scattered around the two buildings.

Beck parked on the patchy asphalt surface outside the office, went to the trunk of the Marauder, and pulled out three thousand in cash from a stash of twenty-five grand in the trunk's hidden compartment. As he stuffed the money in his pocket and closed the trunk, a short man with a healthy gut hanging over his khaki slacks came out of the office flashing a big smile. The salesman wore a white shirt that didn't button at the neck, and a red-and-blue-striped tie that didn't quite make it over his belly. Nor did his comb-over quite make it across his bald head. Beck took an immediate liking to him, shaking his meaty hand, matching the strength of his grip.

"How're you today? Sam Herbert. M and T auto sales. What can I do for you?"

"What's the M and T stand for?"

"Martha and Tom. My mom and dad."

"Are they still with us?"

"Just mom. Dad passed away four years ago."

"And you're carrying on the tradition, Sam?"

The short, stout man nodded with a sincere look. "Doing my best. You shopping for a vehicle?"

Beck got right to it. "I'm going to buy a truck today."

Sam Herbert's face lit up like someone had given him an unexpected birthday gift. It sounded like this fellow was here to buy, not just shop.

Beck let the sales ritual unwind for almost two hours. Like most salesmen, Sam Herbert never stopped talking the entire time. Beck took a test drive of an old Ford Ranger, bargained good-naturedly, made up a story about how he was in food supply and had recently taken on the account for the Ellenville area. Beck claimed he was trying to get more business from Eastern Correctional, asking Sam if he knew anybody who worked there.

"Oh, sure," said Sam. "Done business with a lot of those folks. Good people."

Beck kept his half of the conversation going, asking innocuous questions about the staff at Eastern. He changed the subject and asked about local bars and restaurants. Then circled back to ask about which residents favored what establishments.

Beck ended up with information on where the prison staff hung out, and a dark green Ford Ranger, a 1998 XLT with 147,276 miles he'd bargained down to $5,700 from $6,500, citing the significant rust on the underside of the truck, which Sam explained away as the unavoidable result of "all the gosh-darned salt they have to put on the roads every winter."

Beck used $2,850 of his cash and a New York State driver's license in the name of Tom Tolsen with Beck's photo on it and a rural post office box for a mailing address to close the deal. Sam promised to give the truck the once-over and get all the paperwork done right away.

"I'll be back around four to pick it up. Can you get me plates by then?"

Sam checked his watch. "Shouldn't be a problem. I'll run over to the DMV in Ellenville. I should have 'er all ready for you this afternoon."

Beck left with a smile, a nod, and a final firm handshake from the loquacious Sam Herbert.

34

By the time Palmer dropped off Tyrell and met Ippolito for breakfast at their usual diner it was a little past four in the morning on Thursday.

As they settled into a booth, Ippolito asked, "You get asshole Tyrell tucked away?"

"Yeah. Did you finish all the paperwork for asshole Frederick Wilson?"

"Yep."

"I guess that's all we can do."

Ippolito said, "For now. As soon as we finish here, I'm going to grab some sleep. You better, too, John. Your eyes look like two piss holes in the snow."

"Thank you. That's charming. Especially with breakfast."

"You going to eat?"

"No."

"Don't be a fag. Eat something. That goddam fucking Adderall is taking away your appetite."

Ippolito ordered bacon and eggs with home fries. Palmer settled for a toasted bagel with butter.

Ippolito asked, "So when you figure we'll get ballistics on those guns from dead Derrick's whorehouse?"

"I told them to rush it. Where are you on setting up the meeting with Jackson?"

"It's in the works. I'm figuring by end of day, today."

"Is Bondurant going to be in on it?"

Ippolito said, "One way or another. That spooky freak is always hanging around in the background. By the way, that's another reason we should go in this direction."

"What do you mean?"

"Word is going to get out we arrested Tyrell. I'd prefer Jackson doesn't tell his pal Whitey to rip out your witness's tongue and put a bullet in his head. And I'm not exaggerating about the tongue."

"Christ, Ray, we can't let that happen."

Ippolito answered with a mouth full of bacon and eggs. "Don't worry. Bondurant won't do shit unless Jackson tells him."

"So end of day today, huh?"

"Yeah. What's the matter?"

Palmer grimaced. Shook his head. "Nothing."

"Jeezus, what the fuck, John? I don't want a reluctant virgin on this. Tell me now if you don't want to do this."

"No, no. I just hope Juju Jackson will make a deal."

"What, are you fucking kidding me? How the hell you think that heartless bastard has stayed in business so long? Jackson is fucking ruthless. He'll do what's good for him. Tell me how this isn't good for him."

"Okay, okay."

Ippolito leaned forward. "Listen, you want to worry about something..." Ippolito rotated his fork in the air. "...worry about whatever line of bullshit you're going to come up with about the federal investigations swirling around Jackson. I'll play up the NYPD side of it, but your FBI crap is what's going to sell this thing."

Palmer nodded. "That won't be hard. Once the Feds get wind of the NYPD investigation, they might actually step up their own investigations."

Ippolito pointed a finger at Palmer. "There you go. In fact, you should go have a homo sponge bath with your gay-boy FBI buddy, and see what he's got on Bondurant and Jackson. They're always putting together some massive RICO bullshit plan to take down a million guys. See what they're trying to nail him for."

"You realize as soon as I ask McAndrews about those two in particular, he'll want to know why."

"So? Tell 'em. We're investigating murders connected to guys underneath Jackson. Plant the idea in his noggin that it would be smart to accelerate their moves against Jackson and Bondurant."

"In other words, I go make true the bullshit we're going to feed Jackson by being the one who tips the Feds off about our murder investigations."

Ippolito smiled. "Now you're getting it, Johnny boy."

"But I don't want the Feds horning in on our murders."

"Why the fuck would they? They don't give a shit about an ex-con nobody hiding out in Red Hook, or a two-bit gangbanger pimp who got shot. They want to lock up top guys on a bunch of conspiracy and racketeering shit. If they're going to accuse somebody of murder it ain't going to be Derrick fucking Watkins or this Beck asshole. It's going to be Jackson and Bondurant. Those two have killed more people than Derrick Watkins ever did, or ever would have. I hope the Feds slaughter those two sick fucks. In the meantime, we need those witnesses."

Palmer conceded. "All right. Fuck it. I'll light a fire with McAndrews about Jackson and Bondurant, then we'll tell Jackson the FBI is looking at them, so the sooner we wrap up our homicides, the better for them. Ergo, be smart and give us witnesses to back up Tyrell."

"Ergo, schmergo, what the fuck ever. John, the beauty of this is if the Feds do move against them sooner rather than later, we can tell Jackson 'we fucking told you so.' It's perfect."

Palmer laughed, "Even though we'd be the ones who made the Feds move faster."

Ippolito shot Palmer a disingenuous look. "Fucking cooperation between law-enforcement agencies at its finest. What say we get in early, and keep this shit ball rolling?"

"Sounds good. See you at the precinct, around noon?"

"Fuck no, I gotta get more sleep than that."

Palmer said, "Two?"

"Three. That'll give us plenty of time."

35

Jerome Biggie Watkins was sweating. Not because of exertion. Because he was sitting next to Eric Juju Jackson. They were on a bench facing two basketball courts in a park off Daly Avenue in the West Farms section of the Bronx.

It was late morning on a warm spring day, but there were no basketball players on the court. Or mothers and children in the toddler playground behind them. Or anybody out on the ball fields. For a moment, Biggie thought maybe Juju had arranged for the entire park to be emptied. He knew it seemed paranoid. But he also knew if Juju Jackson wanted the park empty, he could make it happen. Why would he? So he could shoot him and walk away unseen, that's why.

Juju was a slight man. What hair he had left had turned a dirty gray. He wore clothes that belied his wealth: Levi's jeans, a blue button-down shirt, and black, plain-toe shoes. His most prominent feature was his skin. At sixty-two, Jackson's face bore the ravages of the horrendous acne that had plagued him during adolescence. The term "Juju" had nothing to do with African or Caribbean voodoo. It referred to the fruit-flavored gummy candies of his youth called Jujubes. The small, rounded candies resembled the bumps and rivulets of Jackson's facial skin, and became the basis of a cruel adolescent nickname: Juju-face.

The name had been shortened over the years to simply Juju. Nobody dared used the name within hearing distance of Eric Jackson, but the name had long ago done its damage. It was one of several factors that had molded Eric Jackson into the monster Biggie had seen pull a straight razor across the face of a young girl, shoot a young man in the right knee, and when he'd stopped screaming, shoot him in the left knee. And that was only what Biggie had seen himself. He'd heard about much worse.

What really unnerved him about Juju Jackson was the man's absence of emotion. With Juju Jackson there was never a warning or an explanation. Jackson could pull a gun or a knife, shoot and maim someone mid-sentence during a conversation that seemed perfectly reasonable, even pleasant.

That's what produced the acrid sweat.

Biggie had just finished telling Jackson his brother, Derrick, had been murdered by one of his whores.

Juju stirred slightly on the park bench, scrunched his face, yawned.

"Any particular reason the bitch shot him?"

"I don't know. Just happened out of nowhere. I think she was figuring we were going to do her."

"How'd she figure that?"

"Derrick gave her shit about the thing with her father."

"What'd I tell you about that bitch?"

"Told me to have him cut her loose. I was on my way over there when the father showed up."

"You were?"

"Yeah. For real. I didn't know he was going to be there like the next day after you told me. Shit. As it was, Derrick had the bitch out on the street workin'. She wasn't even there to throw out."

Jackson stared straight ahead, lips pursed, nodding. "You see how things get fucked up when you don't do what you're supposed to do when I tell you to do them?"

Biggie couldn't think of any answer that wouldn't annoy Jackson, so he said nothing.

Jackson shifted on the park bench. Biggie's nerves ticked up a notch. He kept a close watch on Jackson's hands.

Jackson asked, "What about the crew that came bustin' in on you?"

Biggie worried about not knowing enough to satisfy Jackson, but he had to say something. "They seemed like they knew the whore's father. The guy Derrick and them beat up. They wanted to know who shot him. They thought Derrick shot him. Or one of his guys."

"How'd they find Derrick?"

"I ain't sure. We heard they was at the Houses lookin' for him. Probably went to Derrick's apartment. I'm figuring the kid Derrick had watchin' the place told them."

"He around?"

"Nobody seen him."

"Then he told them. You find him and you shoot him. In the mouth."

Biggie nodded. He knew however many times they shot Leon Miller, there damn well had better be at least one bullet fired into his mouth.

Juju Jackson squinted, going through a thought process Biggie did not dare interrupt. After a few moments, Jackson spoke.

"Okay, here's what you do. You gonna find that bitch and you gonna kill her. But first you gonna make a mess of her. And then you leave the body somewhere outside where people will see it. You understand?"

"Yes, sir."

"I want you to find Tyrell and get him to help you with the bitch. We got to make sure he knows what his obligations are. I don't blame him for getting arrested, but I blame him for getting released without being booked or arraigned for somethin'. That means he agreed to work with the cops. Probably to testify against the crew that rolled on you all. But it won't stop there. Cops'll use him to come at all of us. So you find him. Let him tell you what bullshit he thinks he's playin' at. Then you have him help you find the bitch and make sure he pulls the trigger on her so we got that on him."

"Okay. No problem. He'll be into it."

"After you do the bitch, stay close to him and find out what he's tellin' the cops. Let me know. I'll give you the word when I want you to kill him."

"Got it. What you want to do about them guys who knew the bitch's father?"

"How many of them were there?"

"Four."

"Probably more behind them." Anger crept into Juju's voice. "This is the shit that happens when people don't do what they supposed to do."

Biggie froze. He could feel Jackson seconds away from pulling a knife or a gun on him. For a moment, he thought about running, but before he could muster the courage, the moment passed.

Jackson said, "We'll have to take care of them."

Jerome knew that meant Juju would be bringing in Whitey Bondurant and his men, which was fine with him. He readily agreed.

"Okay. No problem."

"Yeah, right. No fucking problem for you."

"Well . . ."

Jackson's voice rose a notch. "Well, what?"

Biggie cursed silently. Instead of keeping his mouth shut, he'd ignited the spark again.

I said, "Well, what?"

"Nuthin'. Sorry."

Eric Jackson stared at Biggie for a moment, then turned away. It was the first time he had looked at him in the entire conversation. Biggie had no doubt Jackson was deciding on whether or not to kill him. And then he said, "What time you got?"

Biggie checked his watch. "Almost two o'clock."

"You best get moving, Jerome. You got a lot to do."

36

Manny Guzman sat silently in the front passenger seat as Demarco Jones guided a gray 2008 Chevy Impala north on the Bruckner Expressway. The car had been delivered to Demarco by one of the crew's colleagues, a master thief and security expert named Ricky Bolo.

As they drove north out of Red Hook, Demarco and Manny had come up with several names of ex-convicts and criminals they knew who might be familiar with the gang sets up in the Bronx. They needed a lead on how to find Jerome Watkins.

They hopscotched around the Bronx and Harlem for a few hours, tracking down and talking with associates, but didn't shake loose any solid information about where Watkins might be.

The weather had turned overcast and gloomy. Demarco pulled the Impala to a curb and shut down the engine, got out of the car, stretched, and walked around. Manny stayed in the car making calls on his cell phone.

After a few minutes, he called out to Demarco.

"Yo. Got something."

Demarco climbed back in the Mercury. "What?"

"Friend of mine. Should have thought of him before."

"Where to?"

"East 173rd Street."

"What's there?"

"A church."

"At this point I'm willing to resort to prayer."

Twenty minutes later, Demarco pulled up to a narrow two-story building that looked more like a broken-down social club than a church. The church occupied the ground floor. Fifty-year-old wood siding faded to a dull rust color covered the front of the building. Two holes had been chopped into the wall to accommodate small windows, both protected by ugly iron bars. Next to the windows stood a narrow door. A sign above the two windows announced: True Holiness Church of God in Christ. Pastor Benjamin Woods.

Demarco knew there were hundreds of storefront churches like this scattered throughout the Bronx. He wondered who set foot in such places.

They stepped out of the Impala.

"How do you know Pastor Woods, Manny?"

"Dannemora. He used to be called Big Ben. Lot of the gangs tried to hire him as an enforcer. You did not want Grande Benjamín coming after you."

Without warning, a huge head popped out from a window above the ground-floor church. It happened so suddenly, Demarco reached for his gun, but a boisterous voice called out a Spanish greeting to Manny.

Manny stepped back and looked up at his friend. He waved. Benjamin Woods motioned for Manny to come upstairs.

One short flight of rickety stairs led them to the pastor's small living room in an apartment above the church. Smells of cooking and incense filled the space. The room had enough space for a small couch and a large wingback armchair set near the front window. Next to the chair, a well-worn Bible had been placed on a small end table.

Benjamin Woods sat in the chair, a dark-skinned man who weighed at least three hundred pounds, very little of it fat. He wore a voluminous white shirt, black pants, and a pair of enormous black mid-ankle boots.

Whenever Demarco saw a man who might compete with him physically, he thought about what he would have to do to take him down. With Benjamin Woods, he decided his first move would be to shoot him. Quickly and continuously while backing away from him until his gun clicked empty.

Manny Guzman stepped toward his friend, hand outstretched. "Woody. Good to see you, man."

"Come here, brother." The six foot seven pastor stood and embraced Manny Guzman, gathering in the smaller man. He placed his enormous forehead on the top of Manny's head for a moment, as if extending a benediction.

Once he released Manny, he turned to Demarco and offered a huge right hand. Demarco took hold and felt a solid grip. The pastor did not attempt a show of strength.

Demarco and Manny sat on the couch. Woods returned to his chair and asked, "What can I do for you?"

Manny got right to it. "A good friend of ours was shot dead. We're trying to find one of the people involved."

"Who got shot?"

"Packy Johnson."

The pastor's brow furrowed as he searched his memory. "Yes. I knew him. In Clinton. A righteous man, if I remember correctly. Kept to himself."

"Yes. The one we're looking for is named Jerome Watkins. We've been asking around. His street name is Biggie, but we can't get a lead on him."

"Yes. Biggie Watkins. You believe he had something to do with shooting Johnson?"

"We think so."

"He's been around for quite some time. He has a brother, Derrick."

Manny said, "Right," but didn't mention that Derrick was dead.

Demarco asked, "What's his story?"

"Biggie Watkins is another depraved man outside the circle of the Holy Spirit." Woods raised his right hand. "Although all things are possible in the fullness and sufficiency of God's grace and scripture."

Demarco didn't respond. The pastor looked at Demarco and said, "It was sufficient to save me, son."

"Amen. Can you help us find Watkins?"

Woods turned his attention to Manny. "Do either of you all intend to kill him?"

Manny answered immediately, "No."

"What if he killed your friend?"

"We don't think he did. We think he might know who did."

The pastor nodded. He took a deep breath, narrowed his eyes, and contemplated. Or perhaps he prayed.

After a few moments, he began speaking and spoke for ten minutes without stopping, working himself up into a sweat. He occasionally mopped his brow with a large white handkerchief he extracted from his back pocket. He kept the handkerchief in hand while he recited a detailed history of the evolution of street gangs in the northern Bronx. He named a dozen groups that had emerged from various neighborhood affiliations, morphed, split, and merged again.

He described how the brothers Watkins' affiliation could be tracked to an offshoot of the old Black Spades who had dominated several of the Bronx housing projects in the seventies.

There had been feuds, factions, deaths, and rivalries. Many had died or gone to prison. Woods explained how the current gang scene resembled militias in a third-world country. At the top were older leaders. Under them, in a loosely enforced structure, were hundreds of young men who had, like always, formed into dozens of small groups based mostly on geography.

"It's all a grand pyramid with fewer villains on top controlling young men below and forming the usual alliances for protection. Everything powered by one unending, ever-growing horror."

"Which is?" Demarco asked.

"Guns. Guns are the entry ticket. The young ones all aspire to a gun. With the gun, they can get money. With the gun, they can make a name for themselves and avenge anyone who *disrespects* them. They are willing to shoot each other for the smallest insult. With a gun and money and reputation, they believe they can move up the food chain.

"These boys have nothing else. Most of the men who sired these children ended up among the incarcerated masses. Or died violent deaths. As did their uncles and cousins and older brothers. There are no more role models. The young ones have no god. No religion. No churches."

Benjamin Woods looked back and forth between Demarco and Manny.

"All the power of God and His Word are within the walls of my humble room downstairs. But do you think any of these young men will walk into that space? No, they won't. They are lost to us. They run wild, shooting each other for no good reason. Bragging on the Internet. I don't understand it."

Manny turned the conversation back to their objective. "And Biggie Watkins?"

Woods responded quickly. "He's one of those right below the twin pillars of evil."

"Who are?"

"Eric Jackson and Floyd Bondurant. Jackson is their leader. He's known by the name Juju. Bondurant is called Whitey. He is Jackson's enforcer. A depraved, murderous man. The finger of evil has touched both those men." Woods turned to Manny. "Do you know them?"

"No."

"You won't forget them once you see them. Bondurant is an albino. He has black features, but no color to his skin. He's big. Has reddish white hair. Jackson is . . . well, I'll just say he too is unpleasant to look at."

"Why?"

"His skin was ravaged as a youth. Perhaps God's way of marking him. They've spread the myth they are special. It's not a new tactic. In the past, there were some who used to call themselves the Five Percent or some such nonsense. Now these two call themselves The Chosen. An insult to the Lord himself. I've long ago stopped trying to understand the kinds of evil men can commit. Those two I leave to God's judgment and damnation.

"As for Jerome Watkins, he will be difficult to locate. He's a pimp. He exploits women for money. An abomination in the eyes of the Lord. And he handles money for the sets controlled by Eric Jackson. I believe he has several places around the Bronx to house his whores and play his role as moneychanger. I don't know where these places are located. I assume he moves around between his houses of exploitation and misery. But if you want to find him, I suggest you find his masters."

"Jackson and Bondurant."

"Yes, Emmanuel."

The pastor said, "I won't go near those two. I might fall into the trap of hate."

Manny waited a beat and then stood up and said, "Thank you, Ben."

Demarco stood with Manny. The pastor blessed them and wished them well. The blessing seemed immaterial to Manny, but it unnerved Demarco. If felt like an assumption of his damnation.

They thanked Benjamin Woods and got back in the Impala.

Demarco said, "I appreciate the history lesson, but the good pastor didn't tell us anything that will help us locate Watkins."

"He's pointing us were we're gonna have to go."

"I guess that's his style."

"Yep. Straight at it."

"He's right. That's where this is heading."

Manny said, "But right now, we don't have nearly enough information to take on Jackson and Bondurant. And we can't make a move like that until James returns."

Demarco said, "I think that leaves us one option."

Manny nodded. He had come to the same conclusion. "The girl."

Demarco said, "And now that I think about it, she might help us get to Biggie Watkins."

"And we know of at least one place she might be hiding."

Demarco nodded, "Her grandmother's place."

"Let's go."

Demarco leaned forward and fired up the Impala.

37

Amelia had heard the scratching and skittering of rats before. As she lay wrapped in her car-cover cocoon, hidden in the dark basement of the abandoned house, she remembered her mother's panicked reactions to the rats that always seemed to invade wherever they had ended up living. It was all part of her mother's self-indulgence. The hysterics, the drugs, the neglect, the nearly incomprehensible disregard for her one child.

The anger rose inside Amelia in an all-encompassing spiral. She sat upright, tearing away at the stupid car cover. She ached from sleeping on the hard, cold, floor. She'd slept more than twelve hours and now felt as if she couldn't breathe in the goddam dark, stinking, moldy, stifling hole in the ground.

They'd taken everything from her. Her mother, the foster system, the schools, every man who'd abused her, her father who never nurtured or protected her, but most of all the pimp and his crew who had torn away her last shreds of dignity and turned her into a murderer.

She stood up, done with it now. Done with being taken from. Done with running. There was no way she was going to escape from the Bronx without money. It was time to get out of this stinking hole and take back what they had taken from her.

With the dark night over, Amelia could see more of the basement. She saw a bookcase attached to the back wall with L brackets. Amelia tore it off the wall with the tire iron and dragged the bookcase to the window.

She used the shelves like a ladder, stepping up all the way to the top, high enough so she could push the iron bars out of her way and lean out the opening. The cool air revived her. She breathed deeply and shimmied out the half window.

She found the Jeep where she'd left it. There was a parking ticket shoved under the windshield wiper. Good, she thought. She threw the ticket on the ground. Let them come after that dead piece of shit Derrick Watkins.

She stopped at the same McDonald's on Jerome. Even though it was past one o'clock, she ordered a Sausage McMuffin with Egg and coffee. She ate slowly and methodically as she carefully planned her next moves. She knew they would be staking out her grandmother's place. Good. Let them.

She finished her meal and, to her surprise, Amelia found the bathroom unoccupied. It was the first time she'd smiled in a long time.

Once inside the bathroom, she took as long as she needed to do everything she needed to do, including stripping off her T-shirt and washing again, this time with hot water. Several people banged on the door, but she yelled at them to wait. She walked out of the bathroom when she was good and ready, returning the glares of customers waiting for the bathroom, her hand inside the pocket of the hoodie holding her gun.

Back in the Jeep, she pulled the gun out of her hoodie and looked at it more carefully. She saw the name Ruger etched into the barrel and grip, but it meant nothing to her. She pushed the button she figured would release the magazine, which dropped out of the gun onto her lap. She couldn't tell how many bullets were in the magazine but, by the weight of it, she knew she had at least some. Good enough. She slid the magazine back in, clicked the safety down, and shoved the Ruger back into her hoodie pocket, feeling competent and powerful.

She smiled, remembering the kick and crack of the gun when she'd shot Derrick, the weapon banging into the palm of her hand with each shot.

She pulled out of the McDonald's without any of her previous nervousness. So what if she hit something. Fuck it. She'd just leave. If somebody gave her a hard time, she'd see what would happen when she pulled out the Ruger.

Amelia made it back to her old neighborhood in the Bronx and cruised farther north into West Farms where she knew heroin addicts scored their drugs.

She spotted what she was looking for hunkered down at the back of the parking lot of a Howard Johnson motel. She pulled the Jeep into the lot and jumped out, strolling over to a woman whom she'd known since she was ten. Back then, the kids called her Crackhead Betty, but Amelia knew she had switched to heroin long ago, and from heroin to wine as she had become less and less able to prostitute herself for money.

Crackhead Betty had set herself up in the far corner of the parking lot. She sat propped against the wall, surrounded by a luggage carrier filled with plastic bags, a sleeping bag, and filthy blankets. She also had a grocery-store cart and a two-wheeled shopping cart. The grocery cart held clear garbage bags stuffed with empty soda cans and plastic bottles.

Amelia approached Betty, taking note of how much she had deteriorated. The woman was forty-two, but looked sixty. She wore a baseball cap over a filthy knitted hat and, despite the warm weather, a stained down coat. The skin on her face appeared ravaged from old bruises and years of exposure to the elements.

The bottom three buttons on her shirt were gone, and Betty's stomach spilled over a pair of black tights. She seemed to be in a kind of alert stupor. Crackhead Betty stared at Amelia with a look of anxious paranoia.

Amelia knew that crazed look and called out in a friendly voice, "Hey, Betty, how're you doin'?"

The friendly greeting elicited a crooked smile from the woman. There seemed to be something wrong with her lower jaw. The smile revealed missing teeth.

Betty immediately took Amelia's friendly greeting as a chance to beg for money.

"Oh, chile," she said, "I need a little spare change. I need to get something to eat."

Amelia asked, "What're you drinkin' these days, Betty?"

"Wine. Any sweet wine, honey."

After her second stop at McDonald's, Amelia had less than thirty dollars left. She said, "Okay, Betty, I'll get you a bottle of wine and give you some money, too. But I got to borrow your shopping cart and some cans for a few minutes."

Betty's voice grew shrill, "No, no, don't take my stuff. Don't take my stuff."

Amelia stuffed a five and two ones into Betty's filthy right hand and told her, "You sit still. Don't worry. I'll be right back with your wine."

For a moment, Amelia considered asking Betty for her down coat, but rejected the idea. She'd never give it up, and it might be infested with lice. Instead, she emptied the shopping cart and put one bag of empty soda cans and a filthy blanket into it.

The derelict woman clutched the bills, wincing with worry as she watched Amelia wheel the shopping cart to the Jeep, open the back hatch, and lift the cart, cans, and blanket into the back.

Amelia drove back to her grandmother's neighborhood, but didn't dare cruise past the house in the Jeep to see if any of Derrick's crew were keeping watch out front. Instead, she parked on Vyse Street, one block east of Hoe Avenue.

She pulled the gun out from the kangaroo pocket of the hoodie and shoved it into the waistband of her jeans above her left pocket. She went around to the back of the Jeep and opened the hatch, pulling out the blanket she'd taken from Crackhead Betty.

She rummaged around the jumble of automotive junk in the cargo area, looking for a length of rope. Instead, she found a set of bungee cords.

She quickly took off the pink hoodie. Then she draped the dingy gray blanket over her head like a long shawl. The blanket reached past her knees. She used one of the bungee cords like a belt, gathering the blanket and securing it around her waist. The blanket covering her head cut off some of her peripheral vision, but it also blocked a clear view of her face. She made sure she could still reach under it and get to the Ruger. Perfect.

38

When Demarco turned onto Hoe Avenue from 174th Street, he and Manny spotted a car parked in front of a small playground across the street from Lorena Leon's public housing unit. Two men sat in the front seats. Coming up Hoe, they could see only the backs of their heads, but they had little doubt they were from Derrick Watkins's crew.

Demarco said, "Looks like we've got two of 'em. And I'm betting the big one behind the wheel is Jerome."

As Demarco drove past the parked car, Manny slid down out of view below the window level. Demarco casually scratched the right side of his head, blocking his face.

"Park around the corner, D. We'll come back on foot and take them."

"How you want to work it?"

"We come up on each side of their car from behind. Put guns on them. If one of them is Biggie we throw the other one out, and take Watkins to Red Hook."

"In their car?"

"Yeah. Ricky can drive up here and fetch this one. You sit in the back with him. If he twitches, put a bullet in his damn knee."

Demarco said, "I might do that anyhow. Get him talking right now. Who cares if he bleeds all over the place. It's his car."

*

Amelia could feel the excitement growing as she pulled the shopping cart and bag of cans out of the Jeep. She took a deep breath, telling herself to go slow. She pressed her hand against the Ruger, feeling the reassurance of its solid mass.

As she closed the Jeep's hatch, and set off with her shopping cart and cans, she pictured shooting whoever might be waiting for her to show up at her grandmother's house. She hoped one of them was Tyrell Williams.

She decided if they were parked near Lorena's house, she would come at them straight on. She wanted to see their faces when she shot them. They'd be looking for a whore. She wasn't a whore anymore. She was a stooped-over can-collector dressed like a crazy homeless person.

She walked around to 172nd Street and headed for Hoe, pulling the wobbly shopping cart with her left hand so her right hand would be free to pull the gun.

When she turned onto Hoe Avenue, she made sure to stop and look at the tied-up garbage bags set out for collection near the curb. As she pretended to check garbage bags for cans, Amelia tried to see if any of the parked cars were occupied. She couldn't see much farther than three cars ahead, which meant she'd have to get fairly close before she would spot anybody staking out her grandmother's. She wondered if she should pull the gun out now, so she could shoot more quickly.

Demarco had to drive two blocks on 172nd Street before he found a spot to park. He pulled in to the space, and they hustled back to Hoe Avenue. They planned on coming at them from behind, figuring they could get fairly close without too much risk of being spotted. At some point they'd appear in the side-view mirrors. Hopefully, they could close the distance before Watkins's guys drew their weapons.

At the corner of 172nd and Hoe, Demarco turned to Manny and said, "Let's stay on the sidewalk until we get close. Just two guys walking. Then we'll split up and take them. If they spot us before we get close, do what you have to do. Don't risk getting nailed by these dopes."

Manny gave Demarco a short nod, his eyes on the car midway down the block.

Amelia spotted the two men at the other end of Hoe Avenue coming her way at the same time she saw Tyrell and Biggie sitting in a white Toyota Avalon three cars ahead of her.

She stopped and turned toward the curb, her heart pounding. She kept her head down, but turned to check out the two at the other end of the block. Shit! She recognized them. The tall black guy who had opened the door for her at Derrick's place, and the shorter Hispanic one who had searched Derrick's crew for guns.

They had to be after Tyrell and Biggie, too.

She couldn't move. She bit down to stop herself from screaming in frustration.

Not now. Not when I'm so close. *Goddam them. I'll shoot them first if they get in my way.* But then she told herself, *Take it easy. You barely have enough bullets for Tyrell and Biggie, much less those other two.*

She tried to remember how many times she'd shot at Derrick. Three? Four?

It didn't matter. She was closer. Walk up to Biggie's car and start shooting. That would drive the other two off. Shoot right through the windshield. Grab their money and run. Now. Do it now.

She turned and reached under the blanket for her gun.

Demarco and Manny were about to split apart when they saw the woman on the street with a shopping cart filled with soda cans.

Great, thought Demarco, a damn homeless can-collector walking right into the middle of their play.

Manny saw her, too, and stopped a few steps ahead of Demarco. He turned to him and guided Demarco over to a building near the corner. He leaned back and faced Demarco.

"Let the homeless woman pass by and get off the block, and then we'll take them down."

Demarco stood facing Manny, his head turned slightly to watch the can-collector up the block. And then Demarco said, "Aw, hell."

Amelia kept her gaze down. She held the Ruger under her blanket, eyes on Biggie and Tyrell in the front seat. There were three cars and a stretch of empty curb between her and them.

She had an overwhelming urge to walk faster, but she forced herself to keep a slow pace, pulling the shopping cart behind her.

She felt her heart pounding. The gun seemed very heavy in her hand, held awkwardly under the blanket. She advanced within two car lengths. She saw Tyrell turning to talk to Biggie, who didn't look at him. Biggie kept his attention across the street on her grandmother's place. She saw Tyrell lift a forty-ounce bottle of malt liquor to his mouth. He drained the bottle and in the next second opened the car door, stepped out, and walked toward the small park with the empty bottle in his hand.

Without even thinking about it, Amelia followed him into the park.

Manny said, "What?"

"Guy just got out of the car. The can-collector followed him into that little playground."

"Christ, she probably wants the bottle he's carrying."

"It's not the empty bottle she wants," said Demarco. "That's the girl, Manny. Look how tall she is. Same skin tone. That's Packy's kid. The one who shot Derrick Watkins."

Manny turned to get a quick look before Amelia and Tyrell disappeared into the park.

"Goddammit," said Manny. "Come on."

Manny ran as fast as his bowed legs would carry him, Demarco gliding along right behind him.

There was a toddler-size slide and a set of monkey bars in the center of the small park, and nothing else. Past the play area, a short chain-link fence, a wall of foliage, and small trees blocked the park from the empty lot beyond it. There was nobody else in the park.

Amelia followed Tyrell at a distance. He was oblivious to her presence, intent on emptying his bladder after downing forty ounces of malt liquor.

Amelia hung back until Tyrell found a spot at the back of the little park near the foliage. Tyrell tossed the empty malt liquor bottle into the bushes.

He unzipped his pants.

Amelia waited patiently, then moved within five feet behind him. She carefully aimed at the small of his back, anticipating that the pistol would kick up and the bullet would hit him dead center.

She held the Ruger with two hands, concentrating, ready this time for the sharp crack and recoil. She squinted in anticipation. As she was about to pull the trigger, Tyrell sensed someone behind him. She held off. Amelia wanted him to see her. Still holding his penis, he looked over his shoulder. Amelia pulled the blanket off her head and waited until he recognized her before she pulled the trigger.

The first bullet obliterated Tyrell Williams's lower spine. The impact pushed his pelvis forward. Paralyzed from the waist down, his legs folded under him. He felt hardly any pain as he sagged to the ground in an awkward heap, landing mostly on his back.

Amelia walked to him. She made sure Tyrell was looking at her. She couldn't clearly hear his cries or pleas, or whatever noise came out of his mouth because the gunshot had deafened her somewhat. She carefully aimed the gun at his chest, even as he raised his hands to ward off the shot. She fired three times. Three steady, even shots. The first bullet went through his sternum. The second bullet took out a lung and clipped his heart. The last bullet hit his throat, cutting off any chance of Tyrell Williams finishing the curse he tried to scream at Amelia Johnson.

Biggie Watkins didn't hesitate. When he heard the first gunshot, he came out of his car with not one, but two guns in his hands. He couldn't see into the playground where the gunshots had sounded, but he saw Demarco Jones and Manny Guzman coming at him from down the block.

Without a second's hesitation, he raised his guns and began shooting at them with both hands.

Manny and Demarco veered away from each other so Biggie had to fire in two directions. Watkins spread his arms and kept shooting.

Demarco slipped behind the back of a car for cover, letting off a fast shot that blew out the back window of Watkins's Toyota. He leaned out, took careful aim, and shot at Watkins, but missed as the big man moved around behind the open driver's-side door.

Manny Guzman did not duck, did not take cover, did not stop. He continued advancing on the sidewalk toward Watkins, who remained in the street, using his car door for cover.

Watkins extended his right hand around the door and fired two shots at Demarco. Then he popped up just high enough to get his left hand above the roof of the car and shoot at Manny.

Manny kept advancing.

Demarco leaned out again from behind the car where he was crouched, knowing Manny would not stop, and fired three times to give Manny cover.

Demarco had to shoot with his left hand, leaning out from behind a car thirty feet from Watkins. His first shot went wide. On his second shot he overcompensated, and it hit the trunk of the car. The third shot hit the Toyota's door.

Watkins kept firing blindly and almost nailed Manny. Manny continued toward him without even flinching.

Demarco cursed, slipped out from behind cover, switched hands, and fired shot after steady shot at Watkins mostly to distract Watkins's attention from Manny. Nine-millimeter bullets blew out the driver's-side door window and banged into the car door, forcing Watkins to drop flat onto the street. That meant Biggie couldn't shoot at Manny now, so he aimed both guns from under the car door and fired at Demarco.

One of Watkins's bullets ricocheted up off the street and zinged past the side of Demarco's face. He felt the heat of it sizzle past him. Demarco dropped down and fired back, trying to get a shot under the car door.

Manny Guzman reached the Toyota, calmly stepped around the front of the car, and put two bullets into the back of Jerome Watkins's head.

Demarco saw Manny behind Watkins, heard the two quick shots. He knew beyond any doubt Manny had killed him.

Demarco jumped up and ran forward. Manny pocketed his Charter Arms Bulldog and stood waiting for Demarco.

Manny said, "Come on, let's get him out of the way. We'll take his car."

"What about the other guy?"

"He can't do anything for us and, from the sound of it, she nailed him. Let's go."

Manny bent down and grabbed the left ankle. Demarco grabbed the right ankle, and they unceremoniously dragged Biggie Watkins around the Toyota onto the sidewalk.

Demarco hustled back to the driver's seat. The keys were still in the car. Manny slipped into the passenger seat.

Demarco pulled the driver's door shut, and the remains of the window fell in on him. He peeled out from the parking space, made a hard right, and shot down 172nd Street heading toward Ricky Bolo's Impala.

Manny braced himself in the passenger seat, pointed to the floor on his side, and calmly said, "You see this shit these guys had in here?"

Demarco didn't take the time to look at what Manny pointed at as he raced through an intersection and pulled the bullet-ridden Toyota into a bus stop near where he had parked the Impala. Only then did he look down at the rope and duct tape.

Manny said, "They had some nasty plans for Packy's kid."

"Yeah, well, she had her own plan. Damn fools sitting out there where anybody could find them."

"You surprised?"

"No."

Demarco shoved the Toyota into park. He wiped down the wheel and gearshift, and the door handle on his side, but didn't bother turning off the engine. Maybe somebody in the neighborhood would help themselves to the car and make things tougher for the police.

He waited for Manny to wipe down his door handle and then both hustled into the Impala. Demarco pulled out carefully and drove off at a normal speed.

At the sound of the first gunshots, Amelia Johnson had ducked down near the body of Tyrell. While the gunfire blasted out on the street, she carefully went through Tyrell's pockets, searching for his money. She found a fold of bills in his front pocket. Nothing in the wallet in his back pocket. She replaced it and made her way to the park entrance, keeping out of sight.

She waited a few moments after the shooting stopped, came out of the small playground with her shopping cart, and calmly walked over to Biggie Watkins. The two bullets from Manny Guzman's .357 caliber Charter Arms Bulldog had blown through Biggie's head and destroyed most of his face.

Amelia felt a strange mix of disappointment and happiness. They had killed him. She supposed that was good, but she still felt a need to point her gun at Biggie Watkins and fire a bullet into the dead bulk of the man lying on the street in front of her. The big body twitched. She fired again. And again. But on the third pull, nothing happened. She had no more bullets.

She carefully slipped the gun into her waistband, feeling the heat of the barrel against her abdomen. She calmly squatted near the body and stripped Biggie of his money. She dropped his wallet next to him, and disappeared from the block before anybody emerged to view the carnage.

39

The sight of Eastern Correctional still sent a sick feeling into Beck's gut, but as he watched Walter walk out to the parking lot it seemed as if the prison had hit Walter even harder.

Walter slipped into the passenger seat with a sigh, leaned back, silent for a moment.

"How'd it go?"

"Very much as you suspected. They pretty much stone-walled me."

"Was it the usual closing of ranks, or do you think there was something else behind it?"

"I don't want to think that, but my gut tells me there is. Which makes it all the worse."

"I'll go with your gut, Walter."

"Fortunately, we don't have to."

"Why?"

"I got lucky. They gave me a desk in the social services office to conduct my interviews. One of the women working nearby heard me and came forward. She told me she knew someone who might help."

"Who?"

"A high-ranking correction officer. A female captain. She gave me her cell number."

"Did you call her?"

"Yes, but she refused to talk to me. Especially on the phone. She also refused to let the social services lady act as a go-between. She didn't want to have contact with any-one connected to Eastern."

"Is there any way we can convince her to talk to you?"

"No need. I offered you."

Beck shot Walter a surprised look. "And she agreed?"

"She figured there would be zero chance you'd talk to anybody in the department."

"That's for sure."

"She agreed to meet you at the Mobil station in Ellen-ville at five-fifteen. Said her name was Rita, but I have no idea if it's her real name."

Beck looked at his watch. 4:05.

"Perfect. Just enough time to get my truck."

Walter leaned back in his seat and said, "If you don't mind, James, I'm going to rest my eyes."

"Go right ahead."

Beck drove in silence toward M & T Auto Sales think-ing about Walter's polite euphemism. Resting his eyes. As if he'd been in there reading all day. Within a minute, Walter had fallen asleep.

Beck left Walter napping in the Mercury while he paid the balance he owed on the truck, signed the rest of the paperwork, and collected the Ranger. When he returned, truck keys in hand, Walter was sitting behind the wheel, awake and waiting. Beck leaned into the open driver's-side window and said, "Hey, Walter, you know if you want to head back to Brooklyn now, it's fine with me."

"No. I want to hear what the lady CO says to you."

"All right. I'll meet with her, then we'll have some din-ner, and you can head back."

"Fine."

"As we enter town, you'll see a church on the right. You park there. I'll go to the Mobil station and hear what she has to say."

"All right."

"How will I know who she is?"

"Her friend says she's a blonde."

Beck gave a short nod. "I'll be back as soon as I'm done."

Beck kept an eye on his rearview mirror until Walter pulled in to the church parking lot. He continued on to the Mobil station at the edge of town, pulling in at 5:15 P.M. exactly. There was a single row of two pumps with nozzles for cars on each side. A typical convenience store anchored the station.

A bleached blonde stood at one of the pumps filling up a Subaru Forester that hadn't been washed in a long time. Beck figured her for about two hundred pounds packed into a pair of slacks and the white shirt worn by high-ranking correction officers. Everything about her seemed round, especially her head and face.

Beck didn't know the location of the gas cap on the Ranger. He pulled up to the other side of the pump the woman was using and saw he'd guessed correctly. He knew the truck had a full tank, but he still went through the motions of putting the fuel nozzle into the filler neck.

Beck decided she had set this up pretty well. Even if someone saw them talking, it would look like two people filling up their gas tanks shooting the shit.

Rita watched the man on the other side of the pump carefully. He almost looked like a local. Sturdy. Ordinary clothes. Maybe hands that were too clean for a working-man, but at least he didn't pull up in an expensive car wearing clothes with a bunch of logos.

Beck turned to face the woman laid back against the truck, and said, "Is your name Rita?"

"Is yours Beck?"

She had a voice that sounded like she had been chain-smoking and shouting for decades.

Beck nodded and waited.

"I hear you want to know about Paco Johnson."

"Yes. Did you know he was murdered?"

She said, "As of a few hours ago."

"Do you have any idea why?"

"You served time with him?"

Beck nodded. "At Clinton and Eastern."

"You're the one who got his conviction overturned."

"Because I didn't commit a crime."

Rita smirked. "I never met a con who did."

Beck said, "You have now."

The woman looked at the digital readout of her pump. She seemed to be looking to turn it off at some dollar number, but then decided to keep going until her tank filled.

"Answer me one question. If I tell you what I know, what are you going to do with the information?"

He gave Rita the same answer he'd given Walter. "I'm going to do the right thing."

"What does that mean?"

"It means I'm going to do the right thing."

Beck watched her hover between leaving and talking to him.

"This is crazy, talking to an ex-con about this."

"About what? You haven't told me anything."

The gas pump shut off as Rita's tank reached full. She hesitated. Looked up, looked at Beck. He didn't want a full tank to be the thing that tipped her into leaving.

"Leaving now won't accomplish anything."

Rita had her hand on the fuel nozzle, but didn't pull it out.

Beck said, "I'm guessing there's something going on in that prison you can't tell the bosses about. Maybe you don't have enough information, or enough proof, or if you try to do something about it, you're going to get jammed up. Even with your rank I'm betting it won't be easy going up against the men's club that runs the place."

"And you think you can do something about it?"

Beck thought of Walter's answer. "I can try."

Rita continued to struggle.

Beck said, "Sorry you don't have a better choice."

"What do you mean?"

"You want to do something about the people who caused the death of an innocent man. But you don't want to talk to an ex-con you don't know who might do something outside the law."

Rita looked at Beck. "Well, at least you're not stupid."

"What if I told you I've never committed a criminal act? Never even got a parking ticket. Bounced a check. Stolen a dime. The only thing I have to do with crime was being a victim of it."

"Is all that true?"

In Beck's moral universe every word was true. "Absolutely."

Beck crossed his arms, rested his foot against his truck, and waited.

Rita took out the nozzle and placed it in the pump receptacle.

Finally, she spoke. "I don't know the details. But I do know there's nasty, disgusting shit going down with a group of the guards in there."

Beck nodded, taking note of the word *disgusting*. Beck waited to hear more.

"It's bad," she said.

"How did you find out?"

"You hear things. In passing. It involves a small bunch of guards who think they can do whatever the hell they want."

"Who are they?"

She paused. Beck waited. Either she was going to tell him, or she was going to get into her car and leave. She screwed her gas cap on and closed the cover. Finally, she said, "I'm going to give you one name. One name, and it better not come back on me."

"It won't."

She looked at Beck. For a moment, she looked like she had decided to leave. And then she said, "Oswald Remsen."

Beck nodded. He knew the man. Remsen had been a senior guard when Beck was at Eastern.

The woman continued, "He's an old-time CO who's been around Eastern forever. He has three sons who are guards. Two of them work at Eastern. They are the worst of the worst. I swear I don't know how they ever got through the academy. Somebody up at Albany must have been dumb, blind, and asleep to let them through. I doubt the third son is any better."

"Two of his sons work at Eastern?"

"Yeah. Remsen is high up in the union. Got his sons in there with him, which anybody with a brain should have prevented."

"Where's the third one?"

"Down at Sing Sing."

Beck asked, "So how can I find Remsen without going through a lot of trouble?"

"What are you going to do?"

"Find out if Oswald Remsen is involved in Johnson's murder."

"How?"

"I don't know yet."

She looked at Beck, still conflicted. He saw her struggling. Beck spoke softly. "Rita, we both know you've already decided to help me. You've come this far. You've given me the name. I'm not going to let it drop. But it would help if you gave me something more. You don't have to say anything. Just nod yes, or shake your head no."

"I'm not playing twenty questions."

"How about two? Is he a drinker?"

She nodded yes.

"I hear a lot of the COs drink at a tavern over on Fifty-three."

Rita nodded again. "You hear right. That's two questions. That's all I can do."

"I understand."

Beck turned away and pulled the gas nozzle out of his truck. He didn't look at the tough, angry woman again.

He heard her car door slam shut, her engine start, and a Subaru with a bad muffler drive off.

He replaced the fuel hose and walked into the Mobil station store. He bought two cups of coffee, a pack of generic cigarettes, three scratch-off lottery tickets, and a tin of Skoal Wintergreen smokeless tobacco. He paid cash for everything and left.

He emptied both coffees into the trash receptacle near the pumps, making sure the coffee stained the cardboard cups. He opened the pack of cigarettes, dumped out a few and crumpled the pack a bit.

He climbed into his truck. There weren't any cup holders in the Ranger, so he tossed the empty cups on the passenger-side floor. He opened the Skoal, left the wrapper on the floor, then dropped the cigarettes and dip on the dashboard. He quickly scratched off the lottery cards, not bothering to see if he'd won anything, and dropped them on the dash, too.

He pulled out to rendezvous with Walter Ferguson, wishing Rita had wanted to tell him more, but thankful there wasn't any information that would compromise Walter.

He checked his watch. Not even six o'clock. Enough time to send off Walter, get back to his motel, and decide which weapons to bring with him to the tavern on Route 53.

40

Palmer and Ippolito had been working on their case and getting ready for their secret meeting with Eric Jackson for two hours, when Levitt and Clovehill walked into the detective squad bullpen at five P.M.

Ippolito muttered, "Now, what?"

As they approached, Levitt told them, "We have a problem."

"What?" asked Palmer.

"Somebody shot your witness Tyrell Williams about an hour ago over on Hoe Avenue."

Palmer couldn't believe it. "What?"

"Am I speaking a foreign language? Your witness Tyrell Williams is dead."

"When? How?"

"Palmer, focus. I just said about an hour ago." Levitt handed Palmer a piece of paper with an address written on it. "You better get out there and see what the hell is going on."

"Jeesuz fucking Christ."

"Hey."

"Sorry, boss. It's just . . ." Palmer shook his head in disbelief. "Do you have anything else? Any more information?"

Levitt looked at a report he held in his right hand. "Your guy is one of two dead on the scene. The other one is tentatively ID'd as Jerome Watkins."

"Any witnesses?" Palmer asked.

"I don't know. Go see what you can find out. I want to hear from you two within the hour. Whatever you have. If you don't reach me, report in to Sergeant Clovehill. Go."

"Yes, sir."

As soon as Levitt and Clovehill left, Palmer blurted out, "I can't fucking believe it. This is a disaster. Anything to make sure I never get a goddam break. Fuck!"

Ippolito said, "I wonder if Juju and that maniac Whitey are already cleaning house."

"Fucking hell."

Ippolito said to Palmer, "Hey, look at the upside, John. Now you got two more murders to investigate."

"Upside? Where's the upside with Tyrell dead? He was my key to closing two murders. What am I supposed to do now?"

Ippolito lowered his voice. "The same fucking thing we were gonna do. We'll just get another witness to replace him. There were more guys at that location. Listen, this might be a blessing in disguise. I never trusted shit bag Tyrell."

"Christ, Ray, this is getting nuts. Fucking Jackson's going to squeeze us for everything we got. If I had Tyrell, I'd only need a couple more to corroborate."

Ippolito sat at his desk. "Aw hell, John, in for a penny, in for a pound. You think a guy like Jackson does some complex calculation? One of his mooks is as good as another. There was nothing special about Tyrell Williams except for his unfailing ability to fuck things up. I told you that asshole was going to screw you, John. Didn't I tell you?"

"By getting killed?"

256

"Getting killed is one of their specialties. One way or another these goddam shine, mutt motherfuckers find a way to ruin everything."

Palmer raised a hand. "All right, all right, stop. Let's get the hell out there and see what happened."

"Hang on a second." Ippolito shuffled through the piles of papers and folders on his desk. "Let me get the file Witherspoon put together for you. It's got photos of Beck and his known associates. Maybe they did this. You know, looking to take out more of Derrick Watkins's boys. Let's take pictures and see if we can get an ID."

Still distracted, Palmer said, "What?"

"Photos. From Witherspoon's file. It might have been James Beck or one of his crew who shot Tyrell and the other guy."

"Oh. Right. Right. Okay. Good idea."

Ippolito dug out a folder from the mess on his desk and flipped through the loose pages.

"Here they are." Ippolito pulled out three sets of identification cards complete with mug shots for Beck, Ciro Baldassare, and Emmanuel Guzman. "I'm thinking it's too soon for Juju to be doing this. I bet one of these hard cases are the shooters. Which is good. Could give us more leverage with Jackson."

Palmer stared at the photos and scanned the criminal records.

"Come on, John. Get your head in the game. You lost Tyrell, but this might put us in a stronger position."

"How?"

Ippolito pointed to the mug shots. "I just told you. If one of these guys shot two more of Jackson's boys, he'll be fucking foaming at the mouth to go after them. It gives us more to offer him. If he agrees to play ball with us, we'll point Juju in the right direction."

"Hold on, Ray. Beck is mine."

"Hey, if Beck or one of his guys shot Biggie Watkins and Tyrell, Jackson and Bondurant are going after them, case closed. You want to get witnesses and keep Beck for yourself, you're going to have to make a deal."

"How?"

"Like I said before. Witnesses for information. And now we talk him into laying off Beck if we give him the rest of Beck's crew."

Palmer raised a hand. "Wait a minute . . ."

"John, you already got two murders on your plate. Now there's two more. You want to get credit for solving the Paco Johnson murder and lock Beck up for the Watkins murder, we gotta move fast before borough command steps in and takes over all of it. What do you give a shit if Jackson gets a lead on Beck's crew?"

Palmer shook his head. "I don't know."

"Think about it. In the meantime, let's go see what the hell happened."

41

Demarco drove out of the Bronx thinking about the gun battle with Biggie Watkins and smelling the gun smoke on his clothes. He headed straight to the Cross Bronx Expressway and over the George Washington Bridge into New Jersey. Even though he didn't intend to keep Ricky Bolo's Impala for much longer, he wanted to get out of New York City in case there was an alert out for the car.

Manny asked, "You taking the long way back?"

"Safer. And I figure we should check in with Ciro. After that shootout, we're going to need a place to lay low. Cops are going to come looking for us in Red Hook sooner or later."

"Yeah. Thanks to Packy's mother-in-law the cops know about James. They know about him, they'll know about us. After the war we were in last winter, the Red Hook place is on their records."

Demarco said, "We have to get someone to lock up Red Hook and hide all the guns and anything else we don't want the cops to find. And hang out there if the cops come with search warrants. If someone's not there, they'll break down doors and tear up the place."

"True. Who should hold the fort? Alex?"

Demarco said, "Alex got stuck doing it last time."

"Willie?"

Demarco shook his head. "No. No way. Cops bust in on him he'll start a war. And he's still on parole. They'll lock him up in a heartbeat. I guess Alex."

"I'll call him now. And Ciro. Let him know we're coming."

Manny made the calls while Demarco drove. He didn't expect either of them to pick up. He left messages, pocketed his old clamshell phone, and stared out the windshield, brow furrowed.

Demarco looked over at him.

"What?"

"Cops are only half our problem. This thing is gonna explode now. Three dead, including the two brothers who ran things. Eric Jackson will be coming after us now. And they'll be looking for Packy's daughter even harder."

"So they can use her to find us."

"Yes. Even though she doesn't know us, or have a clue where to find us."

"Which isn't going to help her," Demarco said. "They'll torture her, and she won't have any answers."

Manny shook his head. "First Packy. Now his kid. Shit. We got to find her, D. We can't let them kill her, too."

"Killing her is the least of what they'll do to her."

Manny made a guttural noise, picturing the duct tape and rope he'd seen in Watkins's car.

Both men fell silent.

Finally, Manny said, "We're going to have to take out those guys."

"But how?"

"I don't know, brother. I don't know."

42

Amelia Johnson kept thinking about how to get more bullets as she drove back to the parking lot where she'd found Crackhead Betty. The derelict woman had already finished a pint of cheap white wine and fallen into a stupor. No surprise. Amelia had left her with seven dollars and there was a liquor store nearby.

Amelia returned Betty's shopping cart, blanket, and bag of cans. She folded a twenty-dollar bill and stuffed it into the pocket of Betty's filthy down jacket, hoping she'd find it soon.

She climbed into the Jeep and drove off, still thinking about bullets. She might not have any, but she had a lot more money. She pulled the Jeep to the curb and dug out the bills she had taken from the bodies, quickly counting the money. It amounted to six hundred and seventy dollars. Good, but she needed more.

And in the next instant, Amelia knew exactly where she might get it.

She had been unconsciously driving toward Bronx River Houses. She pulled out and headed toward Tyrell's apartment building on Daly Street. She knew his sister, Darlene, often stayed at his apartment. If she was there, it would make getting into the place easier, and odds were good she hadn't yet heard her brother had been shot dead.

Amelia parked the Jeep almost in front of Tyrell's apartment building. She didn't think about anything, or plan anything. She walked right up to the outside panel of buzzers, all of them unmarked, and pushed 4E.

Nobody answered. She buzzed again and again, and finally a female voice yelled, "Who is it?"

"Darlene, it's me, Amelia. I got something for Tyrell."

"Tyrell not here."

"So buzz me in, and I'll give it to you."

"What is it?"

"A envelope from Jerome."

"Jerome?"

"Yeah."

"What's in it?"

"What the fuck you think is in it? C'mon, buzz me in. Tyrell don't get this he's going to be pissed."

Amelia heard a mumbled curse before the buzzer rang.

She entered the lobby, saw the OUT OF SERVICE sign on the elevator, and headed up the stairs. When she reached the fourth floor, she pulled out her empty gun. Even without bullets, the Ruger made her feel powerful. She walked up to Tyrell's door without hesitation and banged on it.

The door swung open in the middle of a curse.

"Fuck's up with you, bitch? Bangin' on doors and shit . . ."

Amelia overhanded the barrel of the gun right into the Darlene's face, splitting the skin from her forehead down to the bridge of her nose, and knocking her backward into the room.

Darlene was a large girl. As tall as Amelia and fifty pounds heavier. She swung at Amelia, who leaned back away from her fist and whipped the barrel of the Ruger into the side of Darlene's head. Darlene's hands flailed at Amelia as she staggered sideways and fell on her side, unconscious.

Amelia stood over the fallen woman, yelling, "Don't you never, ever call me a bitch. Ever, goddammit. I ain't nobody's bitch."

Amelia knew she was in a blood rage. She took a deep breath and stepped back from the woman on the floor, blinking her eyes, coming back to herself.

She kicked the apartment door closed, forcing herself to calm down and focus. She noticed the ragged, gasping breaths emanating from the unconscious woman. The sound made her angry. She muttered at Darlene, "What the hell you think was going to happen, you calling me that?"

Amelia walked past Darlene and began searching the filthy apartment. There were clothes on the furniture, the floor, even hanging on doorknobs. There were shoes scattered about, cardboard boxes filled with more clothes and household items, dishes piled high in the sink, garbage bags overflowing, empty fast-food containers everywhere. The whole place had a sour smell to it. Amelia had an urge to get out of the apartment, but she walked past everything, straight back to Tyrell's bedroom.

She tossed the pillows off the unmade bed, thinking there might be a gun under one of them. She felt under the mattress, then lifted the entire mattress and shoved it off the box spring. Nothing. She went through the closet, looking at shelves, feeling pockets of coats and pants.

She tore into a chest of drawers. She found nothing except clothes and items she didn't want. In frustration, she pulled out the top drawer and threw it on the mattress. Nothing. But when she did the same to the second drawer, she saw two envelopes taped to the bottom of the drawer. She tore them off, saw cash in both envelopes, and stuffed them into her back pockets.

She moved quickly through the rest of the apartment, checking the bathroom, a room filled with boxes and assorted junk, all the closets, the kitchen cabinets, the freezer.

Darlene had struggled back to consciousness, and had propped herself up against the couch, sitting on the floor holding her shirt to her bleeding forehead.

She saw Amelia in the kitchen. "Why'd you fuckin' hit me?"

"What the fuck you think I'd do, you calling me a bitch? I ain't nobody's bitch, Darlene. Shut up and be glad I didn't shoot you."

Amelia was about to leave when she spotted a set of car keys in a glass bowl on the kitchen counter. She grabbed them and asked Darlene, "Where's Tyrell's car at?"

"I don't know."

"Come on, tell me or I'll start in on you again."

Darlene screamed, "I don't know! He parked it outside somewhere. Leave me the fuck alone. I didn't do nothing to you."

Amelia turned away and walked out of the apartment without another word. She'd find the car in the neighborhood. Time to get rid of the damn Jeep anyhow. Everybody knew it belonged to Derrick, it was too hard to park, and almost out of gas.

Tyrell drove a green Chevy Malibu. She'd find it.

43

Beck pulled the Ranger in to an empty area in the dirt parking lot behind the tavern on Route 53 shortly before eight. He entered through a side door that opened directly into the barroom.

An L-shaped bar dominated the space, the long side facing him, the short side of the L on his left. There were two empty bar stools around the curve at the short end, both empty. Beck walked over to the stools, pushed one closer to the wall, and sat in the other, taking over that end of the bar. This gave him a view of the door he'd entered, all the patrons at the bar, behind the bar, and a seating area past the bar large enough to hold five tables for two. Two of the tables had been pushed together and three men sat at them drinking from longneck bottles of beer. One of the men was Oswald Remsen.

It didn't surprise Beck. Rita had confirmed that Remsen was a drinker. This was where Sam Herbert said the correction officers hung out. What else was there to do on a Thursday night?

Beck looked at Remsen, but only for a few seconds, not wanting to attract his attention. He scanned everyone else at the bar. It seemed like a typical blue-collar crowd. Nearest him sat an overweight fellow drinking beer who seemed friendly enough, prematurely bald, wearing thick glasses resting halfway down his nose. Two stools past the bald guy sat a tall man in a checked shirt and jeans stained with roofing tar. He sipped straight whiskey at a steady pace, occasionally glancing at the old TV behind the bar. Past him sat a couple, both in their forties, both with mixed drinks in their hands. Beck guessed gin and tonics. They were pleasantly drunk. The woman was sloppy and overweight, wearing a faded old red sweatshirt bearing the Coca-Cola logo. Her partner had turned his bar stool to face her. He was bearded, skinny, talked with a raspy smoker's voice, slurring his words and occasionally emitting a harsh, annoying, phlegm-filled laugh.

Beck realized every person in the bar had come here to drink until they were drunk. It both depressed him and made him feel like drinking.

He watched the woman working the bar. She moved with easy efficiency. Beck admired that, and he admired her looks. She was the kind of woman who attracted a male clientele, but wasn't overly concerned by the attention. She dressed in jeans that fitted her well and a white shirt. She had dark brown hair stacked on her head to keep it out of her way, which somehow made her look both business-like and sensual.

She headed in Beck's direction, gave him a quick smile, and asked, "What can I get you?"

Beck smiled back and said, "A Budweiser and a Jameson neat. And a menu."

She dropped a menu in front of Beck encased in yellowing plastic marred by a cigarette burn in the corner. She went to pull a Bud from her cooler and set the wet, cold bottle on the bar, leaving Beck to twist off the cap while she grabbed the Jameson from the back bar and poured a generous amount of the Irish whiskey into a four-ounce water glass. The menu looked so stained and old he didn't even consider ordering food. He scanned the back bar and spied a rack with chips and Beer Nuts.

There was also an old twenty-seven-inch Toshiba TV mounted on a shelf behind the bar. The Yankees were playing the Red Sox, a game that would normally interest Beck, but not on a small screen viewed from the side.

The woman bartender returned and asked Beck what he wanted.

Beck said, "How about a couple of bags of those Beer Nuts?"

She smiled at him, seeming to approve of his decision to avoid anything on the menu. Beck decided he liked this woman.

When she put the two bags of peanuts on the bar next to his drink, Beck asked, "What's your name?"

"Janice," she replied.

Beck extended his hand. "Tom."

She hesitated for a moment, and then reached out to shake Beck's hand. She seemed a little embarrassed. Her hand was cold and wet from reaching into the beer cooler, and her skin was rough. Beck made sure to hold her hand softly and smile back.

"Thanks," he said, not sure what he was thanking her for. The service, or for shaking his hand, or both.

Janice nodded and moved off. As she walked away, Beck took time to enjoy the view of Janice from behind and looked for a wedding ring. There was none.

Beck opened the Beer Nuts, took a large sip of his whiskey, chased it with a swig of cold beer, and tossed a small handful of peanuts into his mouth. It all tasted fine.

He had a fairly clear side view of Oswald Remsen and the man opposite him who blocked his view of the third man at the table.

Remsen had not aged well. He was about fifteen pounds heavier than when Beck had last seen him, and back then he was overweight. His hair had thinned and gone a dirty gray.

When Beck was at Eastern, he had little interaction with Remsen. Oswald Remsen was the kind of guard who always looked to find something wrong so he could give somebody a hard time. Prison guard or prisoner, nobody wanted to fall within his gaze. It rarely turned out well.

Beck sat calmly, drinking his whiskey and beer, eating his peanuts, trying to blend in. He watched Janice. Glanced at the ball game. Kept track of Remsen and the other two. He felt the effects of the booze on his empty stomach and didn't mind it at all.

The tall working guy with the roofing-tar-stained jeans drained his glass and left.

Five minutes later, a heavyset man entered through the parking lot door. Beck recognized him. Another correction officer from Eastern who had worked Beck's tier back in the day. His last name was Morgan. As with most prison guards, Beck never heard his first name. Morgan had also gained considerable weight.

He walked straight to Oswald's table and sat next to him, nodded to the other two, but talked quietly to Remsen. Remsen didn't even bother to turn and look at Morgan. He just nodded a couple of times.

After Morgan finished reporting in, he pulled an envelope from his back pocket and slipped it to Oswald Remsen under the table. If Beck hadn't been watching carefully, he might have missed it.

Remsen took the envelope and shoved it into the inside breast pocket of his tan Windbreaker. Less than a minute later, Morgan nodded to the other two and left. He didn't stay for a beer.

Beck had finished his generous shot of Jameson and most of his beer.

Janice came by and asked, "Another round?"

"Sure."

When she returned with his drinks, Beck said, "Pretty busy for a Thursday night."

"Not really. The usual regulars."

"First time for me."

"Yeah, I haven't seen you in here before."

Beck ripped open his second bag of peanuts and offered the open bag to Janice before he took any.

She said, "No, thanks."

Beck smiled back. "Come on, you burn a ton of calories on your feet back here all night."

"Don't remind me about my feet."

"That's the worst part of it, standing all night."

"You tend bar?" she asked.

Beck nodded. "I've spent a little time behind the stick. How long have you been at it?"

"Too long."

Janice turned away and headed off to the far end of the bar. Clearly, Janice had mastered the art of being friendly while avoiding lengthy conversations with the patrons.

Beck started in on his second round of beer and whiskey. He slowed down, but the arrivals and departures of men bringing payments to Remsen didn't. Over the next forty-five minutes, three more men came in, spoke to Remsen, slipped him envelopes. The last of them stayed for a beer, but he was the only one. It was as if the others really didn't want to be seen with Remsen.

Beck had a few more words with Janice. He kept it casual. Janice responded in kind, but when Beck asked her if the man sitting in the back was the owner, Janice's brow furrowed and she quickly moved off without saying a word.

Son of a bitch. Remsen owns this shit hole. She's not worried about talking to me. She's worried about Remsen seeing her talk to me.

44

By the time Palmer and Ippolito arrived at the murder scene on Hoe Avenue, the Crime Scene Unit had sealed off the entire block.

The detective in charge of the CSU, a man named Hallandale, made sure Ippolito and Palmer wore booties and latex gloves. Palmer wanted to check out the dead bodies immediately, but Ippolito stopped him, saying, "Hang on. Let's try to figure out how this went down."

They walked near the corpse of Jerome Biggie Watkins laying half on the sidewalk, half in the street. Ippolito pointed to the two guns bagged and left on the ground next to Watkins's.

Ippolito muttered, "Fucker came well armed."

Palmer noted all the tent cards placed near shell casings lying on the street. "Looks like he nearly emptied both of 'em."

Ippolito pointed south down the block. "Bunch of casings over there, too. I assume he was shooting in that direction. Let's see if he hit anybody."

They walked to the next set of tent cards. There was no blood in the area. The CSU personnel had started the tedious job of finding where all the rounds fired from Biggie Watkins's guns had landed.

Ippolito stood in the middle of the street looking back and forth. Then he turned and walked back toward the

Watkins corpse, Palmer following. Hallandale met them and fell in step alongside.

Ippolito asked him, "So the big guy who got nailed, what was he doing? Standing over there banging it out with someone down there?"

"Not quite. We found one witness so far. She says he was standing in the street behind the driver's-side door of his car, shooting at two men coming from over there."

"Two?"

"Yes."

"Where's the car?"

"The doers who nailed him got away in it."

"What, they came on foot?"

"Yes, but we found the victim's car three blocks north at a bus stop, engine running. We figure they left their car there, drove to it, and switched. Although we haven't found anybody who saw them."

"And you know it's the vic's car how?"

"Two shots in the door. Two shots in the back of the trunk. One through the back window into the dash. And the driver's-side window was blown out."

"That's a lot of hits."

Hallandale said, "I think whoever put all the shots into the car was mostly providing cover for the second shooter coming up the sidewalk trying to close in on the dead guy."

Hallandale pointed to a dark Camry back down the street. "Shooter number one took cover behind that car. We got two bullets hitting the front of the vehicle, and we're still counting more landing around it."

He pointed to the sidewalk. "Second shooter approached on the sidewalk. Shots were fired at him, but there's no sign he fired back. No shell casings. Could be a revolver, but there aren't any bullet holes in the dead guy's car on that side. I think the second shooter held his fire until he got close enough to nail the big guy."

"Interesting. Guy must've have had some balls walking at some asshole with two guns blazing and not take a shot."

"That's the way it looks."

The three detectives retraced their steps back to Jerome Watkins. Ippolito crouched down and used the gloved forefinger of his right hand to turn the head of the corpse. Most of the face had been blown away by the gunshots to the head.

"Fuck. No open casket for this one. How do you know it's Jerome Watkins?"

Hallandale said, "Credit cards and some other ID in his wallet. But no license or cash."

Ippolito smirked, "I'm not surprised. In this neighborhood, he's lucky he still has his shoes." Hallandale gave Ippolito a look. "Well, relatively speaking," said Ippolito.

Watkins's shirt had been pulled up to reveal the gunshot wounds in his back. Palmer and the CSU detective watched Ippolito squat down and look at the bullet holes.

Ippolito looked up from his crouch and asked, "What do you make of these? You think the guy who shot him in the head put these in him, too?"

"No. Different caliber bullet. I'd say the shots in the back are nines. The head shots are forty-fives, or three-fifty-sevens. I'm guessing now, but I figure while the street shooter is giving him cover, the sidewalk shooter comes around the car and puts two in this guy's head. Then the street shooter comes up and bangs two shots into him for, I don't know, for good measure. Or because he's angry at getting shot at. Whatever. So, two shooters. The body shots were put in him after he was down. One of the slugs went through into the asphalt."

"Two shooters. Two different guns."

"Yep."

Ippolito grunted and stood up straight, his knees creaking. "Fuck. I gotta start working out."

Palmer said, "Let's go make sure the other vic is our guy."

Ippolito and Palmer made their way to the bloody corpse of Tyrell Williams lying in the back of the small park.

"Shit, man," said Ippolito. "I don't think those guys like your buddy, Tyrell. They shot the crap out of him."

Palmer stared at the body. "Fuck. It's Tyrell all right."

"What's left of him? I guess the good news is he doesn't have to worry about his busted nose anymore."

"Very funny."

Palmer examined all the bullet holes, using his pocket Maglite to compensate for the waning daylight.

"Why you figure he's back here?"

"Well, with his dick out my guess he was taking a piss. Somebody follows him. Shoots him in the back. He goes down. They stand over him, bang, bang, bang – make sure he's good and dead. I guess Beck and his boys aren't thrilled about these guys shooting their friend Paco."

"They shot Tyrell pretty much the same way they shot Derrick Watkins."

"These boys don't play around."

Ippolito walked away from the bloody corpse to the center of the small playground and leaned against the toddler-size slide. Palmer followed him.

"So your buddy Tyrell came in here to hose, or else he just likes to walk around with his dick out in a kiddie playground, which I wouldn't put past him."

"Come on, Ray."

"Hey, who knows? Anyhow . . ." Ippolito pointed from the street to Tyrell's body. "I'm figuring sidewalk shooter follows him in here, blasts the shit out of him. Gunshots wake up his buddy Jerome, who gets out of the car, pistoleros in hand."

"Right."

"Street shooter blasts away at Watkins. Sidewalk guy comes out of the park and draws fire."

Palmer added, "And then it went down like the CSU guy said."

"Yep. One shooter gives the other cover while he gets to Biggie and puts two in his head. Second shooter walks up and pounds two more shots into him just for fun. Or maybe cuz he wants to match his buddy."

"Or to send a message, like with Tyrell."

"And Derrick," said Ippolito. "Well, there's a hell of a lot of ballistics and follow-up to do. It'll take 'em days, maybe weeks, but I'm thinking we got it pretty well figured out. Now all we have to do is find out who was doing all the shooting. Hopefully, your pal Beck was one of 'em."

"Yeah. Hey, speaking of ballistics, I'm looking to get the results back on the guns I found up at Derrick Watkins's place."

"When?"

"Probably tomorrow, Friday."

"Okay, fingers crossed and all that shit. In the meantime, we should canvass the area for anybody who saw what happened. Show the pictures of Beck and those other two skels. Plus, show 'em to the witness the CSU guy found. See if we get a match."

Palmer said, "Okay, let's go."

"Hold on a sec. First, ask yourself something."

"What?"

"What the fuck were all these guys doing here?"

"What do you mean?"

"Tyrell was at the Mount Hope apartment. Probably Jerome Watkins, too. Beck and his crew were there. Why are all those same guys here?"

Palmer said, "Because Beck is trying to hunt down the rest of Watkins's crew."

"Okay, let's assume Beck and his guys are looking for the rest of Derrick's boys. How do they know to find Jerome Watkins and Tyrell Williams in this particular place?"

Palmer thought for a moment. "Well, Loretta Leon lives across the street, but why would that bring them here?"

"Yeah, why?"

"I don't know. Maybe we should go ask the old lady what was going on."

"We can, but I doubt she knows anything," said Ippolito.

"Maybe Beck's guys were here waiting for them."

"Gets back to my question. Why would Beck's guys think those two dickheads would show up here?"

"All right, Ray, why do you think?"

"Who's the only person in this whole mess connected to Lorena Leon besides our original vic, Paco Johnson, who started all this shit?"

Palmer finally got it. "The fucking daughter."

"Bingo."

"So you're saying they were all looking for the daughter."

"That's what I'm saying," said Ippolito.

"Why?"

"Maybe she knows something. Something Derrick's brother and Tyrell wanted to know."

Palmer made a face. "What could she know? She's just a whore. Why make it complicated?"

"So, what's your theory?"

"She finds out Derrick, her pimp, is dead. The whole neighborhood has to know by now. So she decides to take a little vacation. Jerome can't let her do that. He gets Tyrell to help him find her so he can put her back to work. Make sure she doesn't think the trouble her father caused got her out of peddling her ass. Tyrell suggests they stake out grandma's."

Ippolito considered Palmer's theory. He tipped his head in acquiescence. "Maybe. Maybe. But how does that explain why Beck or guys from his crew were here?"

"I don't know. If they're looking to finish off Derrick's crew, how many leads do they have to find 'em? The old lady or the granddaughter."

"You're saying they figured Watkins and company would be looking for the girl, so they came here."

"That's what I'm saying. Come on, we have to move fast on this, Ray, because like you said, the borough homicide detectives will be jumping in now, and I for one don't want to be left on the sidelines with nothing to show for our efforts."

"All right, all right," said Ippolito. "This neighborhood ain't filled with a lot of model citizens, but maybe we'll get lucky and find someone who will pick out a photo for us."

"Hopefully. When are we supposed to meet Jackson? How much time we got?"

"Eight o'clock. Couple of hours."

"Plenty of time. Be nice to have some proof Beck, or some of his people, shot Jackson's boys."

Ippolito nodded, noting Palmer had come over to the idea of setting up Beck's crew for Eric Jackson.

"Listen, John, I know I'm the one pushing this thing with Jackson, and I still say it's a necessary evil, but rule number one, and don't forget this – if shit starts to go against you, if Jackson starts pulling something you don't think you can control, do not hesitate to cut your losses and move on. You're just starting out. I'm two minutes from retiring. We get jammed up now with some bullshit, not saying we will, but if it does happen, I could lose everything. It'll hurt you but let's be honest, you got other options. They pull my pension, I'm fucked."

"Understood."

"And let me be right up front here, John."

"What?"

"I'm not doing this for me. At this stage, you know damn well I ain't advancing in rank or position. I'm going way outside the lines on this for you, kid. And I'm counting on you doing what you said when we first partnered up – putting the word in with your father to pull the right strings when I'm out there looking for the next place to land. Are we together on that? Tell me now it's a go or no-go, and no hard feelings."

"It's a go, Ray. Don't worry. We both know I can't get this done without you. I give you my word, I won't leave you high and dry. My father makes three or four calls, you'll have three or four offers. End of story."

Palmer extended his hand. Ippolito shook it, meeting Palmer eye to eye.

"Done."

They ended their handshake, and Ippolito said, "By the way, we gotta find the girl. I haven't a clue how, but we can't have her running around loose out there. Somehow, she's involved. Who knows? Maybe she was at that place when Derrick got popped. We find her, maybe you'll have yourself another witness."

"Hey, maybe so, Ray. That would be fucking great."

"Goddam right it would be."

45

As Janice walked away from him, Beck couldn't help noticing she glanced furtively at Remsen to see if he was watching her. It explained a lot about her reserve and wariness.

Remsen had always been ready to make life miserable for any prisoner or correction officer who came across his path. Having Oswald Remsen as a boss had to be a nightmare for Janice.

Beck felt his antipathy toward Remsen emerging from a deep place. He stared openly at the man, almost daring him to look in his direction. Remsen had spent decades living off the fear and misery he created in prisoners locked up without any means to fight back, guards he outranked, and this hardworking woman taking care of his piece-of-shit bar stuck out in the middle of nowhere.

Beck forced himself to stop staring at Remsen. He looked at the remains of his whiskey. It all made sense now. The fact that Remsen owned the tavern explained why he could sit in the place collecting his payoffs with impunity.

But where was the money coming from? Drugs? Beck couldn't imagine a correction officer with Remsen's years in the system taking that risk. Rita the CO accused Remsen of doing something disgusting. It didn't take much of a leap to figure prostitution might be the source of Remsen's cash under the table. Everything started to fall into place. Packy's daughter was being prostituted in the Bronx. If Remsen was running a prostitution ring upstate, he certainly wouldn't be able to recruit enough women from the locals. They had to be coming from somewhere. If Packy thought his daughter was going to be forced to sell herself for Oswald Remsen, a brutal correction officer, the absolute scum of the earth, he would have hitchhiked through hell and taken on a hundred thugs to stop it.

But how was Derrick Watkins connected to a corrupt correction guard running prostitutes in upstate New York? Had Derrick served time in Eastern? Or somebody he knew?

Beck had an urge to slip on one of the brass knuckles he'd brought, walk over to Remsen's table, and smash him in the face until he told Beck everything he wanted to know.

He turned his whiskey glass between his thumb and forefinger, staring at the bar top. He took another quick look at the overbearing man at the far end of the room, lording over everybody and everything around him.

Beck nodded to himself. He could see it. If Remsen knew Packy was onto him and soon to be released from prison, he would do whatever he could to stop Packy from causing trouble. Paco Johnson was just another ex-con with no connections, no money, no power. Totally expendable. And the fact that Remsen could take care of Packy outside Eastern meant nothing would bounce back on him.

Beck forced himself to stop thinking about it. Turn off the switch and calm down. He'd found out enough for one night. He'd made a lot of effort to conceal his identity and blend in with the locals. It would be stupid to do anything more now, especially alone and more than slightly drunk. He had to suppress his loathing for Remsen before it made him do something reckless. He'd figure this out, but not here, not now.

He finished his last swallow of Jameson and chased it with a swig of beer. The peanuts he'd eaten had done nothing but make him more hungry. Time to get the hell out of this shit hole and find something decent to eat.

When Janice turned his way, he motioned for a check.

While he waited, he took one last quick look at Remsen, now talking on his cell phone. Beck decided the other two who had been with him the whole time were probably the sons Rita had told him about.

Beck paid his bill, leaving double the amount, hoping Janice didn't have to kick back any of the tip to asshole Oswald Remsen.

He headed out of the bar, feeling the effects of the whiskey and beer. He hadn't thrown the booze down quickly. He was fine. Time to get some dinner and figure out his next move.

He wore an old denim work jacket he'd brought with him along with jeans, a khaki shirt, and sturdy lace-up shoes. Clothes that not only made him look like a local, but were also suited to the chill air settling in. Even in May the nights in upstate New York were dipping into the fifties.

Both hands were shoved into the pockets of his jacket. He absentmindedly slipped his fingers into the brass knuckles in his left pocket as he felt around for the truck key in his right.

Despite trying to put everything out of his mind, Beck kept thinking about Oswald Remsen. Trying to make the connections between Remsen, Packy, his daughter, prostitutes, and the Watkins brothers. Brothers. Dammit. Beck cursed, shaking his head at how long it at taken him to put the last part of it together. Rita had given him everything he needed. The third Remsen son working at Sing Sing. He had to be the link. Plenty of men from the Bronx connected to the Watkins's must have filtered in and out of Sing Sing.

Between the booze and being preoccupied by his sudden insight, Beck didn't hear the footsteps behind him soon enough. He didn't turn in time to avoid the baseball bat, only enough so that the bat hit him behind his right shoulder instead of squarely in the middle of his back where it might have shattered his vertebrae.

The wallop knocked Beck to the ground. With both hands in his jacket pockets, he landed awkwardly, but rolled onto his feet quickly, before the next blow from the bat put him on the ground permanently.

On his feet but off balance, Beck staggered back and ducked as the end of the bat whipped past the top of his head.

He continued backpedaling, the adrenaline, panic, and pain burning away the effects of the whiskey and beer. In the dim light of the parking area, Beck saw the man wielding the bat stood at least six six, and well over two fifty. There were two more men advancing along with him, staying back a pace, letting the hulk do the hard work. It was only a matter of time before one of the swings put him down and they all moved in for the kill.

Beck managed to get his hands out of his pockets, but only the left hand held a weapon. He ignored the other two attackers and focused on the one with the bat. He advanced on Beck, the bat held over his head like an axe. Beck knew whatever the bat hit, would break: skull, collarbone, shoulder, or an arm raised to block it.

He couldn't keep dodging the bat. He had to take it away, but how? His attacker was too big, too strong. Was this it? After all he'd been through was he going to end up beaten to death in a dirt parking lot outside a shit bar?

The blow came down at him, hard and fast. Beck changed direction and lunged forward, aiming his left hand, timing his one chance with absolute commitment, ignoring the ridiculous odds, and going for it with everything he had.

The brass knuckles smacked into the aluminum bat with a metallic thunk that surprised everybody, including Beck. The impact nearly buckled Beck's wrist. It reverberated all the way through his arm to his shoulder. Beck's brass-knuckled fist hit the bat squarely, but he only managed to deflect it.

The end of the bat pounded onto the ground. Beck stomped on the handle, forcing the bat out of the bigger man's hands, then he whipped a brass-knuckled backhand at his attacker that missed.

The big man let out a snarling growl, grabbed Beck, and threw him to the ground.

Before Beck could get to his feet, the other two were on him like jackals. The kicks rained down fast and hard, hitting his chest, ribs, back. One kick hit his right elbow. Another, the side of his head. Beck saw flashes of light in a field of black, and swung his knuckled fist blindly, feeling the brass connect with one of his attacker's legs. He immediately threw himself in that direction, rolling into a pair of legs, taking one of them to the ground.

Beck's head cleared as another boot caught him in the back, but he didn't care, he was on top of one of the attackers and landed two brass-knuckled punches as a body dived into him, driving him off the man under him.

Beck shoved off the third attacker as a huge boot hit him in his left side, paralyzing him with pain. Another kick clipped the side of his head and neck, and another his shoulder. There were more of them now. Beck lashed out with his own kick then rolled into a fetal position, hands and arms trying to protect the sides and back of his head. He wondered how many of them there were. He felt himself losing consciousness, thinking *I'm going to die,* but finding comfort knowing that Manny Guzman, Demarco Jones, and Ciro Baldassare would hunt down every one of these bastards and kill them, too.

And then he heard a gunshot, and everything went black.

46

Amelia walked around Tyrell's neighborhood for thirty minutes looking for his green Malibu. The balls of her feet began to hurt. She felt drained from the fight with Darlene and the shooting at Hoe Avenue. Her reaction to Darlene calling her a bitch had unleashed something in her that had shocked her as much as it had made her feel liberated.

After another five minutes without success, she decided the hell with Tyrell's car. Just get back in Derrick's Jeep and drive away. By now Darlene had probably made ten phone calls ratting her out.

Amelia turned a corner to head back to where she'd parked Derrick's Jeep, and there it was, Tyrell's green Chevy. She looked around. Nobody on the street. She quickly unlocked the car and turned the engine over. She navigated over to Crotona Parkway and drove north on the wide boulevard past East Tremont Avenue looking for a place to pull over.

She spotted an empty parking spot near the Happy Land Memorial, a small inconspicuous fenced-in area in the middle of the median across from a twenty-four-hour parking garage. The memorial commemorated eighty-seven people who were killed in a fire that destroyed an unlicensed social club a few blocks south on Southern Boulevard.

Amelia backed into the side-by-side parking space. The people on the street took no more notice of her than they did of the tiny memorial park. She looked through the glove compartment, hoping to find a gun. Nothing. She checked the mesh pockets behind the front seats and found nothing.

She got out and opened the trunk. At first, all she saw was the spare tire and a cardboard box filled with junk. And then she saw the laundry bag. She grabbed the neck of the bag and knew by its weight the bag didn't contain just laundry.

She pulled open the drawstring, pushed aside the dirty sheet, and found two bundles of cash, two guns, boxes of bullets, and two ledger books.

"Damn."

She immediately pulled the drawstring closed and shoved the laundry bag into the back of the trunk. She pushed the cardboard box in front of it.

She climbed back into the Malibu, trying to estimate how long it had been since Biggie had been shot and killed. At least an hour? Maybe a little more. Plenty of time for word to spread. She had to get off the streets. Right now. Lay low. Check the guns, count her cash, get something to eat. Clean up. Figure out her next move.

Amelia fired up the Chevy and headed for a motel in an industrial area almost within walking distance of the Bronx River Houses. It was the only place Amelia knew where she could get a room without a credit card or ID.

Derrick rented rooms for his whores there for short-term stays late at night. There were almost always vacancies. He would make a deal with the night manager to rent the empty rooms until morning for half the normal price. There were times when he rented two or three rooms a night. Derrick had once told her if it weren't for him the night managers would starve.

Amelia could feel her heart racing a little as she drove toward the dreary motel. From the moment she'd pulled the trigger on Derrick, Amelia knew she would have to leave the Bronx forever. If she could take down one more place, she'd be gone. It had worked at Tyrell's. Logic told her to try Biggie's house next.

Juju Jackson and Bondurant would have men out on the street looking for her. And for those guys who shot Biggie. The last place they'd expect to find her would be at Biggie's house. If she moved fast, she might make her biggest score yet. Hit the place around three, four o'clock in the morning. It would most likely only be Queenie and a few of Jerome's wives and whores in there. Hit fast and take whatever money she could find and then get the hell out of the Bronx once and for all.

Amelia told herself, calm down. Get organized. Clean up. One more hit, and she'd be gone. Maybe Atlantic City. Hell, maybe California. Figure it out once she had her stake. She had guns, bullets, money, and a car. She could do this.

47

Manny saw the expression on Demarco's face as they walked through the parking lot heading for a strip club in the back of a small shopping mall near the West Shore Expressway on Staten Island.

"Don't let Ciro see that look on your face."

"What look?"

"You know what look."

"You mean the look you get when you think of stale booze, body odor, and cheap perfume?"

"Guys on your team don't get the attraction."

"You mean the thrill of women with fake breasts and bad tattoos grinding their fat asses into your genitals?"

"My point exactly, *ese*."

Demarco suppressed a smile and asked, "Does Ciro have a stake in this place?"

"If you ask him, he'll say he has an *interest* in it."

Demarco said, "What's the difference?"

"You'd never find his name anywhere."

The club had just opened for the evening when they entered. Ciro must have told the bouncer/doorman they were coming. He waved them in and said, "He's downstairs," pointing to a door located to the right of the cashier's cubicle.

Manny led the way. Demarco wrinkled his nose at the damp basement odor. Was it the proximity to the bay?

The wildlife refuge across the road? Probably both, but the smell reminded him of something.

"By the way, Manny. We have to dump our guns in the wildlife refuge."

Manny made a face.

"Hey, my bullets aren't in any bodies back there. It's really only your gun we have to dump. I'm only tossing in the Glock so you don't feel too bad."

"The only thing too bad is, too bad you can't shoot better. Then some of your bullets would be in that fat pimp, too."

"Just laying cover for you, amigo."

Manny smiled and nodded. Patting Demarco on the back. "I know, D. *Muchas gracias.*"

"*De nada.* But we still gotta dump the guns. We'll buy you a new one out of the house fund."

They walked through a storage area containing kitchen supplies stacked neatly on wire shelving, past a doorway and into a larger area with lockers for the busboys and bartenders. There were several folding chairs set up in front of the lockers. A lingering odor of stale cigarette smoke mixed with the damp basement smell.

A large office occupied the far end of the downstairs space, warmly lit by lights recessed into a drop ceiling. There was a black leather couch, a glass coffee table flanked by two matching leather chairs in front of a large oak desk, and oak wainscoting on all four walls.

None of it quite made up for the fact that the office was in a windowless basement.

Ciro occupied half of the couch, feet resting on the coffee table, dressed in dark slacks, expensive loafers, and a black pob shirt. He pursed his lips and narrowed his eyes at Manny and Demarco when they entered.

"Bad day in the Bronx, huh, boys?"

"How can you tell?" said Manny.

"Experience. How bad?"

Manny sat in one of the leather chairs opposite Ciro. Demarco took the other, propping his feet up on the coffee table, mirroring Ciro. He compared his oxblood Allen Edmonds to Ciro's dark green shoes and decided Ciro's were probably more expensive and made out of an endangered species.

Demarco answered, "Might not be too bad. Might mean a bloodbath coming. Depends on how we navigate things."

"What do you mean by *navigate*?"

Demarco laced his fingers behind his head, concentrating on how to bring Ciro up to speed without taxing his patience.

"Ah, okay, so – there's two more dead guys. We put down one. Packy's daughter shot the other one."

"The girl? You're kidding."

"No. I'm not."

"How'd that happened?"

"I guess she came to the same conclusion we did. The bad guys had to be looking for her because she shot one of theirs. She figured they would probably stake out her grandmother's place to find her. Which they did. She dressed up like a homeless can-collector and was sneaking up on 'em as we arrived."

"What's with that kid?"

Manny answered, "She got guts. And enough brains to figure out it's better to shoot them before they shoot her."

"Hey, she wants to take out the whole fucking gang, good for her."

"Theoretically," said Demarco. "But I doubt she's going to get much further. One of Manny's connections, an old-timer up in the Bronx, gave us the rundown on what she's going up against. The Watkins boys were part of a much larger organization."

"How large?"

Manny interjected. "Pretty much a bottomless glass."

"Of what?"

Demarco answered, "Mostly local young bloods running around with guns trying to build a rep so they can gang up. Plus a few hard-core guys. Could add up to quite a few. Point being, Packy's kid isn't going to last much longer if she keeps shooting people in that part of the Bronx."

Manny said, "And it ain't going to be a clean death. They're going to make an example of her."

Ciro nodded, "So we got two more dead guys, a sixteen-year-old girl looking at a gruesome death, and we don't know shit about who shot Packy."

Demarco said, "I'm figuring the guy who runs this set knows a lot about who shot Packy and why. His name is Eric Jackson."

Manny interjected, "Juju Jackson. His enforcer goes by the name Whitey Bondurant. You ever hear of them?"

"Hell no. So what do you guys want to do?"

Demarco said, "I think we have three options. Let me take you through them. See if you agree."

Ciro whipped his feet off the coffee table and leaned forward.

"Okay. Shoot."

"That's option one."

"Yeah, who exactly?" asked Ciro.

Demarco said, "Jackson and Bondurant would be at the top of my list. They have to be looking to kill Packy's kid. And James. And us. And one way or another, they're behind Packy getting shot."

"Okay, how do we get to them?"

Manny said, "That's the problem. No clue yet."

Demarco said, "We're not even close. We would have to really work it right."

"Okay, so what's option two?"

"Option two is, we find the girl. Losing Packy was bad enough. They're going to do more than just shoot her. Plus, the cops will be looking for her at some point. Better for us they don't get their hands on her. Also, she might be able to help us figure out how to get to Jackson and Bondurant."

Ciro said, "What's option three?"

"Wait for Walter to arrive back and find out what the cops are doing. Then wait for James to return and see where he's at. That might change our priorities."

Ciro said, "I ain't sitting around waiting. We don't know how to get to the big boys yet. So I say we find the kid."

Manny said, "I agree. That's what James wanted us to do while he's gone. Find the brother, or the girl. Brother's dead. Time to go for the girl."

Ciro said, "Any idea how?"

Demarco said, "Yes, I think I know, but we'll have to wait a couple of hours or so."

"Fine by me. That'll give us time to get something to eat."

Without missing a bit, Demarco and Manny both said, "Not here."

48

The gunshot Beck heard before he lost consciousness had been fired by Oswald Remsen. He stepped into the pack attacking Beck, grabbing and pulling men off.

"Goddammit, stop it. Stop! I don't want him dead. Back off, Back off."

He went down on one knee to see if Beck was still breathing. "All right. He's alive." He pulled Beck's hands away from his head and rolled him onto his back. The brass knuckles were still on Beck's left hand. Remsen removed them and slipped them into the pocket of his Windbreaker.

"Straighten his legs. Give him some goddam air."

Remsen stood up and stared down at Beck, waiting for him to come around. He kicked the bottom of Beck's foot. Beck stirred. Remsen kicked again, harder. Beck came to, instinctively tried to sit up, but fell back as a piercing pain shot across the middle of his back. Bruised ribs. Maybe cracked. He gritted his teeth, breathed carefully, dizzy but trying to focus on what was happening.

There were five men standing around him, and one man on the ground, the one Beck had gotten on top of and beaten.

Remsen told the two men nearest to Beck, "Get him on his feet."

They were the two who'd sat with Remsen in the bar. Remsen's sons. They lifted Beck up, causing enough pain that Beck stopped breathing. They propped him against his Ford Ranger.

As they held him, Beck leaned forward and threw up, feeling the acid sting of the whiskey and beer coming out of him. Some of it hit the bigger man's pants and shoe. Both men cursed Beck and shoved him back against the truck, which caused Beck even more pain than vomiting had.

Beck's head cleared a bit.

Oswald Remsen stepped forward, his sons still holding Beck's arms, grabbed a fistful of Beck's hair, and held his head up.

Beck looked back at Remsen without expression.

"You are one stupid, sorry son of a bitch, my friend. You think you can walk into my place and eyeball me, ask questions, and I'm not gonna notice it? I been watching sneaky assholes like you a long time, boy."

Beck didn't respond.

"I recognized you about two seconds after you showed up. You're that piece of shit cop killer who was in my prison awhile back." Remsen paused, trying to remember the name. "Beck. That's right, your name is Beck. I know you. What I don't know is what the hell you're doing in my bar."

For a moment, Beck thought about spitting in Oswald Remsen's face, but he knew another round of fists and feet might finish any chance he had of surviving this.

"I'm gonna ask you one time, what were you doing in my bar?"

Beck croaked out one word. "Drinking."

"Asshole." Remsen shoved Beck's head away and told the others, "All right, let's get him out of here before anybody notices this commotion. Who's got cuffs?"

One of the men on the fringe stepped forward and extended a pair of handcuffs toward Remsen.

"What am I?" said Remsen. "Workin' for you? Go on, cuff him. Joe, empty his pockets."

Joe Remsen yanked out Beck's wallet, money, truck keys, and his other set of brass knuckles. He handed everything to his father. Remsen shoved the contents into the pockets of his Windbreaker without bothering to look at any of it.

Once they were done searching him, Remsen's man pulled Beck's arms behind his back and cuffed him.

Beck made sure to clench his hands into tight fists so that his wrists were a fraction of an inch thicker than they would be when he unclenched them.

After the man finished cuffing Beck, Remsen told him, "Okay, Fred, get Vic into your car and drive him on over to the hospital. Tell them he was in a bar fight."

Remsen told his sons holding Beck, "Put him in the GMC. William, you stay with him in the back. If he moves, knock the shit out of him. Joe, you drive. Follow me."

Remsen's sons pulled Beck toward a new GMC Terrain. As they walked toward the car, Beck opened and closed his mouth slowly to make sure they hadn't broken his jaw. He could feel his left eye swelling, remembering a stinging kick that had hit him on the cheekbone. He opened his left eye wide, hoping it wouldn't close completely. He could breathe normally so his nose wasn't busted. He decided his ribs were bruised, not broken. His right shoulder where the baseball bat had hit him was already sore and swollen. His knees were okay, but his arms, right thigh, back, and hip would be covered with deep bruises come morning. He forced himself to stop thinking about the pain. If he didn't keep focused and concentrate, there would be no morning.

William Remsen shoved Beck into the backseat of the SUV. Beck had to lean forward because his hands were cuffed behind his back. He laid his forehead on the passenger-seat headrest.

William slammed the door. Beck leaned away just in time to avoid being smacked on his throbbing shoulder.

Joe Remsen got behind the wheel.

While William walked around the back of the GMC, Beck slipped his right thumb behind his belt and felt for a small, thin piece of steel taped under a piece of masking tape.

By the time Beck walked out of prison, he so hated being handcuffed he'd made it a point to study every means, every trick invented to escape from them. It boiled down to two methods. Either using a universal key to open the cuffs, or a shim. Universal keys didn't open every brand of cuff and were much harder to conceal, so Beck settled on shims. He taped them on the back of every belt he owned, under the tongues of his shoes, and hid one in his wallet.

Even under the best of circumstances it wasn't easy to blindly slip a shim into the tiny opening where cuff fitted into the lock housing. Beck didn't want to think about how much harder it would be trying to do it riding in a moving car, with his hands cuffed behind him, after a brutal beating.

In the few moments William took to walk around the SUV, Beck had freed the shim from his leather belt. He held it in his right hand, waiting until William climbed in next to him and the GMC stopped rocking.

William leaned forward and spoke to his brother. "You noticed the old man took Austen with him."

"Yeah."

"I bet he's giving him hell for not being able to take out this guy."

"He should."

William sat back. "I guess we're going to the place."

"I guess so."

While they talked, Beck slid the thin piece of metal between his forefinger and middle finger a split second before William jabbed an elbow into his left arm.

"Asshole. Puke on me and now we gotta sit here and smell your stink."

The blow nearly made Beck drop the tiny shim.

Beck stifled a curse. Losing the wafer thin, inch-long piece of steel, barely wider than a matchstick meant losing his life.

Joe Remsen shoved the SUV into drive and accelerated out of the parking lot, sending Beck back into his seat, causing more pain. Dirt and gravel spewed as he caught up to a large Ford F-350 truck in front of him.

Beck tried to ignore the pain and concentrated on relaxing his arms, shoulders, and back. If he stiffened up now, he wouldn't be able to maneuver into position to use the shim.

Beck leaned over so he could see out the windshield. The truck ahead of them looked new, its metallic black paint gleamed in the glare of the GMC's headlights.

Beck took a sidelong glance at William. He resembled his father, with the same bloated piggy face. Joe must have taken after the mother. He was shorter than his father and brother, wiry, with sharp features and dark, stringy hair. He reminded Beck of a weasel.

Nobody spoke during the drive. Beck breathed deeply, slowly, and quietly.

There was nothing to be done except use his mind to seal off the pain. Every breath hurt him, which made it more difficult, but he kept at it, trying to slow his heart rate and stave off the fear and dread over what was coming. He assumed they were taking him someplace where they would beat him until they found out whatever they could. And after that, kill him.

Beck stopped thinking about it. He tried to take note of what direction they were driving in, and how long they drove. But mostly he sat visualizing the shim sliding into an infuriatingly small space where the ratcheted end of the left handcuff slid into the lock housing.

Once he maneuvered the shim into the opening, it would stop where the ratchet on the cuff met the edge of the pawl inside the housing. The shim had to be pushed past that point for it to release the cuff. But the shim was wafer thin. Trying to push it past the pawl would bend it. The only way to do it was to push gently and squeeze the cuffs farther closed. That would move the shim between the ratchet edge and the pawl. Then and only then would the cuff slide open.

But if the person putting the cuffs on made them too tight, there would be no room to close them farther. Beck had clenched his hands to make his wrists a tiny bit thicker, and the CO who'd cuffed him had learned to avoid closing the cuffs tight on the skin to avoid endless complaints. There was room, but for only one more click.

Suddenly, the brake lights of the truck up ahead flared. Joe Remsen braked hard, pitching Beck forward against the back of the passenger seat.

The sudden movement caused a wave of nausea to come over Beck. He thought he might vomit again. A sign of a concussion. He breathed deeply and swallowed the bile rising into his mouth.

The truck up ahead took a sharp right turn into a scrub forest. Joe followed, bouncing off the asphalt onto a rutted tire-track path that cut through the scrub forest. The SUV's suspension jounced and creaked as it traveled over the uneven ground. Every jolt sent pain through Beck's rib cage, but he used it to steel himself and his resolve. Twice the GMC dropped into deep ruts and several times it banged into stones embedded in the ground. The trees and foliage were so dense the SUV's headlights made it look like they were traveling through a raggedy green tunnel.

Beck knew he might die this night. But not as a beaten, helpless, handcuffed ex-con. He was not going to let these arrogant bastards, who one way or another had been responsible for the death of a man better than they would ever be, kill him without a fight.

Finally, they emerged into a circular clearing about the size of an acre. The two vehicles veered away from each other and parked at opposite edges of the clearing, pointing toward the center.

When they cut their engines and turned off their headlights, everything plunged into near darkness, barely illuminated by a half moon obscured by the clouds.

William and Joe got out of the GMC and walked across the clearing to join their father and Austen. As the dome light in the SUV faded to black, Beck could see them gathered around Remsen, who was working on something he'd placed on the hood of his Ford. In a few seconds, a harsh white light flared as Remsen fired up a Coleman lantern. He adjusted the flame inside the cloth mantel, and all four men stood talking in a huddle.

The moment William and Joe got out of the GMC, Beck began to work on the handcuffs. He took one quick breath to focus, turned his right hand over, and slowly opened his fist. Carefully, he brushed the thumb of his left hand over the palm of his right, feeling for the shim. It was there, stuck to his palm.

He inhaled and exhaled slowly, and concentrated on moving carefully and methodically. He picked up the shim from the palm of his right hand with his left forefinger and thumb, and transferred it to the same fingers on his right hand. He gently gripped the tiny piece of metal, feeling the shim's small, round top, turning it in the right direction.

While holding the shim, he used the side of his right thumb to feel for the opening into the cuff housing. Experience guided his movements. He carefully, blindly probed for the opening.

The cuffs were positioned so the keyhole faced out, which meant Beck had to twist his torso to position the shim at the correct angle. It caused more pain, but he ignored it. He kept his eyes closed so he wouldn't be distracted. He didn't worry about Remsen and the others. He put all his attention into visualizing the tiny opening and the tip of his shim edging toward it. Probing. Gently trying to slide the tip of the shim into the impossibly small space.

He couldn't find it. The tension built to a point where Beck stopped breathing.

He was trying too hard. Pushing too hard. He stopped everything. Relaxed his arms, shoulders, neck. He looked up. Inhaled, exhaled. And then began all over again, slowly, patiently.

He tried to forget they would be coming for him any second. Focus everything on the shim. Where the fuck was it hitting? He thought he felt the tip catch the edge of the opening, but it wasn't moving in.

Beck changed the angle. Bent his left elbow, raised the hand behind his back. Twisted around more. Causing more pain. Tried again. And again. He took a breath, held it.

Go slow. Try three times in a row. It's got to be there.

One, two . . . and then, without warning, lower than where he thought the opening was, the shim stopped. Was it in the opening? He couldn't tell.

He rolled his forefinger onto the rectangular top of the shim and pushed. Gently so he wouldn't bend the wafer-thin piece of metal. A little more. It seemed to move into the slot. Relax. Don't screw it up.

Now came the last part. He positioned his right thumb on the top of the cuff; his last three fingers against the bottom. Holding the shim in place with the side of his forefinger, he was about to squeeze the cuffs, when suddenly, without warning, the car door opened.

He fell out of the SUV and slammed onto the ground, all his weight falling on his damaged shoulder, jarring his bruised ribs. His feet were still in the GMC. A hand grabbed the collar of his denim jacket.

It was the big one, Austen, sent to get him.

He pulled Beck out of the car, painfully raking Beck's ankles over the door jamb, turned him onto his back, and dragged him out into the clearing, his cuffed hands underneath him, like Beck was a sack of garbage.

Beck twisted sideways so the cuffs wouldn't grind into the dirt and grass, ripping the shim out. But it was too late, too late. He'd been slammed onto the ground, dragged across the dirt, everything was lost.

The rage that enveloped Beck was so utterly without bounds nothing mattered now. Not the pain. Not the handcuffs. Not even dying. His entire being focused on the stupid, heartless bully dragging him through the dirt, his back turned to him in disdain.

James Beck was not going to be dragged to his death.

He violently twisted around so he faced the ground, pulled his knees under him, and with all his strength, wrenched his upper body backward, stopping his forward movement just long enough to get his right foot under him.

Austen stopped to look behind him. Beck pulled his other foot under him and exploded forward. His head and shoulder hit full force into the back of Austen's legs, which crumpled under the impact. He let go of Beck and tried to get his arms in front of him to break his fall, but he landed hard, face first. Beck instantly scrambled up onto the big man's back. Austen rolled over and shoved Beck off him.

Like a cat, Beck twisted onto his knees. Austen, still on his back, tried to sit up. Beck reared back and snapped his forehead into Austen's face. Beck heard as much as he felt the satisfying crunch of bone and cartilage shattering.

Austen fell back flat on the ground. Beck scuttled forward on his knees, reared back and using the only body part he could hit with, slammed his forehead into the Austen's face again, and again, and again. Beck didn't care if he split his own head open. He didn't care if he knocked himself out. All he wanted to do was to hit and hit and hit.

The big man tried to block Beck's head, but he was no match for Beck's strength and rage. Blood covered Austen's face. He couldn't see. Beck hit him again, and broke Austen's right eye socket, and when he turned away, Beck's slammed his forehead down and fractured Austen's jaw, cracking two of his rear molars as they sheared against each other.

Finally, out of total desperation, the brute managed to blindly block Beck's head and knock him off his knees so he couldn't hit him again. But Beck would not be stopped. He quickly got to his feet, struggling to get his balance with his hands cuffed behind him. Beck heard shouts. He sensed the others running toward him.

Austen, semiconscious, tried to push himself upright with his left hand, but Beck kicked the arm out from under him, and when Austen fell back, Beck stomped his elbow, fracturing the humerus with a dull crack, tearing cartilage and ligaments, fracturing the ulna out of the socket. Austen screamed, his huge arm useless.

Beck heard shouts and footsteps pounding, closing in.

The big man, still on his back, roared out in pain and frustration.

Beck aimed carefully, pivoted, and stomped his left foot into Austen's exposed throat, crushing the larynx nearly flat, putting all his two hundred pounds on the man's throat, pressing his weight against the violent flailing of a dying man as something smashed into the side of his head, sending him into oblivion.

49

A ringing sensation from a deep black void pulled at Beck while his brain remained unresponsive to the hand slapping his face. And then suddenly consciousness crashed onto him as he felt himself choking. He tried to raise an arm to block the water splashing into his nose and mouth, but couldn't, so he turned away from the water, spitting and choking. The pouring stopped.

A voice yelled, "Stand up. Get up, goddammit!"

Beck didn't recognize the voice. He didn't remember where he was. And then everything came flooding back. He realized why he couldn't block the water. He was lying in a field outdoors, in the black of night, handcuffed.

"Get up before I shoot you right now, you son of a bitch."

Now he recognized the voice. Oswald Remsen.

Beck struggled into a sitting position, blinking away the wet until he could make out the three of them standing about five feet away. Remsen and his two sons. William, the larger one, held the Coleman lantern. Oswald aimed a .45 semi-automatic at him. Joe, standing next to his father, pointed his .38 service revolver at Beck.

Beck struggled to his feet, still trying to blink away what he realized was not just water, but also blood dripping into his eyes.

Oswald yelled at him.

"You animal piece of shit. You killed him. You goddam killed him."

Beck didn't answer.

"You had to turn animal, like every fucking piece of shit convict always does. So now we're going to skin you and gut you like the animal you are. I just hope you don't die too soon." Oswald pointed to his left and yelled, "Walk."

Beck turned and saw nothing but darkness until William Remsen stepped in front of him holding the lantern.

The other two fell in behind Beck, both of their guns pointed at his back.

Beck had to walk fast to keep up with William and the circle of lantern light. He stumbled for the first few yards, but walking revived him somewhat. The blood dripping from his forehead channeled down the side of his nose and mostly out of his eyes.

Remsen hadn't shot him after he'd killed Austen, so he still wanted answers. Maybe he could use that to find out why Packy Johnson had been killed. Then he might at least go to his grave knowing the truth of it.

After about a minute walking, the light from the lantern revealed a wooden lean-to about ten yards ahead of them. Beck caught an odor of rotten meat.

"Stop."

William continued toward the structure, which was about ten yards wide, eight feet deep. The open side facing them stood eight feet high. The roof angled down to about five feet at the back where it met a plywood wall. Three sturdy fence poles, each about twelve inches in diameter, supported the two-by-four framing and a roof covered in asphalt shingles.

William raised the Coleman lantern and hung it from an eyehook screwed into the two-by-four supporting the roof. The white light revealed the source of the stench. Drying deer skins hung stretched across the back wall. Various size butcher knives and hacksaws hung from the poles supporting the roof. There was a set of rope and tackle attached to a crossbeam. The dirt under the lean-to appeared discolored and crusted in spots where they'd bled out the animals.

Fifty-pound bags of lime were stacked at one end of the lean-to for covering the guts and organs they buried after dressing deer. About a cord of split wood had been loosely thrown into a pile at the other end of the lean-to.

It didn't take a huge leap of imagination for Beck to picture himself suspended by the rope and tackle. He wondered which of the Remsens would slice him until he told them what they wanted to know. He wondered how far into the forest they would haul the pieces of his body for burial.

He contemplated the possibility of getting his hands in front of him. If he could, he'd try to grab Oswald Remsen's throat and not let go until they killed him. Hopefully, he'd have time to crush Remsen's larynx before that happened.

Oswald pointed his gun at a small tree stump standing on its end outside the lean-to and told Beck, "Sit."

The log was about a thirty inches high, barely wide enough to sit on. Beck straddled the stump and sat on it, spreading his feet to keep his balance with his hands cuffed behind him, his back facing the lean-to. Remsen and his sons stood in a semicircle in front of him, just within the light cast by the Coleman lantern hanging in the lean-to behind Beck. Between them was a pile of ashes and charred wood, the remains of many campfires.

Oswald Remsen said, "We both know you're going to die here tonight, it's up to you how. Answer my questions fast, no bullshit, and we'll finish you with a bullet to the head. You don't, we'll gut you and rip off strips of your skin until we get our answers."

"That simple, huh?"

"That simple, convict."

"How do I know you're not going to torture me anyhow?"

"You don't."

Beck nodded. "How about this – you want to find out what I know. I want to go to my grave knowing a few things. How about you ask me a question, I'll answer it. Then I ask you a question, and you answer it. Get it all out fast and easy."

"You're an idiot. Last chance, a bullet, or knives and pliers?"

"Try the knife if you want, but I fucking guarantee you it'll be hours before you find out anything. If ever."

"Fine by me. We got all night."

"Really." Beck pointed with his head toward the body somewhere in the dark field off to the left. "You going to have enough time for me, and for burying your buddy?"

"Best you don't remind me of that."

"Let's cut the bullshit. You could have killed me back in the parking lot. You could have killed me after I took out your man who likes hitting people with baseball bats. You want information, I'm making a reasonable offer."

"I got half a mind to start slicing you up right now. See how tough you are."

"Up to you," said Beck. "They say people who are tortured will say anything. You never know what's true."

Oswald stared at Beck. Beck returned his gaze. Oswald couldn't see any fear in James Beck's eyes.

"All right, tough guy. We'll play it your way for a couple of minutes. One way or another, I'm gettin' my answers. First question: Why are you up here poking your nose around?"

Beck answered quickly. "Because you're the one responsible for murdering Paco Johnson."

"Who?"

"Paco Johnson. He was released from Eastern on Tuesday."

"Where the hell did you come up with me being responsible for the murder of some worthless convict?"

"Hey, I get a question now."

"Fuck you."

"It's an easy question."

"I'm not playing games."

"Neither am I. Did you, or did you not, arrange the murder of Paco Johnson?"

Oswald Remsen hesitated, then answered. "What the hell, you're not going to be alive to do anything about it. First of all, I couldn't give a shit about that asshole. A goddam pain in the ass. Some new fish transferred in and told him some shit about his daughter getting whored out. So what? That's got nothing to do with me. I didn't arrange for anybody to kill him and trust me, I've paid my dues, boy. I got enough connections to have a piece of shit like him taken out in two seconds if I want to.

"All I did was give some people a heads-up cuz I knew the guy was a troublemaker. What'd he do? Go and piss somebody off? If they killed him, it ain't my fault."

"What people?"

"Not your turn, convict."

"Okay."

Beck cleared his throat and spat into the ground, buying time, carefully clocking the position of each man. The elder Remsen stood in front of him, five feet away. Joe, still holding his revolver, stood about four feet to the right of his father. William stood about ten feet to the left of Oswald, a few steps closer to the lean-to.

"Who told you to come looking for me?"

"Nobody. A man gets out of prison after seventeen years, he's not going to get killed for something he did a few hours after he got home. It had to be connected to something that happened at Eastern."

"You're lying. There's a whole lot of people in that prison, convicts and staff, but you came looking for me. I want to know who put you onto me. And I'm warning you, convict, the next thing comes out of your mouth better be the truth, or I'm stringing you up and cutting it out of you."

Beck had no intention of telling Remsen the truth. It would mean implicating Walter Ferguson and Rita. He shifted his weight on the narrow stump, pictured the possibility of diving to his left to get out of the circle of light, and trying to get his cuffed hands under his legs and in front of him.

He gently pulled the cuffs wide, gauging how many links were in the chain, trying to figure if he could pull his hands far enough apart to get them past his hips and legs. It felt like the cuffs weren't spreading apart much at all. Maybe the links were kinked. He ran his right thumb back and forth along the chain joining the cuffs, and suddenly felt something. Was it true? He ran his thumb over the handcuff housing. He couldn't believe what he felt.

Carefully, he brushed his thumb over the lock housing. It was true. He could feel the shim, still stuck in the slot between the cuff and the lock housing. The top of the shim had been bent over from Austen dragging him, but the rest was in the slot, jammed in with dirt and grass.

He needed time to try to clear away the dirt and straighten out the shim.

"All right. There's more to it."

"What?"

"Like I said, I figured Johnson's murder had to have something to do with prison. So I made a few calls. I still know guys serving time at Eastern. I talked to an old-timer in there who told me Packy didn't have any beefs going on in the population. Cons respected him. Nobody wanted to do anything to jam him up before he was about to be released."

"I'll want to know who you talked to, but go on."

"So if it wasn't the convicts, I figured it had to be something between him and the guard staff."

"Why?"

"Process of elimination. Had to be one or the other."

While he talked, Beck cleared away the dirt and bent back the shim. He shifted on the stump, trying to give the impression that sitting on it was uncomfortable, but really so he could maneuver his hands into position.

"You're trying my patience, Beck. Why me? Of all the guards at Eastern, why me?"

"The truth? I had no real idea you had anything to do with it. I just wanted to talk to some guards, see what I could find out. I've been in town all day. Didn't take long to find the COs watering hole. I went into that bar to see if I could get some information. And then I see you sitting there, fat and happy, collecting payoffs."

"This answer is startin' to sound like total bullshit."

"Why? I went to find Eastern guards and there you were, taking envelopes under the table from guys coming in and out. I asked myself what the hell is Remsen up to? Is he selling drugs? Nah. Too risky. He doesn't have the guts. What else is there? Where's the money coming from? I put that together with Packy getting shot trying to save his daughter who was being prostituted. I figure you're running whores, Remsen. I'm figuring the same guys prostituting Packy Johnson's daughter, Derrick and Jerome Watkins, are supplying women to you. I haven't quite figured out who your customers are. You can't be running hookers through the prison. Where's the business coming from?"

"You're not as smart as you think you are."

"Enlighten me."

"Mostly dumb-ass horny truckers, asshole. We've got whores working truck stops, bars, motels, and dives everywhere between Westchester and Albany. Only thing holding us back is getting more whores from the mud people."

Beck gave Remsen an admiring nod, shifting again on his stump to position his fingers so he could gently

313

squeeze the cuff on his left wrist tighter while pushing the shim in with his forefinger.

"Was Packy's kid going to be one of your whores? Is that why he went after her as soon as he got back to the city?"

"That's two questions, convict."

"Take your pick."

"It was a little more complicated than that, but close enough. But you still ain't telling me the truth. I don't believe you just walked into my bar. How'd you know to come looking at me? Who ratted me out?"

Beck ignored the question. He had to keep Remsen talking, because if he got the damned handcuff off, there would be no more questions and answers. Just blood and chaos until either they were dead, or he was.

Beck said, "And you still haven't answered mine, asshole. Who did you give the heads-up to about Packy Johnson?"

Remsen yelled at Beck, taking a step toward him. "That's it. Enough of this bullshit, you lying piece of shit. William, set up the block and tackle."

Time was up. Beck abandoned all caution. He squeezed the cuff firmly, pushing it all the way closed, hopefully the shim with it. He reared up on the stump and shouted, "Fuck you!" as he twisted his wrist and pulled upward to see if the cuff would slide open. It did, surprising Beck so much that for a moment, he sat motionless.

Oswald had worked himself into a fury, yelling at Beck, "You're going to tell me everything goddam thing I want to know before the night is out." He turned and said, "Joe, get him on his feet."

As Joe Remsen moved, Beck stood up, brought his suddenly freed hands in front of him, bent down, and grabbed the log he'd been sitting on. He underhanded the stump straight at Remsen's face, putting everything he had into it.

Forty pounds of hardwood flew at Remsen, bottom rising upward. Remsen stood immobile, stunned. He didn't even have time to flinch as the bottom of the log shattered his jaw and the top smashed into his forehead. He fell backward, unconscious before he hit the ground.

As soon as the log left Beck's hands, he was already moving toward the falling Remsen. Neither of the sons reacted, too stunned and confused to move.

Beck made it almost halfway to the father before Joe turned to point his gun at him. By the time Joe Remsen pulled the trigger on his revolver, Beck was diving toward Oswald, reaching for the gun in his hand.

William Remsen turned, drawing another service revolver.

Beck slid past Remsen, but at the last second grabbed the barrel of Remsen's gun, pulled the semi-automatic out of Oswald's hand with his left hand, turned it, and grabbed the handle with his right. Joe Remsen opened fire. Beck rolled behind Oswald and fired two fast, focused shots at Joe Remsen. William fired a shot. Beck pointed behind him and fired blindly at William, who flinched, ducked, and ran for cover in the lean-to.

Beck's shots blew Joe Remsen off his feet. William made it to the lean-to and hunkered down near the woodpile at the back corner of the lean-to, behind the lantern light. Beck scrambled away from the circle of light, got to his feet, and stepped back deeper into the darkness.

Beck stood unseen, trying not to make any noise, pulling himself together.

In eight seconds, it had gone from three to one, to one on one.

Beck stood still, positive the light from the lantern shining in front of William prevented him from seeing anything in the darkness. But he couldn't see William, either.

Beck stayed back out of the light and slowly, silently walked counterclockwise toward the lean-to.

William shaded his eyes, trying to see where Beck had gone. He thought he saw movement and fired off two shots, one of which came close enough to make Beck drop to the ground and stop moving.

Beck pointed Oswald Remsen's gun at the lean-to, watching for movement. He was familiar with the weapon, a 9-mm Beretta 92FS that could be loaded with either a high-capacity magazine that held fifteen bullets, or a regular magazine that held ten. With the regular magazine he had seven rounds left, but there was no way to know which magazine was in the gun, or even if it had been fully loaded. Checking the magazine would give away his position.

William had a six-shot revolver, but Beck had no way of knowing how many bullets he might have, or if he'd already reloaded the gun.

Beck fired a shot at where William's muzzle had flashed and rolled to his left. William returned fire where Beck had been, a disciplined single shot. The bullet plowed into the ground, sending up a spray of dirt and grass.

Beck rolled onto his back, took the dangling left cuff and attached it to the closed cuff on his right hand so it wouldn't distract him. He then rolled back onto his feet and quickly angled around past the far end of the lean-to, making sure to stay hidden in the dark. From that position, Beck didn't have an angle to shoot into the corner. If he wanted to take out William, he'd have to step into the light and put himself in the line of fire.

Beck stopped, wiped his face with his sleeve, getting ready.

He pointed the Beretta straight up and visualized the spot where he estimated William would be crouched behind the pile of wood. Beck knew once he started, he could not stop.

He took a deep breath, exhaled slowly, positioned his feet, and came around the corner of the lean-to firing the Beretta, advancing, firing, moving toward Remsen, shooting nonstop, aiming above and to the left of the muzzle flash, all the while angling away from Remsen's return fire.

Wood chips flew, the exploding gunpowder blinded him, but Beck never stopped. All in. Win or lose.

The Beretta clicked empty. Only a ten-round magazine.

Beck kept moving left out of the light, dropped down flat, blinking to get his night vision back, trying to hear any movement with his ears still ringing.

If William Remsen had any ammunition left, Beck knew he'd lost. He strained to hear any sound from the lean-to. Nothing.

He waited. An eerie silence filled the clearing. Still nothing.

Beck stood up and walked quietly toward the lean-to, making sure to remain in the dark. He stopped and carefully leaned around the sidewall of the lean-to. There was just enough light to make out an inert heap in the back corner. William Remsen.

Beck had no idea how close William Remsen had come to hitting him, and he didn't care.

He stepped in, grabbed the lantern off the hook, and placed it on the woodpile in front of Remsen's body. Two of his bullets had hit Remsen. One below his right eye, and one in the side of William's neck. Beck didn't bother feeling for a pulse. The 9mm bullet under the eye had blown a sizeable hole out of the back of William's head, and the other had destroyed a good portion of his throat.

Beck picked up the lantern and walked over to Joe Remsen. His two shots had hit him center chest, both bullets within an inch of each other. Dead man number two.

That left the father. As Beck approached the older man, the lantern casting its white glow out in front of him, he saw Oswald's head moving. The man emitted a low, agonized sound. When Beck got within a couple of feet, he saw why. Two of the bullets the sons had fired at him had hit their father. One near Remsen's groin. A massive amount of blood stained the ground.

The other bullet had hit him in his left side about six inches below his armpit, perhaps taking out a lung, and maybe hitting the spine.

Beck stepped away, letting the man bleed out and die in his own time.

He walked over to Joe Remsen and rummaged around in his pockets to find a key to unlock his right cuff. He got it off in a few seconds, pocketing the cuffs and key. He stood and surveyed the scene in front of him.

A gunfight had occurred here, but Beck realized it didn't have to involve him.

The two bullets in the father were from his sons' guns. And the bullets in the sons were from the father's gun.

Beck walked over to Joe Remsen and took the revolver out of his hand. He brought it over to Oswald and put the gun in the dying man's hand. He aimed the revolver into the night sky so the bullet wouldn't be found, and pulled the trigger so there would be gunpowder residue on Oswald's hand. Then he wiped the Beretta to remove his prints, took Joe's revolver out of Oswald's hand, and replaced it with the Berretta.

He wiped Oswald Remsen's prints off Joe Remsen's gun, and put the revolver back in the son's hand.

Next, he retraced his steps and carefully walked with the lantern to each place where he'd fired Remsen's Beretta, looking for spent cartridges. He found eight out of the ten in the white glare of the Coleman lantern, picked up each one with the tip of a twig he found and scattered them near the fallen Oswald Remsen.

He stood for a moment thinking it through. Okay, but what about the dead big guy over near the GMC? Another body to account for. How? Maybe the sons took him down and then went after the father. Why? Maybe in a fight over the money in Remsen's pocket.

Beck thought about the log he'd thrown at Oswald. He left it where it was. Somebody threw it at the father. Part of the fight. Which gave him an idea. Beck picked up a piece of hardwood from the pile in the lean-to and walked out to Austen's body. He slammed the wood into Austen's face a few times, then laid it across his crushed throat and stepped on it.

He returned to the area in front of the lean-to and lightly scuffed over where his shoes might have left impressions. His footprints really didn't concern him too much. There had been others at this site with shoes making marks different from the Remsens'.

Even if somebody had enough experience in forensics to piece together the horrendous mess, so what? If by some miracle they figured out there had to be a fourth shooter, it wouldn't lead to him.

He reached into the pocket of Oswald Remsen's Windbreaker and retrieved everything of his they had taken from him. Lastly, he took out one of the envelopes of money stuffed into Remsen's inside pocket, leaving the others.

Beck kicked over the lantern as if it had been knocked over in the fight, assuming it would burn out soon.

He rubbed his face with both hands. Took a deep breath. Rolled his head and moved his arms. The cut on his forehead had stopped bleeding. All in all, he didn't feel too bad, mostly thanks to the adrenaline still coursing through him. He'd be feeling the effects of this night soon, and for a long time after.

Didn't matter. He felt able to finish what he had to do.

He angled away from the murder scene and walked across the dark clearing toward Oswald's Ford F-350. He'd leave the GMC, which could have held four men.

The lantern sputtering on the ground gave off enough light to reflect off the truck. He pulled open the driver's-side door, hoping he didn't have to walk all the way back and look for the keys. He didn't. They were in the ignition. Even better, there was a half-full bottle of water in the truck's cup holder.

Beck decided he just might make it through this night.

50

Raymond Ippolito drove. John Palmer sat in the passenger seat, trying to match names in an NYPD file with names on an FBI organizational chart of Bronx gang members. In a horizontal line under mug shots of Eric Juju Jackson and Floyd Whitey Bondurant, identified as Sovereign Commanders aka The Chosen, were eight squares. Two of the squares had the names and pictures of Jerome Watkins and Derrick Watkins, labeled Harrod Avenue Villains, and underneath them a vertical list of twenty-two names.

Ippolito glanced occasionally at Palmer with growing impatience.

"Is that crap showing you anything you really need to know, John?"

"Visual aid, my man."

"For who?"

"Jackson."

"That's part of your pitch?"

"Yeah."

"You're only going to get one shot at this, John."

"That's the twentieth time you've told me that. Where are we meeting him?"

"Chinese restaurant over on 180th. It's a place where I can set up something like this."

"Why?"

"There's a back room that won't be wired."

"You sure?"

"As sure as I can be of anything. I know the owner a long time. Don't fuck around when we have to prove we aren't wired. Jackson knows the drill."

"Okay. What about Bondurant? He gonna be there?"

Ippolito turned to Palmer. "I sure fucking hope not."

"Why?"

"Why? Because he's a homicidal maniac. You ever see that big nasty-looking fucker coming at you, you pull and shoot, no questions asked. I'm serious. He's the enforcer who makes the whole operation what it is. He kills people. That's what he does."

"You really think Jackson can deliver?"

"He can if he wants to. But understand one thing, John."

"What?"

"Once we let this shit out of the tube, we can't put it back."

"Yeah. Well . . . I'd say it's already out."

"True."

Ippolito turned onto 180th Street and parked illegally a few cars away from the Chinese restaurant. He didn't bother to put any identification on the dashboard. Even the dumbest traffic cop would figure out it was an unmarked police car.

Palmer checked his watch. Exactly eight o'clock.

As they headed for the restaurant, Ippolito told Palmer, "By the way, John . . ."

"What?"

"Try not to stare at Jackson's face."

"Why?"

"He's got bad skin."

"How bad?"

"Horrible bad."

"Shit, now you tell me."

The Chinese restaurant was only half full when Ippolito and Palmer entered. The host shook hands with Ippolito and said nothing. He led them through the dimly lit restaurant, the air heavy with the scents of old-style Cantonese cooking, to a back room set up with a table for four.

Eric Juju Jackson sat alone at the table, an untouched plate of beef with oyster sauce in front of him. He sipped from a cup of tea. Even doing something as prosaic as sipping tea, Jackson seemed menacing.

He stood. Without saying a word, he looked back and forth at Palmer and Ippolito. Palmer laid his folder on the table. He and Ippolito emptied the contents of all their pockets. They took off their jackets, draping them over chairs. They proceeded to unbutton their shirts, pull them free of their pants and lift them up. They turned around so Jackson could see they weren't wearing any wires. They unbuckled their pants and dropped them so Jackson could see their bare legs held no wires or recording devices.

Jackson, who wore a plain blue oxford button-down shirt and black jeans, did the same for them. Palmer tried not to stare at the ravaged skin across his back and shoulders. It looked like someone had taken an ice pick to it.

All three zipped and buttoned and buckled, put everything back into their pockets. Palmer and Ippolito sat on either side of Jackson, who still didn't say anything, or look at them.

Ippolito said, "This is my partner, John Palmer."

Jackson made a nearly imperceptible nod.

"I think we have an opportunity to help each other out."

Jackson continued looking straight ahead, as if he held the detectives in such contempt he refused to look at them.

"Why you think I need your help?"

Palmer spoke up. "Because there are a number of investigations focused on people connected to you."

"I got no people connected to me."

Palmer didn't hesitate. "Well, both the NYPD and the FBI say you do."

Palmer slipped the 11 x 17 FBI organizational chart of known Bronx gang members from his folder and placed it on the table facing Jackson. Many of the names were highlighted in yellow. He paired the chart with pages of NYPD files with many of the same names highlighted in yellow.

Jackson glanced at both as if they had nothing to do with him.

Palmer didn't try to convince Jackson. He simply said, "Those are the people under FBI and NYPD investigations. Here is a list of the federal charges they're drawing up."

He laid a typewritten page on the table listing: money laundering, prostitution, exploiting minors for the purposes of prostitution, transporting minors across state lines for purposes of prostitution, conspiracy, racketeering, tax evasion.

"I'm sure they'll include more charges when they start petitioning the federal courts for warrants. As usual, the

Feds will cast a wide net. They'll invoke RICO statutes. They'll arrest everybody connected to those crimes, including you."

Jackson said nothing.

Palmer continued. "That's their side of it. Our side is investigating two murders connected to you involving people on those FBI charts. Warrants are in process. Unfortunately for you, Mr. Jackson, once we start making arrests, it's going to prompt the Feds to move faster than they might ordinarily. They won't want their targets to end up in state courts. They'll rush to get warrants, subpoenas, pull in witnesses, and push for indictments."

Ippolito added in a friendlier tone, "Look, Eric, the FBI has a big hard-on these days about getting convictions on prostitution of minors. Operation whatever. What is it, Detective Palmer?"

"There are several operations in place. All run by their Child Exploitation Task Force. They have a lot of resources they're focusing on the east coast these days."

Jackson finally responded, still looking straight ahead.

"FBI ain't going to find a damn thing on me. All that RICO shit starts with finances. Ain't no financial records connecting me to anything. No way are they gonna prove any exploitation of any minors by me."

Ippolito said, "Maybe yes, maybe no, Eric. The Federal Bureau of Investigation is very good at tracking money. Be that as it may, once they move, they'll grab everybody. They don't even need warrants to start pulling in witnesses. They start squeezing some of these dipshits around you, threatening 'em with no-bullshit for-real sentences of thirty, forty years' hard time in a federal penitentiary, these kids are going to fall over each other trying to make deals. It'll be a race to see who flips first. The FBI will have their choice of rats telling them what they know, whether they know it or not."

Jackson finally turned to Ippolito. "We got ways of dealing with that shit, too."

Palmer leaned in now, getting to it. "Okay, fine. Let's say you do. So the sooner you know when this is going down, the sooner you know who's going to get pinched, and the sooner you can make plans to deal with it."

Ippolito took note of how quickly Palmer had volunteered to give Eric Jackson names of people to kill, and when to kill them.

Jackson had heard Palmer, but wanted to make sure. "What exactly are you saying to me?"

Palmer answered, "You'll know when subpoenas are going to be issued, schedule of arrests, grand jury indictments, and the names."

"From the Feds?"

"Yes."

"How you going to get all that?"

"Same way I got the org chart."

"And I'm supposed to believe you?"

"You'll believe it when you see it."

"And you saying this is coming down because of some murders you investigating?"

Ippolito spoke up. "Yes. Shit's gonna hit the fan once we start making arrests."

"What're these murders you talking about?"

Palmer said, "On Tuesday, an ex-con named Paco Johnson got released from prison. Mr. Johnson had a run-in with one of your associates, Derrick Watkins, who subsequently shot him. As a result, friends of Paco Johnson tracked down Derrick Watkins, and shot him. We have reason to believe those same friends of Paco Johnson shot and killed two more of your men earlier today, Jerome Watkins and Tyrell Williams. We're investigating all four of those murders. They're all connected."

"Who are these people you talking about? The friends of that convict."

Ippolito held up a hand. "Hold off on that for a second."

For the first time since they'd sat down, Juju Jackson looked back and forth between the two detectives, almost catching Palmer, who had been sneaking glances at his ravaged skin.

Jackson said, "All right. Let's cut through the bullshit. You got information I might be interested in. What do I got to do to get it?"

Palmer concentrated on looking directly into Jackson's eyes, and made his pitch in a low voice.

"Okay, bottom line. The friends of Paco Johnson we're talking about are part of a crew run by a guy named James Beck. We had Tyrell Williams lined up to testify that Beck shot Derrick Watkins. We believe Beck, or one of his crew, shot Tyrell this afternoon to eliminate him as a witness. We need a witness to replace Tyrell. Preferably someone who was at the location on Mount Hope Place where Derrick got shot. We also need a witness to corroborate that. We also need witnesses to testify that Derrick Watkins shot Paco Johnson, providing a motive for Beck and his men to attack his crew. We need a minimum of four witnesses who can stand up."

Jackson took a sip of his tea. Palmer and Ippolito waited for a response.

After a few moments, Jackson said, "All this shit you telling me about federal investigations, we all know ain't worth all that much. There ain't one dollar they can trace back to me. Maybe knowing who they're coming after might help me tie up some loose ends, but ain't no big deal. Like I said, I got ways of finding out who's thinking about turning rat and taking care of it."

Ippolito and Palmer waited. Jackson pushed his cup of tea away.

"But this other thing? I can't have no crew from somewhere coming in here shooting my people. Can't have it. I appreciate you giving me a name. But I ain't going to say any more, 'cept I think it's best if you gentlemen go do what you have to do, and I do what I got to do."

Ippolito said, "Eric, why make life hard? You really want to start from scratch on this? We can tee up these guys for you." Ippolito leaned toward Jackson. "Hey, I know what you're thinking – fuck these cops. Let 'em close their own cases. I get that. But let me tell you, it's better for all of us if we wrap up these homicide investigations quickly. Yeah, it's good for me and my partner. But it's good for you, too. We put this shit to bed fast, maybe the Feds go back to chasing their tails, and it's business as usual."

Jackson nodded. Thinking it through.

"Eric, trust me, if we don't make these cases, nobody is going to cry over some poor ex-con. And definitely not over fucking Derrick Watkins, or his brother, and that other mook, Tyrell. We keep gettin' paid.

"You, on the other hand, you're going to be out there all on your own, my friend. The Watkins brothers are connected to you. Their whores are connected to you. If the powers that be decide your time is up, it's up. And whoever these guys are coming after your people, they ain't amateurs. What's it been? Couple days and they've already taken out both the Watkins brothers? Plus Tyrell. Who knows how far they're gonna take this little vendetta? Better we work together to put all this to sleep." Ippolito shrugged and sat back in his chair, trying to look nonchalant. "Join forces. Faster, easier, simpler. Divide and conquer."

"Divide how?"

Palmer chimed in. "There are four guys on this crew shooting your people. You give us witnesses who will let us take down Beck and one other guy on his crew. We give you leads on the other two. That's two for us, two for you. Take yours down however you want."

"How you know it's only four guys?"

"We know. They have connections, but it's only four involved in this."

"That's it?"

"That's it. Seems like they're pretty good at what they do."

"And you know where to find the other two shooting my people?"

"Absolutely."

"Plus, I get a heads-up on the FBI thing."

"Yes."

Jackson nodded to himself. "When you need these witnesses?"

Ippolito spoke. "We're meeting with the assistant district attorney tomorrow at one. We need four witnesses at the Forty-second Precinct by noon, latest, so we can prep them."

Palmer added, "Preferably four with fairly clean records who can take direction."

"And when do I get the rundown on Beck's crew?"

Palmer continued, "Just to be clear. We get Beck and one of his guys I can identify. You get the other two."

"But I gotta have information and whereabouts on every fucking one of them. You guys don't nail Beck and whoever, I got to be ready to defend myself."

Ippolito closed the deal. "All right, Eric, we see four stand-up witnesses by noon tomorrow, we'll give you everything we can on Beck's crew, plus keep you ahead of the Feds. But – you give us a few days to arrest Beck and the other guy. After that, everybody does whatever the fuck they want."

Jackson said, "Today's Thursday. So by Sunday, I'm free to go."

Ippolito said, "No. Today's shot. We need until Monday, earliest."

Jackson nodded, leaned toward Palmer and Ippolito, and said, "I don't like sitting on my hands."

"You'll have the info on that crew tomorrow. If I were you, I'd use the time to make a plan. Monday is reasonable."

"All right, fuck it. And remember, you two don't hold up your end, my witnesses gonna get real hard to find. And if you do find 'em, they'll have amnesia."

"Fair enough." Ippolito stood. He knew when to end the meeting. "Nice talking to you, Eric."

He and Palmer put on their jackets and left without another word.

Thirty seconds after they left, Jackson took out his cell phone to call Bondurant. The cops had no idea who had really shot Derrick Watkins. He wanted to make sure Bondurant had found the girl, or was close to it. He waited for Bondurant to pick up. He didn't.

He wondered what the hell was going on.

"Whitey, call me."

51

They ended up at one of Ciro's favorite Italian restaurants not far from the strip club. A small, unassuming family operation with very good food.

By the time they finished dinner, Demarco had a plan to find Amelia.

"We should get going. We'll leave Ricky's Impala in the strip mall for him to pick up, and drop you off, Manny, so you can meet Walter and retrieve the Merc."

"Okay."

"Make sure to tell Walter to check up on the police investigation first thing in the morning. We have to know what they know."

"Yo, *señor mami,* that's, like, the fifth time. I'm on it."

"All right, sorry."

"You think those *tonto* cops are really gonna have any leads on who shot Packy?"

"I doubt it. We don't. What I really want to know is, if they have any leads on *us.*"

Manny nodded, "Ah, *sí, sí,* amigo. Good point."

Ciro said, "Yeah, it would be nice to know if they're looking at you two for shooting that fat-fuck brother of the pimp."

Demarco said, "I don't think we've ever been in this situation."

Ciro asked, "What do you mean?"

"We're actually innocent. Between all of us, we shot one guy in self-defense who was blasting away at us. That sixteen-year-old girl took out the other two."

"Yeah, she's a whiz. Who knows, maybe she'll shoot more. Don't matter. Cops are gonna pin all of it on us. They lie for a living. How else are they going to do their jobs? Come on, let's go find that child before she causes any more trouble." Ciro dropped a hundred-dollar bill on the table for a tip. He hadn't asked for a check. The waiter wouldn't have dared bring him one.

Ciro dropped Manny off at a bar on Atlantic Avenue where he could sip coffee and rum until Walter was due to arrive.

As they drove up Atlantic to jump on the BQE and head for the Bronx, Ciro asked Demarco, "So what's the plan, Big D?"

"Okay, here's how I see it. It's a process of elimination."

"Go ahead."

"A girl gets turned out at the age of sixteen, it's unlikely she has any straight friends who can help her. Any of the people connected to her street life will turn their backs on her, because they won't dare cross Jackson and Bondurant. She's not going to stay at the grandmother's after that shootout. She sure as hell isn't going to stay in the Bronx River Houses. So my guess is she holes up in a motel."

"Sounds right, but where? What motel?"

"Someplace she already knows. A place where she won't need a credit card and ID. Which means a motel in her neighborhood. Probably someplace she turned tricks in. There are two in that area."

"Which one you want to check first?"

"The one farthest from her grandmother's – the Howard Johnson Motor Lodge in West Farms."

It was 8:40 when they drove past the bare-bones motel occupying a triangular lot bounded by Boston Road, the Cross Bronx Expressway, and West Farms Road.

Ciro circled the motel to check the surrounding area. There wasn't much to see. He bent over his steering wheel, scanning the forlorn industrial area, taking note of the oppressive elevated subway track running in front of the motel.

"Why the fuck would anybody stay around here? There's nothing here."

"There's some nice empty lots, abandoned buildings, a lovely liquor store right there. Hey, if you have a boiler you want welded, you can get that done here, too."

"Or if you want to lay some pipe."

Ciro pulled in to the small parking lot next to the motel. Both men walked around to the front entrance. Night had fallen, invisible clouds had rolled in from the west, covering the stars and moon, but high-intensity sodium lights hanging out over the sidewalk provided enough light to read small print.

They entered a small lobby built to be functional and damage-proof. On their left, the hotel clerk sat barricaded behind a fake-wood-veneer divider, topped by a narrow counter and a Plexiglas barrier.

Demarco stepped up to the reception counter. Ciro stood next to him, adding even more bulk.

The possibility of two customers prompted a small Bengali man with thinning dark hair to quickly step over to the Plexiglas barrier. He wore the same white shirt and dark dress pants he'd worn since Monday.

"Good evening," said Demarco.

The clerk took a moment to check out Demarco and Ciro. Demarco had to rest an elbow on the counter and bend over slightly to get below the top of the Plexiglas barrier. These were not typical customers. About all he could muster in response to Demarco's greeting was, "Yes."

He said it without inflection. The clerk glanced at Ciro before looking back to Demarco. He seemed worried about the amount of protection his plastic barrier provided him. Before Demarco said anything else, the clerk announced,

"We're full."

Demarco frowned.

"Did I ask for a room?"

"No."

"Did you think saying that would make me leave?"

"I don't know."

"Just say you're sorry. It's offensive."

The clerk hesitated and then said, "Sorry."

"Thank you. I want to know if a young woman checked in here. She's about five foot seven, slim. Looks to be in her twenties. Skin a bit lighter than mine."

The manager blinked. "Are you police?"

"Yes," Demarco said, "we're police. We are looking for this young woman I described to you. Is she here?"

"Do you have identification?"

Ciro calmly took out his forty-five and laid it on the counter. The clerk spluttered, "I'm not sure. I came in at six. I didn't check everybody in."

"Have you seen anybody like I described?"

"No."

"Do you have any women staying here?"

"I don't know."

"Go check."

Demarco watched him scurry to his desk and start clicking through the records on his computer. It took him almost a full minute. He returned to the window.

"No. No women registered."

"Why are you so nervous?"

"You make me nervous. The gun makes me nervous."

"You should be nervous. Particularly if you're lying to us. Are you sure there isn't a woman staying here who fits that description?"

"We don't do that business."

"What business?"

"We don't rent rooms by the hour. Only by the night."

Demarco paused, looked over at Ciro, turned back to the manager. He held up a hand before the man could say anything. "Listen to me carefully. If we find out the girl is here, and we *will* find out, we will cause you enormous problems. Do you know what the word 'enormous' means?"

The man nodded four times. "Yes."

"So – are you sure?"

"Yes."

Demarco stared at him.

"Yes. I'm sure."

"Okay."

Demarco and Ciro walked back out onto the street.

Ciro said, "She ain't there."

*

The shower and shampoo in the bare-bones bathroom at the Expressway Motel helped, but when Amelia put her clothes back on she wished she could have washed them, too. She kept smelling the rancid, moldy smell of Crackhead Betty's blanket and the acrid scent of gun smoke.

Amelia tried to ignore her dirty clothes as she sat on the bed and inventoried everything from the laundry bag she'd found in Tyrell's car. The guns were a .40 caliber Taurus 840, and a 9-mm Glock 17. The two boxes of ammunition were all 9-mm bullets. She checked the magazines in the guns. Both magazines seemed full. She ignored the ledger books and counted the cash. Adding it to the money she'd taken from Biggie Watkins and Tyrell, she had a total of $4,272. More money than she'd ever had in her life.

She remembered with a Glock you just had to squeeze the trigger all the way back to shoot it. She pulled back the slide to chamber a round and looked at the little lever next to the trigger. She gently pushed it with the point of her finger, released the trigger, and laid the Glock on the bed next to her. She stuffed all the cash into the pockets of her new jeans, and placed the red laundry bag on the floor with the ammunition, the second gun, and the ledger books.

The queen-size bed filled most of the room, which needed cleaning, but at least there wasn't any garbage in the wastebaskets. And the two small towels in the bathroom had been laundered. She'd made sure to leave the bedcover on the bed.

It was too early for the hookers and pimps to be gathering and conducting business, but not too late for the smell of marijuana to drift by, or to hear a door slam, or voices arguing through the thin Sheetrock walls.

She checked the time on the room's digital alarm clock. 9:02 P.M. She stretched out on the bed, thinking about the money. More than four thousand dollars. She thought about robbing Biggie's house. Picturing who might be there. No, she told herself. No way. There's got to be some of Juju's guys there by now. Why risk it? She had enough to get the hell out of the Bronx. She had an urge to stand up and leave now, but she ached for sleep. And her hair was going to take at least a couple of more hours to dry. Just a couple more hours.

She looked out the window. She thought she heard thunder. The bed felt so comfortable after a night on the concrete floor of that basement. Maybe drive by Biggie's house and check it out. If it didn't look right, leave. Plenty of money. But hair still wet. Don't have a hat. And then Amelia Johnson fell asleep.

"Christ, I think this neighborhood is even worse."

Demarco smiled. "I'd call it a tie."

"What the hell is behind all this corrugated metal fencing?"

"Scrap metal, I think."

"And look, D, another boiler-welding place."

"Yes, but that one is for marine boilers."

"What the fuck does that mean? Is there water near here?"

"The Bronx River?"

"I can't believe there's a motel here."

"Maybe sailors stay there while their boilers are being welded."

The motel sat in the middle of a U-shaped parking lot. There were two driveways leading into parking areas at the north and south sides of the motel. The south lot was half the size of the north lot. As Ciro approached the south entrance, they saw a brand-new silver Lincoln MKT approaching the north entrance. Both men took notice.

"That car doesn't belong here."

"Neither does mine," said Ciro. "Looks like somebody's got the same idea as you."

"Process of elimination."

Ciro quickly turned in to the lot and took the first parking spot he found.

Demarco opened his door. "C'mon. This could be interesting."

As they hustled toward the motel entrance, Ciro slipped on a pair of leather sap gloves. Each finger was filled with four ounces of steel shot. Demarco pulled a retractable-steel baton from his back pocket and carried it out of sight behind his wrist and forearm.

They rushed through a set of sliding-glass doors into a small foyer, turned right, and walked through another set of glass doors into a lobby crammed with a small couch, two armchairs, and a table. The check-in counter occupied the far wall.

There was no sign of the hotel clerk. They took seats on the couch. Ciro folded his arms, hiding his hands, trying to look as if he often sat in the poor excuse for a lobby in a bad hotel in the Bronx. Demarco kept his steel baton under his right hand and wrist.

Four black men walked into the lobby. One average size, one large, two extra-extra large. The cramped space had suddenly filled with dark clothes, tattoos, bling, and muscle. The smallest of them seemed to be the leader of the group. He wore a tracksuit, leather coat, and sunglasses even though the sun had set hours ago. They all stood in the lobby posturing, glaring, accustomed to intimidating people, especially in a gang of four.

Tracksuit headed toward the check-in counter, but stopped to look at Demarco and Ciro.

"Who the fuck are you?"

One of the XXLs, wearing a three-quarter-length leather coat, loomed over Demarco, arms crossed over a huge chest to make himself look even bigger.

Demarco spoke before Ciro answered. "Nobody. We're just waiting for a friend."

Tracksuit turned to Demarco and said, "Well, wait someplace else, you dumb-ass nobody motherfucker. Go on. Get the fuck out of here. Both of . . ."

Before he finished the sentence, Ciro exploded off the couch and punched him in the face, breaking his nose, cheekbone, and sunglasses. Tracksuit's head snapped back. A line of blood splattered the wall behind him. He fell unconscious onto the table between the two armchairs, breaking the glass top.

Demarco rammed his foot into the knee of the man standing over him, buckling his leg. He jumped off the couch as the man fell sideways, leveraged his right elbow into the big man's jaw, breaking it with a muffled *snap*. Demarco twisted away as XXL fell toward the couch and backhanded the steel baton across his head, cracking the back of his skull and knocking him out.

The man closest to Ciro swung at him and hit the side of Ciro's head. Snarling, Ciro threw a roundhouse punch into the man's forearm, breaking the ulna bone. Ciro followed it up with punch after punch to the body, breaking ribs and rupturing internal organs with his steel-shot covered fists.

The fourth man, the last one into the lobby, managed to draw his gun. Demarco whipped the flexible steel into the man's wrist, his long reach extending another seven inches. The baton cracked the radius bone and broke the scaphoid bone, but not before the thug got off a shot, firing a bullet into the side of the couch. Demarco took one step and hooked a full-force heavyweight knockout punch into the man's temple.

Four down, four out, multiple broken bones, one ruined knee, a bruised liver, a ruptured spleen, a collapsed lung, seven seconds.

Ciro kicked the leader, asking, "Who's getting the fuck out, now, huh?" Kick. "Huh?" Kick, kick. "Who's getting out now, tough guy? Motherfucker!" Stomp. Kick.

Demarco deftly stepped over the heaps of men and rushed to the check-in counter. He leaned over to find the hotel clerk crouched down out of sight, hands over his head. Demarco grabbed his shirt collar and pulled him to his feet.

"What room is she in? A black girl. Tall. Young. What room?"

The man yelled back, spluttering, "Four eighteen, four eighteen."

"Stairs?"

The clerk pointed south.

Demarco ran toward the first-floor corridor, yelling to Ciro, "Get rid of the surveillance disc, then get the car. If you see her, stop her."

Three blocks south on the Sheridan Expressway service road, Floyd Whitey Bondurant thought he heard the faint crack of a gunshot. His driver was already headed toward the Expressway Motel. Bondurant had been driving around the Bronx, checking in with his men, who had been trying to find Amelia Johnson without success. The two motels in the area were logical choices, and when he heard the gunshot he yelled at his driver, "Punch it!"

Bondurant's men never questioned him. The driver floored the accelerator on the 2009 Lexus RX 350. The car leapt forward. Within a block, they had reached sixty-seven miles an hour.

A look of fierce concentration and anger descended on Bondurant. He had very prominent cheekbones, a massive forehead, a pronounced chin. He would have looked more frightening if his eyes showed, but he always wore sunglasses to protect them from the light. He pulled out a large-frame Taurus PT 24/7 loaded with .40 caliber bullets. There were fifteen rounds in the magazine and one in the chamber.

Bondurant sat in the passenger seat. His deep voice rumbled at the man in the backseat, "Elliot, get your shit ready."

Elliot already had his gun in his hand.

The gunfire awakened Amelia instantly. She did not hesitate; she did not look out the window. She grabbed the

Glock, picked up the red laundry bag, slipped into her ballet flats, and ran out of the room.

The door to the back stairs was only fifteen feet away. She smacked the release bar and hit the stairs, running down so fast she almost ran out of her shoes.

By the time Demarco emerged on the fourth floor, Amelia had burst out the ground-floor door into the parking lot. She ran toward the green Malibu parked on the north side of the motel.

Ciro came running out the front entrance on the south side, looked right and left, saw nothing. He made a fast decision. Instead of running to check the other side of the motel, he sprinted for his Escalade.

Demarco glanced into Amelia's room just long enough to confirm it was empty. He raced down the back stairwell almost twice as fast as Amelia had, taking the stairs in huge three-step strides, grabbing the handrail and jumping down the last third of each flight.

Amelia had parked the Malibu far back from the street. As she ran for it, a clap of thunder sounded and cold rain suddenly lashed her face.

Out on the service road, Bondurant's driver braked hard trying to make a turn into the south driveway, but the Lexus slid past the driveway on the rain-slick street. Bondurant pointed with his gun, "Go in the next driveway. Go."

The driver wrestled the car straight and headed for the north side of the motel.

Amelia made it to her Malibu as Demarco emerged into the lot, his Glock in hand. He ran toward Amelia's car, trying to get close enough to block her from pulling out.

Amelia saw Demarco. She saw the gun in his hand. She floored the Malibu and scraped the car next to her making a Y-turn. Demarco got close enough to bang on the trunk of the car and yell, "Stop!"

Bondurant's Lexus reached the north driveway as Amelia accelerated toward the street. Bondurant yelled at his driver. "Stop!"

The Lexus slid into the driveway, blocking more than half the exit.

Bondurant stepped out of the passenger side and calmly rested his Taurus on the roof of the Lexus as Amelia accelerated toward the space between the Lexus and a painted brick wall dividing the parking lot from the sidewalk.

Bondurant tracked the car, and fired at the Malibu.

Demarco took aim at Bondurant, firing at the strange-looking man in the sunglasses. Bondurant turned in the direction of the gunfire.

The Malibu surged toward the small opening. Bondurant's driver dived sideways onto the seat. Elliot was out of the back door, bringing his gun into position to shoot.

Inside the Malibu, Amelia hunched over the steering wheel, aiming for the small opening.

Bondurant returned fire in Demarco's direction as the front of the Malibu simultaneously smashed into the Lexus and the wall with a deafening *bang*. A chunk of the brick wall exploded. The Lexus spun counterclockwise, away from Bondurant toward Elliot knocking him down, shattering his right pelvis.

The Malibu continued forward, scraping past the wall and the Lexus because the terrified Amelia had jammed her foot down on the accelerator. Scraping past the Lexus slowed her enough so Amelia was able to turn right onto the service road without colliding head-on into the guardrail.

Bondurant remained on his feet as the Lexus spun away from him. Demarco advanced on him, firing the Glock. Bondurant returned fire as he climbed into the Lexus, yelling at the driver, "Follow her. Go. Go!"

The steering on the Lexus had been compromised by the impact of the Malibu, but the driver managed to turn onto the road, swerving and wobbling as he accelerated after the green Malibu.

Ciro screeched around the corner and braked next to Demarco, who emptied his gun at the disappearing Lexus. He jumped into the Escalade.

Demarco reloaded his Glock and calmly told Ciro, "We're not losing her now."

"No fucking way."

52

By the time Beck pulled the Ford F-350 into the dirt parking lot next to Remsen's bar, there were only two vehicles left in the lot. His Ford Ranger, and a blue 2001 Volvo V40 Beck assumed belonged to Janice the bartender.

He parked Remsen's truck exactly where it had been and wiped down everything he'd touched with a microfiber towel he found behind the passenger seat. He climbed out, dropped the keys in the cup holder, threw the towel in the back, and closed the door with his elbow.

Beck headed for the bar, but had to stop as a wave of fatigue and nausea hit him. He bent over, hands on knees, waiting for the weakness to pass.

"Shit!"

He straightened up and continued walking until he got close enough to the bar's front door that he could see inside. There were no customers. Most of the lights were off. Janice stepped out from the kitchen, turning off those lights. She walked quickly behind the bar, grabbed her purse, and headed for the front door with a bundle of keys in her hand.

Beck walked over and sat against the front fender of the Volvo. Janice stepped out and locked the front door.

She turned toward the Volvo, stuffing her keys into her purse. When she finally looked up, the sight of Beck startled her.

He held up a hand and said, "Sorry, I need to talk to you."

She remained standing on the front porch of the bar, two steps up from the dirt parking lot. She looked out into the lot, saw Oswald Remsen's truck, but no sign of him or the others. She looked back at Beck.

"What do you want?"

"Just a minute of your time."

"Did you drive Remsen's truck here?"

"Yes."

"Where's Remsen?"

"It doesn't matter."

She stared at Beck, bloody, beat-up, dirty. She asked again, "What do you want?"

"I want to give you some money and ask you a few questions."

"Money? Why?"

"You might need something to tide you over for a while."

"What are you talking about?"

Beck answered with a shrug.

"I saw what Remsen and his men did to you."

"You did?"

"Some of it. I heard a gunshot and looked out."

"You didn't call the cops?"

"Not on Remsen. I'm sorry. You left the bar before I could warn you."

"So make it up to me by answering a few questions."

Janice looked around again and said, "Get into my car. I don't want anybody seeing us out here."

Beck walked around to the Volvo's passenger door, steadying himself on the body of the car as he made his way. He climbed into the passenger seat, still feeling depleted and woozy. He began to think he might not be able to drive back to his motel.

Janice slid into the driver's seat. When the car's dome light came on, she got a better look at Beck.

"Good Lord. You should get to a hospital."

"I don't need a hospital. Just let me get through this with you."

"Through what?"

"Some questions." He reached into his pocket and took out the envelope of cash he'd taken from Oswald Remsen. "Here, take this. For your time and trouble."

"Trouble?"

"Well, your time then. If you keep your mouth shut about seeing me, or even remembering me, you shouldn't have any trouble at all."

"Wait a second. If you have Oswald's money and his truck, that means he's dead or near to it. And his sons, too."

"You're right. And so is that big son of a bitch who likes baseball bats."

Janice sat back in her seat, clearly stunned.

"My God. How did . . . ?"

"It's much better for you if you don't know anything about it."

She didn't respond for a few moments, absorbing what Beck had said.

She turned to Beck. "What do you want from me?"

"A few answers, and I'll be on my way. I know Oswald Remsen and his sons were running prostitutes servicing truckers. Correct?"

She paused, looked at Beck for a few moments, made a decision.

"Yes."

"Do you know how many men besides his sons were in on it?"

"No. But I know there were others involved."

"All prison guards?"

"Five of the ones I know are prison guards."

"Four men came in tonight to give him money. Are they all guards?"

"Yes."

"Do you know who the big guy is?"

"He's a cousin or something. Austen White. He's the one who isn't a guard."

"There were two others with the big guy who jumped me. One was named Fred. Do you know his last name?"

"Yes."

Janice pulled a pen from under her visor. She took the cash out of the envelope Beck had given her and shoved the money into her purse. She wrote on the empty envelope.

"You're not going to ..."

"No. I'm not. And don't assume I killed Oswald Remsen or anybody else. What do you know about Oswald's third son?"

"Not very much. He works downstate. Sing Sing."

"What's his name?"

"Edward. Edward Remsen."

"Do you know where he lives?"

"I think he lives in the Bronx. I'm not sure."

Beck nodded.

"About these prostitutes, do you know where the women come from?"

She finished printing the name Fred Culla on the envelope. "No. I hear Remsen talking and laughing about mud people, which I guess means black people, but I don't know anything about how he recruits women."

"Okay, last question. Do you know how Remsen recruited those other guards? The ones besides his sons?"

Janice looked at Beck, thinking it over.

"Not for sure," she said. "But Oswald Remsen has been a steward in the union at Eastern for a long time. And he's a captain. So I expect he'd know most of the guards and has some influence."

Beck nodded, taking it in. "Okay. Thanks."

Janice handed him the envelope. "I don't know much. I try to avoid hearing their conversations."

Beck nodded. "I understand." He put the envelope in his shirt pocket, turned carefully so as not to aggravate his bruised ribs, and opened the car door.

He stepped out of the car and stood up. Another wave of nausea and dizziness hit him. He thought, I have to get some food and more water. That was the last thought Beck had for ten hours.

53

Demarco calmly finished reloading his Glock as Ciro roared after the Lexus, fighting to keep control of the big Escalade slaloming up the Sheridan Expressway service road. Fortunately, there was no other traffic except the Lexus in front of him.

The Escalade's wipers could barely keep up with the wind-lashed torrent of rain. Ciro concentrated on the red taillights of the damaged Lexus. As he closed in on the it, he yelled to Demarco, "Save your bullets. You'll never hit him with us sliding all over this fucking road."

"We can't let them or the girl get on the Expressway."

Ciro's answer was to accelerate even more. He angled right and banged the corner of his massive bumper into the rear left corner of the Lexus, sending it into a violent counterclockwise spin on the wet asphalt. It banged into a guardrail, bounced clockwise, and smashed into the base of a streetlamp pole. As the pole crashed onto the roof of the Lexus, Ciro wrestled the Escalade straight and roared past. He clipped a DO NOT ENTER sign, bumped over a grass divider, and straightened out onto the service road.

Amelia heard the crash, looked in her rearview mirror and saw the rainwater spray into the air and debris fly as the Lexus smacked the guardrail. But taking her eye off the road was a mistake. With the Malibu wobbling so badly, she had veered toward a fence running along the expressway. In a desperate move, she wrenched the steering wheel right, hit a curb, and slalomed off the road into an open construction site.

Ciro saw the Malibu leave the road up ahead and barely managed to brake enough so he could follow Amelia.

Amelia just managed to keep control of the Chevy. She slammed on the brakes and slid into a concrete partition. The engine died. She tried to start the car, but the key was already turned in the ignition. She turned the ignition off and then tried again, grinding the starter. She pumped the gas pedal, desperately turning the ignition key. Suddenly, the passenger door opened. Rain blew in. Before she realized what was happening, a large hand covered her hand turning the ignition key and a calm voice said, "Hold it, kid. Don't you smell the gas? Turn the damn thing off before you start a fire."

Amelia looked over at Demarco Jones smiling at her.

"That was some driving. But I think those guys put a couple of bullets in your gas tank. You've been spewing gas all over the road, which was good. They slid all over the place once we hit them."

Amelia sat frozen. Demarco gently, but firmly, turned off the ignition. She didn't know what to do or say.

"Come on, we gotta get out of here before the cops find us." Demarco flashed a dazzling smile. "Hey, how much worse off can you be with us? Come on. You have anything in this car that will track back to you?"

He had already found the empty Ruger from Mount Hope Place in the glove compartment and the laundry bag on the floor. He dropped the Ruger into the bag.

He held up the laundry bag and asked, "Anything else?"

"No."

"You hear those sirens? We don't have much time."

Demarco had to go around to the driver's side and help Amelia get the bent door open. They climbed into the Escalade, both Demarco and Amelia in the passenger seats behind Ciro.

Ciro killed his headlights, put the big SUV into all-wheel drive, and carefully navigated across the excavated rock and rubble to the far end of the construction site. He managed to squeeze between huge boulders that had been dug up at the site and set in a line to form a barrier between the construction area and a footpath that ran alongside a soccer field. He meandered through the park paths, under the 174th Street overpass, across a footbridge, and under the Cross Bronx Expressway until he emerged on Devoe Avenue.

Once on Devoe, Ciro switched on his headlights and announced, "That was fun."

54

Manny Guzman stood across the street from Walter Ferguson's apartment waiting patiently.

It was a warm, almost sultry evening, the air pregnant with the feel of a rainstorm coming. He'd called Walter while waiting in the bar on Atlantic. Walter said he should arrive by nine. Sure enough, two minutes before nine the all-black Mercury Marauder pulled up in front of Walter's apartment on Livingston Street.

Manny strolled across the street and slipped into the passenger seat.

"Hey, Walter."

"Hello, Emmanuel."

"How'd it go?"

Walter rubbed the back of his neck to release tension from the long drive. He'd stopped only once for a bathroom break.

"I think I found some information that helped James."

"Which was?"

"It seems this thing with Packy might involve correction officers."

Manny scowled. "How?"

"It's not completely clear. I made contact with a guard on the staff who seemed to know something, but all she did was give us a name of another guard who works at

Eastern. He was there when James was there. Name of Oswald Remsen."

"But you don't know how he's connected to Packy."

"No. That's what James stayed to find out."

Manny stared out the windshield of the Mercury, nodding to himself, then he turned to Ferguson and said, "Well, I'm glad you're back, Walter. I wanted to check in with you, remind you to follow up on what the cops are doing. See where those two detectives are on Paco's case."

"Yes, James told me the same thing when I left him. I've already called them, but I haven't heard back. Not all that surprising. Before I left Ellenville, I put in a call to their precinct. Got the name of their supervisor and left a message for him."

"And?"

"He hasn't called me back either."

"What you going to do?"

"Head up to the Bronx in the morning and find the man. His name is Levitt. I'm going to sit in that precinct until I find him and get answers."

"Good."

Walter turned again to Manny. "Anything I should know about that happened while I was gone?"

Manny pursed his lips. "Like usual. Things gets worse before they gets better."

"Any details you want to share?"

Manny paused, squinted for a moment.

"Walter, we both know a man gets murdered the way Paco did, it most likely ain't a simple thing. We're finding out what's behind it. When it's all over, you'll know everything we know."

"That's what James said to me."

"He told you the truth."

"But why not tell me what you're finding out as it happens?"

"Things keep changing."

"Why not keep me up with the changes?"

Manny turned to Walter. "I understand what you're trying to do, my friend. You're trying to decide if you're doing the right thing. But you won't know until this is all figured out."

"By then it might be too late."

Manny shrugged.

"So I have to have faith that you all are doing the right thing?"

"Yes."

"And after it's all over, what if I decide you didn't do the right thing?"

"Walter, you're gonna do what you think is right. Now, later, whenever. That's the kind of man you are. And when this is over, you're going to go to your church down the street, and kneel down, and think it through. Maybe you talk to your priest, or maybe you talk in your mind to your beautiful wife. Or maybe you ask God. And then you will decide if you did the right thing. Maybe you get the answer. Maybe you don't."

Walter sat silently for a few moments. "And if I decide I did not do the right thing?"

"Then you ask for forgiveness, amigo. You ask for forgiveness."

"From whom?"

Manny tipped his head. "Yourself."

Walter frowned, nodding. After a few moments, he said, "Thank you, Manny. I'll let you know what I find out tomorrow."

Manny patted Walter's shoulder. "*Gracias.*"

They both stepped out of the car. Walter retrieved his carry-on from the backseat and headed for his empty apartment. Manny took his place in the driver's seat and headed for Red Hook.

55

The sound of a dresser drawer closing woke Beck up.

Struggling into consciousness felt like swimming up from a deep pond filled with dark, viscous liquid. The soapy scent of a woman fresh out of the shower helped to dispel the dull buzz in his head and pulled him awake.

Beck blinked his eyes open. They felt like they had been sealed by a thin film. He rolled his head and stretched under the blanket covering him. The resulting pain pulled him fully awake.

He cursed silently. *Shit.*

Translucent pull-down shades softened the light in the small bedroom. Above him, Beck saw a ceiling fixture with a frosted cover. It had a floral peach-colored decoration around the bottom.

He looked to his right in the direction of the soft sounds.

Janice the bartender stood in front of a mahogany dresser wearing a thigh-length kimono-style robe, untied, choosing between two folded bras in her hand. She had already selected a pair of panties she'd placed on top of the dresser.

Beck didn't move. He didn't want to feel the pain that would cause, or attract Janice's attention and embarrass her.

He had no memory of getting into a bed, yet here he was, under a wool blanket. He felt around under the blanket. He was wearing everything but his jacket and shoes. It concerned him that his dirty clothes were making her bed sheets dirty.

Janice slipped off her robe and dropped it on the bed behind her. She had very white skin. Her backside was nicely shaped, her thighs defined with long muscles. Beck would have looked away, giving Janice her privacy, but he couldn't take his eyes off an elegant, sinuous tattoo that ran from under her full right breast, along her ribs, across her hip, ending where it encircled part of her firm right buttock. The tattoo consisted of fine black lines with beautiful highlights depicting the plumage of a peacock.

She turned sideways to Beck, revealing more of her breast and flat stomach. She swept the panties up off the dresser, leaned over, and stepped into them gracefully and efficiently. Beck watched her breast sway and noted the muscles along her rib cage.

Beck closed his eyes. Don't be a jerk, he told himself. Give the woman her privacy.

He remained still, listening as she pulled open another dresser drawer, closed it, and moved around the small bedroom. Finally, when he figured she was fully dressed, Beck took a deep breath and stirred. He heard her walk over to his side of the bed and felt her presence hovering over him.

He stirred again, and the pain made him wince and exclaim, "Jeezus."

That was end of his sleeping act.

Janice said, "How bad is it?"

Beck opened his eyes and focused on her. She wore a pair of faded jeans that fitted well and a simple black turtleneck top that didn't.

Beck croaked, "How'd I get here?"

"It wasn't easy. You passed out after you got out of my car. I couldn't rouse you completely, but I got you awake enough to get you back in the car and into my house. It's a good thing my bedroom is on the ground floor. I don't think you would have been able to walk up any stairs, and I sure as hell couldn't have carried you."

Beck thought about sitting up, but held off.

"How long have I been out?"

Janice looked at her watch. "About ten hours. I finally got you into the bed around midnight."

Beck pulled aside the blanket.

"I'm making a mess of your sheets. Sorry. Where'd you sleep?"

"I have a guest room upstairs."

"I feel bad I put you out of your bed."

Janice waved off the apology. "Don't worry about it. I didn't try to clean you up. I put antibiotic cream on your cuts and scrapes, but you should wash up. You think you can stand up and take a shower?"

"Sure."

"Don't pass out on me again. I nearly broke my back trying to get you on your feet. How much do you weigh?"

"Couple hundred. I haven't had anything to eat in a while. Except those peanuts at your bar."

She smiled at the reference to the peanuts. "Plus four drinks."

"Three and a half. I didn't finish the beer."

Janice extended her hand to Beck. "Come on, see if you can get up. There's a bottle of hydrogen peroxide in the bathroom. I'd dump a bunch of it on that gash on

361

your forehead, and everywhere else where your skin's broken."

"You sound like a nurse."

"I'm not. But I was raised on a farm. We didn't run to an emergency room every time someone got a bump. It's too late for stitches in your forehead, but I can put some butterflies on it and bandage it for you."

"Thanks."

"You better wash those clothes. You know how to use a washing machine?"

Beck gave her a look.

"What? I know men who think they'd grow breasts if they did laundry."

"I know how to use a washing machine."

"It's down the hall from the bathroom. Don't put too much soap in."

"Yes, that's a common error amateurs make."

Beck managed to sit up and get his feet on the floor. He paused to get a breath.

"What's the worst?" she asked.

"Ribs. Right side in back."

"I don't think they're cracked or broken. Otherwise you wouldn't have been able to sleep like you did."

Beck answered with a grunt.

Janice motioned with her outstretched hand. Beck took it. He felt the rough skin on her palm, reminding him of when he'd first met her. She grabbed his elbow with her other hand and helped him onto his feet, impressing Beck with her strength.

Beck grimaced, but felt better now that he was standing. "Thanks. For everything."

"I couldn't leave you in the parking lot. And the nearest hospital is a pretty long drive. I didn't think you wanted to go there anyhow."

"I'm okay. Hey, what about my truck? Is it still in the lot?"

"Yes, but not where you parked it. Before we left, I drove it out back behind our Dumpsters. Nobody will see it from the road."

Beck looked at Janice. "You're . . ."

"What?"

"You're doing a hell of a lot for me."

"And you wonder why."

Beck tipped his head as if to say yes.

"Two reasons. I feel guilty I didn't warn you in the bar. But I was afraid Remsen would see me and I didn't want to face him if he caught me warning you."

"I understand."

Beck waited for the second reason.

"But mostly because I hate Oswald Remsen enough to make me sick. So, if you did what I think you . . ."

Beck held up a hand to stop her.

"Well, I think I owe you."

"No you don't."

"If you say so." Janice stepped back to give Beck room. "I have to go to the store. What do you want for breakfast?"

"Whatever you're having, but more."

"I'll shop accordingly. By the way, if you start rummaging around in my medicine chest for pain medication, all I have is Tylenol. If you have a concussion, I'm not sure you want to take anything else."

"I'm all right. I've got a hard head."

"Go clean up, and I'll be back soon. There's a robe that might fit you in the back of my closet."

"Okay. By the way, I remember your first name. Janice. But you didn't tell me the rest of it."

"My last name is Elkins. What's yours?"

"Beck."

"And you said your first name was Tom?"

"I did. But it's James."

"Why'd you tell me Tom?"

"Sort of obvious, isn't it?"

"Yeah, now that you mention it."

Janice headed out. Beck followed and went into the bathroom across the hall. The first thing he did was swallow four Tylenol, finishing the glass of water.

The low-ceilinged bathroom was just big enough for one person. There was a small window with white curtains above the toilet. The powder-blue tiles in the tub and shower were too old to ever be matched.

Beck emptied his pockets, finding his cell phone. The battery was dead.

He stripped off all his clothes, walked naked to the bedroom, and found his denim jacket hanging on a chair. He emptied the pockets and found everything he'd taken back from Oswald Remsen. He took the clothes filthy with dirt, grass, bloodstains, and sweat to the laundry room, shivering slightly against the chill. He would have thrown everything away, but he had nothing else to wear so he had to wait for them to be washed.

Beck squirted stain remover on the bloodstains, and made sure not to use too much detergent. He set up the machine carefully and started the wash cycle.

He took his time in the shower, soaping over everything twice, inventorying his bruises and scrapes. His wrists were raw from the handcuffs, particularly his right wrist. The area under his left eye was bruised and swollen. His forehead was a mess. There were scrapes and swollen areas, and a cut at the hairline where the skin had split. There were bruises on his arms where he'd blocked blows, and on his back, legs, and thighs where he'd been kicked. It would be days and days of progressing from red to purple to green to yellow. He didn't want to think how much it was going to hurt driving an old truck back to Brooklyn.

The dull headache he'd woken with had eased off by the time he stepped out of the shower and dried off with a blue towel Janice had left on the toilet for him.

He found the hydrogen peroxide in Janice's medicine chest and poured the disinfectant on his wrists and knuckles, holding his hands over the sink. He watched the hydrogen peroxide bubble and foam up where there was raw skin.

He cleaned the cut on his forehead, then rinsed the sink and went to find the bathrobe Janice told him about. It was a heavy terry-cloth robe, dark blue, big enough to fit him.

Beck wondered who it belonged to. Ex-husband? Boyfriend? What was her story? She was a good-looking woman, and seeing her nearly naked had made her more attractive to him.

"All right, take it easy," he told himself. *Get your clothes washed, eat, thank her profusely, and get the hell out of here.* Beck wanted to be as far away from Ellenville as possible when those bodies were discovered.

He found his way into Janice's kitchen. Again, a flashback to rural fifties. Worn linoleum floor, old appliances, but everything clean and functional. The scent of fresh-brewed coffee filled the kitchen.

Beck found a cup in a cabinet to the right of the sink. He filled it and left the coffee black, sipping it carefully since there wasn't any milk in it to cool it down.

The clock on an old Sharp microwave read 10:47.

He reached for a faded yellow wall phone with a long, twisted cord and punched in Demarco's cell number.

He sat at a rough wooden table big enough to seat four, gathering the robe around him, wishing he had something on his bare feet to keep them warm.

Demarco answered on the first ring. "This is an upstate area code so I guess you're still alive."

"More like half alive. How're you?"

"Half?"

"Things went bad."

"How bad?"

"Very."

"You okay?"

"Okay enough."

Demarco asked, "When you coming back?"

"As soon as I get my clothes back."

"Let me think about that for a second. Okay, I give up, where are your clothes?"

"In a washing machine. What's going on at your end?"

"Long story, but Derrick Watkins's older brother, and one other lowlife, are no longer with us."

"Jerome?"

"Yes. Street name, Biggie."

"Not very inventive."

"Nope."

"So I take it you didn't learn anything from him."

"No time."

"You find Packy's daughter?"

"Twice. We found her the same time we found the bad guys. Turns out she was stalking them. She shot the low-life, we took out Biggie. Second time at a motel."

"Sounds like she's her father's daughter. Where is she now?"

"Sleeping in the front bedroom upstairs. Interestingly, I'm washing her clothes, too."

"You never offered to wash mine."

"Who's doing them for you now?"

"Nobody. I'm doing 'em myself, like always. Anything else I should know?"

"Somehow the girl came up with two ledger books tracking Derrick Watkins's prostitution business. Believe it or not, from a quick look at the numbers, the guy was netting about three hundred grand a year."

"Just him?"

"Looks that way."

"Shit. Anything else?"

"Manny and I found out the Watkins brothers were part of a bigger crew. Run by a couple of guys been around in the Bronx a long time. Eric Jackson and Floyd Bondurant."

Beck nodded, adding Demarco's information to what he knew. "Okay. Where's Walter?"

"He came in last night. Talked to Manny. Went up to the Bronx this morning to talk to the supervisor in charge of those two detectives about their investigation."

"Good. Is he there now?"

"I think so."

"Well, if he calls to warn you about warrants for anybody's arrest, be ready to make yourself scarce."

"Ciro's getting a house for us in Staten Island in case we have to abandon ship. Alex is gonna house-sit here."

Beck checked his watch. "All right, I should be leaving here in about an hour. That puts me in Red Hook around two. Call Alex, have him come in. See if he can run down information on Jackson and Bondurant. Ask him to help Walter with anything he found out about the cops' investigation. Make sure Walter stays there until I arrive. And get ahold of Ricky and Jonas."

"You want them here, too?"

"Yes. Also, tell Alex to track down a man named Edward Remsen. He's a CO, works at Sing Sing. I think he lives in the Bronx. Have Alex do that first."

"Okay."

"We'll need Ciro, too."

Demarco asked, "Anybody else?"

"Willie Reese. Ask him to be there."

"Full-court press, huh, James?"

"Yes."

Beck heard footsteps outside the kitchen door. He told Demarco, "Get things rolling, my friend. I'll see you soon."

He hung up Janice's phone as she entered carrying two plastic bags of groceries. Beck took the bags out of her hands and placed them on the counter while Janice slipped out of her coat. She hung it on a peg next to the door. Beck took a carton of eggs and other groceries. It all felt very domestic.

"That fits you," Janice said.

"What? Unpacking the groceries, or the robe?"

"Both I suppose."

"I'm not going to ask who the robe belongs to."

"It belongs to me. He's long gone."

"I had to use your phone."

"You didn't call China or anything, did you?"

Beck smiled. "No. Listen, I . . ."

"If you're going to thank me again, don't. I'll start break-fast." She stopped and listened for a moment. "I think your clothes are on the first spin cycle. Keep track of them and get them in the dryer. Not that I'm rushing you, but the sooner you get out of here the better."

"I understand."

"No you don't. I already got a call from the sheriff ask-ing if I know where Oswald Remsen is. Remsen didn't make it home last night. I don't think that's entirely un-usual, but his wife called the sheriff a couple of hours ago."

Beck didn't respond.

Janice asked, "Any other wives going to be calling the sher-iff this morning?"

"Depends on how much they miss their husbands."

Janice stared at Beck. He looked back at her without expression. He watched her thinking it through, worry and concern clouding her expression.

He said, "Janice, there are two things you have to know. What happened last night, had to happen. There was nothing I could have done to stop it."

"Okay."

"And the other thing is, don't jump to any conclusions. Don't assume anything."

"I'm not sure I know what that means."

"It means don't try to figure out what happened to Remsen and his men. In fact, don't even think about it. No matter what you hear over the next few days, it'll take time for everything to emerge. In the meantime, it's not your responsibility. And you know nothing about it. Nothing. If anybody asks you about a stranger in the bar last night, you tell them you think there was, but you can't remember anything specific about him. Just an ordinary guy. Did you hear fighting in the parking lot? Not really. You were busy. Stick to that, don't draw conclusions, you'll be fine."

"All right."

"Was there anybody else in the bar who saw anything?"

Janice thought for a moment. "By the time you left it was just me and Albert Collins. He's not a problem. Albert is a little slow. Nobody will bother asking him anything."

"Then you're fine."

She nodded. "All right. I got it. Thanks. How do you like your eggs?"

"Any way you want to cook them. One other thing."

"What?"

"Do you have an Internet connection? I want to look something up."

She almost asked Beck what, but didn't. "My computer is in the living room. All I have is satellite out here. It's slow, but it works."

"That makes two of us," said Beck.

56

This time Palmer, Ippolito, and Levitt met with the assistant district attorney, Frederick Wilson, in the precinct's community affairs office on the first floor. The precinct commander, Dermott Jennie, was there, too. Wilson's Asian assistant was not.

Juju Jackson had delivered four eyewitnesses, as promised, shortly before noon on Friday, in time for Palmer and Ippolito to prep them. The four did reasonably well when Frederick Wilson questioned them. One of the witnesses, Johnny Morris, actually sounded convincing when he claimed to have driven Derrick Watkins along 174th Street looking for Paco Johnson, and swore he saw Derrick shoot him. And he also managed to sound outraged when he told Wilson he saw James Beck shoot Derrick Watkins at the Mount Hope Place apartment.

The other witnesses followed Morris's lead, backing up his claim that Beck shot Derrick Watkins, and swearing they heard that Derrick shot the guy who had been at Bronx River Houses.

Wilson didn't bother pointing out he couldn't use hearsay testimony, or pressing the witnesses on why they were all in the Mount Hope apartment, or on what had transpired at Bronx River Houses. He'd worry about all that if they were still around when it came time for a trial.

Ippolito ushered Jackson's stooges out of the community affairs room where they had been meeting, and Palmer took over. He continued his presentation by pointing out there was a possibility one of the guns found at the Mount Hope Place apartment could turn out to be the murder weapon in Paco Johnson's death.

Wilson asked, "How would you link the gun to Derrick Watkins?"

Palmer answered, "Trace the ownership. Maybe find people who saw him with that particular weapon."

Wilson didn't bother to argue the point.

Palmer continued, "We're also working on obtaining witnesses who saw the initial altercation at Bronx River Houses."

"Hopefully witnesses without criminal records."

Palmer didn't respond to Wilson's gibe. He slid paperwork toward Wilson and said, "Here's my affidavit identifying Ciro Baldassare as the man who fired on me at the Mount Hope murder scene. With the help of other detectives in the squad, we've identified him as an associate of James Beck. He's still on parole. If nothing else, we can violate him right now for possession of a weapon and attempted murder of an NYPD detective."

Ippolito returned to the meeting, but hung back letting Palmer take the spotlight.

"And here's more information we worked up on known associates of James Beck. One of them is a man named Emmanuel Guzman. You can see his record there. He matches the descriptions provided by a witness who saw the shooting of Jerome Watkins on Hoe Avenue. We'll follow up and see if she can ID Guzman."

Palmer continued. "Here's an image from a security camera in the Housing Authority parking lot near the scene." He slid a copy over to Wilson. "The shorter man looks like Guzman. The taller black man we believe is an ex-convict by the name of Demarco Jones. Both of them served time with Beck. Both are still on parole. We should be able to get them locked up just on suspicion, and for being in the company of a known felon."

"Where'd you get all this information on Beck and the others?"

"Most of it is from a report filed by a detective in the Seven-Six. There was a major incident with Beck last winter. Deaths, injuries, a fire. It's all in there."

By the time Palmer finished, Wilson had no choice but to agree he would get arrest warrants for Beck, Guzman, Jones, and Baldassare. But Wilson was no fool. He said, "Tell me gentlemen, putting aside James Beck, do you want these men arrested for parole violations, or the crimes you've accused them of?"

There was a moment of silence, and the wily Ippolito said, "Either, or. One way or another they're off the streets."

"Well, if you intend to convict them for new crimes, you've got a lot of loose ends to tie up. Particularly Beck. He's not on parole. I'd prefer not to issue warrants and arrest any of them until you deliver everything you've promised."

Palmer attempted to say something, but Wilson talked over him.

"Hear me out. Today is Friday. I suggest you take the weekend to get what we need to make these arrests stick.

I need murder weapons, timelines, hopefully corroborating witnesses who aren't known associates of the victim, witnesses or affidavits explaining how Beck tracked down Derrick Watkins. I'll need the crime-scene report from the shootings on Hoe Avenue. And at some point, I'll need an explanation as to why Watkins, Williams, Guzman, and Jones were all at the same location. And, of course, by the time we get to trials, if we get there, I'll need more."

Lieutenant Levitt broke in., "Mr. Wilson, it's a complicated case, but we should get these men off the street and in jail as soon as possible. Right now you have more than enough to get indictments. We'll have much more by the time you go to a grand jury. And everything we've promised by the time this gets to trial. We need arrest warrants to get things rolling."

"You'll have them. But let's be clear. I am not interested in cases involving parole violations. I'm not interested in bringing charges against a dead man. Beck is the prize here, gentlemen. But he has no criminal record, and he'll have first-rate representation, not some overworked Legal Aid lawyer. And there's every chance a judge will grant him bail, which he very likely will be able to post. I want everything I can get before I have to arraign him.

"And, don't forget, you could end up arresting these fellows in three different boroughs, so you're going to have to coordinate with at least three precincts. And with whatever division chiefs are going to supply you with ESU, or whatever else you need.

"Not to mention, if I can't get them all into the Bronx system, we could be arraigning them in three different courts. You're going to need time to organize the arrests."

For the first time, the precinct commander, Captain Jennie, broke in. "Agreed. We'll pull everything together over the weekend, but will you agree to get us warrants Monday the latest?"

Wilson nodded. "Yes, depending on your progress."

Frederick Wilson didn't waste any time leaving. He shoved his legal pad and documents into his briefcase, said, "Stay in touch," and left Levitt's office.

As soon as the office door closed, Jennie said, "All right, listen up. The word has come from on high. The department wants to take down Beck. Obviously, certain people aren't happy with him being a free man. So you two get out there and get as much done as you can. Levitt and I will start coordinating with borough command and the detective division and everybody else we're going to need. Where are you two going to start?"

Ippolito said, "Back at the Bronx River Houses for more witnesses."

Palmer said, "And with CSU and ballistics."

Jennie asked, "Do you need any more bodies on this?"

Levitt broke in, "I've got one other detective on the squad helping out. Mostly coordinating all the paperwork."

"Ask for what you need to make this happen."

With that, Jennie left.

Ippolito and Palmer exchanged surprised looks. Levitt said, "You heard the man. It's on. Get to work and let me know what you need."

Ippolito said, "Will do."

"All right, I gotta meet with that parole division supervisor."

Palmer asked, "Who?"

Levitt looked at his notes. "Walter Ferguson. Paco Johnson was assigned to him."

"What's he want? We interviewed him on the day of the murder."

"He wants to know where we're at. He's got to file reports with the Department of Correction." Levitt headed for the door. "Don't worry about him. I'll take care of it. Get going. Touch base with me by end of day."

Levitt found Walter Ferguson sitting patiently on a molded plastic chair near Sergeant Clovehill's desk. Levitt motioned for him to come to his work area.

Walter presented his identification and told Levitt, "Lieutenant, I appreciate your cooperation. I know you're very busy. If you agree, I think the simplest thing to do is to give me whatever documentation you have and let me read through the material. And afterwards, a couple minutes of your time if I have any questions."

Levitt thought about it for a moment. Ferguson seemed organized and reasonable. He decided the quickest way to get rid of him would be to do what he asked.

"Fine."

Levitt gathered all the case material, including his notes from the Wilson meeting, and handed the pile to Ferguson. "We're still in the middle of this. I'll be here for another hour or so. You can take notes, but nothing goes out of this office. Everything stays between us and the Department of Correction. In fact, I'd prefer if you waited until Monday to file your reports."

Walter nodded. "It'll take me at least until Monday to prepare them."

"Good. I'll check with you if you have questions before I leave."

"Thank you."

Levitt escorted Walter back to Clovehill's desk and told him to find Mr. Ferguson a place where he could work.

57

Beck parked his truck across the street from his Red Hook bar later than he had hoped, a little after three P.M. on Friday. The last forty minutes of stop-and-go traffic on the BQE had been excruciating. By the time he walked across the street and into his ground-floor bar, he still wasn't able to stand up straight.

Demarco Jones and Willie Reese were in the barroom. Demarco said nothing, but Willie Reese reacted with concern and confusion when he saw Beck. Reese was a very large, muscled-up, menacing ex-con who at one time had gone head-to-head with Beck and had suffered a broken nose, cracked ribs, and nearly lost an eye.

"Yo, Beck, what the fuck?"

Beck wasn't in the mood to explain anything. "There were six of them."

Willie narrowed his eyes and frowned.

"Four dead, one in the hospital."

Reese made a noise of approval, but he didn't look any less concerned.

Beck made his way up to the second-floor loft, Demarco and Willie trailing after him.

Manny stood in the kitchen, as usual, cleaning and preparing food.

The Bolo brothers, Ricky and Jonas, were also hanging out in the kitchen area. They were wiry, compact men. Ricky, the more talkative, more animated of the two, stood describing a small piece of electronic equipment to Manny, whose disinterest didn't dissuade Ricky at all. His brother, Jonas, stood leaning against the large island work counter, scanning the room as if he were casing it for a robbery.

Alex Liebowitz sat at Beck's desk with Walter Ferguson, downloading photos from Ferguson's smartphone.

Beck told everyone he'd be back and headed for the stairs at the west end of the second floor.

When Beck disappeared up the back stairs the others exchanged looks, but only Demarco spoke.

"He's gonna tell us it looks worse than it is."

After changing his clothes and dosing himself with pain relievers, Beck reappeared.

He headed toward the large rectangular dining-room table opposite the big kitchen area and waved for the others to join him. They assembled, bringing whatever material they had.

Beck took a seat at the head of the table. Alex Liebowitz and Walter Ferguson sat to his immediate right and left. Then Demarco and Willie opposite each other. Ricky and Jonas were next, facing each other. Manny sat at the other end of the table.

Beck asked, "Where's Ciro?"

Demarco answered, "On his way."

"And the girl?"

"Upstairs."

"All right, so we have a lot of catching up to do. What's happened since I left?"

Demarco started, but knowing Walter was at the table he spoke cautiously.

"I already told you we located Amelia. But here's something you might be interested in. She can tell you how she came up with them." Demarco slid two ledger books toward Beck. "These will give you an idea what Derrick Watkins was earning running his prostitutes. My quick run-through of the numbers puts his profits at about three hundred thousand a year. That doesn't include what his brother was doing. And like I mentioned on the phone, those two were part of a much bigger crew run by a longtime gang leader named Eric Jackson. We got the run-down on him and his main enforcer, Whitey Bondurant, from a friend of Manny's up in the Bronx. You might have known him. Benjamin Woods."

"Yeah, I knew Big Ben. What's he doing now?"

"Turned into a pastor. Has a storefront church."

"God bless him."

"If Derrick was doing three hundred K, Jackson's whole operation could be in the millions. Be nice to get proof of that, but thanks to Packy's kid we have something to go on."

Beck nodded, adding the information Demarco gave him to what he had learned about Oswald Remsen's prostitution business.

"Thanks. What else?"

Jonas Bolo spoke next.

"You asked us to track down a CO named Edward Remsen. He lives in the Norwood section of the Bronx. We made a few inquiries. He's working today. His shift at Sing Sing ends at six. You want us to tail him from his job, we should leave now. Or, we can wait for him at his home address."

Beck checked his watch. Nearly four o'clock. He assumed the last surviving Remsen might have already heard his father and brothers were missing. Once he found out they were dead, there was no telling what he would do."

"Go now. You know where to pick him up in Ossining?"

Ricky spoke up. "Yeah, we know the lot where the COs park. Alex got the make and model of his car and his license plate. We should make it in time to catch him. Don't worry, we'll find him."

"Okay. Call me as soon as you do. And stick with him."

Without another word, both Bolo brothers stood and left.

Alex Liebowitz began talking next in a calm, methodical manner, which contrasted with his disheveled appearance. Alex looked like a Brooklyn hipster – thick black eyeglass frames, shirt untucked, cuffs unbuttoned, skinny jeans – but he had none of the verbal affectations that plagued his generation. He never said "like" or "sort of" or up-talked. He had a hard enough time speaking slowly and carefully with a mind that moved at warp speed.

There was a stack of pages in front of him.

"Okay, so those IDs Demarco e-mailed me – I verified all the names, two of the addresses didn't match. Did a quick search for arrest records. They're all in the system. Let me know if you want more." He slid two pages to Beck.

"Next, here's the information I got for Ricky and Jonas on Edward Remsen." Alex slid two more pages toward

Beck. "Home address, relatives, age, car registration, social security, credit history. No liens. No lawsuits. Not a deep dive. Again, let me know if you want more."

Alex picked up another set of pages.

"I ran the names Jerome Watkins, Derrick Watkins, Eric Jackson, and Floyd Bondurant through three of the crime databases I can access. All of them are in the NYPD and FBI gang files. Bondurant and Jackson's files go back to the mid-eighties. I can check more databases if you want me to, but bottom line, those guys are responsible for a lot of crime. If the Feds ever move on them and make a case, Jackson and Bondurant will go away for a long time.

"Last, here is all the information Walter brought in on the NYPD investigation into Paco Johnson's murder. They wouldn't let him make copies of anything so he took photos. I downloaded them and cleaned them up. He can tell you about it."

Walter cleared his throat and leaned toward Beck.

"Alex helped me put together a summary page on top." He waited for Beck to take a quick look at it. "Earlier today, I read through reports filed by Detectives Raymond Ippolito and John Palmer, and a page of notes about their meeting with an assistant district attorney named Frederick Wilson written by their supervisor, James Levitt. I'm not entirely sure Levitt intended for me to see his notes, but they were on the pile of documents he handed to me. As Alex said, I couldn't make copies, but I guess Levitt figured an old civil servant like me wouldn't know how to take pictures.

"Ippolito and Palmer were the two who interviewed me on the morning Packy was shot. Palmer seems to be the one writing all the reports.

"There's also a ballistics report on the bullet and gun that killed Packy. And a preliminary report on the bullets that killed Derrick Watkins, but no match yet to a gun."

"There's also an initial CSU report and Palmer's write-up on a shooting that took place on Hoe Avenue. Victims were Jerome Watkins and Tyrell Williams."

Beck carefully checked the ballistics report on Packy while Walter continued.

"Of course, the detective's reports aren't up to date, but I had a chance to talk to Levitt after I went through everything. He supervises the precinct detective squad. As I said, they had a meeting at one o'clock with the assistant district attorney assigned to Packy's case. Levitt confirmed his detectives have witnesses that will testify that James shot Derrick Watkins, and that Derrick Watkins shot Paco Johnson, which they claim is your motive for shooting Watkins."

Beck asked, "Where'd they get these witnesses?"

"Levitt didn't explain, but when he asked me to help locate Demarco and Manny, who are listed on my parole roster, I pushed him about the witnesses. He wrote their names on a Post-it. I stuck it on Palmer's last report."

Beck compared the names on the sticky note with Alex's printout of the IDs they'd taken from the crew at Mount Hope Place.

Walter said, "I'm sorry to say, the assistant DA will be issuing arrest warrants very soon. Levitt wasn't exactly forthcoming about when, but I'm guessing Monday, latest. They want to arrest you for the murder of Derrick Watkins. Ciro for the attempted murder of Detective John Palmer. Manny and Demarco for shooting Jerome Watkins and Tyrell Williams."

Beck held up the Post-it note. "And their proof I shot Watkins are these bullshit witnesses?"

"Apparently."

"And they're saying they were in that apartment at the time?"

"Yes."

Demarco said, "Doesn't matter if they were there or not, James didn't shoot Derrick Watkins."

Walter said, "Then I guess all four are lying. Which begs the question, who *did* shoot him?"

Demarco interrupted. "Which begs the better question, where did they get those fake witnesses?"

Manny spoke up, "I'd say from the boss, Eric Jackson. How else they gonna come up with witnesses so fast in a neighborhood where everybody learns to keep their mouths shut? I'm betting all those stooges are part of his set."

Ciro emerged from the stairwell and headed for the table. "Wouldn't be the first time cops and crooks conspired."

Ciro took a seat, and Walter asked, "Why? What does Jackson get out of it?"

Manny answered, "Jackson gave them witnesses. They probably gave Jackson information on us."

Beck interrupted, "And their proof Derrick Watkins shot Packy are these same witnesses?"

"One of them. I think the one named Morris. Says he saw Derrick Watkins shoot Packy. Two others are hearsay witnesses. But also important, James, according to the ballistics report the bullet removed from Packy matches one of the guns the police found at the Mount Hope Place apartment. They're saying it belonged to Derrick Watkins. Has his prints on it."

Beck nodded. He'd already read that in the report.

"As for Manny and Demarco, they claim to have one eyewitness at the scene, a woman who gave a description that fits Manny and Demarco as the shooters on Hoe Avenue. Plus, they have an image from a security camera about a half block away. I took a picture of it. It's in that pile."

Beck shifted his gaze from the ballistics report to the blurry image of Manny and Demarco. He held it up. "They actually think this is evidence?"

"Well, it's my picture of the photo in the report. But it's not much different from what I saw. Plus, of course, their witness at the scene."

Beck frowned and sat back. He folded his arms, retreating into himself.

Walter didn't add any more information or interrupt Beck's thoughts.

After a moment, Beck said, "And the case against Ciro is Detective Palmer claiming he can identify a man from a block away shooting at him with a twelve-gauge shotgun."

Walter answered, "That's what his affidavit says. There's a note in there about them still canvassing for more witnesses in all the locations.

"James, minimum they can violate Ciro, Manny, and Demarco for multiple parole violations. Levitt wants me to contact Ciro's parole supervisor on Staten Island. And they're going to arrest you for murder. They may never convict any of you, but they have grounds. I don't see any of you avoiding jail until it gets sorted out."

Beck leaned forward and said to Walter, "I know you've been put in the middle of this, Walter. You've got your obligations to the NYPD and Department of Correction, and your loyalties to us, and to the truth. But I don't want you to worry. This information you've given us will make it possible for us to get to the truth and defend ourselves against what I'm sure you realize are false charges. It's much appreciated."

Beck stood and reached his hand out to Walter. Walter stood and shook hands with Beck.

"Walter, thank you. For everything. You've had a long day, especially after yesterday."

"I'm fine. You look like you had a terrible time after I left you. What happened?"

Beck waved it off. "There were some very unpleasant people up there. Don't worry about it." Beck motioned toward the papers on the table. "Between what I found out upstate and all this, there's a lot going on here, Walter. It's going to take a while to sort it out. I want you to get some rest."

Walter grimaced. "I should have gone up to the Bronx the minute I heard Packy had pulled that stunt hitchhiking in."

Beck said, "Walter, what's done is done. I promise you, we're going to take care of this. Just get some rest. We're going to need you."

"Yes. Yes, of course."

As he walked out of Beck's loft, the men thanked Walter. Nobody spoke until they heard the door downstairs close. Demarco broke the silence with an uncharacteristic curse.

"Shit! Minimum they're gonna try to send us back to prison and nail you for a murder, James."

"None of us is going anywhere. How's the girl? Is she all right?"

Manny spoke, "She's in one piece. Keeping to herself."

Beck said, "We're not the only ones jammed up here. If we get rid of the murder charges against us, that leaves the girl open for the murders."

Demarco said, "You're right. If they stop looking at us for it, at some point they might figure out it was her."

Ciro said, "Fucking hell, we got a piece of shit who's running a crime empire on the backs of women, the same fuck behind Packy gettin' popped, and now he's jamming us up supplying witnesses to the cops."

Demarco said, "And looking to kill Packy's kid."

Manny said, "And us, amigo. You know they're coming after us, and they got lots of young guns with them trying to make a mark."

Beck sat, arms crossed, frowning.

Everybody fell silent, waiting for Beck, who appeared to be falling into a darker and angrier mood with each passing moment.

Finally, Manny asked, "You got a way out of this, James? Or is it time to close shop and disappear?"

Beck looked up, breaking out of his reverie.

"We're not running, and we're not going back to prison."

"So what are we gonna do?"

"First I have to decide if I'm going to tell that young girl I'm going to kill the man who murdered her father."

That caused a moment of silence. And then Demarco asked, "You know who?"

"Yes. Detective John Palmer."

58

Detective John Palmer and Raymond Ippolito parked on 174th Street, within sight of the Bronx River Houses. Juju Jackson sat in the backseat of their unmarked car. Ippolito at the wheel. Eric Jackson had called them ten minutes after they'd finished their meeting with Frederick Wilson, demanding a meeting.

Jackson started the conversation.

"You got my witnesses, right."

Ippolito said, "Yeah. It looks good. What's the problem?"

"Time for you to keep up your end of the bargain. I got to move on that crew, now."

"Jeezus Christ, Eric, we just met with the ADA. We're getting everything worked out."

"You didn't hear what happened last night?"

Palmer asked, "What?"

"That crew took out four of my best guys at the Expressway Motel, and nearly killed another one who was with Whitey."

Ippolito said, "That motel isn't in our precinct. It's in the Four-Three. What the hell happened?"

"I just told you what happened. I got to hit that crew. Now."

"How do you know it was Beck's crew? What were your boys doing?"

"It was Beck's crew. You going to give me what you promised or not?"

Palmer turned around to talk to Jackson.

"Listen, we're setting this up for you perfect. You're going to be able to clean house in one shot."

"What the hell you talkin' about?"

"I said we're setting this up."

"How? When?"

"Couple of days, max. All you're going to need is one car of good shooters."

Ippolito looked at Palmer. He couldn't believe what he was hearing.

Jackson said, "How? Where?"

"All right, we're taking a huge risk, but here's the plan. Like we told you, Beck's crew consists of four guys. That's it. Only four."

Jackson said, "How do you know?"

"Trust me. We've scraped all the NYPD files. It's just the four of them. Like I said before, they probably have connections to other guys, but that's the crew."

"Go on."

"Our original deal was two for us, two for you, right? I'm going to deliver three of them to you, unarmed. The whole crew except for Beck, okay? Unarmed, in one place where you can set up to take them out. You'll have a clear shot at all three. You can plan escape routes and be gone in five seconds. How's that sound?"

"Like bullshit."

"It isn't. We just now got word from our precinct commander. The top brass has stepped in. The NYPD wants James Beck taken down, whatever it takes. Today is Friday.

We've been running around getting everything organized. We're getting arrest warrants for all four. Tomorrow, Saturday, there's going to be an all-day meeting to organize the arrest teams serving the warrants. The troops go in after them Sunday, early Monday morning, latest. They'll get processed initially wherever we pick them up, but at some point, all of them will be sent to Bronx Criminal Court on 161st for arraignment."

"I still ain't heard how we gonna get a shot at them."

Palmer spoke slowly and precisely. "Once they get arrested and into processing, they obviously won't be armed. They won't be anywhere near a weapon. I'm going to know where they are every step of the way. I'm going to mess with the evidence a little so that Guzman, Baldassare, and Jones will make bail."

"Bullshit. Them guys gotta have heavy records. How's the judge not going to remand them?"

"Trust me, all I gotta do is lose a few pages of material. They'll have a good lawyer. And money. But if the judge doesn't let 'em post bail, so what? They'll be sent to Rikers and be out of your hair. You'll have plenty of time to take care of them inside if you want."

Ippolito knew Palmer was lying about Baldassare. He'd already supplied Wilson with an affidavit he'd signed. But he might be right about Jones and Guzman.

Jackson asked, "What about Beck?"

"Forget about Beck. I told you, he's going down. He's not getting bail. Nobody really gives a shit about the other three. All you have to do then is be ready when they walk out of court. You can have men on the street, or do it as a drive-by, or both. Whatever way you want. I leave that up to you. They walk out of the Bronx courthouse, unarmed, all three in one place, and your guys take 'em out. End of story. Done."

Jackson muttered, "Christ."

"What?"

"Outside the courthouse? Place is crawling with cops."

"No it's not. Not out front. Cops come in and out, but rarely through the front. And they don't guard the front. There's more correction officers or court police than NYPD, but they're mostly inside, too. Out front is a bunch of losers smoking and drinking coffee waiting to go into court.

"If you don't want to do it in front of the court, fine. Wait for the three of them to come out. They'll probably have a car waiting for them. They get into their car. You follow the car. Pick the best place. Take 'em all out. Blast the crap out of the one car. Kill them all. We're done. You won't get a better opportunity, ever. You can't get in the way of these arrests. But you can take your shot if you want it."

Silence descended in the car. Ippolito looked at Palmer. In twenty-two years on the force he had never seen, or even heard of a cop conspiring with a criminal to assassinate three men. His only thought was how to get as far away as possible from John Palmer.

Jackson asked, "And you can track 'em every step of the way?"

"Absolutely. I'll be in the court. I'll have to be available if they want me to appear at the arraignments. I'll know when they're heading out. When they make bail, I can even go behind the courtroom and find out when they finish their paperwork."

"And this ADA ain't gonna get them remanded?"

"Can I guarantee he won't? No. Yeah, they all have records, but like I said they're going to have a damn good lawyer. And I'll make sure he has grounds. Nothing is guaranteed, but this is a hell of a lot better than your people running all over trying to find these guys."

Jackson looked at his watch.

"It's Friday. When you say they're going to start arresting these assholes?"

"Sunday, early Monday morning. You won't have to wait long."

"Good, cuz I ain't. And if we find any of these assholes beforehand, we'll shoot 'em down like dogs, and you can use your warrants to wipe your asses with."

59

Demarco knew better than to doubt Beck, but he still couldn't believe what he'd heard.

"You're saying that cop shot Packy?"

"Yes. Detective John Palmer shot Packy."

Beck held up the copy of the ballistics report on the bullet removed from Packy. "According to this, the bullet that killed Packy was a twenty-two from a gun they found in Watkins's apartment at Mount Hope Place." He held up another page. "Here's an inventory of the guns." He held up a third page. "Here's a photo of all the guns laid out next to the pillowcases I put them in." Beck pointed to one of the guns in the picture. "This gun is a Phoenix Arms HP twenty-two. The gun ballistics says it fired the bullet that killed Packy."

Beck paused, waiting for any reactions. There were none.

"I wiped down every gun we took off those guys and put them in those pillowcases. None of 'em was a twenty-two. They were all nines, except for one forty caliber. So how the hell did the Phoenix twenty-two get into one of those pillowcases?"

Manny Guzman asked, "It was in the pillowcase with the others? Cops didn't find it somewhere else in the apartment?"

"No. The report says all those guns were in the pillowcases. If the cops found that twenty-two someplace else in the apartment, why put it in a pillowcase? And, it's the only gun with the serial number filed off. And, the only gun with prints on it."

"Derrick Watkins's prints."

"Correct, but remember, I wiped down every gun. Palmer's report says he led the search of that apartment right after we left. And all of a sudden a small caliber untraceable gun appears? That's the perfect cop throwaway piece. He was the only cop on the scene who knew about Derrick Watkins's involvement with Packy. He brought the gun into the apartment. He saw Watkins dead . . ."

Demarco broke in, "And used it to pin Paco's murder on Derrick Watkins."

"Exactly." Beck held up more pages. "He knew that gun killed Packy, because he used it to shoot Packy. With Derrick laying there dead, he had a chance to put Derrick's prints on the twenty-two. Then he adds the Phoenix to the other guns. Now he's got someone to take the fall for shooting Packy. A dead man who can't deny it. *He* had the gun that shot Packy. *He* shot Packy. *He* used it to solve his case."

Manny asked, "But why? What was his motive? He didn't know Packy. Packy hadn't been in that neighborhood for seventeen years."

"You're right. It doesn't make sense unless there's a connection between John Palmer and Packy Johnson."

"What's the connection?"

"Walter helped me find a senior guard at Eastern, Oswald Remsen, who was running a prostitution ring with his two sons, both of them guards at Eastern. I can't prove it yet, but I'm betting his third son, Edward, worked with Eric Jackson to supply Oswald Remsen with prostitutes."

Manny asked, "How? What's the connection?"

"Edward Remsen is a guard at Sing Sing. Plenty of guys from the Bronx are in that prison. I'm figuring one or more of them connected to Eric Jackson hooked up Edward Remsen with Jackson. The Watkins brothers have been recruiting and running prostitutes for years, Jackson was their boss. I got Oswald Remsen to admit a new inmate up at Eastern tipped Packy off about his daughter prostituting for Jackson's crew. I think Packy knew about Oswald's prostitution business. I think he believed his daughter, Amelia, was going to be shipped upstate to prostitute for Oswald Remsen."

Manny said, "Shit, his daughter getting whored out for a corrupt CO – that would've definitely sent Packy over the deep end."

"It did. That's why he headed straight for Bronx River Houses to get his daughter. But I still haven't explained Palmer's motive." Beck held up the ledger books Amelia had found. "If Derrick Watkins was making three hundred thousand a year with his stable, Oswald Remsen had to be making much more. Maybe millions. Now here's where it connects to Palmer. Turns out Oswald Remsen was also a big wheel in the correction officers' union. When things went down up there between us, he denied ordering anybody to kill Packy, but said he had the connections to do it. Said he'd 'paid his dues.'

"I didn't know what that meant. Who he was connected to? Before I came back here, I went online. It took about five minutes to figure out the correction officers' union does a ton of lobbying in Albany. The chief lobbyist for the New York correction officers' union is John Palmer Senior."

"Fuck."

"I'm betting Oswald Remsen put a lot of money into that man's pocket. It all fits. Oswald knew an inmate had tipped off Packy about his daughter being turned out by those pimps in Eric Jackson's set. Remsen knew Packy was getting out on parole. He wanted to make sure Packy didn't make any waves. I believe Remsen called John Palmer Senior, who, in turn, called his son, an NYPD detective working in the Bronx, and told him to make sure Paco Johnson didn't cause any trouble for them."

Demarco asked, "By killing him?"

"No. I don't think Palmer Senior ordered his son to kill Packy. He wouldn't want his golden boy to do that."

Demarco asked, "Then why did he?"

"At first, I didn't see it. I remembered back when we found Derrick Watkins, I didn't think he'd shot Packy. I thought one of his crew did it. Trying to make a name for himself. But there was someone else trying to make a name for himself."

Demarco said, "John Palmer Junior."

"Exactly. His father tells him check on this guy Paco Johnson who might be causing trouble about his daughter living with a pimp at Bronx River Houses. I think the plan was to intervene and violate Packy back to prison. Simple. Problem solved.

"But Packy moved too fast. Next thing he knows, Palmer hears a bunch of 911 calls about a disturbance at

Bronx River Houses, which is in the precinct right next to his. Palmer makes a beeline over there. Or maybe he was already snooping around Bronx River Houses trying to find the daughter before his midnight-to-eight shift.

"Packy is calling out Derrick Watkins. Trying to find his daughter. They beat the shit out of him. Cops start arriving. Palmer doesn't want to disappoint Daddy. He has to make sure this doesn't get worse. He follows Packy out of the complex until he walks into Palmer's precinct. Now Packy is on his turf. What does Palmer see? The guy his father warned him about, already making trouble. A broken-down ex-convict, already half dead from a beating. But he sees more. He sees an opportunity to take care of a problem for his father, *and* a chance to advance his career. He walks up behind Packy, puts one in his head with his throwaway piece."

Beck pointed his forefinger like a gun barrel. "Opportunity. Impulse. Pop. One shot. Packy is dead in the gutter. Daddy's problem is taken care of, and John Palmer is on the way to solving his first murder.

"Palmer had the weapon. He had the opportunity. He had the motive. In fact, two motives."

For a few moments, no one said a word. And then Manny Guzman spoke. "He should have gotten away with it. Packy was a nobody."

Beck said, "He should have, but he's not."

There were a few moments of silence while everybody at the table absorbed what Beck had told them. And then Ciro Baldassare asked, "How's Palmer not going to get away with it?"

Beck didn't answer.

"Hold on, boss. You really thinking about takin' out a cop?"

Beck sat back. "Let's not worry about that now, Ciro. First, we have to figure out how to get Manny and Demarco off the hook for shooting Jerome Watkins and Tyrell Williams. And me for shooting Derrick Watkins, and you for the attempted murder of an NYPD detective. And, we have to do it in a way that doesn't implicate Amelia for shooting Derrick Watkins and Tyrell Williams."

Manny added, "And we gotta make sure Jackson's crew doesn't kill her. Or any of us."

Demarco said, "Plus, we have to do it fast, before the NYPD comes down on us and locks us all away, maybe this time for good."

Willie Reese rose his big hand.

Beck said, "Yeah?"

"Plus that other guy."

"What other guy?"

"You said there were six. You took care of five."

Beck smiled. Willie Reese never failed to surprise him. He reached in his back pocket and held up the envelope with the name Janice Elkins had written on it. He tossed it onto his pile of documents.

"Plus that other guy."

Reese nodded and told Alex Liebowitz, "Computer man, don't lose that name."

Manny said, "So back to my question. What's first, James?"

"First, I talk to Amelia."

60

Beck left the others sitting at the table and headed for the third floor, where there were several bedrooms for guests. Amelia had picked the one at the far end.

The room had a double bed, a single window facing southeast, a closet with sliding doors that took up most of the wall opposite the window. There was a bed, a dresser, a mirror, and under the window a small round table with a club chair upholstered in brown leather. Amelia sat in the chair, her long legs stretched out, her bare feet resting on the edge of the bed. The Glock 17 on the table next to her.

Beck knocked lightly on the open door.

"Amelia?"

She quickly pulled her feet off the bed and sat up.

Beck stayed in the doorway.

"I'm James Beck. Your father was a very good friend of mine. I'm happy to see you here. May I come in?"

"Yes."

Beck entered the room and extended his hand.

Amelia hesitated. Shaking hands wasn't something she did. Beck was about to forget it when she leaned forward and put her hand in his. It was more like allowing Beck contact than actually shaking hands.

Amelia was dressed in her jeans and gray Levi's T-shirt, but all her clothes had been washed and dried by Demarco while she had waited in her room, napping, wrapped up in an extra-large flannel bathrobe.

Beck said, "Can I talk to you for a minute?"

"Okay."

Beck sat on the edge of the bed. Amelia in the chair. They both made believe the Glock wasn't on the table.

Beck tried to gauge Amelia's mood. This was a very different version of the young woman he'd seen shoot Derrick Watkins. That woman had looked like a caricature, a perverse attempt to manipulate and heighten the sexuality of an adolescent. The young woman who stared back at him seemed reserved to the point of austere. She wore no makeup at all. She had combed out her hair and tied it into a tight pony tail. She looked like a high school athlete holding herself in a tense state of composed readiness.

For a moment, Beck thought about asking her to put the Glock in one of the dresser drawers, or just do it himself. Instead, he asked, "How are you?"

The question confused Amelia for a moment. She couldn't remember anyone ever asking her that. She replied, "All right."

"I'm sorry you've been going through a hard time."

"When?"

Beck felt foolish. This girl's entire life had been a hard time.

"Lately."

"Oh."

"Well, at least you're with us now. Assuming you want to be."

"I got no place else to go. Even if I did, I'd probably get killed before I got there."

Beck looked directly at her. "We won't let that happen. You're safe with us."

"Why? You think Juju Jackson and his guys ain't gonna find you? Or the cops?"

"I'm going to take care of that."

"How?"

"Let me ask you a couple of questions first."

"Okay."

"The gun you used to shoot Derrick Watkins, where did you find it?"

"In the freezer, back in the kitchen. I got it when you asked me to get a towel for him."

"I'm sorry you had to go through that."

"What?"

"Shooting him."

"I didn't have no choice. They was going to kill me."

"Do you know why?"

"Pimps don't need no reason. Maybe cuz of the trouble my father caused."

"You should know why your father caused them trouble."

"Why?"

"He was trying to save you from being forced to work for people in a situation even worse than in the Bronx."

"Who?"

"I'll explain later. Point is, we have a lot to deal with. First thing I need is information on Eric Jackson's operation. Where his money comes from. Who was running his women. Do you know any way I can find out about that? Where'd you find those ledgers tracking Derrick's prostitution business?"

"I found 'em in Tyrell Williams's car. He must've ripped off Derrick's place after I shot him."

Beck nodded. "You think there might be more information like that somewhere? More ledgers?"

"Yeah. Most likely at Biggie's house. Whatever Derrick did, Biggie did more. Biggie has, well had, a house where his wives and kids live, and where he has his phone lines for the in-call hookers."

"Where is it?"

"Crotona Avenue near 178th. I don't know the exact number. I know it by sight. I'll show you if you want."

"I don't want to take you up there."

"You gonna hit the place for Biggie's records?"

"Yes."

"You got a lot better chance of gettin' in there if I'm with you."

Beck struggled with his decision.

Amelia said, "Hey, I don't want to go up there very much either, but sooner or later Juju or Whitey Bondurant going to go in there and clean out the place. They might've done it already if they ain't too busy looking for me. I know some of the women in there. I show up, I'm pretty sure they'll open the door for me."

Beck checked his watch.

Amelia said, "You ain't got much time. Biggie been shot for a while now. Juju probably already got people up there watchin' the place."

"Okay. We should move fast on this. I guess we could use your help. We'll figure out how to play it as we head up there."

They stood up to leave. Amelia slipped on her hoodie and shoved the Glock into the kangaroo pocket.

Beck asked her, "By the way, when you were looking for a gun to shoot Derrick, were there other guns hidden in that apartment?"

"Not that I could find. I didn't want to use a frozen gun, but it worked."

"You still have that gun?"

Amelia pointed toward the closet. "In the closet. In a red laundry bag. Why?"

"I might need it later."

"You can have it. But it's empty."

"Empty is fine."

61

Sitting in their van on Hamilton Avenue overlooking the employees' parking lot outside Sing Sing, the Bolo brothers spotted a hunched-over man walking toward the car registered to Edward Remsen. Although the car was a gleaming new Lexus GS 350, in his rumpled uniform and scuffed work shoes, Remsen looked like the last person who would own such a car.

Ricky, talking out of the side of his mouth as usual, commented to his brother, Jonas, "That shit bag definitely has a second stream of income."

They tailed Remsen to a bar frequented by guards located on Main Street in Ossining. While he was still in the bar Ricky called Beck to report on his progress.

Beck answered the call while he, Amelia, and Demarco were heading to Biggie Watkins's house.

"What's going on?"

"Remsen's been in a local watering hole for about forty minutes. Looks like the usual TGIF-activity for law enforcement personnel – getting piss drunk."

"Interesting. Either they haven't found his father and brothers, or they haven't notified him yet."

"Maybe he likes to turn his cell phone off while he's drinking."

"Whatever. Stay with him. Ciro and Manny are heading to Norwood. Call them and let them know when and where they can take him down."

"Will do. If his next stop isn't home, I'll let them know."

"Good. Tell them where he's headed, and they'll catch up to you. Don't lose him."

"No way."

Beck cut the call and turned around in the passenger seat so he could talk to Amelia.

"Thanks for doing this."

"This is going to help you take down Juju, right?"

"Yes."

"Then you don't got to thank me." Amelia turned to stare out the car window. "If you don't do somethin' about Juju Jackson and Whitey Bondurant, I'll have to look over my shoulder the rest of my life. If they get me, they'll kill me. After they rape and beat me. Simple as that."

"That's not going to happen."

"You only two guys. Or four guys. Every damn thug in the Bronx want to be on their crew."

"That's why they're called wannabees. What can you tell me about this place we're going to?"

"It's Biggie's main house. He has other places, but I don't know all of 'em."

"What about Jackson?"

"What about him?"

"Does he own part of this place?"

"Juju owns part of everything. He's behind a lot of shit."

"How many women you think will be there?"

Amelia shrugged. "I don't know. Four, five, maybe more. And most likely Queenie."

"Who's she?"

"She was one of Biggie's women. Maybe even one of Juju's before that. She got passed on. She's a smart whore who always found a way to be useful. She was helping Derrick run his deal. Watched over his whores."

"Who else might be there?"

"Some of the ones that lived with Biggie, and probably the girls that can't stay at Derrick's place in the Houses anymore."

"Any children?"

"For sure. And probably some of Juju's guys in there watching over things. Got to be. They wouldn't leave all those women alone. And they got to watch over Biggie's stuff."

Beck said, "I wanted to ask you about that gun you have."

"I ain't giving it up."

"I'm not asking you to. I want to know if you ever fired it."

"No."

"Then you don't know if it works properly. Please don't shoot the gun unless you absolutely have to. And, if you have to, be careful. We don't really know who's in there, or where they might be. You fire that gun, bullets could go through walls. You don't want to shoot any babies, do you?"

Surprisingly, Amelia thought for a moment before she answered. "No. I guess not. Then again, if they're Biggie's babies, maybe they be better off dead." Amelia paused a beat, staring out the window. "Especially if they're girl babies."

After a few moments, Beck said, "I'm thinking you should help us get in the house, then hang back while we do what we have to do."

"Fine with me."

A few minutes later, Demarco drove past a two-story house, three windows wide with faded yellow wood siding on Crotona Avenue between 178th Street and East Tremont. The house stood behind a rusting chain-link fence set into a two-foot concrete base painted a garish red. All the doors and windows were secured by wrought-iron bars. Next to the house stood a four-story brick apartment building. A driveway ran between the house and the apartment building leading to a backyard.

Demarco drove around to Belmont Street and stopped directly behind the house. He pulled over to the curb next to a four-foot chain-link fence that bordered the yard.

Beck said, "Give me a minute to get in place behind the house."

"If someone comes running out the back door, just show him your face. That should stop them."

"That might be all I can do. Don't shoot anybody in there unless you have to. I don't want any kids hurt. We've been leaving enough dead bodies behind us as it is. Take 'em down, or drive 'em out. I'll take care of anybody who comes out back."

"Then what?"

"We search the house for evidence on Jackson's operation and get the hell out."

Beck watched as Demarco pulled away. He wasn't worried about sending Demarco alone into the house. It would be like releasing a mongoose into a nest of snakes.

Demarco parked on Crotona up the street from the house. He and Amelia stepped out onto the sidewalk.

Demarco told her, "See if you can get someone to open the door. I'll handle it from there."

Amelia nodded. She put her right hand in the pocket of her hoodie. Demarco slipped his steel baton out of his back pocket and into his right hand. He walked alongside Amelia in his usual effortless way, dressed in dark slacks and a dark blue Dolce & Gabbana jacquard dress shirt. He noticed the way Amelia shuffled along and said to her, "We have to get you some decent shoes."

"You got that right."

"In fact, we should shop for a whole new wardrobe."

She looked at him and said, "How come you talk so white? You look like a damn hard case, but you sound like you ain't at all."

"I speak the way I do because I prefer it. The way I look sometimes makes people nervous, so it helps disarm them."

"Disarm? Like they gonna lay down their guns or something?"

"Something like that."

"Why you want to do that?"

"It usually makes things easier."

"And what's all this about a *wardrobe*. It sounds gay, man."

"I am gay." Before Amelia responded, Demarco said, "Go do something useful. Get me into that house."

Demarco softly kicked the unlatched fence gate out of Amelia's way and motioned her forward. She walked past broken toys, a rusty lawn chair, an open garbage can, and up a short flight of stairs to the front door. The heavy wrought-iron gate in front of the main door stood half open, but the front door was closed and locked. An oval window set high on the front door showed there were lights on in the house.

Amelia pushed the security door out of her way, stepped to the front door, and knocked hard, twice. Demarco positioned himself next to her. He had to stand sideways as there was barely room for him on the landing.

Amelia knocked again, harder. An outside light mounted on the wall next to the door came on.

A voice asked from the other side of the closed door, "Who's there?"

Amelia said, "Is that you, Queenie?"

"What the hell you doing here, Princess?"

"I need a place to stay."

Queenie opened the door a crack and spoke in an angry whisper. "Are you crazy? Everybody's lookin' for you. You don't want to be coming in here."

"C'mon, Queenie. I need a place to stay."

"What? There's three of Whitey's boys in here right now. They say you shot Derrick. They gonna kill you, Princess. Go on, get the hell outta here."

Demarco moved Amelia aside and shoved the door open, knocking Queenie back. Queenie opened her mouth to yell out a warning, but Demarco covered her mouth with his left hand and pushed her back against the wall with his right.

"Don't move. Don't say . . ."

Before he could finish, a male voice shouted out from upstairs, "Who the fuck is that?"

Demarco motioned with his head for Amelia to come in. She stepped into the house with her Glock in her hand.

Demarco whispered to Queenie, "Tell him nobody."

Amelia stepped forward and pointed her gun at Queenie's face.

Demarco took his hand off her mouth, and she yelled back, "Nobody."

The voice upstairs yelled, "What the fuck you mean, nobody?"

Demarco was already running for the set of stairs on his right. He heard heavy steps pounding down from above. He hit the stairs running and almost made it up the first flight when a large man holding a gun at his side turned into him. Before the man could react, Demarco rammed the point of the closed steel baton into his solar plexus. The gunman doubled over, paralyzed. Demarco grabbed the back of the his head and slammed it into the stairway bannister, breaking his nose. He jammed the butt of the baton into his temple, knocking him out.

It had taken all of three seconds. Demarco paused to pull the gun out of the unconscious man's hands and continued rushing up the stairs, gun in one hand, his expandable steel baton in the other.

He heard crying and whimpering from children awakened by the yelling.

He reached the dark second-floor hallway just as someone burst out of a room to his right. Demarco slashed the steel baton across the side of a tall man's head, then back-handed it against his jaw. Two out of three, down and out.

Demarco couldn't see much in the dim light, but at the far end of the hall another figure leaned out of a room and fired a shot at him. The sudden gunshot caused an eruption of screaming and crying.

Demarco jumped into the room the tall man had come out of. It was lit with only a night-light. Demarco could make out three cribs, but the noise from the children awakened by the gunshot was horrible. He leaned out and back for a split second and the shooter fired two more times. Now the screaming turned into hysteria, with women on the floor yelling and crying out. Demarco was trapped, but somehow he had to get to the gunman without returning fire.

He moved to his left to get a view of the hallway. There was another doorway on the opposite side, halfway down the hall. He took one step back and went for it full speed, bursting across the hall, banging the door open, and almost falling into the room. Several women had taken cover behind a bed that couldn't possibly stop a bullet. They screamed and yelled. Demarco yelled back, "Shut up!"

Demarco had moved like a pawn on a chessboard, getting one step closer to the guy with the gun, but he still couldn't risk shooting at him.

One of the women was cursing, another whimpering. Demarco ignored them. He pulled out the gun he had taken from the first attacker, leaned out into the hall, and threw it into the wall at the end of the hallway. Shots rang out. The shooter leaned out from the doorway to see if he'd hit anything and Demarco overhanded his steel baton at him. The handle of the baton cracked into the shooter's forehead. He stumbled backward and disappeared down a set of stairs leading to the kitchen on the first floor.

Demarco let him run. The first man was still unconscious. Demarco walked back to the other end of the hallway, wincing against the cacophony of crying children and babies, and checked him for weapons. He found a small revolver stuck in his waistband. He pulled the gun out and shoved it in his back pocket. He ripped the man's belt off his pants, tied his wrists with it, and kicked the side of his head.

He continued back along the hallway, leaning into bedrooms, yelling at the women to be quiet and take care of their damn babies, and headed down the back stairs.

Outside, Beck heard the gunshots. He stood motionless, waiting in the shadows of the small backyard, cluttered with empty spackling buckets, bags of garbage, cinder blocks, scrap wood, and other junk.

Beck picked up a concrete masonry block.

He heard footsteps running down stairs. The back door flew open. He braced himself and swung the concrete block into the body mass running his way, timing it just about perfectly.

The man fleeing the house stopped so suddenly, his feet flew out from under him and he hit the ground with a loud thud. Beck kicked the gun he had been holding into a pile of rubble. As the downed man groaned and struggled for air, Beck dragged him back into the house, the effort making him groan, too.

He called upstairs, "Demarco? Any more in there? Where are you?"

Demarco stepped into view on the back steps.

"That was the last one. You get him?"

"Yeah."

Beck and Demarco found a roll of duct tape in the kitchen. Beck used it to immobilize Bondurant's men, taping them from ankles to knees, wrists to elbows, and around their mouths. While he did that, Demarco, Amelia, and Queenie settled down the women and children, collected all their cell phones, and then brought the women into the large front room.

Amelia, Glock in hand, watched over the women as Beck and Demarco searched the house.

They found one ledger book on the dining room table, along with two cell phones and two landline phones. They found four rifles and five handguns stashed around the house. Beck went out into the yard and retrieved the last handgun. They piled everything on the dining room table.

In the closet of the largest bedroom, they discovered a safe bolted to the floor.

Beck said to Demarco, "Hey, bring that woman in charge up here. I don't want to waste time on this safe if there's nothing in it."

Demarco returned with Queenie. She stood in the middle of the messy bedroom, a sullen look on her face. She wore jeans that fitted her fifteen pounds ago and a white top with a red stain above her right breast. The years had added weight, softened her body, and hardened her attitude.

Beck said, "Thanks for getting the kids settled."

"What you want with me?"

Beck held up the ledger book he'd found in the dining room.

"You're the one who made all the entries in this, aren't you?"

"So what?"

"Are there any more ledger books in that safe?"

Queenie's mouth turned into a firmly shut line. Her expression told Beck everything he needed to know.

"What else is in there?"

He got the same reaction.

"Okay, there's two ways you can play this, ma'am. You can take a share of all the cash we find in that safe and come with us. Or, you can stay here until Jackson, Bondurant, or more of their men show up and deal with what they do. Which way do you want to go?"

Queenie stood where she was, unresponsive.

"And just so you know, in terms of Jackson and Bondurant, their time is over. One way or another, they're done. I guarantee you that."

Queenie sneered. "You trippin', man."

"I won't tell you again. Their time is over. You want to go in with us and take your share of what's in the safe, or you want to stay here and wait for Bondurant?"

"What do you mean 'go in' with you?"

"I don't have time to explain everything. Decide now."

Queenie refused to make a choice about going with Beck, but she did say, "I don't know exactly what's in that safe. But if I were you, I'd find a way to open it."

62

Ciro and Manny sat in Ciro's Escalade parked about a half block from Edward Remsen's house on Hull Avenue in the Norwood section of the Bronx. Manny's cell phone rang.

"Yo."

"It's me," said Ricky Bolo. "We're about five, six minutes out heading your way. Coming down Mosholu Parkway. Where are you?"

"Parked at a hydrant a half block from his house."

"Good. Looks like this useless drunk will be home soon. You set?"

"Yes. He's got his own parking area. A driveway leads up to it from the street. Nice little gate and all. He pulls in there, it should be easy."

"I'll leave it to you. We'll tail him until he turns onto his block and then be on our way."

"Good."

"Over and out, sweetheart. Have fun."

Manny hit the End button on his phone and turned to Ciro.

"He should be here in about five. How you want to play this?"

Ciro squinted at Remsen's house down the block. Night had fallen. Five-story apartment buildings occupied the north side of Hull Avenue except for two small houses, one of which was Remsen's. The other side was mostly modest two-flat houses. Only three streetlights illuminated the long block, so there were plenty of shadows under the trees and between houses.

Ciro stepped out of his car and looked down the block. He came back and said, "I can't get between his house and the one next door. Gate is blocking the way, so I'll wait in the doorway across the street. What'd Ricky say he's driving?"

"New Lexus. Dark blue."

"Okay, you get behind the wheel. Fall in behind the Lexus. When he turns into his driveway, you pull in and block the driveway. I'll do the rest."

Ciro pulled a two-pound, nineteen-inch fish bat made of molded glass-filled polypropylene from under his seat.

"Don't kill him, Ciro."

"I'll just give him a tap."

"Make it half a tap. And don't hit him in the stomach. He's been drinking. He'll puke all over himself. I don't want to haul away a stinking mess."

"Jeezus, maybe I should give him a fucking written invitation to come with us."

Ten minutes after the Bolos ended their tail on Remsen, Ricky Bolo's cell phone rang.

Ricky said, "You get him?"

"It's me, Beck."

"Oh, we just left Ciro and Manny. They were doing that thing."

"I know. They called me. It's done. Listen, I have a safe needs opening."

"Cool. What kind?"

"A Diebold."

"With a dial or a touchpad?"

"Touchpad."

"You have the model number?"

"Uh, no, you need it?"

"Not really. Where is it?"

"In the Bronx. On Crotona near 178th Street."

"Is that a house?"

"Yes. The safe is in a closet. A fairly big one."

"The closet or the safe?"

"The closet. Safe isn't very big. Two by two by three."

"Good. In a closet will help cover the noise. If it matters."

"It does. We have sleeping babies here."

"What?"

"Just hurry."

Demarco joined Amelia downstairs keeping watch.

Beck and Queenie roamed the second floor, making sure doors were closed and the babies and children were sleeping.

Jonas did most of the work. Ricky changed drill bits; handed him tools; adjusted the chain holding the frame that kept the drill in place. It took thirty-eight minutes to remove the touchpad, drill a hole, and set up an electronic box that made the connections to open the lock.

The safe turned out to be a bonanza.

It contained eighteen thousand dollars, fifteen ledger books going back over a period of ten years, and a Western Digital one-terabyte external hard drive, along with three more handguns and six boxes of ammunition.

Beck said to Jonas and Ricky, "Get those guns and ammunition out of here. And the weapons downstairs on the dining room table. Do what you want with them." Beck handed Ricky Bolo six thousand dollars. "Here's your share. After you take care of the guns, head back to Red Hook. There's more to do."

"On it."

Beck turned to Queenie, who had been napping in a large wingback chair in the bedroom. He tapped her on the shoulder.

Queenie cleared her throat, took a moment to get her bearings, and stood up.

"What?"

"Gather the women in the living room downstairs. I want to talk to them." Beck handed Queenie three thousand dollars. "Here's your cut from the safe."

Queenie looked at the money, said nothing, and shoved the cash into her bra.

Beck went downstairs and asked Demarco, "Those guys squared away?"

"Yeah, I put them in three different rooms."

"Good. Time to get out of here."

Demarco left to get the Mercury. Beck found Amelia in the front room with the other women. He motioned for her to step out in the hallway.

"What?"

Beck handed her three thousand dollars. "This is yours. We found it here."

Amelia took the cash without comment.

"We're leaving now. You take Queenie out to the car when Demarco pulls up. Get in the backseat with her.

Keep an eye on her. I know she's not your favorite person, but try not to show it."

Amelia nodded and went to wait by the front door.

Queenie came out of the front room. "They all here."

"Good. Thanks. Queenie, go with Amelia please. It's time."

Beck waited for pushback, a comment, but Queenie just looked around once and left.

Beck walked into the front room. Six women looked at him, perfectly willing to let him be in charge. Some stood, some sat. Some were dressed for bed, others were in street clothes. Beck stood at the dining table, quickly counting the remaining money into one-thousand-dollar piles. Beck found himself a hundred dollars short for the last pile. He wasn't sure where he'd miscounted. He didn't have time to recount. He added the difference from his own pocket, picked up the piles, and handed them out to each of the women.

Beck wasn't sure how he felt as each woman looked at him and took the money. None of them asked any questions. None of them said anything. After he handed the last pile of cash to the last woman, Beck said, "When Jackson's men come, hide that money. Tell them I took it all. I'm sorry for the disturbance. Good-bye."

Beck turned and hurried out, unable to count all the things he was sorry about.

He closed the door quietly as he left so as not to wake any of the children.

63

On the drive back to Red Hook, Amelia and Queenie sat in the backseat of the Mercury as far apart as they could. A few minutes into the drive, Beck heard Queenie muttering to Amelia, "What the hell you doing with these two? Comin' in there tearing the place up."

Amelia kept her voice low. "What do you care?"

Queenie said, "Girl, don't give me no damn attitude. I tried to help you when you needed it."

Amelia's voice rose. "Help me how? Help me get raped and beaten and locked up in a closet? Help me be a whore?"

Queenie folded her arms and harrumphed, talking as much to herself as to Amelia. "You think you the only one? My name is in them books, too. Long before yours. You ain't the only one got prostituted. Uppity . . ."

Amelia spun toward Queenie, ready to punch her, but Beck turned to them.

"Ladies, please!"

Turning sent a bolt of pain flashing across his lower ribs. He grimaced. The pain put an edge in his voice.

"We don't need any arguing."

Queenie couldn't stop herself from announcing to everyone in the car, "I hope you all know what the hell you doing. Juju Jackson and Whitey Bondurant got a hell of lot more men than you got. And everyone of 'em is looking to kill this girl."

Amelia yelled back, "And everyone one of 'em tried is either dead or busted up, so fuck you and fuck them."

Beck raised his voice to interrupt them. "Queenie."

She turned to face him, cocking her head back and forth with each word. "What? What you got to say to me, mother-fucker?"

Beck softened his voice. "You're an intelligent woman. This is the time to stop talking and start thinking. Time you got on the right side of this thing whether you like it or not."

"What side is that?"

"The side against Eric Jackson."

"Yeah? And how's that gonna work?"

"We'll discuss it in the morning."

Queenie made a face, crossed her arms again over her chest, and shook her head. It took a great deal of effort for her to stop talking.

When they arrived in Red Hook, Beck asked Demarco to get Queenie settled in a room.

He stood outside his bar while Demarco and Queenie went inside. Beck hadn't asked her to, but Amelia stayed with him. It was nearing one-thirty on Saturday morning. A cold front had moved in and the moist air off the bay seemed to be hovering right at the dew point.

A bone-deep fatigue had seeped into Beck. The constant pain from the beating outside Remsen's bar had drained him. Amelia stood next to him, tall and straight, her silent presence lending gravity to the early morning surroundings.

She asked, "Are you okay?"

Beck turned to her, surprised at the question.

"I'm okay. Just tired."

"Sorry about that shit in the car. She just reminds me . . ."

"I understand. Try to forget about that. It's all going to be over soon."

"How?"

"Step by step."

"I hope you know what you're doing."

"So do I. Do me a favor, can you reach in and get those ledgers and the hard drive in the front there?"

Amelia moved quickly to do as Beck asked.

Beck picked the hard drive off the pile and let Amelia carry the rest. He'd aggravated something in his back slinging the masonry block into the guy running out the back door at Watkins's house. He didn't want to risk bending over to get the ledgers, or carry them.

When they reached the second floor, Alex Liebowitz and Willie Reese were the only ones present. Alex sat at Beck's computer. Willie napped on one of the couches.

Beck took a seat at the dining table.

"Amelia, can you put those ledgers on the table?"

She did.

"Try to get some sleep."

Amelia understood that was Beck's way of politely asking her to leave. As she walked upstairs, Alex came over and sat next to Beck. Willie Reese woke up and joined them.

They waited for Beck to finish typing text messages into his smartphone. One for Walter Ferguson and one for his lawyer, Phineas Dunleavy, asking both of them to please come to the Red Hook headquarters at eleven A.M.

When he'd finished, he looked up and said, "Okay, guys, I don't have a lot of gas left." He handed the external hard drive to Alex and said, "See if you can open this."

Alex went off to check the drive.

Beck turned to Willie. "Everything okay?"

"I got a lot of eyes and ears out there. It's quiet, boss."

"I don't think anything will happen until Sunday or Monday. Tell your guys to watch for two things. Cops moving in a group, and any rough boys they don't know. In particular, a black albino guy, big, wears his hair in dreads. He'll probably be wearing sunglasses."

Reese scowled. "What do you mean? Like a white black guy?"

"Yes."

"Never seen one."

"Hopefully, you still won't. From what Demarco tells me, he's dangerous."

"Then if we see him, we should put him down. Fast."

Beck thought about his answer for a moment. "If it gets to that, agreed. Main thing right now, Willie, I want you to keep an eye on Amelia. I'd prefer she doesn't leave the place, but if she gets restless and wants to take a walk, or really needs something, you stick with her. Nobody bothers her."

"Done."

"Last, before I forget, when Demarco comes down, ask him to make sure and secure the gun Amelia has in a red laundry bag in her closet."

"Got it."

"Thanks. I've got to sleep."

On the way to the back stairs Beck passed Alex.

"Any luck?"

"I haven't gotten through the password protection yet."

"I need what's in there, Alex."

"Go get some sleep."

When he stripped for bed, Beck avoided looking at the purplish bruises blossoming all over his arms and torso. He did check out the wound on his forehead, gently pulling off the large three-by-four-inch adhesive pad. Janice Elkins had done a good job squeezing the split skin closed and securing it with butterfly bandages, but there would still be a scar. Beck spread a finger of antibiotic ointment on it and covered it with a fresh adhesive pad.

He rummaged around in his medicine chest, deciding he'd better take a Vicodin or he'd never sleep. And he knew he had to stop his mind from constantly wrestling with his seemingly intractable, interlinked mess of problems. The worst of which was how to take out an NYPD detective, a politically connected one to boot, without creating a firestorm of investigations that would bring all of them down.

Beck would not risk allowing any of them to have any contact with the judicial system. Despite their resources, one mistake, one misstep, one person in the monstrous machinery of law enforcement, and they could be incarcerated for years. And if things went really bad, for the rest of their lives.

And now Beck had two wildcards to deal with: Amelia Johnson, a young woman more volatile and unpredictable than most adults he'd ever met. And Queenie, a woman who had much of her humanity leached out of her first by years of being abused, and then by years of being the abuser.

Beck lay down on his bed, trying to clear his mind while a dozen questions, concerns, and thoughts swirled into a blur that slowly pulled him into a deep, merciful sleep.

64

At 6:50 A.M. the Vicodin had worn off. When Beck rolled over, the pain pulled him out of his sleep. He forced himself to get up and move. Shower, coffee, food. He pushed through it all, step by step.

When Beck emerged on the second floor, he saw Manny at the stove, heard the soft sizzle of eggs frying, and smelled the tang of maple-honey ham frying in a skillet all mixed with the scent of strong coffee brewing.

Amelia and Demarco sat side by side at the work island, eating and sipping coffee from oversize mugs. It sounded to Beck like they were talking about clothes.

Alex sat at Beck's computer, printing out documents on Beck's high-speed laser printer. He'd been working steadily for six hours.

"How'd you get it open?"

"I went in through the BIOS and disabled the password, but it didn't get me very far. The files are encrypted."

"That doesn't sound good."

"Especially since I don't have the original computer they used to encrypt the files. Were there any computers where you found this hard drive?"

"I didn't see any, and we searched the place pretty thoroughly. So what did you do?"

"I had to reach out to a hacker group that has the fire-power and software to search the drive sector by sector, find the encryption keys, and open the files."

"How much did that set us back?"

"Ten K. They got about eighty percent of the files open."

"You find anything we can use to nail these guys?"

"How about bank accounts in Kansas City, Missouri; Roslyn, Long Island; and a TD Bank in Toronto?

"Really?"

"Yep. I got bank statements and deposit images. I'm printing out everything now."

"How were the deposits made?"

"U.S. postal money orders via snail mail."

Beck smiled. "We got 'em."

"Uh-huh. All kinds of federal crimes connected to moving money between states and a foreign country. We also busted open a folder showing a bunch of properties, along with the titles and deeds."

"Who owns them?"

"I'll tell you who doesn't."

"Who?"

"Eric Jackson." Alex handed Beck a single page. "Here. I printed out the names of the straw owners and the addresses."

Beck scanned the names.

"Holy shit."

"Interesting, huh?"

"Very." Beck's voice trailed off, as he thought through the implications. "You find any information on other properties?"

"I think that's it. It was all in one folder."

"Okay, can you destroy that folder? After you copy the information?"

"Sure."

"Do it. How long before you open the rest of the drive?"

"Couple hours, but I think the rest of the drive is empty. I'm making sure now."

"Okay. Finish printing the bank stuff. Wipe out the information on these properties and leave everything else. Can you do it without leaving a trace?"

"No. But I'll make sure there won't be any way to figure out when it was done."

"Good enough. Thanks."

"You're welcome."

Beck paused and looked at Alex. "The ten thousand was worth it."

"Yep."

Beck headed up to the third floor and knocked on Queenie's door.

"Who is it?"

"Beck. Can I come in?"

"It's your house."

Beck stepped into the room. Queenie had raised the window wide open. Beck could smell the sea air chilled by the cold water in the bay. A bright sun lit up a blue sky cleaned by a high-pressure system. But there was nothing fresh or sunny about Queenie. She sat on the bed, slumped over, her short hair uncombed, her clothes wrinkled from wearing them all night.

"How much sleep did you get?"

Her answer was a smirk.

"What do you want for breakfast?"

She looked at Beck, annoyed. "What the fuck am I doing here?"

"That's what I want to talk to you about. How about we take a walk? Might do you some good to get outside."

Queenie shook her head as if this were simply another bother to endure.

"You want some coffee? I'm going to get some coffee to walk with."

She frowned at Beck, but hoisted herself off the bed and followed him down the back stairs to the kitchen area.

Queenie remained sullen, refusing to look at Amelia while Beck prepared coffee in two stainless-steel travel mugs. The tension between the two women ended all conversation in the kitchen. Queenie took her coffee with milk and three spoons of sugar.

Beck and Queenie made their way outside and walked toward the waterfront without speaking until they settled on a bench with a view of New York Bay.

Queenie broke the silence. Pointing out across the bay, she asked, "What's out there?"

"Jersey. Bayonne. Over there is Staten Island."

Queenie nodded, pointed, "And the so-called Statue of Liberty."

"Yep." He paused. "I'm sorry I had to pull you out of your place last night."

"Ain't my place. Ain't got no place."

"Well . . ."

Queenie turned to Beck. "Well what, dammit? What'd you bring me out here for? You lookin' to turn me into a

428

rat? I been ridin' this bitch for a long time, son. You ain't going to make me no rat now."

"I'm not asking you to rat out anybody, but why the hell would you stay loyal to those pimps?"

"Juju Jackson is a hell of a lot more'n a pimp. And Whitey Bondurant ain't no pimp. He's Jackson's enforcer."

"Wrong. Whatever else he does, Eric Jackson makes millions from prostituting women. He's a pimp. And anybody who helps him is a pimp."

Queenie looked at Beck askance.

Beck said, "Don't give me that look. It's millions. Maybe hard to believe, but it's true."

"If you say so."

"I do. You can put a number on the dollars, but you can't measure the pain and misery behind it. Anyhow, this is all beyond you ratting out anybody. There's no cops involved. I already told you, they're going down."

"Uh-huh. And how's that gonna happen?"

"It has to. It's either them, or us."

Queenie leaned back and said, "I ain't gonna argue with you. But what's it got to do with me? Why you need my help?"

"To get to Jackson."

"And how I'm gonna do that?"

"Call him on his phone."

"And say what?"

"Are you willing to help us?"

"I help you, are you gonna take care of me?"

"You can take care of yourself. All you need is a fresh start."

"Shit. What I'm gonna do? Go work for Google?"

Beck's voice hardened. "You're going to have to do something, because what you've been doing with Eric Jackson is over."

Queenie shook her head. "You keep leavin' out Whitey Bondurant and his thugs."

"I'm not leaving him out. Why is everybody shitting their pants over that guy?"

"Cuz he's a damn monster. I seen that man do things will give you nightmares for the rest of your life. I seen him burn people. Break bones. Cut people. Shoot people."

"Then it's long past time he went down. There are more dead bodies piling up around this mess than you want to know about. All connected to Eric Jackson. The thing you should know, what you have to understand, is that you don't want to go down with them."

"I ain't done shit they can pin on me."

"I hope you really don't believe that, Queenie. You've been mixed up in their business for a very long time. The cops and the Feds are going to start arresting everybody they can get their hands on, including you."

"How do you know?"

"Because I know. They're the ones who'll force you to turn rat, not me. They'll threaten you with so much jail time, you won't have a choice. They will not have a drop of mercy for you, Queenie. They don't care if you sit out at Rikers, or in a federal detention center, and rot for months or years before you even go to trial. A trial that will put you away for decades, maybe for the rest of your life."

"You tryin' to scare me?"

"No. I'm trying to warn you. If the NYPD or FBI don't lock you up, Juju Jackson and Bondurant are going to kill you. You know too much."

Queenie stared out at the bay, frowning, sullen. But she had stopped arguing with Beck.

After a few moments of silence Beck asked, "What's your real name, Queenie?"

She turned, surprised at the question. "Why you want to know?"

"Because Queenie was your working name. I don't want to use that name."

She stuck her chin out, rummaging up a vestige of pride in her name and herself.

"My real name is Queen-Esther Goodwin. Sometimes I used my middle name, Karen. My first name is two names. Queen-Esther. The pimps changed it to Queenie a long time ago. Like a goddam dog's name."

"Time to let it go. Queen-Esther sounds a lot better."

She looked at her coffee mug, but didn't sip from it.

"Used to take a lot of shit for my name when I was a kid. Mostly just used Karen." She shook her head. "I wondered if this day was ever going to come."

"It has."

She finally took a sip of the coffee Beck had prepared for her.

"You sure, Mr. Beck?"

"I'm sure your other life is over. I'm sure there has to be a way to start over. You have any relatives or friends someplace else?"

"I got people in Florida. A sister if she ain't forgot me. She's married. Had two daughters. They grown up now."

"Husband still around?"

"Far as I know."

"Will she give you a roof for a while?"

"Maybe."

"Did you manage to put any money away?"

"About sixteen hundred dollars hidden in one of Biggie's apartments I'll never see again." Queen-Esther shook her head and frowned. "Sixteen hundred dollars. You know how long it took me to save that?"

"No."

"Shit. In one night you give me almost double that. Enough to get a plane ticket out of here."

"You'll need more than that to start over. But I don't think it'll be a problem."

"Why's that?"

"I've got to look into some things a bit more, but one way or another I'll get you what you need to start over. Hell, Esther, all those years you worked for that scum, you earned it."

She paused, thinking about whether or not she could believe the man sitting next to her. "What I got to do for it?"

"Help me do what I have to do."

"What's that?"

"Take down Jackson and Bondurant. And save the girl."

"Princess."

"Amelia."

"And how you gonna do that?"

"I'll explain when we get there."

"How long it gonna take?"

"I don't think we have much more than twenty-four hours."

"You think they comin' for you that fast?"

"I know they are. The cops for sure, if Jackson and his crew don't get to us first."

Queen-Esther Karen Goodwin continued staring out at the expanse of water in front of her and spoke as if she were talking to herself as much as to Beck. "Man, I run now it won't be easy. Even with the money you say you gonna give me."

"You have any warrants outstanding?"

"Some old stuff nobody is lookin' at. Still, I can't be bringing heat on my sister."

Beck nodded. "Not these days. Every jurisdiction has access to everybody else's records. These days they stop you for a traffic ticket, unpaid bill, anything, warrants in New York will come up. You won't be able to get insurance, a driver's license, credit cards, ID, go to a hospital, or work under your real name. Even if you buy some ID, it can blow up if someone rats you out."

Queenie nodded. "You know what you talkin' about, don't you?"

"Yes."

"Well, so do I. I been duckin' police my whole life. You really think you can get me a decent stake and help me get away clean without Juju and Whitey comin' after me?"

"It's either that, or we all die."

"All right, Mr. Beck, whyn't you tell me exactly what I got to do for you."

Beck checked his watch.

"I've got to prepare for a meeting with a couple of gentleman at eleven. After that, we'll get to work. Okay?"

"All right."

"In the meantime, start with one thing."

"What?"

"No more fighting with Amelia. You two are going to have to get along for now."

Esther pursed her lips. "That girl wasn't never cut out to be no whore. Girl like her woulda been beaten down by now till she broke, or died. I don't know how she thought she could play with the likes of Derrick Watkins. It don't work like that."

Beck listened, saying nothing.

"But it ain't my place to teach her anything. All right, Mr. Beck, no more fussin' with her. She's your problem now."

65

Except for two hours of sleep grabbed when he couldn't function anymore, John Palmer had been working nearly nonstop from late Friday afternoon until just after twelve noon on Saturday, first running down as much proof as he could to bolster the case against Beck and his men, and then making himself available to the police officials cycling in and out of meetings at One Police Plaza.

Clearly, the word had come from on high to go after Beck and his crew. Palmer was fairly sure his father might have had something to do with it, but they hadn't discussed it.

Cops cycled in and out of meetings from multiple divisions bearing ranks all the way up to assistant chiefs. Palmer and Ippolito, their squad commander, James Levitt, and their precinct commander, Dermott Jennie, presented material over and over again. Also included were Bronx Borough Commander Assistant Chief Edward Pierce, precinct commanders based in Brooklyn, the Bronx, and Manhattan, the assistant chiefs in charge of the Warrants Squad, NYPD Emergency Services Unit, and lawyers from the Bronx District Attorney's office led by Frederick Wilson.

During the whole time, more information had been filtering in from the other detectives in the 42nd Precinct Levitt had assigned to work on the cases. But finally, by two o'clock Saturday, everybody had been briefed and plans agreed upon.

A meeting was scheduled for 3:00 P.M. Sunday afternoon to finalize the personnel who would execute the arrest warrants on Beck and his men at locations in Brooklyn, Staten Island, and Manhattan.

Even though most of the participants had left, Palmer was too tired to gather his things and leave. Ippolito sat next to him. He'd stuck it through with Palmer, mostly keeping in touch with other detectives and organizing information while Palmer presented. But now with the interminable meetings ending, Ippolito knew his final exit had come. Time to get as far away as possible from John Palmer and his plot to assassinate Beck's men.

He turned to Palmer and said, "Well, I guess that's it. However this turns out, you made your mark, John. There's a hell of a lot of brass who know your name now."

"Thanks, Ray."

"Listen, I'm not officially out until Friday, but the skipper told me to clean out my stuff and use personal days to take the rest of the week off. So now that all this bullshit with the brass is done, I'm gone, unless you need me for something."

Palmer knew what Ippolito was doing, but he didn't care. Raymond Ippolito had served his purpose.

"Sure, Ray. No reason for you to hang around. There's nothing else to do. I'm gonna be sleeping until tomorrow's meeting and then be on call for Wilson when he needs me. I was you, I'd be on a beach somewhere sipping a margarita this time next week."

Palmer pushed himself out of his chair. Ippolito stood and they shook hands.

"Let me know when you want me to put the word in with my dad."

"Will do."

Lieutenant Levitt saw them and headed toward them. A moment before he reached them, his cell phone rang. They all stopped and stood in place while he answered his phone.

He stood listening, brows furrowed.

"Wait, who called you?" He paused to listen. "And what did he say?"

Levitt's expression turned dark.

He kept nodding, saying, "Uh-huh," and "Okay."

He ended the call and looked at Palmer and Ippolito. He closed his eyes for a moment, shook his head, and muttered the closest thing to a curse they'd ever heard him speak.

"God almighty."

Palmer asked, "What's the matter?"

Levitt stared at Palmer and Ippolito with an expression neither of them could interpret. After a moment, he said, "Nothing. It's just another meeting I have to go to."

Palmer said, "You want me to come with you?"

"No. No, this is on something else. You two are done here."

Levitt headed out of the conference room. Ippolito watched Levitt leave. His gut told him Levitt had lied to them. He grabbed Palmer's shoulder and said, "Hey, don't forget my send-off. Wednesday night. We're starting at the Pine. Plan on an all-nighter, kid. I ain't going out with a whimper."

"Yeah, yeah, sure, Ray. Wednesday."

Ten seconds later, John Palmer stood alone in the conference room, wondering what the hell had just happened.

66

Beck left Queen-Esther Goodwin watching New York Bay with decisions and courses of action spinning in his head.

Alex had disappeared to grab some sleep.

As Beck passed Demarco and Amelia, Demarco called out, "James."

"What?"

"I want to get the girl some clothes."

Beck stopped, checked his watch. His Saturday morning was disappearing.

"Two hours max. And please take Queenie, I mean Esther, with you. She needs clothes, too. A few days' worth."

"We're calling her Esther now?"

"Yes."

Amelia said, "I once heard her square name was Karen."

Beck said, "Queen-Esther Karen Goodwin."

"I'm not sure it's a good idea we go together."

Beck's patience for the Amelia/Queenie feud had run out. "You have to change that. At least for the next twenty-four hours. She's sitting outside by the barge. Go ask her to come with you. Please."

Beck headed downstairs. He found Manny sitting at the old wooden table in the downstairs bar kitchen, sipping coffee. He took the seat across from him.

"It's coming down."

Manny asked, "How soon you figure?"

"Next twenty-four hours."

"Who's first? The cops, or Jackson's crew?"

"I have to stop the cops first. They have to be coming at us with everything this time. But Jackson will be right behind them. Have to deal with that, too."

"You got a plan, right?"

"If you call a suicide mission a plan, yeah."

Manny said, "What else is new?"

"Problem is, it won't just be us."

"Meaning what?"

Beck avoided answering. "What shape is Edward Remsen in after Ciro took him down?"

"Ciro got that drunk *cabron* right after he parked his car. Popped him in the liver, right under the ribs."

"From behind?"

"Yeah."

"With his fist?"

"No. With one of those fish clubs."

"Shit."

"He just gave him a tap."

Beck said, "I hope he doesn't bleed to death internally. I need him alive."

"Too bad. He deserves to die. There's something foul about that guy, James. Dirty. You know what I mean?"

"This whole thing is foul. We're going to have to take down a lot of them, Manny."

"How?"

Beck leaned forward and told the grizzled old gangster his plan. Making it clear what he needed Manny to do. Listening if Manny had any suggestions.

By the time Beck finished, he had three minutes before Walter Ferguson and Phineas Dunleavy were scheduled to arrive.

67

Palmer told himself to forget about Levitt and his damn phone call. It didn't matter. Nothing was going to stop the machinery that had been unleashed to go after James Beck and his men. Too many heavyweights had signed off. Too many divisions had come on board and a ton of personnel. It would take the commissioner himself to shut it down.

And then, when Palmer was about to leave the One PP conference room, his own phone rang.

The caller ID told him it was his father. All his suppressed worry and anxiety flared up again.

"Dad."

"John, there's something I need to tell you. Get to a pay phone. Call me on the private number."

"What's going on?"

"It may be nothing. Just call me. I'm waiting."

By the time Palmer made it out of police headquarters and found a working pay phone on Broadway and Duane Street, he was grinding his teeth.

When his father answered, he spoke without even saying hello first.

"All right, John, here's the situation. I don't think this should have anything to do with you, but I want you to be aware about an incident upstate. Four men were found dead outside Ellenville. There is a connection between me and one of those men. Nothing I can't explain, but nobody wants to be connected to four men who met violent deaths. Fortunately, the initial reports seem to indicate the deaths are the result of a falling out among family members. The state police are investigating."

"Who are they?"

There was a pause on the other end of the line.

"No need to go into details. It's been on the local news, and will go national by this evening. The state police are going to release their initial findings sometime later today. If anybody asks you anything, your answer will be you heard something about it on the news, but don't know anything else about it."

"All right. But is anything going to connect to me?"

"Very doubtful."

"Dad, Ellenville is right near Eastern Correctional."

"Yes, but you told me the situation with that man on parole had been covered."

"It's all in the works, Dad. It led to another investigation, but that's not a problem. It's covered."

"John, I'm aware of what's going on at One Police Plaza, but listen to me carefully. If anything doesn't go according to plan, just let it go. Walk away."

"What do you mean?"

"If the district attorney gets cold feet. If the arrests don't go right. If complications arise, don't push it. Don't try to make a case. Let it go."

Palmer knew exactly what his father was saying. It would tear his guts out to let it go, but he could do that. What he couldn't do was stop Juju Jackson. If he double-crossed Jackson now, who knew what he would do? How the hell could he shut down Jackson and his crazy enforcer Whitey Bondurant?"

His father interrupted Palmer's thoughts.

"You understand, right, John?"

"Yes, yes, I understand."

"Okay, son, I'll call you in a few days."

Palmer listened to silence on the other end of the line, replaced the receiver, and stood unmoving in front of the pay phone. *Now, what?*

And at that exact moment, the throwaway cell phone he told Juju Jackson to use buzzed in his suit-coat pocket.

68

Two hours before Palmer talked to his father, Beck sat with Walter Ferguson and Phineas P Dunleavy at the table in his large bedroom on the third floor where they wouldn't be disturbed.

Although it was a Saturday, Beck had asked both men to wear business attire. Walter, tall and trim in a dark blue suit, white shirt, and tie looked like a university professor. Phineas Dunleavy, shorter, broader, with his unruly head of white hair, wore a bespoke brown glen-plaid suit, blue striped shirt, and yellow tie. He looked like a well-groomed bulldog ready for a fight.

Beck had printouts of information, the external hard drive, and the ledgers of Derrick and Jerome Watkins. He selected a single piece of paper from the top of his pile and slid it toward Phineas.

"Phin, Walter and I are ahead of you on what's going on. Let's get you up to speed with this list of charges the Bronx District Attorney's office is going to arrest us for, plus a summary of the evidence they claim to have."

Dunleavy quickly scanned the page without showing any reaction.

"Walter has provided us with that. I expect the cops will try to arrest us tomorrow, or Monday. We can't let that happen."

Phineas looked up and said, "These are serious charges, James. How do we stop them?"

"You and Walter are going to present evidence to the Bronx ADA and the NYPD captain in charge of the homicide investigation that will show them someone else committed those crimes."

"Will they believe it?"

"Right now, all I need is for them to believe we have enough evidence to undermine their cases against us. But that's only part of what I want you to present."

"Go on."

"I also have information about criminals already known to the NYPD and FBI who have been prostituting hundreds of women and girls, and committing a long list of crimes associated with prostitution including money laundering, tax evasion, racketeering, and murders. This is way beyond what they're charging us with. I want you to get both the NYPD and the FBI to open investigations into those crimes."

"How did you obtain this evidence, James?"

"Through a private citizen who came forth voluntarily with evidence that led to me discovering the rest."

"And you can present this citizen?"

"Yes, with the right protections and immunity. But that's a negotiation for later."

Phineas frowned in concentration. "They'll be questions about illegal searches and all. I'll have to go over everything. And interview your source."

"I know. But for now, Phin, here's the order of attack. Stop the arrests. Present the evidence that will point them to the real criminals. Make a deal to keep my witness safe."

"Understood. How do we get to these law enforcement people? It has to be done quickly."

"As soon as I finish briefing you. Walter can put you in touch with a lieutenant in the Forty-second Precinct. And with the Bronx ADA assigned to prosecute. Right, Walter?"

"Yes."

"As I recall, Walter, you also know people in the FBI who might be able to help us with what's going on in terms of the women and children being exploited."

"I have one contact who might. Her name is Julia Sanders. She's on the Innocence Lost Task Force."

"Good. Can you call all of them now to set up meetings while I go over everything with Phineas?"

Walter answered, "You want me to tell the cops they're being set up to make false arrests?"

"Yes. And tell both the NYPD and the FBI we have evidence of serious crimes they should pursue?"

"Okay."

When Walter stepped out of the room to make his calls, Beck gave his lawyer more explicit information so Phineas would know exactly what he'd be navigating. He was wrapping up when Walter returned.

"I talked to Levitt's sergeant. He says Levitt is in a meeting. I told him if Levitt wants to avoid a disaster, he should call me as soon as possible. I spoke to the ADA's assistant. Gave her enough to convince her Frederick Wilson needs to meet with me. She said he'd call me soon. It took me a few calls, but I got through to Julia Sanders. We have a meeting today at FBI headquarters, two P.M."

"Great. Let's keep going."

Beck started with Packy's release from prison. He carefully presented the evidence proving Detective John Palmer shot Packy Johnson. He explained how Palmer framed Derrick Watkins for the Johnson shooting by planting the murder weapon at the Mount Hope apartment. He explained Palmer's motive, his father's connection to Oswald Remsen, Remsen's prostitution ring, and his connection to Eric Jackson through his third son at Sing Sing.

Walter interrupted. "James, do you know that Oswald Remsen, two of his sons, and a fourth man were found dead outside Ellenville?"

"No. I've been concentrating on all this."

"I got a call this morning from the facility parole officer at Eastern I was working with. He told me."

"Walter, whatever happened up there had nothing to do with you."

"What about you, James?"

"What about me? If those men were killed, I'm assuming it had something to do with the criminal enterprise they were running. The world is better off without them."

Walter looked down, struggling with Beck's explanation. He steeled himself, looked up, and asked, "Can you tell me you didn't shoot them?"

"Of course I can. Who's investigating the deaths?"

"State police."

"Wait to see what they find out. It won't involve you, or me."

Phineas looked up from the paperwork and said, "James, what about Palmer's accusation and his witnesses who say you shot Derrick Watkins in revenge for Packy?"

"It's bullshit. The witnesses are lying. I didn't shoot Derrick Watkins. You shouldn't have any trouble casting doubt on those witnesses. Ask the police how they came up with four witnesses so quickly in a neighborhood where nobody ever cooperates with the police. I guarantee those stooges were provided by Eric Jackson."

Phineas asked, "Of course, but can you prove that?"

"I will. Let's keep going. You could drive a truck through evidence they have against Manny and Demarco for the shooting on Hoe Avenue. The security camera photo is a joke. And the description from their eyewitness is so vague it could be anyone. Everything becomes tainted once we show them Palmer is a murderer manipulating evidence."

Phineas checked the eyewitness statement and photo.

Walter asked, "If you didn't shoot Derrick Watkins, and Manny and Demarco didn't shoot Jerome Watkins or Tyrell Williams, who did?"

"My guess is Eric Jackson's enforcer, Floyd Whitey Bondurant. Everything connects back to Eric Jackson. Jackson is cleaning house. He's eliminating everybody that connects him to Packy Johnson."

Phineas asked, "Again, can we get any proof of your theory, James?"

"I'm working on it. Present my theory to the police, Phin, you'll be on solid ground. Let's keep going."

Beck slid the ledger books to Phineas and Walter.

"These ledgers show in detail the profits earned by Derrick and Jerome Watkins from prostitution. They go back years. There are hundreds of women and underage girls involved. A good portion of that income went to Eric Jackson, and many women connected to Jackson and the Watkins's brothers ended up working in the Remsen prostitution ring."

Phineas started to speak, but Beck raised a hand.

"I know – where's the proof? My witness will confirm that but, more important, Oswald Remsen had a son who works at Sing Sing. I believe he was the connection between his father and Eric Jackson, who supplied women for their prostitution business. At least some of those women came from the Watkins brothers. I have no doubt Edward Remsen will cooperate with the FBI and testify to these facts when he bargains for a plea.

"Even without Edward Remsen and my witness, right now I have proof that Eric Jackson violated federal banking laws trying to hide profits from his illegal operations."

Beck slid the external hard drive across the table.

"That hard drive shows that millions of dollars have ended up in bank accounts controlled by Eric Jackson. One of them is out of state. One in New York. One in Canada. All the money was deposited in the form of U.S. postal money orders. All signed by Eric Jackson."

Phineas smiled. "You're right, James, we don't even have to prove the money came from prostitution right now. The FBI can start with tax evasion and banking-law violations."

"Exactly. They want this guy. Now they have a reason to move on him. These bank records, the ledgers, the testimony of my witness and, if the FBI is diligent, I'm sure they'll find women who worked as prostitutes for Jackson and Remsen. There's more than enough for them to arrest Edward Remsen and Eric Jackson. And like I said, the Feds will turn Edward Remsen. He's looking at decades in a federal penitentiary unless he cops a plea and rats out Jackson."

Phineas said, "I just hope the FBI can find Jackson and Remsen. I wouldn't be surprised if Edward Remsen is on a plane somewhere by now. He has to have heard about what happened to his father and brothers."

Beck said, "I'm confident they'll find them."

Walter asked, "What about Bondurant?"

"Don't worry about him, right now. First things first. Right now, you simply have to point the NYPD and the Feds away from us and in the right direction."

Walter wanted to press Beck for more answers, but Phineas said, "Walter, you and I should go over all this before we meet with all these law enforcement people. We have to present this carefully and we don't have much time."

"Yes, I know. But . . ."

"But what?"

The moment of truth had arrived. Despite Beck's denials, his bruised face told Walter he must have had something to do with the deaths of Oswald Remsen and the other three men upstate. Nor did Walter believe Beck had obtained all his evidence without resorting to violent means.

But he also knew Beck was right. And that the terrible exploitation of women and girls had to be stopped, and the murderer of Paco Johnson brought to justice.

Beck watched a good man, Walter Ferguson, struggling with the eternal dilemma: Did the end justify the means?

Beck leaned toward Walter and spoke softly.

"Walter, I promised you I would give you everything I discovered. I've done that. You said you wanted the chance to work this through the legal system. I'm giving you that chance. I'm asking you to take everything to the police, the Bronx DA's office, and the FBI. What more can I do? Please help me stop people who have caused unimaginable misery, who have raped and beaten and prostituted women and girls barely in their teens. Who have murdered people. I wish we had more time to talk it over, my friend, weigh the pros and cons, address your concerns, but I don't."

Walter nodded. He sat silent, thinking. Beck and Dunleavy waited. Finally, Walter said, "I understand. Let me keep trying to contact Levitt. I expect you two have more to talk about."

With Walter gone, Phineas Dunleavy turned to Beck and said, "James, I believe we can move this where it has to go. And I think I'll even be able to discredit that murderous cop's testimony against Ciro."

"Good."

"But, James, you realize the NYPD and the Bronx DA will never make a case against John Palmer for murdering your friend, Paco Johnson. I agree Palmer had motives and opportunity. But it all hinges on the gun you say he planted and as sure as I sit here, lad, we both know Palmer will lie and deny, and never stop lying. He'll say he found the gun under a bed, in a drawer, someplace in that apartment. You won't be able to prove he planted that gun."

"I know that, Phin. At this point, I'm only asking you to throw enough sand in the gears to stop them from arresting us, and make Palmer a plausible suspect."

Phineas knew Beck was trying to steer him away from the bitter reality facing Beck, but the wily old lawyer wouldn't be dissuaded.

"James, you can't go where I think you're going. You can't. We can get Palmer for perjury, suborning witnesses, whatever. But you're going to have to live with the fact that a bent, corrupt, murderous bastard is going to get away with killing Paco Johnson. Tell me you can live with that, James. Can you do that, lad?"

Beck stared at Phineas, pleased and grateful that his friend and protector knew the ultimate danger underlying everything, and was trying to protect him from it.

"I'll do whatever I have to, Phineas."

Dunleavy knew a non-answer when he heard one. He dropped his voice and leaned toward Beck. "James, you can't take out a cop, not even a rotten cop like this one who murdered your friend and tried to put you and the boys back in jail. You can't."

"Phin, put that out of your mind. Concentrate on what we need to do now. You're going to have to persuade these law enforcement people to stop what they're doing and change course. You have to make sure Ciro, Manny, and Demarco are protected from prosecution. The rest is going to take time. I know I'm asking a lot. But you have to do this."

Phineas struggled with his implacable drive to fight and argue and debate until he won his point. He wanted to make Beck promise something he knew Beck never would.

Beck said to him, "Phin, please. Don't get sidetracked."

"All right, all right, lad. I'll buy you time and make sure nothing will happen to the boys. I promise you."

Beck shook hands with Phineas. He thanked him for his promise to keep his men safe, struggling with the bitter irony that he was going to ask every one of them to risk death come morning.

69

As soon as he left Phineas and Walter, Beck sat with Alex Liebowitz.

"Where are you on the property search?"

Alex handed him printouts. "I looked at variations of that name for properties in all five boroughs and Westchester County. Didn't find anything beyond the stuff on the hard drive. Two houses, one apartment building with eighteen units, and a commercial building on Southern Boulevard. All in the Bronx. Owned by Queen-Esther Goodwin, Karen Goodwin, Karen Esther Goodwin, and Esther Goodwin."

"You think Jackson owns more?"

"Probably. But do we have time to do a nationwide search?"

"No. What's the ballpark value of them?"

"Based on a few quick online comparisons, the two houses, say about a half million. I don't know the rent roll on the apartment building, but it's got to be worth at least four or five million. The commercial building is pretty small; I'd say maybe a million. So, somewhere between five and six million."

"No mortgages, right?"

"Nah. I'm sure Jackson bought them to soak up his cash."

"What do you think we'd net if we sold them? Fast."

"What do you figure, about a month?"

"Max. We have to dump them before the Feds start doing a deep dive on Jackson's assets."

"Okay, we could dump them in that time if we asked forty, fifty cents on the dollar. We ain't paying any capital gains, that's for sure. I doubt they filed any returns for the various incarnations of Queen-Esther Karen Goodwin. Have you asked her about any of this?"

"No. I seriously doubt she knows she's the owner of record."

"She's going to have to disappear if we do this."

"She has to anyhow. And we have to spread rumors that Jackson and Bondurant killed her and hid the body. And Amelia Johnson, too."

"I assume you want to set up a corporate entity to hold the titles and launder the money for safety sake."

"Yes."

"That'll cost us."

"Hey, this is found money. Let's minimize the risk. What do you have in mind?"

"China. It's the easiest and fastest these days. Buy some steel or something. Wash the money with a sale. Pocket the balance. I'll reach out to Ming the Merciless."

"Don't let him squeeze you too hard. See if he knows a lawyer who'll act as front man and paper the sales. Maybe someone who has connections to a broker who specializes in distressed properties."

Alex said, "*Distressed.* That's a nice way to put it."

Beck heard the voices of Demarco and Esther downstairs. "Okay, Alex, let's move fast on this."

Alex went back to work as Demarco, Amelia, Willie Reese, and Queen-Esther stepped into the second-floor loft space. Between them, they had seven shopping bags, none carried by Willie Reese.

Beck said, "All set?"

Demarco answered, "We did what we could under the circumstances."

Esther announced, "I got to change."

Beck said, "Okay, but hurry. We have to talk. And we don't have too much time."

While Esther headed upstairs, Beck motioned for the others to take a seat at the dining table. While they waited for Esther to return, Beck went over to one of the couches and lay down, covering his eyes with his forearm. The others couldn't tell if he was sleeping or thinking.

It took thirty minutes for Queen-Esther to return, showered, with fresh lipstick, dressed in black tights and a print tunic top that reached past her ample hips. She looked and acted like a very different person. She took the chair at the head of the table as if it were her right.

Willie sat next to Amelia. Beck sat with Demarco on the other side of the table.

They all waited for Beck to speak.

70

John Palmer grimaced and answered his buzzing burner phone.

"I hope this is important."

Eric Jackson didn't waste any words.

"Beck and his crew took down one of my houses last night. They got information that can hurt me. I ain't waitin' until Monday. I ain't waitin' another fucking minute. I need to know where I can find him. You can't arrest him now. Not with him having this information. I got to take them out now. Right the fuck now."

Palmer said, "Hold on. You can't . . ."

Jackson interrupted. "Hey, copper, get it through your fucking head, you ain't telling me what I can and can't do. You got your witnesses, you got me to hold off, and now I'm fucked. Beck has got to be dead before the day is out. Give me a way to find him, and all this bullshit is over."

Palmer thought furiously. It was all going to hell. Everything he had done, all the scheming and lying and conspiring with criminals – all for nothing.

Palmer said to Jackson, "All right, hang on a second. I'm standing in the street. Let me get somewhere I can talk."

Palmer ducked into the lobby of a nearby building.

He wasn't giving Beck up to Jackson. No way. Fuck Eric Jackson. Jackson knew too much. Jackson controlled

455

his witnesses. Everything connected back to Jackson. There was only one thing to do now. He had to kill him. With Jackson gone, this could work. With Jackson gone, he wouldn't have to risk helping him assassinate the rest of Beck's crew. He could get credit for taking down all of them. He'd find a way to keep Jackson's witnesses on board. He should have thought of this before.

He spoke into the cell phone.

"Okay, are you there, Eric?"

"Yeah, I'm fucking here. Tell me what I need to know."

"You sure you want to go this way? I'm telling you, we're arresting Beck tomorrow. Monday, latest."

"I told you I ain't got time. He's got to go, now."

"All right, all right, the hell with it. I'm not going to argue with you. But we're not doing this on a phone. Where are you?"

"Never fucking mind where I am. I ain't recording shit. Just tell me where to find Beck."

"No. Not on a cell phone. I'm not fucking standing in public running down all the addresses for Beck and his men in Brooklyn, Staten Island, and Manhattan. I'll meet you outside that Chinese restaurant in an hour. Just you. I don't want any witnesses or trouble. I'll have everything written out for you. No discussion. No stripping-down bullshit. I hand you a piece of paper, and we never see each other again. In fact, I never, ever saw you."

Palmer cut the connection. He didn't want to hear any more threats or arguments from Eric Juju Jackson. He'd hand him a piece of paper and put a bullet in his head. End of story.

71

Beck looked at Amelia and Esther before he spoke. Even though Willie and Demarco sat at the table with them, what Beck had to say, he was going to say to them.

"There are facts I read, but I can't really comprehend what they actually mean." Beck paused. "Over two hundred thousand children in this country are being sold for sex. Some as young as twelve or thirteen. Maybe younger. Children. Drugged. Raped. Beaten. Murdered.

"I can't understand how that happens. Not even to one kid, much less hundreds of thousands. I can't imagine what it feels like to be a twelve-year-old girl and have that happen to you." Beck paused and looked at Amelia and Esther. "I think, perhaps, you two can imagine that. But I can't." Beck paused again. "But there is one thing I do understand." Beck punched a knuckle onto the dining-room table, hitting the table with more force with each sentence.

"I understand how it feels when scum like Juju Jackson and Whitey Bondurant, and their pimp underlings like Derrick and Jerome Watkins believe they have the right to terrify and brutalize people. I understand that because I spent eight years surrounded by dehumanized men like them who thought they had the right to brutalize me. To stab me. Or beat me. Terrify me. Kill me." Beck pointed and said, "Everyone at this table knows how that feels.

"And I know one more thing. I know those murderers have to be stopped." Beck leaned forward. "Eric Jackson and Bondurant might rule their own horrifying little worlds, but they do not rule your world, or mine. Not anymore. I'm going to stop them. I'm going to make sure they never harm you, or anyone, ever again. And I'm going to make them pay."

Beck leaned back.

Amelia asked, "How, Mr. Beck?"

"With your help. Every one of us will have to step into harm's way. Particularly you, Amelia, and you, Esther."

Beck nodded toward Demarco and Willie Reese. "We'll do everything we can to protect you. But I can't guarantee you'll come out unharmed. I believe we can take them down. But not without you two. So I have to ask – will you help me?"

72

The caller ID surprised Eric Jackson.

"Queenie, where the fuck you been? Why you ain't answered my calls?"

Queen-Esther Goodwin shot back, "Because my goddam battery was dead and I just got it charged up. Goddammit, Eric, I been through too much bullshit last night and today for you to be jumpin' all over me. You wanna talk to me like that, I'll hang up this phone right now."

The pimp in Eric Jackson told him to come down hard on the old whore, and guarantee her if she dared to talk to him like that ever again he would kill her. But the cunning part of him told him he didn't have time for the usual run.

"All right, all right, take it easy you cranky old bitch. What's going on?"

"What's going on? First you tell me to get the hell out of Derrick's place up at the Houses. Then last night I got run out of Jerome's place by that crew been battling with you. Maybe *you* want to tell *me* what the fuck is going on. What I'm supposed to do now?"

"Look, Queenie, I don't have time for your bullshit. Where you at? You can come up and stay at my place. I'll send someone to get you."

"First of all, I ain't nowhere. I been on the move since last night. I hid out in a place up at the Houses. Then I had to move early this morning to a friend of mines. Now I'm out here scuffling around trying to get something to eat and trying to convince people to help me. And it's all been made worse by the simple fact that I been dragging around goddam Princess, who no-fucking-body will help because they all afraid of you and Whitey hearing about it."

"You have Princess?"

"Yes, I have Princess."

"How'd that happen?"

"Who you think told them guys about Biggie's house? She the one led them to it. She came up to the house, pounding on the door, asking for a place to stay. Before I could even deal with it, when I cracked the door open to talk to her, two guys busted in. They took down Lattrell and them other two like nothing. I grabbed Princess and ran the hell out of there into the middle of the night without a damn thing but the clothes on my back. Not even my purse. I'm lucky I had my cell phone in my damn pocket."

"Why'd she go with you?"

"Why? Cuz she didn't want to be with them guys, that's why. She don't know who the fuck they are, 'cept they say they was friends of her father, who she don't know either. She told me she was holed up in the Expressway Motel, heard a gunshot in the lobby, and ran the hell out the side exit. She said she barely got away from Whitey, and then these other guys grabbed her when her car went out of control as she was trying to get on the expressway."

"Why'd she tell them about Biggie's place?"

"She said because they put a gun to her. Maybe she's lyin', I don't know. Maybe she figured they might get shot goin' in there, and she could get away. Who gives a shit? She with me now. The girl been on the run for days. She's a mess, Eric. She got no ID; nobody to help her; she don't know what the fuck to do. I'm all she's got except for a few bucks she stole from Tyrell."

"Tyrell?"

"Yeah, she told me she shot his ass. You didn't know that?"

"Goddammit."

"Eric, you slippin'. She shot Derrick, too."

"I know that. So she's with you because you told her you'd help her?"

"Damn right I did."

"Where are you now?"

Esther lowered her voice. "Hold a sec. No bullshit now, Eric. I know you want this girl, and I can't be out here running around homeless on my own, so you got to promise me it's gonna be worth it for me to turn her over."

"I promise you'll be dead if you don't."

Queenie yelled, "The way this shit is goin' down I might as well be. What I got to lose? Go on. Keep threatening me."

"All right, shut the fuck up, Queenie. You deliver the girl, I'll make it worthwhile."

"I'm gonna tell myself I believe you, Eric, cuz I don't have much choice. I'm sick of all this shit." Queenie dropped her voice. "Listen here, I know damn well what you gonna do to her. You gonna make an example of her. You gonna mess her up so bad none of them other bitches will even think about doin' anything like she done."

"That's none of your damn business."

"Don't treat me like I'm stupid, Eric. If I do this, we both know I'm burned. Word gonna get out with your whores I turned over Princess. No way I'm gonna be able to deal with any more whores. I got to square up, Eric. I got to do something legit. I know you have other businesses. You got to promise to give me a real job."

"You trying to shake me down, Queenie? You really want to play it this way?"

"Ain't no shakedown, Eric. It's just the reality. If I turn over this girl, what do I have left? I got to have something, or I might as well walk away now and take my chances."

Queenie forced herself to stop talking. She had to wait for Jackson to make a decision.

Finally, he said, "All right, Queenie. I can't see you going straight, but I ain't going to argue with you. You deliver the girl; I'll give you a shot at something. You have my word on it. Where are you? I'll come for you now."

"It ain't going to be that easy. The girl is skittish as a colt. She's got a gun she took from Tyrell's car. I got to keep buildin' her confidence. Sell her on a story. I can't risk her shootin' me and takin' off if she gets suspicious."

"Queenie, don't make this complicated."

"Take it easy. I got this figured out. I told her I know some people outside of Charleston who can take her in. She can't fly down there cuz she don't have no ID. So I promised her I'd bring her to Port Authority and put her on the next bus, which leaves tomorrow. That's when I'll get her out in the open, and you can take her."

"I ain't got time for that."

"Dammit, Eric, I already sold her on this. I showed her the bus schedule. It leaves at eleven-ten tomorrow, Sunday. I convinced her we should take a car service downtown. Sneak out of the Houses around nine and meet the car on 174th outside the project. Have one of your boys in a car. I put her in. You got her. It's done."

"Are you in the Houses now?"

"Yes. And I ain't telling you where. You gonna have to go through all twelve buildings to find us. Cops will be here long before you find me."

"Fuck, I don't have time to mess with you on this."

"You got a better idea, go for it. But I already got it all set up."

After a few moments, Jackson spoke. "All right, here's how this is gonna work. You call me at nine A.M. tomorrow. You tell me what building you're in. Ten minutes later, you walk out. You're gonna be tracked all the way to a car on 174th. You get in that car with her, you understand? You tell her you're gonna make sure she gets a ticket and finds the bus and all. We'll take it from there."

"I don't want to see what you do to that girl."

"Don't worry. As soon as you two are in the car, we'll put a gun on her. My guy will drive you a couple of blocks. I'll meet you and take you up to my place. We'll work on setting you up with something."

"Okay, Eric. Tomorrow at nine."

Esther put down the phone and looked around the table at Beck, Amelia, Demarco, and Willie Reese, along with the Bolo brothers.

"It's done. Tomorrow morning at nine, Bronx River Houses."

Beck said, "You think he bought it?"

"Hell, no. He's gonna kill me and the girl the second we get into that car. And he sure as hell don't think an old whore like me would go at him like I just did. No sir,

Mr. Beck, he knows a set up when he hears it. Juju Jackson's gonna fill the Bronx River Houses with Whitey Bondurant and all his thugs, plus every single punk with a gun who want to get with him.

"I hope to God you know what you're doing, Mr. Beck, because I don't think anybody going into Bronx River Houses on Sunday morning is coming out in one piece unless Juju Jackson says so."

"I already told you, Esther. He's not calling the shots. We are. Here's how it's going to work."

Eric Jackson turned to Whitey Bondurant, who sat with his size-fifteen feet on Jackson's coffee table, sharpening a knife.

Bondurant's deep voice rumbled, "That was Queenie?"

"Yeah. Can't believe it, but that old bitch Queenie finally turned on me."

"How?"

"I'm bettin' she's setting somethin' up with that crew who's been hitting us. And even if she ain't, the damn bitch thinks she can tell me what's what. Demand shit from me. She forgot how this works. She forgot who I am."

"Then she has to go."

"She shoulda been gone a long time ago. Damn bitch knows way too much." Jackson sat silent for a few moments, and then told Bondurant, "Okay, Whitey, we gonna play this out. If I'm right, this is our chance to take care of all this mess and be done with this shit."

"When?"

"Tomorrow morning."

"Are we still meeting with that cop over by the Chinks?"

"Fuck him. I don't need him now."

73

All Saturday afternoon into the night and throughout Sunday morning, Beck kept working, tracking everything, getting information, evaluating it, issuing instructions, planning, re-planning.

At five P.M. he'd gotten a text from Phineas: *Def stopped Brx DA plans. At minimum have delayed NYPD. Walter pushing FBI. Probably nothing final til Mon. Still working on everything.*

By eight P.M. both Manny and Demarco had checked in, telling Beck they were making progress, but slowly.

By one A.M. the Bolo brothers had called in with their final report.

By two A.M. Ciro had called to tell Beck, "Everything is jake. See you at seven."

At three A.M. Beck forced himself to trudge up to his bedroom, where he slowly settled onto his bed in sections, trying to find a position that didn't hurt, trying to stop his racing mind. He set his cell phone to wake him at six so he could go over everything one more time before he and Ciro were scheduled to head out for Bronx River Houses.

Beck would have slept until noon, but when his phone woke him he forced himself to sit up and get his feet on the floor. By the time Ciro arrived to pick him up, he hadn't done much more than shower, dress, and drink enough coffee to get him functioning.

He and Ciro arrived at the Bronx River Houses shortly before eight A.M. Ciro parked his Escalade on Harrod Avenue, while Beck listened to the first call from Ricky and Jonas Bolo telling him they had already spotted eleven men they judged to be part of Juju Jackson's crew stationed around the perimeter of Bronx River Houses.

Beck had no way of knowing how many more were inside the housing project. Nor did he know where Jackson and Bondurant were.

He had less than thirty minutes to make a crucial decision, and he felt his concentration faltering. He'd stopped taking pain medication so he could stay sharp, but the pain from the upstate beating and lack of sleep continued to drain him.

He sat in Ciro's Escalade, staring at a satellite image of the Bronx River Houses and a detailed street map of the area. He kept looking back and forth between the two, trying to predict all the moves that might happen, all the lines of action.

Beck took another swig of coffee, rubbed his face, and told himself, fuck it. He folded the satellite image and map, and shoved them under his seat. Either this will work, or it won't. They were all about to walk into a trap. He'd done what he could, but he knew there were so many variables that a large part of what happened next was out of his control.

Juju Jackson's cell phone rang at exactly nine A.M.

"Where you at?"

Esther said, "Gonna be walking out of building twelve at the north end of the complex in one minute. The one off Harrod and the expressway." And then she ended the call.

Jackson and Bondurant were in a silver Range Rover on Bronx River Avenue. Jackson behind the wheel, Bondurant in the passenger seat. Behind Bondurant sat one of his men by the name of Amir.

Jackson shoved his phone into his shirt pocket and pulled out onto Bronx River Avenue heading north, circling quickly around to Harrod Avenue, while Bondurant called his men, telling them to head for the last building at the northeast end of the housing complex and spread the word.

Amelia and Esther emerged from the building facing Harrod Avenue and walked without hurry toward a semicircular plaza south of the building. At the back of the plaza, a concrete platform rose up three steps, forming a rectangular stage. Behind it rose the twelve-story back wall of the next building south.

As Jackson pulled over to a fire hydrant on Harrod, Bondurant spotted Amelia and Esther. It looked like they were going to cut across the plaza and take the path that led to 174th Street.

"There they are."

"I see 'em."

Bondurant looked around, trying to spot any of Beck's men lurking.

Jackson said, "If this is an ambush, you'll see them soon enough. Just get in there and pull them bitches out. You'll have at least twenty guys covering you in a minute."

"I hope it is an ambush. We see any of that crew, we gonna shoot 'em down like dogs. I put the word out, as soon as we finish off the last one, everybody gets paid."

"Good. Bring the bitches out fast, load 'em up, and we're gone. If you can't make that happen, you shoot 'em both, and get the fuck out of there."

Bondurant and Amir stepped out of the Range Rover, drawing their guns. Bondurant held a .45 caliber Colt 1911 out of sight against his leg. Amir's small Taurus .38 six-shot revolver was almost invisible in his hand.

Bondurant pointed south and told Amir, "I'm going to head that way and get in front of them. You hang back and move in behind."

Bondurant, wearing his sunglasses, scanned the surrounding area. He saw five of his men heading his way from the north. More would be coming in from the south, and more converging from the west perimeter of the complex.

Everything looked normal for an early Sunday morning. He saw only one couple who looked like residents, probably heading for church. Maybe Queenie was playing this straight. Either way it didn't matter. He'd already decided he was going to shoot both women as soon as he got close to them. If anybody showed up from the crew who'd taken out Derrick and the others, he wanted to be free to kill as many of them as he could.

Bondurant hustled to get ahead of Queenie and Princess, keeping an eye on them as he moved into position. He'd forgotten how good Princess looked. He smiled. *She has no fucking idea she's got about one minute before she takes a bullet in that pretty face.*

*

Beck and Ciro had seen the silver Range Rover come racing around the corner onto Harrod Avenue and pull in next to the fire hydrant. They were parked across the street from the Rover about five car lengths south. Both of them slumped down in their seats and watched two men get out of the Range Rover, one of them a hulking black albino – Whitey Bondurant. Beck had little doubt the third man sitting behind the wheel was Eric Juju Jackson, hanging back to let others do his dirty work.

Bondurant watched Princess and Queenie moving almost parallel to him. But instead of continuing across the plaza toward 174th Street, the two women turned and walked up onto the platform at the far side of the plaza. Once there, they stopped and stood in the middle of the stage.

That didn't make any sense. What the hell were they doing?

Bondurant's men were converging from every direction, including several of his hard-core gangbangers, and still Bondurant couldn't see anybody who looked like one of Beck's crew.

Bondurant turned west and headed directly for the platform, confident nobody could stop him now, but before he reached the middle of the plaza, he saw one of his crew gesturing and pointing behind him.

Bondurant turned and spotted the massive shape of Pastor Benjamin Woods heading in his direction, three men on his left, four on his right, all of them serious. Six were deacons in Wood's church. The seventh was Emmanuel Guzman. A crowd of at least forty, most of them men, followed Woods and Manny. They were residents of Bronx River Houses, their number growing as more people from the surrounding buildings joined them.

Bondurant looked south and saw another procession, this one mostly women, led by Belinda Halsted Smith, rolling along on her Rascal scooter, chin high, staring straight ahead through her thick glasses, a determined look on her aged face. On one side of her walked Ms. Margaret and Ms. Maxine. On the other side, Demarco Jones. And behind them, more of the older female *sentinels* of Bronx River Houses along with many of their daughters and granddaughters.

All told, there were three generations of women and men converging on the area, their numbers swelling with every step while Amelia and Esther stood alone bravely waiting for them.

In the face of the marching residents, almost all of Bondurant's crew heading toward the plaza had stopped. They were both confused and exposed as the residents engulfed them.

Windows were opening. Heads leaned out to see what was going on. More and more residents were coming out to either join the marchers, or watch what was happening. Many of Bondurant's men who hadn't made it to the plaza were being engulfed by the crowd of well over a hundred people and growing.

Bondurant yelled and waved for his men nearby to continue toward the plaza. More were coming in from the periphery. Bondurant had no intention of letting anybody stop him. Maybe he couldn't shoot Queenie and Princess in front of so many witnesses, but he could damn well drag them out of the complex with his men clearing the way. Let these fools try to stop him. All they had to do was make it fifty yards out to the street, get them in the Range Rover, and get the hell out. A couple of gunshots in the air and all these assholes would duck and run. Why the hell did any of them give a shit about these damn whores anyhow?

Bondurant ran toward the stage, yelling for his men to come forward, but by now there were five or six residents for every one of his. The two groups of residents merged into a throng that surrounded Bondurant's men. Several of Bondurant's crew tried to push their way to the stage, but the residents stood firm, blocking them. A few of the older women from the complex who had known some of young men since childhood yelled at them, reprimanding them as if they were their own children, warning Bondurant's bullies not to dare push them aside.

Demarco had walked with Belinda as she drove her Rascal toward the stage, but now he broke and moved fast to get to Amelia and Queenie.

Big Ben Woods, the fearsome enforcer from Dannemora, head and shoulders above the crowd, also strode toward the stage, holding his Bible over his head with his left hand while using his massive bulk and powerful right hand to push aside any of Bondurant's men in his way, all the while excoriating them and promising damnation to anybody who dared oppose him.

Bondurant made it to the steps of the platform, gun in hand. In two strides he ascended to the stage. When they saw him, Esther and Amelia backed up until they were trapped against the wall. Bondurant headed for Amelia. She yelled, "Get the hell away from me!"

Out on Harrod Avenue, Beck and Ciro were about to step out of the Escalade when Beck said, "Wait. We can't both be on the street while he's in a car. If he tries to drive out of here, run the son of a bitch off the road."

Beck slipped out the passenger door. In one hand he carried Ciro's fish bat. In the other, his Browning forty-five. The only way to get to Jackson without being seen was to duck down and walk hidden by the cars parked along his side of the street. But the damage Remsen's men had done to him made walking bent over excruciating.

By the time he reached a spot across the street from Jackson, he had to take a knee and recover. He leaned out past the front bumper of a parked car. Jackson stared off to his right, trying to make out what was happening in the roiling mass of people gathering in and around the plaza.

Beck saw Bondurant emerge from the crowd and make it to the platform. He saw Jackson shifting in the driver's seat as if about to make a move. Was he going to flee the scene to save himself? Get out and help Bondurant? Start firing into the crowd?

Juju Jackson shoved the Range Rover into gear.

Amelia's shout stopped Bondurant for a moment. And in that split second Demarco Jones leaped onto the concrete stage and yelled at Bondurant.

"Hey!"

Whitey Bondurant turned toward him. There wasn't much distance for Demarco to cover, but it was enough so that Bondurant had time to raise his gun into firing position. Even though he was a trigger pull from taking a bullet, Demarco kept coming. As Bondurant's gun came level with Demarco's chest, he heard a primal scream as Amelia Johnson threw herself at Whitey Bondurant. She hit him hard, knocking him back, but only a step. Bondurant was much too big to go down. He shoved Amelia away, sending her sprawling onto the hard concrete. It took only two seconds, but time enough for Demarco to close the distance and grab the barrel of Bondurant's Colt, twist the gun out of his hand, and backhand the butt of the gun across Bondurant's face.

Bondurant's sunglasses flew off, his cheek split open, and this time he staggered backward.

Demarco casually looked behind him and underhanded the gun to Manny Guzman who had stepped up onto the platform. Manny caught the Colt, then turned and joined Big Ben Woods and his deacons, who had taken up positions on the top step, ready to hold back Bondurant's crew. But none of them tried to storm the stage. Every person in the plaza stood where they were, waiting to see the fight about to happen between the feared Whitey Bondurant and someone who almost matched his size.

Demarco circled between Bondurant and the women as Esther helped Amelia to her feet and moved her out of the way toward a door set into the wall bordering the back of the stage.

Demarco taunted Bondurant. "You like hitting girls, you nancy bitch?"

The crowd stood, transfixed. For years, every one of them had dreaded even hearing the name Whitey

Bondurant. It didn't seem possible that someone had taken away Bondurant's gun and stood taunting him, goading him to fight.

Bondurant's men called out, telling him to kick the guy's ass. To kill him. To tear him up. They wanted to see what Whitey could do. They needed to see it.

Without warning, Bondurant rushed Demarco, throwing all of his two hundred fifty pounds at him. Demarco countered. He met the force of Bondurant's rush with a forearm rammed into Bondurant's chest. He grabbed Bondurant's right arm, turned, and threw him onto the concrete stage.

Bondurant hit the concrete hard. He rolled over onto his hands and knees. Demarco took a step and kicked him in the ribs.

Demarco yelled, "Get up, bitch!"

Blind with rage, Bondurant rushed Demarco again, this time shooting in low, trying to get his long arms around Demarco and take him down.

Demarco absorbed the force of Bondurant's rush, sprawled backward, grabbed Bondurant's left arm, dug his right arm under his chin, and dropped all his weight onto Bondurant's neck and back, forcing the bigger man to the ground.

He leaned close to Bondurant's ear and whispered, "You can't beat me. I'm not a girl."

Bondurant tried to twist away, to get out from under Demarco, but Demarco pulled up on his choke hold and kept him under control.

One of Bondurant's hard guys rushed the stage, pulling his gun. Ben Woods slapped the side of his head hard enough to send him flying back off the steps. Another made it to the second step, but Manny cracked the barrel of Bondurant's Colt across his jaw, and he went down. Pushing and fighting broke out among the residents and a few of Bondurant's men. A third man pushed past one of Woods's deacons and made it onto the top step, and then Beck's final line of defense appeared. The door behind the stage opened and Willie Reese stepped out holding a Serbu Super-Shorty 12-gauge shotgun.

He raised the weapon with one hand and aimed it at Bondurant's man who had tried to join the fight. The man froze. Willie took two steps toward the man, planted his huge foot on his chest, and sent Bondurant's thug flying off the stage.

Willie stood at the edge of the platform, sweeping his shotgun back and forth, keeping back anybody else who might want to help Bondurant.

Behind Willie, in a desperate move, Bondurant managed to grab Demarco's left elbow, pull down and twist out from under Demarco, landing with his back on Demarco's chest. A flurry of motion exploded. Demarco tried to counter and push off the bigger man. Bondurant surprised Demarco with his speed. He twisted and landed on top of Demarco, scrambling forward, avoiding Demarco's guard, straddling his chest. He reared up and landed a huge punch to Demarco's forehead, driving Demarco's head onto the hard concrete.

Everything went black. Demarco blocked most of the next punch, he turned away from another punch, but Bondurant landed a fist that caught him on the side of his head. Another hit his left eye. Demarco cursed himself for throwing Bondurant around and taunting him instead of taking him out fast. He knew he was only one or two more punches away from Bondurant beating him to death.

Eric Jackson shoved the Range Rover into reverse.

Beck stepped out from behind the parked car and awkwardly ran toward Jackson as fast as he could. He had to catch him before he could back up enough to clear the parked car in front of him, but Beck already knew he didn't have enough time to get to Jackson. It would be up to Ciro to block Jackson's escape. And the only way to do that would be with a head-on crash.

And then Beck skidded to a stop.

In a move Beck hadn't predicted, instead of backing up to get out of his parking space, Jackson made a Y-turn into the middle of the street toward Beck. He braked and reversed into Drive. Jackson wasn't fleeing. He intended to drive over the sidewalk and mow a path through the crowd with the Range Rover to clear the way for Bondurant.

Desperate to stop him, Beck threw the fish bat toward the driver's-side door. The nineteen-inch bat, weighted at the end, spun end over end and smashed into the window. Glass shattered. Jackson slammed on the brakes, turned, and saw Beck coming at him.

He put the Range Rover into Park and calmly stepped out into the street, pulling his gun.

Beck wanted him alive, but it was too late. Too late for his plan. He went down on one knee, raising his Browning into firing position as Jackson pointed his gun at Beck.

*

Bondurant was big. He was strong. He had the controlling position. He tried to shove aside Demarco's arms, getting ready to deliver a final knockout punch.

Maybe it was the clarity that comes before death. Maybe it was because Demarco Jones knew if he lost this fight Amelia and Esther would die, too. But mostly it was Bondurant making one mistake. He rose up so high trying to deliver a final, killing blow, that Demarco had enough time to free his left arm and block Bondurant's downward fist with a sweeping block, followed by one ferocious right hook that hit Bondurant squarely on the temple.

The blow paralyzed Bondurant, not quite knocking him out, but gave Demarco a chance to land two hammer blows to Bondurant's ribs and shove him off. Demarco scrambled to his feet. He staggered away from Bondurant, trying to clear his head from the damage he'd taken, shaking off the pain in his right hand.

Bondurant also made it onto his feet, wobbling and stepping back, trying to recover from Demarco's punch that had sent his brain banging from one side to the other of his massive skull.

Both men circled each other. Both knew the fight wouldn't last much longer. No more taunting. No more unmasking Whitey Bondurant in front of his men. And no more risking broken fists.

Bondurant edged forward. Demarco leapt forward, closing the space between them before Bondurant could react. He twisted from the hip and torqued the edged of his right wrist and arm into the vagus nerve and carotid artery on the side of Bondurant's neck. The blow paralyzed

Bondurant. Another twist of legs and hips whipped Demarco's left elbow into the Bondurant's jaw, cracking the right mandible. In almost the same move, Demarco brought his left fist up, around, and down, landing a hammer blow that broke Bondurant's collarbone into two pieces, followed by a last twist, which brought Demarco's knee slamming into Bondurant's floating ribs, crushing his liver.

Demarco stepped back. Bondurant, already unconscious, dropped onto his knees, his eyes dead, his brain shut down, he fell forward and his face smacked into the concrete platform.

Four moves. Three seconds. Fight over.

The sound of Bondurant hitting the stage made Willie Reese turn for a second to confirm what he already knew. He turned back to the crowd struck silent at the sight of Whitey Bondurant down, out, maybe dead. Willie walked slowly backward, shotgun aimed at the crowd.

Demarco placed a hand on Willie's shoulder, guiding him back toward the door held open for them by Amelia. Willie waited for the other three to step into the open doorway, shotgun still ready, and then he disappeared with the others behind the closing door.

Manny Guzman quickly made his way to Bondurant's prone body. Behind him Bondurant's men, shocked at having seen the feared assassin take such a beating, began leaving as police sirens filled the air.

Big Ben Woods, his deacons, and several of the residents remained on the steps, blocking the view of Bondurant, who had yet to move.

Manny rolled the still-unconscious albino onto his back, and pressed a gun into his lifeless hand. But this wasn't the Colt 1911 Bondurant had come with. This was the Ruger 9-mm Amelia Johnson had used to shoot Derrick Watkins, Tyrell Williams, and Biggie Watkins, fully loaded with the ammunition Amelia had found in Tyrell's laundry bag.

The first police cars appeared moving slowly through the crowd as they converged on the plaza. Woods and his deacons motioned for the cops to come to the stage. Manny pointed to Bondurant and yelled at the nearest cop, "Careful, he's got a gun."

The cop drew his own gun. Manny melted into the crowd.

Juju Jackson stood behind the Range Rover door, calm, aiming, not a hint of emotion in him. He knew the man in front of him had to be James Beck. He knew he had the drop on him. He almost smiled knowing he was going to put a bullet into Beck's heart.

Beck's only hope was that maybe he wouldn't take a direct hit. Maybe he could get a shot off, maybe he could hit Jackson even though he was covered by the Range Rover's driver's-side door.

And then, suddenly, inexplicably, Eric Jackson disappeared with a sudden, metal-crushing bang as Ciro's Escalade slammed into the Range Rover's door, knocking Jackson off his feet. Ciro backed up, jumped out, wrenched the bent door out of his way, and kicked Jackson's gun out of his hand.

Ciro lifted Jackson up with one hand and threw him against his Escalade. Jackson hit the front fender and slid onto the street.

It took a moment for Beck to realize he hadn't been struck by a bullet. And a few more seconds to stand up. He checked out the scene in the plaza. He couldn't tell much about what had happened beyond seeing the police cars rolling into the area and the crowd dispersing.

Ciro asked Beck, "So?"

"Looks like they made it out."

"Good. Let's get this piece-of-shit pimp off the street and get the hell out of here."

74

Beck and Ciro quickly tied up Eric Jackson, pulled a garbage bag over his head, and dumped him into the cargo section of the Escalade. Since Jackson didn't scream in pain and Beck didn't see any blood leaking from his ears, he assumed he'd survived Ciro's intervention with a six-thousand-pound vehicle without suffering any life-threatening injuries.

They emptied Jackson's gun, tossed it into the Range Rover, and left the vehicle in the middle of the street where the police couldn't miss it.

They were halfway to the entrance of the Cross Bronx Expressway with their captive when the first police car flew past them heading toward Harrod Avenue.

Ciro and Beck drove to Sedgwick Avenue, where Jonas and Ricky Bolo were waiting parked under the cover of a viaduct. They quickly transferred Jackson into their van. Ciro confirmed with Jonas where they were to take Jackson – a motel outside the Lincoln Tunnel where he'd already stashed Edward Remsen. In less than two minutes, the Bolos were heading for Jersey while Beck and Ciro continued driving south toward Manhattan.

Beck checked his watch. A few minutes after eleven. He asked Ciro, "So we're set, right? Alex's information was accurate?"

"Yeah. Noon."

"He answered your call?"

"No. I had to leave a message telling him either he calls me, or I'll show up at his apartment on Arden Street. He called back ten minutes later."

"Did he need much convincing?"

"Not really. He picked a restaurant on Broadway and 103rd Street."

Beck checked his watch. "We have time to look around. Make sure he didn't do anything stupid like call in the troops so they could arrest me."

Ciro nodded and then lapsed into silence. After a few moments, he turned to Beck and said, "You sure you want to do this, James?"

Beck nodded.

"This ain't some Bronx pimp, Jimmy. There's going to be a hell of a lot of heat over it."

"Ciro, I know what can happen. I'll do what I can to make sure nothing blows back on you guys. I know I might have to disappear. I know what this means. I know it all, Ciro."

Ciro nodded. Saying nothing because there was nothing more to say.

When they arrived at Broadway and 103rd, Ciro circled the surrounding streets until he was sure there were no cops lying in wait to arrest Beck. He pulled up across the street from the restaurant and told Beck, "I'll wait here. If the cops show, I'll drive this fucking tank into the restaurant if I have to, and get you out of there."

"The cops won't show. This is too far from his precinct. And he thinks there's already a plan in place to arrest us. He sure as hell won't try it by himself. Not in a restaurant filled with Upper West Side yuppies and their kids."

"All right. Be careful."

Beck dodged traffic getting across Broadway, entered the restaurant, and took a seat at a table for two adjacent to the outside seating area. He ordered coffee to revive himself, and watched the patrons at the other tables while keeping an eye out for Raymond Ippolito.

His phone signaled a text message had come in. It was from Phineas: *Starting our 2nd meet with Levitt, Wilson. Higher-ups involved now.*

Beck slipped the phone into his pocket. The timing seemed to be working.

He noticed a few people looking at him surreptitiously. The swelling under his eye and on his forehead had subsided, but the bruises were very visible. There was no hiding the fact that he'd been in some sort of fight.

He was about to order a second cup of coffee when Raymond Ippolito appeared at the restaurant doorway. Beck immediately pegged him for the cop. He wore his shirt hanging out of his slacks to cover the gun at his hip, a pair of too-shiny loafers that looked like Gucci knock-offs, and too much gel on his slicked-back hair. He walked directly to Beck's table, stood over him, and said, "I almost didn't match you with your mug shot. Looks like you took a beating."

"Ippolito."

"Yeah, what's this all about? You got some balls setting up a meet with me."

Beck looked up at Ippolito, calculating the precise angle and point of impact necessary to break his nose with a short right hook. The expression on Beck's battered face made Ippolito sit.

Beck said, "Did you ask me what this is all about?"

"Yeah."

"Murder, conspiracy, perjury, aiding and abetting known felons, prostitution, exploitation of minors, torture, rape, money laundering, tax evasion, and whether or not you and your career are going to survive the next twenty-four hours."

Ippolito shot back, "What the hell are you talking about?" But beneath the bravado, Beck saw fear flickering in Ippolito's eyes.

"Do us both a favor and drop the act. You know exactly what I'm talking about."

The waiter appeared. Ippolito faked a smile and ordered a Bloody Mary. He turned to Beck, trying to keep up the façade.

"Yeah, well, whatever the hell you're talking about, it sounds like you're threatening an NYPD detective."

"Sounds like? This isn't *like* threatening you, Ippolito. I *am* threatening you. You've aided and abetted in enough crimes to send you to prison. Now keep your mouth shut and listen to my proof."

Beck began a careful, concise explanation of the evidence that proved John Palmer had killed Paco Johnson and had planted the murder weapon to frame Derrick Watkins for that murder. Beck told Ippolito he knew the witnesses claiming he shot Derrick Watkins were phony, and that they would fold when Eric Jackson went down, which he assured Ippolito was going to happen soon.

Beck continued on, trying to keep his rage in check as he described the depth and breadth of the criminal enterprises run by Eric Jackson. Without going into details about Remsen's prostitution ring, Beck explained the evidence he had that would allow the FBI and NYPD to send Jackson and Bondurant away, most likely for the rest of their lives.

Ippolito tried one last attempt at bluster. "So what's all that got to do with me?"

"I told you to keep your mouth shut." Beck continued. "All the evidence on Palmer is being presented to Assistant District Attorney Frederick Wilson, your supervisor, Lieutenant James Levitt, and other police bosses as we speak. It will go right up the line to the chief of detectives, and all the other brass who have been lied to by John Palmer. The FBI will be reviewing evidence against Jackson starting at two o'clock today."

Beck's speech had taken five minutes. Ippolito's Bloody Mary had arrived and remained untouched the entire time.

Ippolito blurted out, "Hey, I swear, I didn't know anything about Palmer shooting that guy. I would have . . ."

Beck held up a hand. "If I thought you did, I'd have already killed you. I wouldn't be offering you a way out."

Ippolito tried to say something, but Beck said, "Stop. Don't say anything that might make me change my mind. The time for bullshit is over. You and I both know what's going to happen now.

"The NYPD is going to go after you and Palmer. They'll never get Palmer for murdering my friend, but they'll know he did it, so they'll go after you and Palmer on everything they can. When Eric Jackson starts singing to save his ass, they'll have enough to charge both of you with witness tampering, perjury, falsifying records, colluding with a known felon, aiding and abetting. We both know it'll be a long list.

"You'll hang tough and deny it. But what do you think Palmer will do? Daddy isn't going to let his golden boy's career go down in flames. He'll tell John Junior to turn on you. It'll be all your fault. You're the senior guy. You're the one with all the connections. Palmer will play innocent and blame you. By the time he and Daddy are done, little Johnny will be a hero and you'll lose everything, and end up in prison. You're going to take the fall, Ippolito. You know it, and I know it."

Ippolito picked up his untouched Bloody Mary and nearly drained it. He gripped the glass, thinking it through. A sick, sour feeling formed in the pit of his stomach.

Beck said, "So, Detective, time to decide. You want to save yourself, or take the hit for John Palmer?"

Ippolito couldn't look Beck in the eye. Head down, he cleared his throat and said, "What are you going to do?"

"You know goddam well what I'm going to do. Are you in, or not?"

With his head still bowed, Ippolito muttered, "Yes."

"Yes, what?"

Ippolito looked up. "Yes. I'm in."

Beck nodded. "I'm assuming Palmer is home now."

"Yeah. He's home. He worked almost two days straight."

"What's his next move?"

"He has to be at One Police Plaza today at three to finalize everything for the arrests early Monday morning."

"Are you in that meeting?"

"No. They were done with me yesterday."

"Why?"

"I'm out. I put in my retirement papers weeks ago. My last day is Friday."

"If you want to make it to Friday, you'll do exactly what I tell you."

Ippolito poked at the bloody-looking ice cubes in his glass with the wilted stick of celery.

"What do you want me to do?"

Beck checked his watch. It was 12:40 P.M.

"I assume you've been to Palmer's apartment."

"Sure. A few times."

"I had his building checked out. His intercom has a camera. If you ring him, what does he do?"

"Checks the camera, usually says hi or something and rings me in."

"Does he leave his apartment door open for you, or make you wait for him to open it when you get up to his place?"

"Usually leaves it open."

"We're going over to Palmer's place. You're going to buzz him, and tell him you have to talk to him about the meeting at One PP."

"Then what?"

"Then that's it. He buzzes you in, you walk away with one of my associates. You wait with him until I tell him to let you go."

"Let me go, or put a bullet in my head?"

"No, Mr. Ippolito. You do what I've said, and you won't die today."

"What do you mean, today?"

"If you don't keep your mouth shut, if you don't play this out to the end, you get a bullet right between your fucking eyes."

Ippolito stared across the table at Beck. The dangerous, grim reality of what was happening robbed Raymond Ippolito of all expression. He looked as if he'd aged ten years since he'd walked into the restaurant. He opened his mouth, tried to say something, stopped, and then forced out the words.

"You'll never get away with it, Beck. He's a cop for chrissake. You know who his father is? They'll turn over heaven and earth . . ."

Beck pitched forward and snarled. "And I'll turn over heaven and hell if I have to. He pays for killing my friend, for trying to put my friends back in jail, for conspiring with criminals who torture and prostitute women and girls. You've got one chance to pay for your part in this. Stand up, walk out of here, and take it."

75

John Palmer lived on the eighteenth floor of a building on Columbus Avenue near 100th Street that had been thoroughly vetted late Saturday night by the master burglars Ricky and Jonas Bolo.

The building had been designed to provide housing for up-and-coming singles and young marrieds who were content with living in hundreds of identical Sheetrock boxes stacked on top of each other, floor after floor.

In order to squeeze the maximum amount of profit from the absurdly high rents, instead of doormen and lobby staff, the building provided a large cage in the basement manned round-the-clock by minimum-wage workers who signed for an endless stream of deliveries from Amazon, UPS, FedEx, FreshDirect, local restaurants, dry cleaners, and other merchants. They, in turn, sent texts to the residents, who then made the monumental effort to ride an elevator downstairs to get their *stuff*. The building euphemistically dubbed this their *concierge service*.

Security in and out of the building depended on a video intercom/buzzer system and cameras in the lobby, elevators, and stairwell.

At five minutes after one P.M., John Palmer stood in his kitchen making coffee. He planned on being dressed and ready to leave for the meeting at One PP by two o'clock. His intercom buzzer rang. Barefoot, he padded out to his small foyer, checked the flat-screen display, and saw Raymond Ippolito staring into the camera.

"What's up, Ray?"

"Gotta come up and talk to you."

"About what?"

"Something I shouldn't be yelling about out on the street."

Palmer was already unnerved by what his father had told him, plus Juju Jackson never showing up for their meeting. Ippolito appearing unannounced felt like more bad news, but Palmer wanted to hear what he had to say.

"Okay. C'mon up."

Palmer leaned on the buzzer, opened his apartment door, and then headed back to his kitchen.

Down on Columbus Avenue, when the buzzer rang, Ippolito remained standing in front of the intercom, while Beck, who had stood out of range of the intercom camera, pushed open the door and slipped into the lobby, head down, his face covered by a ball cap.

A couple walked past him while two women returning from their Sunday morning yoga class walked in behind him. He continued past the security camera in the mailbox area, and into the main lobby. Beck had been briefed by Ricky and Jonas about the location of the security cameras in the lobby and near the elevator banks. He made sure to stand out of camera range, mixing with others waiting for one of the building's four elevators to arrive.

Outside, Ippolito faked another ring of Palmer's buzzer, waited for ten seconds, checked his watch, and walked away. He did this exactly as instructed, knowing Ciro Baldassare stood on the other side of Columbus Avenue watching him. Ippolito continued uptown to 101st Street and turned east, heading toward Central Park. When he reached Central Park West, he crossed the street and waited for Baldassare to join him, where they would wait until Ciro told him he could go.

Beck stood aside as four people stepped out of the elevator, then he followed the gossiping yoga ladies into the cab, along with a man carrying grocery bags and his wife talking on her cell phone. Just before the elevator doors shut, a woman with a dog and a two-year-old in a stroller rushed on board.

Beck waited until everyone had pressed their floors so he could pick a floor higher than the others. He leaned forward and pressed twenty-two, keeping his head down so the baseball cap hid his face from the elevator's security camera and nobody noticed the formidable guy with a lumpy, bruised face.

On twenty-two he exited the empty elevator, turning to his right, knowing that like most apartment buildings there were no security cameras in the hallways. The only cameras were at the top and bottom of the emergency-exit stairwell.

He walked quickly down a typical high-rise hallway: low popcorn ceiling, nondescript carpeting, inexpensive down-lighting, long rows of doors painted a deep maroon, each with a security peephole.

Beck found the exit to the stairwell and walked down to eighteen. The Bolo brothers had already taped open the latch on that door with a tape that would leave no residue.

Beck opened the door, removed the tape, and stuck it in his back pocket. He peered out, making sure the hallway was empty. He stepped out, closed the door carefully, and quickly walked to apartment sixteen.

Ippolito had been right. The door was open for him.

Beck stepped quietly into the apartment, carefully closing the door behind him.

There was a small foyer that opened onto a minimally furnished living room/dining area, kitchen on the left, a hallway leading to the bedroom and bathroom on the right.

Palmer stood fifteen feet in front of Beck, backlit by the living room window, holding a cordless phone next to his leg. He was barefoot, wearing a white T-shirt and black workout pants with a stylish red vertical stripe running along the side of each leg.

He turned at the sound of his front door closing and flinched when he saw James Beck.

Beck said, "I'm guessing that phone call wasn't good news."

Palmer looked at the phone in his hand, then back at Beck, confused. "Who are you? Where's Raymond?"

Beck took off his baseball cap and tossed it on the floor. "You!"

"Yeah, me. I assume that was your boss, Levitt, on the phone. What did he say?"

"How did you – Why are you here?"

"To make sure you go down for shooting Paco Johnson, for trying to frame me, for colluding with Eric Jackson, for lying about what you saw at Mount Hope Place, and everything else you've done."

Beck had no gun. He took a few steps toward Palmer, his empty hands at his sides, calm, focused, and aware of Palmer's holstered SIG Sauer sitting on the glass-topped dining room table six feet to Palmer's left along with keys, cell phone, and a wallet.

Palmer stood with the couch between him and the dining table. He took a step back, getting clear of the couch. Beck moved forward and stopped. They were equidistant from the gun on the table.

Beck said, "You have to choose."

Palmer looked at him, confused.

"You can sit and wait for the cops to come arrest you, or you can go for your gun and shoot the guy who's giving them the evidence to take you down."

"You're crazy."

Beck took a half step forward.

Palmer's eyes flicked toward his gun. He'd have to get to it first, pull it out of the holster, chamber a round, and shoot Beck.

Beck seemed to read Palmer's mind. He held up both hands, palms open. He turned halfway around to show Palmer he had no gun behind his back. He patted his pockets to show they were empty.

"You can shoot me just for being in your apartment."

Beck took a step back, giving the advantage to Palmer.

"I know you're a murdering, lying, ruthless, pampered piece of shit, but even for an asshole like you whose had everything served up for him it's a no-brainer. Go for the gun, coward."

Before Beck finished his sentence, Palmer made his move. Rage and desperation made him fast. Very fast.

Two steps, and he had his right hand on the butt of the SIG before Beck made it halfway to the table. He pulled the gun free from the holster and pulled back the slide to chamber a bullet while Beck was still three feet away. For a split second, Palmer thought Beck might be setting him up. Sacrificing himself so he'd be prosecuted for shooting an unarmed man. But in the same split-second it took him to think that, he realized he could plant a weapon on Beck after he shot him. A knife. Easy. He raised the SIG, but too late now. In fact, it wasn't very close.

Beck already had a weapon in his hand. A five-inch tapered Kubotan stick made of aircraft aluminum he'd carried in under his watchband, covered by his shirtsleeve. He'd pulled it out with his first step. Two more steps put him within arm's length of Palmer. Close enough to ram the pointed end of the Kubotan stick into Palmer's right temple with so much force it punched a hole into Palmer's skull, sending shards of bone into his brain.

Palmer's head snapped left. Beck stepped back. Palmer tried to straighten himself. He looked like he was moving underwater. He tried to point the gun at Beck, who continued stepping back, avoiding contact. Palmer blinked rapidly, lost his balance, tottered, and collapsed as a massive hemorrhage formed under his punctured skull.

Beck put the Kubotan into his front pocket and withdrew a pair of latex gloves from his back pocket.

He slipped on the gloves, squatted down, carefully removed the SIG Sauer from Palmer's hand, and laid it on the floor. He grabbed Palmer under the armpits, lifting and maneuvering him over to the couch, setting him down on it, muscling him into a sitting position. He picked up the cordless phone Palmer had dropped and replaced it in its receptacle.

Palmer slumped forward, dying.

Beck went to the kitchen, brushing the marks out of the rug he'd made dragging Palmer to the couch. He checked to make sure no coffee or food were being prepared. He came out of the kitchen and made sure there was no blood on the floor near where he'd hit Palmer.

Palmer's temple was oozing blood as he sat slumped on the couch, but that didn't matter.

Beck made his way to the bedroom. The room was unkempt. The bed unmade. There was a desktop computer set up on a small desk. It was turned off. Beck ignored it.

He found a stack of printer paper on the shelf over the desk and took one page. He pulled open a file drawer and looked through Palmer's papers until he found a sample of his writing. It wasn't really script. Mostly printing. Beck sat at Palmer's desk and from a pen he found next to the keyboard he wrote a simple note, mimicking Palmer's almost childish handwriting: *I'm sorry. Can't do this anymore.*

He pulled a piece of paper from his shirt pocket on which Alex Liebowitz had printed out an enlarged image of the signature on Palmer's driver's license. Beck scribbled a reasonable likeness of the signature on the suicide note, left the pen on the desk, returned to the living room, and pressed Palmer's thumb on one side of the signed page and forefinger on the other. Remembering that Palmer had held the gun in his right hand, Beck pressed the heel of Palmer's right hand onto the page below the signature. He set the page on the end table.

Beck retrieved the SIG from the floor. He positioned himself in front of the slumped-over corpse and put the gun in Palmer's lifeless right hand, placing Palmer's index finger on the trigger.

Then he surrounded Palmer's hand with his, and pushed the tip of his thumb over Palmer's index finger. He placed his right hand under Palmer's chin and lifted the head and body into an upright sitting position. He raised Palmer's right hand and pressed the muzzle of the gun on the wound he'd made in Palmer's temple.

James Beck leaned left a bit, but did not look away. He watched to make sure he'd set everything correctly. Breathing short breaths under the strain of holding the head, body, and gun in position, Beck felt a grinding, sick feeling in his stomach. He wasn't sure what caused it. All the misery created by the ruthless, narcissistic young man in front of him, the pain caused by holding him in position, or the knowledge of what was about to happen.

Beck squeezed Palmer's finger against the trigger.

The SIG Sauer emitted a sharp crack. The hot, empty shell flew up and away, and a great deal of John Palmer's skull and brains exploded outward, splattering everything to the left of Palmer's shoulder: couch, window, wall. And the suicide note.

The 9-mm bullet plowed into the Sheetrock wall, just below the window, penetrating into the brick that separated John Palmer's private eighteenth-floor perch from the rest of the world beneath him.

76

In the aftermath, Beck lived in a strange limbo, waiting to flee if necessary, but staying to make sure his men remained safe from arrest as all the investigations played out.

Even though none of the crew kept their distance or acted differently, Beck felt isolated, because he had to be ready to leave everything behind if anything about Palmer's death turned the attention of the police on him and the others.

After the shooting, he'd wiped off the blood that blew back on him with Handi Wipes, folded everything into his latex gloves, and placed the gloves and wipes in his pocket.

He put his baseball cap on and left the apartment, shutting the door firmly behind him, covering the door handle with his sleeve. He walked two flights up to the twentieth floor. The Bolo brothers had taped over that door lock, too. Beck pocketed the tape and stepped out onto the floor, taking the elevator all the way to the basement. He waited near the service entrance until he could slip out with two FreshDirect deliverymen exiting past a kid delivering a stack of pizzas.

Finally, after weeks of intense investigation, the NYPD ruled John Palmer's death a suicide based on the physical evidence at the scene, the stress Palmer's crimes must have caused him, and Levitt's last phone call. Investigators decided that when Levitt told Palmer to remain in his apartment until further notice, Palmer concluded his arrest was imminent.

The investigators also took note of all the other factors pointing to Palmer's guilt: the evidence Walter Ferguson and Phineas Dunleavy provided, the fact that Palmer's witnesses recanted within minutes after hearing Juju Jackson was in federal custody, Raymond Ippolito's testimony blaming everything on Palmer, and the Bronx DA dropping any prosecutions that had anything to do with Palmer's evidence – all of which convinced the NYPD brass to sweep everything linked to John Palmer as far under the carpet as possible.

Ippolito avoided prosecution, but that didn't prevent the commissioner from stripping him of his rank and pension. He fled to Venice Beach, California, got a job as a bartender, faded into the woodwork, but never stopped watching for James Beck or Ciro Baldassare.

The FBI initiated an investigation against Edward Remsen and Eric Jackson, both of whom they picked up on a tip that led them to a motel in New Jersey where the pair had been hiding out. The charges against them were extensive.

Remsen negotiated a plea bargain, which included forfeiting almost three million dollars in assets, agreeing to testify against Eric Jackson, and identifying all the men in his father's prostitution ring, including Fred Culla, the sixth of Beck's five attackers who had been found beaten in the parking lot of Remsen's old bar shortly before his arrest by the FBI.

Eric Jackson pleaded not guilty to all charges and remained in the Federal Metropolitan Detention Center in

Brooklyn awaiting the trial that would eventually send him to prison for the rest of his life.

Patrolmen in the 43rd Precinct arrested Floyd Whitey Bondurant at Bronx River Houses after his fight with Demarco for possession of a firearm. An anonymous tip prompted the cops to test the gun, and ballistics confirmed it was the weapon used in the murders of Derrick Watkins, Jerome Watkins, and Tyrell Williams. Bondurant's reputation as Eric Jackson's assassin, plus the intense pressure to find someone responsible for the killings, led the Bronx District Attorney to charge him with all three murders, which meant dropping charges against Emmanuel Guzman and Demarco Jones.

Amelia Johnson never became a suspect in the Watkins or Williams shootings.

It took three years and multiple witnesses who came forward to testify against Whitey Bondurant, but eventually he was convicted of multiple homicides and other felonies, which earned him four consecutive life sentences.

The New York State Police investigation concluded that the deaths of Oswald Remsen, his sons, and Austen White were the result of a bloody falling-out over money connected to a prostitution ring. The Department of Correction pushed the state investigators and prosecutors to close the case as soon as possible.

Beck made good on his promise to Queen-Esther Karen Goodwin. He fronted her $100,000 in relocation expenses, promising her more when he finished selling the properties in her name. Esther didn't believe Beck's promise of more money, but once he gave her the first hundred grand, she quickly signed over power of attorney to the lawyer fronting the sale of Eric Jackson's Bronx properties.

Phineas negotiated a witness-protection deal for her that provided both immunity and help setting up a residence far from New York.

Two months later, when all property sales were completed, after fees paid to Phineas, the real estate lawyer, Alex's hackers, and the Bolo brothers, plus repairs made to Ciro's Escalade and new guns purchased for Demarco and Manny, the net was $1,725,000 and change.

Beck wired Esther an additional $331,250 – the balance of her one-quarter share of the sales. That left one share for Beck and his men, one share to fund a trust for Amelia, and one share Beck donated to organizations that helped women and girls escaping from prostitution.

During the time Beck and Alex helped Esther plan her new life, she argued less about testifying for the FBI than she did about her new name.

Beck and Alex insisted she pick a name completely different from her current name. Esther was adamant that Queen remain part of her name, explaining that her mother had named her after the Queen of the Persian Empire.

After a good deal of debate, everyone finally agreed on Tamara Elisabeth David, after Tamar, the daughter of King David. This, of course, was a downgrade from a queen to a princess, ironic in its connection to Amelia's working name, but Queen-Esther allowed it because she had grown fond of Amelia, even though she never admitted it. She also liked the biblical connection to Tamar, and the inclusion of Elisabeth, which was her mother's name.

Although everything had worked out as Beck had hoped, there were still loose ends. Ippolito was alive and able to connect Beck to Palmer's death, but he had no proof, the building security-camera recordings were long gone, and he had no interest in implicating himself in the murder of an NYPD detective.

Quite a few in Jackson's crew escaped the FBI sweep, but none of them were big players. There were still three young men alive who knew Amelia had shot Derrick Watkins, but Beck couldn't see why any of them would come forward, and the cops weren't looking to reopen the case.

What exceeded Beck's expectations was how effortlessly Amelia became part of the Red Hook household. She became the kitchen assistant of the baleful Manny Guzman. Not in his private downstairs bar kitchen. Manny would never allow that. But he did let Amelia shadow him in the second-floor kitchen. It gave him almost daily pleasure to have someone to pass his skills on to. And Amelia made him very proud when one night in late June she single-handedly prepared an evening meal for everyone in the house, plus the formidable Willie Reese.

Willie's role as personal bodyguard evolved more into the role of an overprotective older brother. He let it be known in the neighborhood that no one was to bother Amelia. Not a look, not a comment, and certainly not a touch. It took someone of Willie's size, demeanor, and reputation to enforce his edict since Amelia effortlessly attracted male attention, but it held, and gave Amelia an opportunity to thank Willie Reese for something she had never experienced in her entire life – the freedom to walk in a neighborhood without fear of being harmed or harassed. Her gratitude gave Willie a sense of pride and satisfaction he'd never experienced.

When it came to Ciro, who visited the Red Hook headquarters the least, Amelia kept her distance. She had concluded correctly that Ciro Baldassare was not a man to be taken lightly, and also the least susceptible to her charms. However, Ciro knew Amelia Johnson had *made her bones*, so he treated her with a good deal of deference and respect, which she returned in kind. He enjoyed making a point about how Amelia had saved Demarco by taking on a giant albino assassin. He called her *The Kid*. She called him *The Italian*.

The deepest bond of all blossomed between Amelia and Demarco. She couldn't quite understand how someone who looked like him and was able to beat down a man like Whitey Bondurant could be gay. And perhaps she felt obliged to test him every once in a while by being softly seductive around him, which both pleased and amused Demarco. Amelia became his little sister/ makeover project/co-conspirator. When it came time to buy clothes for her father's memorial and burial, Demarco took Amelia directly to Bergdorf's, where he helped her pick out a beautiful, Akris Punto jacket in black, a dark purple embellished-edge silk blouse, and black Francoise-twill fitted pants, all of which fitted her long-limbed figure beautifully, making her look effortlessly elegant.

Walter, as promised, had made all the funeral arrangements. He joined Beck, his men, and Amelia for the burial at Woodlawn Cemetery in the Bronx, not far from where all the troubles had started. It was a pleasantly warm day in June, the sun shining softly in a bright blue sky dotted with lazy clouds. Woodlawn had the reputation of being one of the most beautiful cemeteries in the world, and so it was, although Packy's plot occupied a spot in a rather plain corner of the graveyard.

As they laid Packy to his final rest, Beck thought about that day at Port Authority, waiting for his friend who had never appeared. Not having been able to spend one second of Packy's freedom with him, and knowing he would never see Packy again had caused a deep, permanent ache in Beck's heart. Thankfully, some of that pain was assuaged when he gazed at the calm, statuesque Amelia standing at the grave site. They had saved her, Beck told himself. At least they had saved her.

In the safety of the Red Hook headquarters, they all continued caring for Amelia. Demarco took her shopping for clothes until she was outfitted to his satisfaction. They talked about makeup, hairstyles, movies, YA books, and the latest TV shows. Willie continued to watch over her. Manny tutored her. Ciro made her feel formidable and confident.

Beck separated Amelia from her Glock, explaining the risk it presented. He had his doctor friend Brandon Wright, gently and carefully do a thorough evaluation of Amelia's health. The good doctor maintained doctor/patient confidentiality, but he let Beck know Amelia had not emerged from her life of abuse unscathed. Among other things she had contracted a common sexually transmitted disease that had to be attended to. She had several vitamin deficiencies, and had never received the immunizations and vaccinations she should have had as a child. The good doctor also discovered that Amelia needed glasses, which, of course, gave Demarco another reason to shop.

As they approached two months, Beck became anxious to get Amelia out of New York. There were still witnesses from Mount Hope Place. Jackson, Bondurant, and others were all awaiting trial, and there was always a possibility her name might come up in the ongoing investigations. He knew the farther away from him and the others she got, the safer she'd be.

Most important, Beck was determined to give Amelia a chance to live the life she deserved. To attend school regularly, to have a boyfriend, to simply be a teenage girl. It was time to guide Amelia on to the next phase of her life, even though it meant he would have to bear the loss of saying good-bye to her for a very long time.

Beck didn't look forward to breaking the news to Amelia. She acted reserved around Beck, treating him as an authority figure, something akin to the father she'd never had. Nevertheless, they had fallen into the habit of sitting together at the bar downstairs while Beck read the morning paper and sipped his coffee. Sometimes Beck would talk about a piece of news he came across, or ask Amelia what she thought about a topic. But on the morning of July fifteenth, Beck cleared his throat, suppressed the emotion churning inside him, and said to Amelia, "I think it's time."

"For what?"

Beck found himself unable to answer.

Amelia pressed. "Time for what?"

He cleared his throat. "For you to meet someone."

"Who?"

"A friend of mine."

Amelia gave Beck a look. "You going to tell me what's up, or make me be patient and wait until you're ready to tell me what's really going on?"

Beck put down his coffee cup, turned to Amelia, pleased at her perception and straightforwardness. He spoke to her calmly and carefully. He told her his thoughts, his concerns for her safety, his hopes for her future. He told her about Janice Elkins and about the restaurant/bar she now owned, although he didn't tell Amelia how he had let Janice know she could buy the place from Edward Remsen at a good price because he needed cash for lawyers, and lent her the money to do so. He explained to Amelia that Janice Elkins needed help with her restaurant, and suggested Amelia might like working for her, and perhaps living with her in Ellenville, while she attended high school. He told Amelia about the demographics, the school system, all the information he had carefully studied and wanted her to know.

Amelia asked, "Why all the way up there?"

"We need to put some distance between you and New York City, Amelia. If something happens, it would be too easy for them to find you. And it seems like, everything considered, Ellenville might be a good place for you."

Amelia didn't argue. Beck didn't try to sell her on his plan.

He told her it would be up to her. He asked her to try it out. Then explained how he had set up a trust fund for her from the sales of Eric Jackson's properties, and how they would invest her money so she wouldn't have to worry too much about supporting herself, or paying for college, or maybe even buying a house or starting a family someday. Beck knew these were things Amelia couldn't quite grasp, but he spoke of them anyhow.

Finally, he explained to her that it would be safer for her to start out with a new name.

"Really?"

"Yes."

"Like what?"

"Well, we were thinking Amelia Jones. Alex already has it all set up. If you like it."

"Jones?"

"It's Demarco's idea. What do you think?"

It was then that Amelia felt the depths of what had gone on between her and Beck and his men, and the bittersweet sting that came with knowing this brief, secure interlude in her life was about to end. Tears filled her eyes.

Beck patted her arm and tried to console her, even though he felt like he might cry, too. "Hey, c'mon. It's because he loves you. We all do."

She blinked back the tears, wiped her cheeks, and forced a smile. "I ain't cryin' just about the name. You know that."

"I know."

"When I gotta go?"

Beck shrugged. "Soon. Demarco says you're going to take your driving test this week."

"With my new name?"

"With your new name. I traded in the Ranger for a nice used Subaru Forester you can have. You're going to need wheels up there."

"I like that truck. How come you traded it?"

"Well, I don't want that vehicle anywhere near Ellenville."

She nodded. "Some bad shit happened up there, didn't it?"

"Yes."

"You ain't comin' up there, are you?"

"Not for a while. I can't take the chance of ruining things for you in that town."

"How long before I get to see you again?"

Beck tried to hide the pain that made him grimace. "I don't know."

Amelia nodded. Thinking her own thoughts. After a moment she said, "You all did so much for me."

"And you for us, Amelia. You know that, right?"

Amelia tried to say something, but didn't, for fear she might cry again. After a few moments she steeled herself, sat up straighter, and turned to Beck.

"Before I go, you gotta do one more thing for me."

"Name it."

"I didn't know my father, but I know he was tryin' to help me. And I know you all thought he was a good man."

"He was."

"So, I think I should know about him. And about what happened to him. Will you tell me? All of it?"

Beck nodded, thinking over her request. And then he began to talk about his friend, his true friend and her father – Packy Johnson. He told Amelia about Dannemora and Eastern Correctional, about how Packy had saved him, and how angry and tortured he had been about Packy's death. He went through all of it, telling her things he'd never told anybody, but only as much as necessary.

Beck explained how he'd figured out Palmer had shot Packy. He tracked everything through for Amelia from the moment he'd discovered Palmer had planted the murder weapon in the Mount Hope apartment, describing how that had enabled him to frame Derrick for Packy's murder, and provide a phony motive for Beck to shoot Derrick.

He told her how Walter had found out what the cops were doing and provided ballistics evidence that had helped him figure out Palmer's crimes.

He explained how the ledger books and computer files from Derrick and Biggie had led to discovering the scope of Eric Jackson's criminal enterprise. He assured her justice had been done without giving her any details that might compromise her.

They talked about how Beck would never get over the loss of his friend, and how helping her had helped him. But Beck didn't tell her about how separating from her now pained him deeply.

When he finished, Amelia seemed to be deep in thought.

She said, "You figured out the cop did it."

"Yes."

"Cuz there wasn't no twenty-two up at Derrick's apartment."

"Right."

"What kind of gun did you say it was?"

"HP Phoenix. All black. Three-inch barrel. It wasn't there when we took the guns off Derrick and his crew."

"Yeah, none of them guys in Derrick's crew would bother carrying a gun like that."

Amelia became even more silent and inward. Beck worried that talking about how her father died hadn't been a very good idea, but he didn't try to console her, or ask how she felt. He sat silently with her, giving the young girl time to absorb everything he had told her. At one point, she turned and stared at Beck.

He asked, "Did you want to ask me anything more?"

For a moment, Beck thought Amelia was going to say something, but all she said was, "No. We don't need to talk about it anymore."

Beck nodded. "Good."

Amelia changed the subject. "So, anybody driving upstate with me?"

"Demarco. He wants to make sure everything is cool with you up there."

"And if it ain't?"

"Then we'll figure something else out. We're not getting rid of you, kiddo. We're never going to stop looking out for each other."

Again, a serious mood descended on Amelia.

"You're right, Mr. Beck. We got to look out for each other. Always. No matter what."

77

On the morning when they were to drive up to Ellenville, Demarco helped Amelia load up her Subaru. The day was overcast and unseasonably cool.

She wore skinny jeans, new Nike cross-trainers, and a long-sleeve raglan top. And, of course, her new glasses. Demarco had picked out the blue Prada frames with her and made sure her prescription lenses were perfect.

Amelia drove. Shortly after they set out, she said to Demarco, "I want to ask you a favor."

"What?"

"I want to stop by my grandmother's. Say good-bye."

"Okay. It's on the way."

Amelia said very little on the drive to Hoe Avenue, which didn't surprise Demarco. The young girl was leaving a place where she had learned to feel safe, for an unknown life in a place she'd never been.

When they arrived in her old neighborhood, instead of parking in front of her grandmother's building, she drove to 173rd Street and parked the car next to a brick wall that bordered the south end of the courtyard behind the public housing unit. The wall had an overlapping section that allowed entrance into the courtyard.

Amelia told Demarco, "I won't be long. Can you stay and watch the stuff?"

Demarco tilted his seat back and said, "Sure."

Demarco didn't think about why Amelia chose to go in the back way, and Amelia didn't explain why she didn't want anybody to see her entering the building. She quickly made her way through the courtyard, found the hidden key she always used to sneak into her grandmother's apartment, and let herself in. She ascended to the second floor and knocked on Lorena's door.

After a few moments, she heard Lorena shuffle toward the door and yell, "Who is it?"

"It's me, Amelia."

"What do you want?"

"Let me in."

Lorena opened the door. At first she didn't recognize Amelia dressed in her new clothes, wearing glasses. Amelia stepped past Lorena into the stuffy, dark apartment, the air heavy with the cooking smells and the general odor of the old woman. For a moment, the aromas brought back the stifling memories of her previous life, which added to the anger roiling inside her.

Lorena turned away from Amelia, ignoring her, oblivious to how dangerous it was now to stoke Amelia's anger by once again making her feel rejected.

The old lady sat by herself on her plastic-covered couch, but Amelia refused to let Lorena rebuff her. She sat next to her, turning sideways to face her grandmother.

"I'm leaving the Bronx," Amelia said.

"So?"

"So I wanted to say good-bye. And ask you something."

Lorena looked down, a sour expression twisting her face.

"Why you leaving?"

"I have to."

"Because of him."

"Who?"

"You know who."

"My father?"

Lorena looked up and sneered at Amelia. "Father? What father? Paco never see you. What he ever do for you? You leaving because he come here and ruin everything."

"*He* ruined everything?"

"Yes."

"How? He tried to help me. What did you ever do for me except make me feel like I was worthless?"

"I give you a place to stay. Food. Clothes. I give you everything."

Amelia stared at the Lorena's sneering, angry face and had to stifle the urge to slap her.

"Yeah, well, now I need something else from you."

"What?"

"A gun."

Lorena looked at her for a moment.

"Why you come to me?"

"Cuz you got one."

Lorena grew quiet. She glared at Amelia.

Amelia raised her voice. "Get it."

Lorena stood up and walked to the bedroom. She returned holding the old .38 Colt revolver she'd tried to shoot Beck with. She sat on the couch, the gun in her right hand.

Amelia asked, "Where's the other one? The Phoenix twenty-two."

Lorena's expression hardened. "I no have the other gun."

"Where is it?"

Lorena turned the Colt toward her granddaughter. "I lose it."

"Why you pointing that at me?"

"You should go. I don't want you here. I don't want to see you anymore."

"What happened to the twenty-two? Where is it? What did you do?"

No response.

Amelia shouted, "What did you do, you goddam, crazy, useless, murdering bitch?"

Lorena screamed, "You don't talk to me like that!"

Amelia yelled, "Why did you shoot him? Why? Why goddammit?!"

Lorena shouted back, "Because he come here after seventeen years thinking he can push me around. Shouts at me – 'Where's Amelia? Where's Amelia?' Like what you do is my fault. He goes out to do what? Be the big *tipo duro*. Show everybody. Get you killed." Lorena leaned toward Amelia, shouting, shaking, still holding the revolver. "He was crazy. I go after him. I see what he does. Starts a fight. They beat him. *Tan estupido*. So now what he gonna do? Get a gun? Go back and shoot them? Because of you? Kill them, and then what? You think they let you live after he does that?"

Amelia watched her grandmother leaning toward her, her face twisted in rage rooted in decades of anger and pain and loss, still holding the revolver.

Amelia demanded through clenched teeth, "Tell me what you did."

"All he knows is killing. Killing for what? He couldn't hardly walk after they beat him, but I know he was coming back to my house. I know he would take a gun. I run ahead of him. Waited in the little park. He come up the street. Passes me. No, I tell myself. No. He can't come here and do this."

Amelia felt her throat tightening. She blinked, pushing down the pain and rage until she finally heard the truth.

"What did you do?"

"I come behind him, I point my gun to his head, and I shoot him."

Amelia's face twisted in anger. How? How could this pathetic, hateful, wasted old woman have caused so much pain and death and sorrow? Amelia shook her head from side to side, consumed by the horrible revelation, ready now to see it through.

"And then what did you do?"

Lorena pointed the old revolver at Amelia as if to keep her away.

"I drop the gun, and I ran."

"You left him there in the street?"

"Yes."

"And the twenty-two?"

She stared at Amelia, defiantly. "Yes."

"Why? Why did you drop the gun?"

"I see the car coming. Not a regular police car. From nowhere suddenly the flashing lights. He must have followed Paco, too. Heard me shoot him."

"The police?"

Lorena's voice lowered, remembering it.

"Yes. A policeman. No uniform. I was scared. I drop the gun and ran." She looked at Amelia. "Same policeman come here next morning. I thought to arrest me. But he didn't. I think maybe he never saw me. He left. And then I think he changed his mind and come back to take me to jail. I was going to shoot him, too. But it wasn't him."

Amelia felt like she couldn't breathe. The moment Beck had described the Phoenix twenty-two, she knew it was Lorena's gun. She knew Lorena must have shot her father, but she hadn't fully believed it until now. And now she would do what she had come to do. She would make sure what Lorena had done would never be known, would never hurt Beck or the others. And she would make sure the person who really murdered her father would pay for her crime.

Lorena saw the murderous look in Amelia's eyes. She raised the thirty-eight, pointing it now at Amelia's chest, her hand shaking.

Amelia grabbed the barrel of the Colt, determined to twist it out of Lorena's hand, but the old woman lunged at Amelia, fighting back with desperate strength, grabbing Amelia's wrist.

Amelia fell back off the couch, Lorena on top of her, both fighting for the gun. Lorena pulled the trigger.

Demarco had been waiting for Amelia's return, growing increasingly anxious thinking about Amelia dealing with the volatile old woman. And then he heard the unmistakable sound of a gunshot. A sound exactly like the one he had heard when Beck had come to Lorena's apartment.

He burst out of the car and ran into the courtyard, but he had no idea which door led to Lorena's apartment. He raced toward what he thought was the right door, a heavy metal-clad door. He kicked it, doing nothing more than denting it. He kicked it again, and again, helpless, choking with dread.

The gunshot sent a surge of fear and strength through Amelia. Still holding the hot barrel, she grabbed the flailing Lorena by the throat, pushed her off, turned and forced her down onto the dirty green carpet. She straddled Lorena, a violent rage coming over her. She ripped the Colt out of the old woman's hand and tightened her grip on Lorena's throat. She wanted to choke her to death. She wanted to shoot her. Amelia pointed the gun at Lorena's face.

Lorena stopped moving. Staring at Amelia with hate. Lying still beneath her. Waiting for her granddaughter to pull the trigger and end her miserable life.

Amelia held her down and pressed the muzzle of the Colt into the middle of Lorena's forehead. She tightened her finger on the trigger.

And then Amelia heard Demarco Jones yelling her name over and over.

"Amelia. Amelia. Amelia!"

She froze. The sound of her name cut into her, bringing her back from the brink. She felt her heart pounding, her ragged breaths coming in gasps.

What was she doing? How could she let this bitter, hateful woman make her kill her own flesh and blood, commit a murder that would bring more death, more misery, more police and danger into Beck's life and the lives of the men who had saved her? How could she let Lorena prove once and for all that she really was worthless?

No. No. She tore herself away from the old woman, turned toward the heavy coffee table, and smashed the gun down on it, over and over. Slamming it against the hard wood. The cylinder popped open. Bullets flew. The barrel bent and the handle split.

Amelia threw the ruined gun away from her and stood up, backing away from Lorena. She was breathless, crying, everything pouring out of her – the loss, the pain, her fear, anger, confusion. Her shame. Letting it all out. Leaving it all behind. Turning her back on the life Lorena Leon represented once and for all.

Demarco was just about to run around to the front entrance when he saw Amelia emerge into the courtyard, wiping her face with her sleeve, replacing her glasses, blinking back the remains of her tears.

He stopped, his heart still pounding from exertion and fear, fear that she had been shot by that crazy, unstable old woman. But no. There was no blood. No look of pain. Amelia walked toward him without expression. He had no idea what had happened in Lorena's apartment, but it didn't matter. Amelia was alive. She was safe.

He went toward Amelia and took her hand. Before he could ask her anything, she shook her head and grabbed his arm. Demarco walked her out of the courtyard, neither of them saying anything.

When they reached the car, Amelia walked to the passenger side. Demarco looked at her over the roof.

She said, "I'm sorry. We shouldn't have come here."

"What did she do? Did she try to shoot you?"

"Worse. She tried to make me as bad as she is. But I'm not. I'm done with her, Demarco. I'm done with all of it. It's over. It's finally over."

Acknowledgements

I'm pleased to have an opportunity to acknowledge and thank the people who have supported and encouraged me in my writing efforts. First, thank you to my wife, Ellen, but those words seem terribly inadequate. Also, thanks to Dave Rutkin, who's supported me every way he could think of, ever since the first book. Thank you, Josh Bank, for years of support and invaluable advice. Thank you, Mike Greene, Norm Siegel, Lorenzo Carcaterra, Dermott Ryan, Dave King, Franklin Tartaglione, Emily McCully, Liz Diggs, Billy J. Parrott, Richard McMahon, Nick Utton, Jamie McClelland, Richard Weininger, Victor Schiro, Dan Barrett, Deborah Brunetti, Ernie Boone, Robert Bidinotto, Craig White, Paul Faulds, Richard Guerin, Robert Stuart, Mark Luetschwager, Buddy Baarcke, Lydia Condrey, John Glendon, Tom Campbell, Steven Wiencek, Jeffrey Scott Beckerman, Frances Jalet Miller, Judy Collins, Sunny Solomon, Joe Hartlaub. And deeply felt thanks to Keith Kahla, my editor, and the team at St. Martin's.

He just wanted a decent book to read ...

Not too much to ask, is it? It was in 1935 when Allen Lane, Managing Director of Bodley Head Publishers, stood on a platform at Exeter railway station looking for something good to read on his journey back to London. His choice was limited to popular magazines and poor-quality paperbacks – the same choice faced every day by the vast majority of readers, few of whom could afford hardbacks. Lane's disappointment and subsequent anger at the range of books generally available led him to found a company – and change the world.

'We believed in the existence in this country of a vast reading public for intelligent books at a low price, and staked everything on it'
Sir Allen Lane, 1902–1970, founder of Penguin Books

The quality paperback had arrived – and not just in bookshops. Lane was adamant that his Penguins should appear in chain stores and tobacconists, and should cost no more than a packet of cigarettes.

Reading habits (and cigarette prices) have changed since 1935, but Penguin still believes in publishing the best books for everybody to enjoy. We still believe that good design costs no more than bad design, and we still believe that quality books published passionately and responsibly make the world a better place.

So wherever you see the little bird – whether it's on a piece of prize-winning literary fiction or a celebrity autobiography, political tour de force or historical masterpiece, a serial-killer thriller, reference book, world classic or a piece of pure escapism – you can bet that it represents the very best that the genre has to offer.

Whatever you like to read – trust Penguin.